THE VALLEY BEYOND

A Daughter's Bond

TS Nichols

Fulton Books, Inc.
Meadville, PA

Published by Fulton Books 2020

This book is a work of fiction set in late twelfth century Spain. The names of places used in the book are fictitious: Segoia, Donato, and Gustavo. The main character of the book, Doña Lucía, is a fictitious character, and was not in reality a member of the royal families of either England or Castile as portrayed in this publication. If there are any references to real people, places, and historical events, they are used for fictitious purposes only. If in the story, there are any similarities to real events, places, or actual people either alive or dead, this is to be considered a coincidence and not meant to be intentional.

ISBN 978-1-64654-008-2 (paperback)
ISBN 978-1-64654-009-9 (digital)

To Maddy, Sydney, AJ, Sawyer, Jaycob, and Harmony.

Acknowledgement

I would like to thank my wife, Barbara, for her technical support and patience in the writing of this publication. It's always good to have a second set of eyes to read your written work, and her eyes were the best in discovering certain errors that went previously unnoticed. Once again, thank you for all that you do.

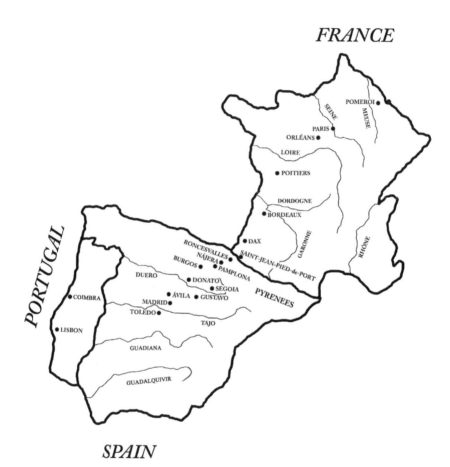

Chapter I

Don Fernando looked over the battlefield where an intense struggle had just ensued on the flat desolate wind-blown plain in La Mancha. The hue of the straw-colored grass and rocks of the plain had turned bloodred as bodies of soldiers, Christian and Moor, lay strewn across the vast expanse. He saw the terrible carnage and asked himself a simple question: What future lay forth for a child born in violence and warfare? He thought of Lady Margaret, his wife, who was with child, and wondered if it would ever find love and happiness in such violent times and whether Castile and the rest of Spain would ever find permanent peace by vanquishing their enemy and settling its own differences.

Suddenly, his thoughts were interrupted by a cry from a familiar voice. Don Fernando eyed carefully the rocky terrain and saw his friend Don Alfonso Coronado, the Conde of Gustavo, behind an area of brush, waving his hands in the air frantically with a cry of "Over here! Over here!" He was about thirty yards away through a line of low brush and thicket. Don Fernando rushed over to his friend, jumping over the bodies of the dead. To his dismay, he was surprised to see an injured Don José, an old knight, with a severe wound to his left side. Both Don Fernando and Don Alfonso Coronado brought their friend back to camp and placed him against a wooden wagon wheel while three Moorish warriors leaped over the wagon hitch, followed by three archers fast firing their crossbows. They killed one, while the other two galloped away unimpeded.

"Hold your fire!" shouted a voice. "Save your arrows for the next battle." The battle was over, and the Christians had won. However, the soldiers in the field were confused as Don José was not on his white charger waving his sword in the air, which usually proclaimed victory and retreat from the battlefield.

Don José was considered a master knight since the time of King Alfonso VII. Now he was an old man, and his demeanor was that of a battle-worn warrior: old, tired, and cranky but always ready to come to the aid of Castile. His presence on the field of battle was sorely missed. One knight actually stopped in the middle of all the carnage and confusion, took off his barrel helmet, looked around, and cried out, "Is the battle over? If so, where is Don José?" Other knights and soldiers on the field asked the same question. Finally, the sound of a trumpeter broke through the confusion, as both sides retreated.

One soldier happened to notice their hero lying against a wagon wheel, as he passed by on his way back to his tent. He cried out, "Here is Don José! Over here!" Neither Don Fernando nor Don Alfonso Coronado had left his side and had called for a physician. Soldiers and knights gathered around in disbelief to see their old war hero so severely wounded.

Don Fernando tried to make Don José as comfortable as possible and removed his chain mail cowl that revealed a man way beyond his prime with a long drawn leathery face full of wrinkles attached to a gray unkempt beard that came to a point. His hair was gray and fell along the side of his head and revealed a large bald spot in the middle of his scalp. Don José, whose lips were tightly pursed, suddenly opened them and cried out, "I thirst."

"Someone throw him a waterskin!" shouted Don Fernando.

A soldier quickly threw one to Don José, who removed the cork, took a drink, and spit it out.

"What sort of drink is this? I need wine!" he cried.

Another skin was thrown in, and Don José wasted no time. He removed the cork and guzzled down a large quantity.

"Don José, save some for the rest of us," said a soldier who stood in front of him.

"You'll have to fight him for it," said a voice from the crowd, which initiated a roar of laughter among the throng that stood before Don José. It put the seriousness of the situation into a lighter mood.

"*Sí*, but you'll never win that battle," said another soldier, which provoked another round of additional laughter.

Don José waved off the sentiment.

Suddenly a knight shouted, "Make way for the king! Make way for the king!"

King Alfonso walked through the crowd and made his way to Don José. The king stood in front of him in his entire splendor, from his chain mail to the boldly emblazoned yellow castle on his red surcoat. King Alfonso VIII was truly the king of Castile and Toledo.

The king looked upon Don José with a concerned look but was able to force a smile. "What happened to you, my friend?" asked the king loudly.

"He found himself on the wrong end of a scimitar," shouted a voice from the crowd. "But that didn't stop him. He pursued the Moor, cut off his head, and threw it as far as he could. It will take the slain Moor many years to find it." Again laughter ensued.

"Is that true, my friend?"

"Ah, I should have retired several battles ago," said Don José in complete disgust with himself. "I'm getting too old for this." Suddenly, Don José winced in pain.

"Where is the surgeon?" shouted the king.

Moments later, the surgeon hurried over and knelt in front of Don José; he moved a portion of the chain mail from the wound, viewed it for several seconds, looked up at the king, shook his head, and hurried off to another patient.

The king sighed and whispered to one of his knights who stood beside him to find a priest. He then looked down at Don José. "I remember, old friend, when I was but fifteen years old and had to defend the kingdom from the warring noble families, you were there and, on several occasions, even rescued me from certain danger and saved my life."

"*Sí*, you did seem to be rather impetuous in battle," interjected Don José. "You were often too careless, charging into the center of the enemy, hacking your way through without regard for life or limb. But despite that, I knew that you were someone worthy at such a young age to hold the title of king."

The priest that had been summoned appeared and knelt down in front of Don José, only to be waved off, as Don José refused to believe that the grim reality of his death was certain.

"Sire," interrupted Don Mendoza, one of the king's knights, "you're needed in your tent."

"Caballeros, you'll have to excuse me. Apparently, I'm needed elsewhere," said the king as he glanced out among the gathered crowd.

"Take care of yourself, old friend," said the king as he put his hand on Don José's shoulder and sadly walked away.

"May I get you something?" offered Don Fernando, as both he and Don Alfonso Coronado were still by his side.

"No, this old dog doesn't require anything from this earth anymore," said a weakened Don José.

By this time, the crowd around their fallen hero had dispersed, but some spent time to gaze upon Don José one last time and showed their respects to a man, as had many before him, who had given his entire life in the defense of Castile and the Christian religion against the nearly five-hundred-year war against the Moorish invaders.

"Ah, see how they treat me as if I was already dead," said Don José as he turned to his right, to Don Fernando. "So much for talk of death. Let's talk about you, Don Fernando. I understand that Lady Margaret is with child."

"Sí, anytime now."

Don José now turned quickly to his left. "And you, too, I believe, Don Alfonso?"

"Sí, but Doña Teresa will not give birth for several months."

"I imagine that both of you are in desire for strong boys for heirs to take your place on the battlefield someday. I would want it no other way if it were my sons."

Suddenly, there was a twinkle in Don José's eyes and a big smile on his face. "What would you do if God granted you daughters instead to mind your castles?"

There was silence.

"Ah, no response. Just as I thought. Two daughters, I predict," joked Don José, who still was able to keep his sense of humor even though near death. "I know that both of you will be blessed with children who will honor your name." Don José started to groan, and his expression turned to one of grimace.

"Are you all right?" asked Don Fernando.

"Of course, this old dog feels much better and soon will be going back to battle the Moors," said a determined Don José. "Both of you are good friends, so will be your children. This I know." Don José's voice weakened.

Before the conversation could continue, the king came back and asked both Don Fernando and Don Alfonso Coronado to join him a short distance away within earshot of Don José. However, before Don Fernando was able to leave his side, Don José blocked his departure with a weakened hand.

He said in a soft voice, "And now the sword has been passed to you, my friend. Swing it hard until its bloody red with the blood of the Moor."

Don Fernando did not say a word. He stood up and patted Don José on the shoulder and went to join the king and Don Alfonso Coronado and left Don José alone.

The three let their friend rest but knew he was awake and could hear the conversation, as they discussed a matter of state. The king realized that he was probably listening to the conversation, as Don José had big ears and did not let any matter go undiscussed.

"Don't you agree, Don José?" said the king with a smile, trying to catch him off guard.

Instead of the usual immediate feedback that Don José was notorious for conveying, there was complete silence. At this point, all three turned to see that Don José had slumped over to the ground. Don Fernando quickly went to his side and listened to his heart. He looked at his comrades and shook his head.

The king was deeply saddened. "Castile has lost a great warrior this day never to return, and I have lost one of the closest friends a man has ever known."

Both knights and soldiers alike walked by to see for themselves the fallen hero of Castile, some in tears, others in shock. Here lay a man that had survived so many battles in his lifetime that it was believed he was invincible. A priest followed forth to administer the last rites of the church, and there was utter silence throughout the camp as word spread about his death.

As the army of Castile was mourning the death of Don José, a boy ventured into camp and broke the silence.

"I'm looking for Don Fernando Alvarado, the Conde of Segoia!" shouted a voice at some distance away.

Don Fernando followed the voice and saw a boy about fifteen years old walking in his direction. He yelled to the boy, "I'm over here!"

The boy quickly ran to him and said, "I'm a squire from Segoia who has come to fetch you. Lady Margaret is about to give birth," said the boy, who was trying to catch his breath from his frantic ride from the palace.

Don Fernando glanced in the direction of the king.

"Go and take care of your new family. I'll be along as soon as I take Don José home."

With the king's blessing, Don Fernando mounted his horse, took one last look at Don José, and galloped off at great speed.

Chapter II

From a distance, beyond the wooded area on the banks of the river Duero, Don Fernando saw the city of Segoia with its high towers and walls, seated on the edge of a cliff, overlooking the river. The city had been the capital of the Condado of Segoia for many centuries, and its high walls and towers were a blend of Visigothic, Roman, and Moorish architecture, as each culture expanded the walls and added their own motifs.

As the Conde of Segoia, he ruled over a vast area of cities, towns, and villages, but home was the city of his birth, the same as his father and his father's father, which went back many centuries. Now, a new birth would someday add to his family's legacy, which Don Fernando hoped beyond hope would be a male heir. Don Fernando galloped ardently down a slow rising incline and onto a wide wooden bridge and up another wooded hill that was on the city road that passed the family vineyard to his right and the peasant village across the road to the left. The village was complete with its own church and white adobe huts, which, like the city walls, glistened in the sun.

About a mile beyond the village, Don Fernando took a right turn and galloped up a hill that led to the city gates. After he waved to a guard on the gate tower, he entered the city, which bustled with its shops, taverns, and inns. The very people who manned those shops also lived in the city. The many narrow, winding side streets were filled with houses and balconies with flowers of all kinds, especially roses and lavender, which gave the city a colorful hue and a pleasant scent.

The pride of the city was its large city square, complete with its large fountain of spring water from the mountains beyond. It was originally constructed by the Romans, who once occupied the area and built the high walls of the city as a fortress to protect the Roman citizens against invaders and other miscreants. Across from the fountain to the right was the beautiful Catedral de la Santa María de La Montaña, originally built in the tenth century before Castile became a kingdom in its own right and was a county under the lordship of León.

It had been said that Fernán González, the first Count of Castile, had laid the cornerstone of the cathedral on the ruins of the old one. Over the two centuries, additions had been added onto the cathedral, which now stood as a beautiful tribute to the old Romanesque style, along with its two tall bell towers. Across from the cathedral was the bishop's palace, complete with its rich gardens and elegance.

Don Fernando rode on through the tower gates of the enclosed palace, which was at the back of the city, and into the large stable. He had an attendant tend to his horse, which had had a tiring ride home. He climbed the narrow three-story winding staircase, which led to the living quarters, and when he entered the hallway outside the bedchamber, he was surprised to see Leonor, the queen of Castile, who appeared completely demoralized, with her hands rested on the back of a chair. Her complexion was flush, and her eyes were reddened by sadness. This was in contrast to the beauty and regality she was renowned for throughout the kingdom. She told Don Fernando that Lady Margaret, her sister, was near death and had been waiting to see him. He should hurry.

Don Fernando entered the bedchamber where Lady Margaret had given birth and was aghast at what he saw. Blood was all over the bed linen, on the curtain lining the bed, and on the canopy above.

"What butchery is this!" yelled Don Fernando. "I saw less blood on the battlefield from which I have just come."

The physician, who had been on the other side of the curtain along with a nurse, had not been aware of Don Fernando's entrance.

"*Mi señor*, please forgive me. I did not hear you enter."

Don Fernando climbed the three steps of the platform, which led to the bed, where Lady Margaret lay near death. He sat down in a chair next to the bed and saw his young wife, all of fifteen years. Her face was pallid and virtually blended into her white pillow, and her eyes were closed. He happened to look on the wooden floor and saw a puddle of blood dripping from the mattress. She had been covered by a sheet, which was completely bloodstained. He uncovered the sheet, which revealed a sight that almost made him gag. He was a warrior who had seen some vile wounds on the battlefield, but this sight he had been completely unprepared to witness.

Lady Margaret was drifting in and out of consciousness, and her eyes were shut, as Don Fernando bristled with anger.

"Physician!" screamed Don Fernando. He hurried down the platform, took the physician by the neck, and held a dagger to his throat. "If you value your life, you had better have a good explanation to the butchery I just witnessed."

"Please, mi señor," said the physician, pleading for his life. "The baby was badly breached. It was either the baby's life or Lady Margaret's. I had to operate, but I did give her a choice. She realized the consequences of her decision, and she chose the life of the baby."

Don Fernando released the physician, as Lady Margaret called for her husband.

"Fernando, are you there?" asked Lady Margaret in a very weak voice.

Upon hearing her voice, Don Fernando walked back up the steps of the platform, sat in the chair next to her bed, and took her delicate hand, which felt cold and limp.

"Sí, I am here," said Don Fernando, whose anger now turned to sadness.

"Did we win the day?" asked Lady Margaret. It was a question she always asked her husband after a battle.

"Sí," said Don Fernando, who tried desperately to hold back his emotions.

"Good. I had no doubt," said Lady Margaret, whose voice was now practically a whisper.

At this point, the physician carried the newborn, wrapped in a small blanket, up the steps of the platform and placed it next to her.

"You have a beautiful healthy daughter, *mi señora*."

Both Don Fernando and his wife carefully studied the child and commented on her long blondish-red hair and blue eyes, just like her mother.

"I'm sorry that I was not able to give you a son, Fernando."

"It doesn't matter. She is beautiful."

There was a pause, as Lady Margaret winced in pain.

"It hurts me to see you in such distress," said Don Fernando as he tried again to hold back his emotions.

Lady Margaret turned her head toward her husband in a serious demeanor. "Fernando, I have little time left, and I need for you to promise me something."

"Of course, anything," said Don Fernando with a forced smile.

"Promise me that you will name her Lucía, as she is the light of my life."

"You have picked a beautiful name that describes her well, my dear."

"Promise me that you will love her and not give her to the church."

"How could I otherwise?"

"Promise me that she will receive a good education and inherit my wealth and titles."

"Of course."

Lady Margaret smiled and, with all her remaining strength, positioned herself on her elbow, bent over, and gave the baby a kiss.

Once again, Don Fernando took her wife's hand as she lay back upon the pillow, and with a deep sigh, she took her last breath, her hand falling limp and motionless.

"Physician!" yelled Don Fernando.

The physician came immediately. Don Fernando put his wife's hand carefully down at her side, sadly gave her a kiss on the lips, and arose from the chair. The physician examined Lady Margaret, turned to Don Fernando, and shook his head.

With that, little Lucía started to cry, as if on cue with the death of her mother, which gave everyone in the room a startled chill. Don Fernando carefully picked up the child from the side of her deceased mother and held her in his arms. He tried to comfort her while walking down the steps of the platform.

"She must be hungry," said the physician. He took the baby from her father. "Bring the child to the wet nurse," said the physician to the nurse at hand.

Before she was able to leave the bedchamber, Father Sierra Piña, Lady Margaret's confessor from the peasant village, came through the door. His face was thin and had a ruddy complexion, which appeared worn from years in the sun and highlighted by long strands of thin gray hair that fell from his tonsure down the back of his neck. He wore a simple brown hooded robe tied by a cord of hemp and walked with a slight limp.

"I came as quickly as I could, but it appears I'm too late."

"Even in her present state of repose, she still needs you, *padre*."

Father Piña shook his head in agreement and, with a slight smile, climbed the platform, stood over Lady Margaret and said several prayers in Latin. After the prayers, he gave her the final blessing of the church and put both her arms gently across her chest in a rest position.

As Don Fernando watched him in action, he quickly realized why Lady Margaret loved the simplicity of this truly holy and gentle man.

Don Fernando met him at the bottom of the stairs of the platform. "*Gracias* for coming, padre. I know in my heart that she is now truly at rest."

"She was a wonderful young woman, Don Fernando, who was loved by all her people. The love of God was truly in her soul, and we can all do no less than to follow her worthy example." Then Father Piña paused and, in a reflective tone, said while he rubbed his chin, "Strange that we had a conversation a couple of days ago where she had reservations about her life after giving birth, as if she knew she was going to succumb after the ordeal. I tried to reassure her that she had many happy years left, but she was adamant." Then he noticed the baby in the arms of the nurse. "Is this the child, Don Fernando?"

"Sí, padre."

While the child waited patiently to be fed in the arms of the nurse, Father Piña smiled at the infant and gave the child his blessing.

"You have a beautiful daughter, Don Fernando. I'm sure she will have a long and fruitful life."

"Gracias, padre. I'll take your statement as an omen for her future."

"If I can do more for you, Don Fernando, you know where you can find me."

"In the loft of the peasant village church, padre. Is that correct?"

Father Piña smiled, shook his head, and without another word said, opened the door and left the room.

As the nurse once again started out the door of the bedchamber, the queen entered the room and, having noticed the baby, said with a saddened heart, "I assume that this child is my new niece."

After a courtesy with child in hand, the nurse responded, "Sí, Your Highness."

"What is her name?" asked the queen.

"Lucía, Your Highness," responded Don Fernando.

"Lucía," repeated the queen as she gave the baby a kiss on her forehead. "What a beautiful name for such a beautiful child. And now I wish everyone to leave so I may have a final moment with my dear sister."

"Of course," said Don Fernando, and he left the bedchamber along with the physician, the nurse, and the household servants who had just arrived to clean the room.

Chapter III

Don Fernando was seated at a table on the dais in the anteroom of the great hall, grief-stricken over the death of his young wife. As he moved sundry documents around the large oak table, he noticed a black silk bag under a scroll. A saddened smile came to his face, as he opened the bag and emptied the contents on the table. It contained a necklace that was purchased from an Arab merchant from Cordoba to celebrate Lady Margaret's fifteenth birthday, but Don Fernando never had the chance to present it to her due to the battle in La Mancha.

As he examined the piece, he started to reminisce how he and Lady Margaret had met and the odd circumstances that surrounded her birth. Lady Margaret was actually born in Poitiers in 1168 and was the daughter of King Henry II of England and Queen Eleanor. At the time of her conception, according to what was told to Don Fernando, Queen Eleanor had been escorted to Poitiers by King Henry after she had agreed to a separation and left there as Henry continued his business in the realm.

Unfortunately, over the years of her marriage to King Henry, she had developed much enmity toward him, especially due to his philandering. However, Queen Eleanor found herself pregnant again after she had become estranged from the king. After her son John had been born, she vowed never to have any more children, so this truly disturbed her. She already had little to do with him due to the animosity she had felt against King Henry, and now here was another child due to a lack of discretion on her part. What to do?

Eleanor had remembered her friend from England, the Lady Jeanne, Countess of Bickford, and her husband, Sir Charles de Crécy, Duke of Pomeroi. Lady Jeanne was barren, and her infertility became a major source of unhappiness, as no heir had been produced in their marriage. So Queen Eleanor cleverly devised a plan. Very early on, Eleanor made arrangements with Lady Jeanne to disappear from public view on the ruse of an alleged pregnancy. Eleanor would feign illness and would also disappear from public view while she stayed at the palace in Poitiers. All personal servants would be sworn to secrecy upon pain of death.

Upon the birth of the child, a certificate was issued that showed the nascence of Lady Margaret Clare d'Anjou, the daughter of the king and queen of England, and witnessed by several notables and close friends of the queen at her court. Three copies of the document were made: one kept by the royal house, the second sent to Rome to record the royal birth, and the third given to the Crécy. No public record of the birth was filed, which meant she did not exist.

As soon as the documents were signed, the child was whisked away in secrecy, accompanied by a nurse who doubled as the mother and a trusted court official who doubled as the father. From Poitiers, they traveled to Pomeroi, north of Paris, to the court of Sir Charles and Lady Jeanne de Crécy. Upon arrival in the dead of night, Lady Jeanne pretended to go into labor with a midwife present. After a time, the midwife came out of Lady Jeanne's bedchamber holding the child, who was presented at court as Lady Margaret Clare de Crécy, daughter of Sir Charles and Lady Jeanne. A birth certificate was issued in her name. Queen Eleanor had already sent a letter to Pope Alexander with a complete explanation of the ruse, which expressed fear for the life of the infant if she was known to be the daughter of King Henry and a possible contender for the crown of England.

Lady Margaret had had a normal childhood in Pomeroi. The grounds of her childhood home contained several acres of apple orchards, which were used for income. She was a happy child and would often be seen running among the trees and helping with the fall harvest. When Margaret was nine, Lady Jeanne died, and Margaret inherited her title as Countess of Bickford, with the permission of King Henry.

When Margaret reached the age of twelve, due to the upcoming dynastic struggles, it was decided for her protection that she leave France, out of the range of King Henry's sons, who by this time knew of Lady Margaret's existence. A marriage was arranged between Lady Margaret and Conde Don Fernando Alvarado of Segoia through King Henry II and King Alfonso VIII of Castile and Toledo, King Henry's son-in-law. Lady Margaret was told of her true identity, and arrangements were made for her sojourn to Castile.

In the spring of 1181, Sir Charles de Crécy set out with his daughter to the city of Segoia in Castile. After several months of traveling, they reached the city and into the welcoming arms of Don Fernando Alejandro Diego Alvarado de Martínez, Conde of Segoia.

When he first laid eyes on Lady Margaret exiting her transport, Don Fernando remembered a young countess of magnificent pulchritude. Her oval face, wide smile, and blue eyes reflected the very depth of the beauty of her soul. Her reddish-blond hair that framed her face only served to enhance her indisputable charm and beauty. However, he remembered when he was introduced to his bride-to-be by Sir Charles on the day of her arrival how shocked he was that such a beautiful mature-looking creature was only twelve years old, a mere child. He was twenty-one.

But notwithstanding, within weeks of her arrival, Don Fernando and Lady Margaret were married at La Catedral de Santa María de las Montañas in the city of Segoia, followed by a banquet that lasted several days and a tournament where the dashing young Don Fernando displayed his prowess. Don Fernando smiled as he remembered Lady Margaret's infectious laughter when he lost one joust and was dragged by his horse on his seat out of the tournament.

Even though it was love at first sight, it was decided, due to her age, that they wait a couple of years before consummation of their marriage. During this time, Lady Margaret enjoyed the companionship of what she called her dashing young warrior. Her older sister, Queen Leonor, enjoyed her company immensely, as she was intelligent and quite engaging in conversation. Often, they would be joined by Doña Juana Mendoza, a good and trusted friend of the queen.

Lady Margaret enjoyed her new exotic life in Castile but did miss the cool summer breezes of home and especially her horse, Gelder, which was not allowed to make the trip, as Lady Margaret was given her own mount. Treated royally by Don Fernando, her life was easy. However, Lady Margaret did enjoy staying busy and was often seen in the vineyard helping her husband with the annual harvest. Also, she performed flawlessly in fulfilling her other duties as condesa.

In late January 1183, Lady Margaret became pregnant and voiced her fear to her sister, Queen Leonor, and Doña Juana Mendoza, a good friend, of a premonition that she would not survive childbirth and would succumb in the ordeal. Both women thought her fears were utter nonsense, but Lady Margaret was adamant and made sure that her husband was not aware of her fear.

Suddenly, Don Fernando was interrupted from his deep thoughts and grief by a voice that startled him. He slowly put down the necklace, raised his head, and languidly laid eyes on a figure of a man dressed in black. It was Don Raimundo Ortega Díaz, the Conde de Donato, a neighboring condado bordering the Condado of Segoia. Don Fernando had not heard him enter the anteroom to the great hall.

The relationship between the two condes had been strained for some time due to a land dispute. The land in question included several thousand acres—or to be precise, twenty-five square miles—and a castle that Don Raimundo seized and claimed as his own. Apparently, the claim was based on a past document that was dated several hundred years before and conveniently discovered in a wall of his palace during a renovation. Don Fernando believed the document to be a fraud, but Don Raimundo always had a knack for protecting his own interests, fraudulent or not.

Don Fernando did not go to war with Don Raimundo over the land in question due to the fragile relationship that existed between the nobles in the kingdom, which could have led to an all-out civil war to the benefit of the Moors. In order to keep the peace among his high-ranking and most trusted nobles, King Alfonso made Don Raimundo pay what amounted to be a token payment for the land, which was only a fraction of the true value of the rich farmland that was seized.

It should be noted that Don Raimundo had the love of the king due to his prowess in having helped the young teen defeat his enemies who vied for the kingdom after King Sancho's death and thus helping him claim the throne. As a result, King Alfonso, due to the proven loyalty of his good friend, was blind to his sometimes treacherous behavior. It also had been rumored that Don Raimundo poisoned his own brother to inherit the Condado de Donato, and he married his sister to a nobleman so far in the north of Germany that it would take a lifetime for her to find her way back home.

Don Fernando, still seated at his worktable on the dais, appeared across the table with a face full of anger.

"What do you want, Raimundo?" asked Don Fernando abruptly.

"I came to simply offer my condolences on the loss of your wife. I happened to be in Segoia on business and at the tavern nearest the palace when a servant burst in and stated loudly that the condesa had died in childbirth. Since I had concluded my business, I decided to come directly here," he exclaimed, with his dark piercing eyes showing little emotion.

Don Fernando rose from his seat and, with his hands rested on the table, bent over and gave his guest a choleric look.

"No reason to look at me in such a harsh manner, señor. I came as a matter of courtesy to pay my respects."

"Respect?" responded Don Fernando. "Do you really expect me to believe that you have respect or care for anything else besides your own self-aggrandizement?"

Don Raimundo raised his eyebrows, turned, and started to walk away, irritated by Don Fernando's remarks. Suddenly, he stopped in his tracks, turned, and faced Don Fernando. "I came here in good faith to pay my respects to a young woman for whom I had the deepest respect and admiration for both her loveliness and her pleasing temperament, not to be chided like some small child."

As Don Raimundo turned away again, he heard Don Fernando shout loudly, "And why weren't you at La Mancha? The king could have used you to control the right flank, and maybe Don José would still be alive."

"I shall overlook your remarks, Don Fernando, due to your loss. However, they do sound like some type of accusation that I find both insulting and troubling. I merely came to hold out my hand in the spirit of sympathy and compassion, but since you have decided to bite it off, it is time for me to leave. Good day, señor," said an agitated Don Raimundo, who opened the door and left.

Don Fernando sat down at his desk and poured a cup of wine. Queen Leonor entered the room.

"I hope I'm not disturbing you, Fernando."

"Not in the least, Your Highness," replied Don Fernando as he rose from his chair and left the dais to greet the queen.

At twenty-one years of age, the daughter of King Henry II of England was as beautiful as she was charming. He could not help but gaze upon her regal yet enticing face framed by a white wimple. Her white bliaut featured a low neckline, the sleeves, the hem, the belt, a scarlet background emblazoned with yellow lions, the heraldic emblem of her family.

Was this the same twelve-year-old princess who had come to marry his king to cement an alliance between England and Castile and was homesick in being in a foreign land with its different customs? She had truly grown into her role as queen, thought Don Fernando.

"I was just greeted by that sinister-looking Don Raimundo, who appeared to be in a hurry to leave the palace. Be careful, Fernando. I don't trust him despite the fact that my husband holds him in such a high regard."

"Believe me, I neither trust nor hold him in any regard. He is simply an opportunist with a despicable nature," said Don Fernando, who had turned to pour a silver cup of wine for his guest.

Don Fernando handed the cup to Queen Leonor. "Here, drink this, Your Highness. It is Segoia's best and will cure any ills."

"Except a broken heart. Nothing can cure that, except time itself, I'm afraid," said the queen as she carefully sipped the wine.

"You look tired, Your Highness. Why don't you rest here in the palace before returning to Burgos?"

Queen Leonor's eyes were red and swollen, and tears ran down her cheeks as she thought about her sister, who would be unknown in history due to the circumstances of her birth, yet known to her real family, many of whom she had had never met.

"Oh, I am so angry at my mother and saddened that she hated my sister so much as to give her away. People are not objects that you can give away like a necklace or a gold coin," cried the queen, wiping her eyes with a piece of linen.

"But she did have a happy childhood. She told me many times," said Don Fernando as he reached over to take the cup from the queen.

"Well, that's a godsend for sure," said the queen with a slight smile.

The queen pulled herself up in the chair and turned her head toward Don Fernando, who was seated next to her. "I'm afraid that I have been selfish, Fernando, going on without regard to your feelings. How are you doing under the circumstances, and is there anything I can do to help?"

"Frankly, I don't know what I am going to do without her. Not only did she take care of me but also the household staff, which she ran so smoothly. She was a natural with people and made everyone feel at ease. All of Segoia loved her. She had won their hearts over such a short time and will never be forgotten."

"Have you discussed the funeral arrangements with the bishop?" asked the queen.

"The bishop! That fat pompous cleric! No, I'm going to ask Father Piña, her confessor, to take care of the arrangements. However, there will be a commemorative Mass at the cathedral, and I am going to commission a sarcophagus with an effigy of Lady Margaret to be built and placed in the crypt of the chapel here in the palace."

"And the baptism of my niece?" asked the queen.

"Within a couple of days, Your Highness, when she will also be introduced to the people of Segoia."

"Have you decided on her full name yet, Don Fernando?"

"Sí, I believe I have. She will be named Doña Lucía María Margarita Diega Alvarado de Crécy, the Duchess of Pomeroi and the Countess of Bickford, the titles from her mother's inheritance."

"She is also an Anjou, from my family's household, and this must also be added to her name as well," added the queen.

"Of course, Your Highness," said Don Fernando.

A couple of days later, Doña Lucía was introduced to the people of Segoia in a ceremony following her baptism on the steps of the cathedral, and alongside Don Fernando, who held the infant, were King Alfonso, Queen Leonor, the bishop of Segoia, and Father Piña. When her name was announced, the crowd roared with approval. Even the baby, Lucía, after having had been held up to the crowd for all to see, appeared to have given a smile of approval by kicking her little legs in the excitement of the moment. She was a beautiful child with long blondish-red hair and blue eyes, which held a hint of mischievous. The queen predicted to Don Fernando that her daughter would be a handful, given her mother's beauty and her father's stubborn nature.

Not noticed in the crowd, however, was Don Raimundo, who gave a sinister smile upon the introduction of the future condesa. A sense of foreboding was in the air unbeknownst to Don Fernando. That sinister smile, along with the evil behind the dark penetrating eyes, was a precursor of what was to come.

Chapter IV

Four years had passed since Doña Lucía's birth, and she was taking on the characteristics that would suit her well later in life. She was a beautiful child with fair skin, an oval face, a wide smile, long reddish-blond hair, and blue eyes the color of a bright azure fall sky. She could be stubborn at times and cooperative at others, depending on what was at stake.

Her nurse, Yamina, originally from Cordoba, was a Mozarab who came north to escape the strict laws of the Moors of al-Andalus. Both her parents were superbly educated and provided for her education as well. She came highly recommended by the Mendoza family, where she was nurse to all four of their children. She was a strict disciplinarian who loved to work with the young.

An empty room in the large palace served as both learning and play area for the young condesa. Yamina taught Lucía her letters and numbers, as well as basic Latin, French, and Arabic. At night, she read Bible stories to Lucía in French or told lurid stories of her homeland in Arabic. Lucía was a very bright girl who loved to learn. In her spare time, when Lucía was not learning her letters or the basics of how to run a household, she would dance to whatever lyrical note would come to her head from the music of the troubadours who would frequent her father's court in Segoia or from her aunt's court in Burgos.

Although she loved to dance, she also enjoyed her dolls. Her favorite was a rag doll named Cassandra, which had belonged to her mother. The doll's name was based on a Greek myth, a story told by Yamina, about a young girl from ancient Troy who was given the gift of prophecy but was cursed by Apollo. As a result, her prophecies were never believed. Lucía related to Cassandra because sometimes people would not believe her when she got into trouble. The doll had dark curly hair of yarn and dark painted brown eyes just like Cassandra.

One day, Lucía did not pick up the toys that she had played with and wandered off on her own and could not be found. She was playing hide-and-seek. As a result, a commotion occurred, and the household guards, under Captain Gómez, as well as Yamina and Don Fernando, looked high and low but could not find the child. She had hidden in a tight place where no one would find her, and she would giggle every time someone passed by. She then, when no one was around, sneaked out to the large fountain in the garden, where she sat in the cool water on a hot summer day and played with her toy boat.

Lucía was eventually caught and punished for having had committed three offenses: not picking up her toys, wandering off without having told Yamina, and playing in the fountain. Lucía's punishment consisted of three wallops on her backside with a wooden spoon and three days in her room. Lucía often said throughout her childhood that if Yamina was as handy with a wooden spoon in the kitchen as she was on her backside, she would have the makings of a very great chef. When Don Fernando addressed her bad behavior and told her he was very disappointed in her, Lucía was very apologetic, as she did not want to disappoint her father.

One day, Lucía was walking along the arcade with her doll, enjoying the spring air, when she noticed a girl who appeared to be the same age as her seated on a bench in the palace garden, which ran between the great hall and the living quarters. Lucía had a nose for curiosity and walked over to meet her. As she approached the girl, she noticed that she was also playing with a doll. Lucía sat on the bench next to her.

"What is your doll's name?" asked Lucía.

"Aldonza," responded the girl, who glanced over to Lucía.

"That is a pretty name," said Lucía as she eyed the doll with its black yarn hair and two buttons for eyes.

"You have a pretty doll too," added the girl, who was trying to be complimentary.

"I'm Lucía. What is your name?"

The girl turned to Lucía. "Isabella. My father said for me to wait for him here while he takes care of business and to enjoy the garden. Everything smells so nice here," said Isabella with a big smile.

After several minutes of sitting on the bench and swinging her feet back and forth, Lucía gave a deep sigh and turned her attention to Isabella, who was calmly minding her doll.

"Would you like to play a game, Isabella?"

Isabella turned to Lucía and, with a smile, said emphatically, "I would like to, but Papa said for me to wait for him here."

Lucía, taken aback by Isabella's statement, was in a state of ennui. She wanted to play with her new friend but wondered how to engage her. Suddenly, she had an idea on what to say. "We could play in the garden, and you would be where your father could find you," said Lucía, confident that would be a reasonable solution to the problem. However, Isabella didn't say a word, and Lucía became fidgety for a response.

She finally turned to Isabella with her eyebrows raised and, with a big smile, said, "Well, what do you say, huh?"

"Well, I guess it would be all right," responded Isabella, unsure of herself.

"What do you want to play?" inquired Lucía.

Isabella shrugged her shoulders. "I don't know."

Lucía thought for a moment. "How about hide-and-seek?"

"All right," said Isabella, who sounded more confident. She put her doll down and rose from the bench. "So pretty. Now I can hide among the pretty flowers and trees," she cried in joy.

The palace garden was a great place to play. It measured one hundred yards by fifty yards. There were four potted palm trees on each of the four corners of the garden. There were also three gray-stone pathways, one vertical and two horizontal. Each pathway was lined with a small hedge with an opening that led to a smaller garden. In each of the smaller gardens, there were various nut and fruit trees, along with a floral bouquet of fragrant scents that tickled the nose of all those who ventured into this oasis. In the middle of it all was the great fountain surrounded by various hues of blue tile in a geometric design. An enclosed arcade surrounded the entire garden, along with benches in each of the smaller gardens, the pathways, and the great fountain.

While the girls were having fun hiding among the trees and behind the hedges, the king's council was busy discussing certain matters of state in the anteroom of the great hall. The council was seated at a table to discuss any matter of state that could be of importance to the kingdom.

The king was seated at the head of a polished oak table, which seated about eight people. Since Don Fernando was the host, he sat at the other end with Don Alfonso Coronado, Don Raimundo and the Conde de Ávila all seated in the middle. A candle chandelier hung over the table. The walls of the one-hundred-by-fifty-foot room were masterfully covered with woolen tapestries depicting Bible stories in vivid color. The floor was covered in smooth gray stone, and under the table was a woven Persian carpet with a geometric theme in orange, blue, and gold. A dais with a wooden worktable was in the background, along with two chairs below. Off to the right of the dais in the corner of the room was another more decorative carved chair, which Lucía loved to climb on and sit in.

Among the affairs to be discussed was a delicate matter concerning the settling of Lady Margaret's estate, which involved the two countries of England and France.

"Señores," said the king as he put down his silver cup of wine, "as you are probably aware, it has been four years since the death of Lady Margaret, and we have been waiting patiently to settle her estate. It becomes difficult when a deceased person of noble rank has property outside the realm in foreign countries, especially in England and France. Unfortunately, there are political considerations, which take time, as we do not want to upset our allies. If not properly handled, it could lead to a misunderstanding and embarrassment. However, just yesterday, I have received notification from King Henry, my father-in-law, that Doña Lucía will be able to inherit her mother's land in England and the title of Countess of Bickford. I also received notification from King Philip of France a short time ago that she will also be able to inherit her mother's lands in France and the title of

Duchess of Pomeroi. Her lands in both countries will be administered by a trusted official who has been appointed by royal authority, and all income from rents, tolls, fees, and tribute minus taxes, fees, and scutage will be sent to her treasury in Segoia by any conveyance thought safe and feasible at the time.

"Since Lady Margaret did not spend any large amounts, Doña Lucía has an untold amount of wealth. Don Fernando and I both agree that if anything unfortunate should happen to Doña Lucía, her wealth will be taken to Burgos for safekeeping until an inheritor is named. It is also up to you as council members to be aware of this and to ensure that this be done if anything were to happen to either myself or Don Fernando."

"Why doesn't Don Fernando take charge of his daughter's treasury personally, and how much is in this so-called treasury? Don't you think we should know if we are to have such a responsibility?" asked Don Raimundo.

"If Your Highness will permit me, I would like to answer Don Raimundo."

"Very well, Don Fernando," said the king.

"First of all, let there be no misunderstanding. I am in charge of my daughter's wealth until such time as she marries, which then becomes part of her dowry. Also, unlike some people," said Don Fernando, who stared directly at Don Raimundo, "I am involved in the defense of the kingdom, and if anything should happen to me, it is reassuring to know that there are trusted friends honest enough to take care of this matter in my absence. As far as the sum of gold coins involved, we have not fully counted the two chests that have arrived from France, but it is substantial. I hope that answers your question satisfactorily, Raimundo."

Don Raimundo shook his head in the affirmative with a polite bow.

"If there is no other business, this meeting is concluded. Good day, *amigos*," said the king as he drained his cup of wine.

Don Fernando and Don Alfonso Coronado entered the palace garden and found the girls had entertained themselves joyfully.

Isabella ran over to her father upon seeing him enter the garden and said with great enthusiasm, "Can we stay longer, Papa? I love it here, and I have made a new friend."

"Well, I see that you have," said Don Alfonso Coronado with great enthusiasm as he lifted Isabella high in the air.

Lucía was close behind her new friend, running at such a speed and echoing the same sentiment that she almost ran into her father. Don Fernando was able to catch her as she wrapped her arms around him. As she pulled away, he noticed that Lucía had a couple of leaves and a small twig in her ankle-length hair, which she refused to have cut. Also, her blue garment had several tears in the shoulder and back.

"What have you been doing?" asked Don Fernando as he pulled the debris from her hair.

"Isabella and I have been hiding. We have been playing hide and seek, Papa."

"I see, and I do hope that is not a new dress," said Don Fernando, who inspected the garment.

"Hmm," responded Lucía.

"I see. Well, another garment to be repaired and sent to the poor," said Don Fernando, not wishing to start an argument with guests present.

"Lucía, this is my good friend Don Alfonso Coronado, Isabella's father."

"I know, Papa." Lucía tried to curtsy but fell on her backside, to the amusement of all. Lucía, although embarrassed, laughed and tried again successfully.

Don Fernando looked over to his guest. "As you can see, Lucía needs more practice in the finer points of courtesy."

Don Alfonso Coronado bent down, took her small hand, and kissed it, which caught Lucía slightly off guard. "It is a pleasure to make your acquaintance, Doña Lucía."

Don Fernando extended the same courtesy to Doña Isabella, who giggled.

Suddenly, Don Fernando turned to his friend and said with a big smile, "Remember, Don José stated that our children would become good friends."

"Ah, sí, my friend," said Don Alfonso Coronado as he nodded in agreement.

"Who is Don José, Papa?" asked an inquisitive Lucía.

"He was a good friend who gave his life for Castile and the Christian Church."

"And now we must be going, Isabella. Say goodbye to Lucía."

The girls said their goodbyes with the promise of seeing each other again.

Lucía had finished her studies in time for supper, and she now walked down to the great hall with Yamina. As Lucía and Yamina entered the hall, servants were precipitately in preparation for the evening meal. Lucía noticed that her father was seated at the head table on the dais, already having indulged in eating stuffed olives.

Lucía and Yamina joined Don Fernando and took their places at the table. Don Fernando always sat on the right, Yamina on the left, Lucía in the middle. The household servants sat at the tables below. Don Fernando always had Yamina join him at the head table for supper so he could obtain from her on how Lucía had progressed that day with her studies.

"Ah, would you like some grape juice, *mi pequeño sol?*" asked Don Fernando as Lucía was busy squirming to get seated in her chair.

"Sí, please, Papa," responded Lucía.

Don Fernando motioned to a servant who stood to the side of the dais, holding two pitchers. The servant immediately came to the table and poured a cup of grape juice for both Lucía and Yamina and a cup of wine for Don Fernando. At the same time, servers appeared with their platters of food for the evening. Lucía watched as the large silver serving platters, heaped with food, came around. The servers holding the platters would stop if she was interested in a particular dish. However, Lucía was a very picky eater, and sometimes either her father or Yamina had to intervene to ensure Lucía had as balanced a diet as possible. They both realized the importance of eating greens and vegetables.

The evening's menu was simple and consisted of a creamy lentil soup, roasted chicken or mutton, greens, chickpeas, and carrots. Bread and dipping sauce were readily available, along with both Lucía's and her father's favorite stuffed olives. Supper was served on trenchers so they could be given to the poor. Servers would always check and refill cups of wine or grape juice. Lucía enjoyed the bowl of lentil soup but only took a very small piece of chicken, a small carrot, and a couple of stuffed olives. Yamina looked at what was on her trencher.

"Lucía, you have to eat more than that."

"But I am not hungry," said Lucía, whining.

"Well then, I guess you are too full for dessert," snapped Yamina.

Lucía had a sweet tooth, and the prospect of not indulging in dessert was out of the question. She knew that if Yamina said no to dessert, her father would agree.

"All right," said Lucía, agitated at the prospect of her dessert held hostage to a larger piece of chicken and a few more greens.

While the table was being cleared for dessert, Don Fernando discussed the progress of Lucía's studies with Yamina.

"Hmm," said Don Fernando after having listened to Yamina's critique. "It sounds to me as if you will have to spend more time on your Arabic. It is important to be able to speak the language of the Arabic people in your condado."

"Can you speak Arabic, Papa?" asked Lucía, who turned to look at her father with her inquisitive blue eyes.

"A little from what I learned here and there. But, Lucía, you have an opportunity to study the language in depth, an opportunity I never had and one that could prove invaluable to you in the future. Don't you agree?" asked Don Fernando, who looked at Lucía with the hope that she had paid attention.

"Sí, Papa. I will try harder," responded Lucía in a bored tone.

"That's mi pequeño sol," responded Don Fernando.

Lucía began to fidget with her fingers and squirm in her chair. "Papa, what do you suppose is taking dessert so long to be served?"

Don Fernando motioned for a servant and told him that they were ready for the next course.

Lucía looked with glee to see the assortment of sweet tarts, a beautiful prepared flan with cinnamon on top, and various assortments of cheeses and dried fruits, along with almond milk to wash it all down.

When the tray came around, Lucía had no problem helping herself to her favorite sweet tarts. Sometimes her overindulgence would lead to a look of askance from Yamina, which meant that she had to put a second helping of sweet tarts back on the server's plate, to the utter frustration of her sweet tooth.

"Papa?"

"Sí, Lucía."

"Do you suppose that we could visit with mother after supper?" asked Lucía, who was chewing on a sweet tart.

"Sí, of course. I think that your mother would appreciate that very much."

With supper over, Lucía left the dais to walk with her father to the crypt of the chapel to visit the sarcophagus of her mother, but on her way, she noticed an unattended tray of sweet tarts left inadvertently on a serving table. As she walked by the table, she quickly assessed the situation to make sure no one was watching and quickly grabbed several of the sweet delicacies, putting them in her pocket for later. A real feeling of satisfaction came over her for being astute enough to find such an eating treasure and to having had put one over on Yamina.

As they entered the chapel, a font filled with holy water awaited them, which they dipped their finger into and blessed themselves. Then they followed the corridor to the end of the chapel, where they turned and went down a series of steps, which led to the rough stone floor of the crypt, a foreboding place lit only by several torches that lined the walls of the underground chamber, casting eerie shadows. Two braziers on tripods stood on either end of the sarcophagus, emitting a sweet smell of aromatics for both heat and additional light.

Don Fernando and Luca knelt on the kneeler on the side of the sarcophagus and, after having blessed themselves, put their hands together in prayer, resting them on the prayer stand attached to the kneeler. A bench was in the back of the kneeler, where Don Fernando and Lucía sat for reflection after prayer.

"Papa, do you suppose Mama knows we are here?"

"I am sure she does, and I am also sure she looks proudly upon you, as I do," said Don Fernando, who rubbed her back lightly as a sign of comfort.

Lucía turned to her father with a smile and said softly, "Sometimes when I come down here by myself, I swear I feel her presence, Papa."

"That means your mother is and will always be with you," responded Don Fernando.

"Do you miss her, Papa?"

"Very much," said Don Fernando, clearing his throat. "Very much, Lucía."

After a while, it was time to leave the crypt, and Don Fernando accompanied his daughter to the care of her nurse and tutor, Yamina, who was waiting to read Bible stories to her before bedtime and maybe, if Lucía was cooperative, to tell a tale from her homeland.

Chapter V

Lucía and Isabella were two girls who truly relished being with each other. Lucía was coeval with Isabella, and the two shared much in common. However, Isabella was a bit shyer, soft-spoken, and a noncomplainer; and her oval face and soft brown eyes, along with a small frame, which she covered with her long brown hair, gave the impression of a fragile and weak child.

As the two girls spent more time with each other, Yamina also became Isabella's tutor on occasion. Yamina offered instruction and was very strict on matters that concerned courtesy and how to manage household staff. The girls learned to stand erect and not to slouch, how to properly curtsy, and the art of the dance, which the two girls enjoyed on their own.

Despite their chores and instruction, they did manage to spend time with each other; they talked and giggled in their shared bed until they fell asleep. However, their favorite pastime was climbing the steps of the tallest tower in Segoia to look out over the countryside. From the tower, they could see the city below and the sparsely wooded grassy plain that stretched to the mountains on the horizon. As they turned, they could also see the peasant village in the distance and to the left of the village, across the road, the family vineyard. As they looked down from the tower, they could see the cliff that the city rested upon and the long drop to the River Duero below.

On occasion, Lucía would spend time at the castle of Gustavo, the home of Isabella. The castle was much smaller than Lucía was accustomed to, as it had only one tower to the left of the castle wall and a thick oak door that led to the courtyard; it was high enough for a man who sat on a horse to pass through. Below, to the left, outside the living quarters, was a dry riverbed that meandered by the castle wall, which was filled with water in the late winter and spring but dry in the summer on the hot dry, dusty plain. Down the road beyond the castle lay the town village.

While at Gustavo, Doña Teresa, Isabella's mother, would also instruct both Lucía and Isabella on how to properly manage a household staff and how to act as host to notables who attended court. She was a very kind soul with an easy disposition and, when time permitted, would laugh and play with the children, at which time her brown eyes would light up, along with a wide smile from ear to ear. Lucía loved Doña Teresa, who became like a surrogate mother and a wonderful role model for Lucía to follow. Lucía also discovered that Doña Teresa had been one of her mother's best friends.

One day, Lucía and Isabella were seated, doing their lessons with Yamina, when a messenger from Gustavo presented Isabella with a message from her mother. Isabella broke the wax seal and, with Yamina's help, read the message. The message instructed Isabella to pack her clothes and be ready to leave in two days as the family had received a personal invitation from King Sancho to visit her relatives in Portugal.

"Do you wish me to wait for a return message, mi señora?'" asked the messenger, who addressed Isabella.

"Tell Mama that I will be ready," said Isabella sadly.

"Very well," said the messenger, who then turned and left the room.

"How long will you be away?" asked Lucía, who pouted at the prospect of the loss of her friend for quite some time.

"I do not know. Mama did not say how long." Isabella was sad at the prospect of having to leave her friend but was also heartened to be going on an adventure. "Don't be sad, Lucía. I will be back in several fortnights, and then I will tell you all about my time in Portugal."

Lucía was very concerned, as she had heard stories at court about the hazards of traveling and overheard her father tell a visiting knight to be careful, as trouble was beginning between Portugal and Castile.

Lucía helped Isabella pack her trunks, but she was still concerned about the hazards she might encounter en route to Portugal.

The day of dread finally arrived, when Isabella's parents appeared with a long entourage of wagons loaded with supplies and servants. The entourage was accompanied by twelve soldiers who wore over their coat of chain mail a surcoat that displayed the coat of arms of Gustavo: three silver swords lying on top of one another on a dark-blue background. Each soldier was fully armed and carried a lance with a dark-blue pennant, which was flying in the breeze. Such an impressive display had not been seen in Segoia for quite some time.

Along with Lucía were Don Fernando, Captain Gómez, and Father Piña, all on hand to welcome Don Alfonso Coronado and Doña Teresa and to wish them well on their long trip to Portugal.

Isabella was torn between having an adventure and staying with Lucía but really had no choice in the matter. Lucía broke down in tears and found it difficult to say goodbye to her best friend and confidante, but Doña Teresa embraced Lucía, comforted her, and told her that they would only be gone for no more than six to eight fortnights. She promised Isabella would write to her about her adventures.

The area in front of the palace became busy as servants hurried to bring down Isabella's trunks from Lucía's bedchamber. Once the trunks were packed onto a wagon, the entourage was ready to leave, but not before Father Piña gave a blessing for a safe journey. Isabella then gave her final embrace to a sniffling Lucía, who once again made Isabella promise to write. Isabella climbed into the wagon and waved goodbye. Then the entourage started to leave the palace grounds into the city, through the city gates, and to the horizon beyond. Lucía ran to the tower, where the two girls would often be found, and watched as the cortege disappeared into the horizon.

More than two fortnights had passed before Lucía received her first letter from Isabella. Lucía broke the seal and started to read the letter, proud of the fact that she could now read with only a little help from Yamina or her father.

"Papa," yelled Lucía as she ran into her father's study outside his bedchamber, "I have a letter from Isabella." Lucía tried to catch her breath. "A messenger brought it from Coimbra, and I read it with only little help from Yamina."

"Good for you, mi pequeño sol. What did Isabella say in the letter?" asked Don Fernando, seated in front of his worktable.

"Isabella said that the journey went smooth but had some difficulty in crossing the mountains, but everyone is okay. One night, several Knight Templars joined them for supper but left early the next morning for Jerusalem. When they arrived in Coimbra, they were greeted by family members and the next day met King Sancho. They had a large welcome banquet at an uncle's castle outside of Coimbra. They will be going to visit another uncle and more cousins in Lisbon soon. She remembers us in her prayers at night and hopes all is well with us. The letter is signed Isabella."

Despite the letter, Lucía still missed Isabella, as they had become very close and their friendship had run deep. Lucía would often lie awake at night in wonderment of what adventures Isabella might have had during the day, until sleep finally cloaked itself around her, like a thick mist that obscured all thought.

The days and weeks passed, and Lucía was kept busy with her studies until one day Don Fernando told Lucía that it was time to harvest grapes in the vineyard and asked if she would like to help pick them as her mother had done on many occasions. Lucía was excited and, as a surprise, was given her very own straw hat to protect her from the sun.

Yamina helped Lucía find suitable clothing to wear in the vineyard and found an old green undergarment and a matching green sleeveless surcoat to serve as an outer garment. Lucía put on her straw hat with the cord tight under her chin and walked down to the stable, where her father was waiting.

"Ah, are you ready, mi pequeño sol?"

"Sí, Papa," said Lucía.

Don Fernando mounted his horse and, with one hand, lifted her onto the saddle. "Now you hold on to the horn tightly with both hands."

"Sí, Papa. Can we go now?" inquired Lucía, who was very enthusiastic about the prospects of a new adventure.

Don Fernando held on to his daughter and the reins of the horse as they rode out of the palace gate, through the city, out into the countryside, down the long winding road, and to the vineyard below. Lucía noticed the peasant village across the road from the vineyard with its many white huts and the beautiful village church. In the middle of the village was the precious well of spring water from the mountains beyond.

Upon arrival at the vineyard, Lucía saw that it was indeed a busy place, with peasants who scurried about, picking grapes in the each of the rows. There were also several men who went up and down the rows with mule-driven carts and picked up the full woven baskets of grapes ready to be taken to the winery to be crushed into juice.

Before Don Fernando proceeded into the vineyard to help with the harvest, he decided to take advantage of Lucía's eagerness to learn and show her around the complex. He realized that she was still quite young, but he felt this was a good time to introduce her to the family business and her future inheritance. He first took her to the winery, where wine was crushed into juice by a wine press and by peasant women who used their feet to crush the ripe grapes. Lucía was taken by the women who ran around in purple feet, and she wondered if the purple stain ever washed off. He then showed Lucía how the stems and other debris were filtered out and how the juice was stored in sealed wooden oak barrels for fermentation.

Finally, he took her to the cooper shed, where the oaken barrels were made. Once the wine in barrels was properly sealed, it was placed in the underground chamber by the winery for storage. Lucía was impressed by the dimensions of the underground chamber and the number of barrels contained inside it. Lucía was told that from the chamber, wine was delivered to all the inns, taverns, religious, and noble houses that were contracted. The remainder was for the palace.

Segoian wine making went back many centuries and had a superb reputation for quality and taste. Although Lucía seemed somewhat confused and bewildered by it all, Don Fernando reassured her that she would come to understand it all in time.

The vineyard was filled with peasants, who were engrossed in their work, and their assiduousness was seen not only in the woven baskets they filled but also in their sweat-laden faces. Lucía noticed that most of the workers were either wearing coifs or straw hats to protect them from the sun, and they wore their garments tucked into their belts so as not to interfere with their work.

Lucía was with her father when he spoke to the peasant leader of the village in charge of the vineyard. "Buenos días, Zito."

"Buenos días to you as well, mi señor," said Zito.

"This is my daughter, Doña Lucía, Zito."

"Buenos días, mi señora. What a beautiful young daughter you have, Don Fernando. She is certainly worthy of a highborn rank."

Lucía smiled with a slight bow of her head to acknowledge such a nice compliment.

"Gracias," said Don Fernando, who beamed with pride.

While Don Fernando and Zito discussed the state of the vineyard, Lucía went over to a row to examine a cluster of grapes, pulled a grape off a cluster, wiped it off on her garment, and ate it.

"Did that taste sweet, Lucía?" asked Don Fernando, who surprised his daughter.

"Somewhat," said Lucía.

"Good," responded her father. "That is what we look for in checking whether grapes are ripe enough for picking."

Don Fernando examined the grapes at hand and showed Lucía the color they should be when ripe, and then he gave one to Lucía and tasted one for himself. Lucía finished chewing on a grape but was curious as to whom Zito was.

"Papa?"

"Sí, mi pequeño sol," said Don Fernando, who had bent down to examine another cluster of grapes.

"Who was that man you were speaking to?"

Don Fernando turned to his daughter and responded, "That was Zito, the peasant leader of the village."

"What does he do?" asked Lucía, who was stuffing her face with another grape.

"His job is to maintain the vineyard and make sure the peasant workers are properly doing their job. He is responsible for the weeding, the grafting, and the picking of grapes, as well as the proper making and storing of the wine once it is made."

"Why is the top of his head bald like Father Piña?"

"Because Zito was a former monk."

"What is a monk, Papa?" asked Lucía.

"A monk lives in a monastery, gives his life to God, and helps the poor. They live in poverty and have very few possessions."

Lucía bobbed her head and made a face that manifested understanding.

"Zito is very knowledgeable about the growing of grapes and the making of wine. I have deep respect for his judgment, which someday, perhaps, you will also have as well."

"Papa?"

"Sí, Lucía," answered Don Fernando, who was beginning to get annoyed at so many questions but felt it important to answer them.

"What does *highborn* mean? Was I born in the sky? I thought Mama was lying on a bed when I was born?" asked Lucía, who showed concern.

Don Fernando laughed. "Lucía, it is only an expression that means that you are of noble birth and destined for leadership someday as a condesa."

Lucía nodded in understanding but made a face that indicated not completely. "Papa?"

Don Fernando interrupted her, "Lucía, why don't you save your questions for later so we can concentrate on the matter at hand—the picking of grapes."

Lucía agreed, and Don Fernando explained in detail the procedure of picking grapes by using a device called a pruning knife, which looked like a small scythe. He showed her how to cut the grape clusters and then put them in a woven basket next to him. Once the basket was filled, it was put at the head of the row, which was wide enough for a mule cart to come by to pick it up, and take it to the winery for crushing and to exchange it for an empty one.

Lucía was also introduced to several of the peasants who were working in the vineyard. They would curtsy or bow to Lucía and tell Don Fernando how absolutely beautiful she was and how much she resembled her mother, whom they all adored. Lucía was happy being compared to her mother.

After a while of helping her father pick grapes, she noticed several of the children who were her age playing across the road, rolling a cooper's hoop with a stick down the hill. "Papa, may I play with the children across the road?"

"I see no reason why not. You have been quite helpful today putting the grape clusters in the basket. We'll continue with this tomorrow," said Don Fernando, who wiped his brow and stripped down to his untied white shirt.

"Gracias, Papa," said Lucía, and she quickly ran off to join the group of children who were having races with their hoops.

"Lucía, make sure you remain in my view. Don't wander off!" shouted Don Fernando.

"I won't. I promise!" yelled Lucía on the run.

Don Fernando wanted Lucía to get to know the people of the village, and interacting with them was a good way of doing so. Yet he was very mindful of Queen Leonor always reminding him that Lucía was the granddaughter of a king and should not be allowed to take such liberties with peasants.

Don Fernando watched with a smile as Lucía fit in with the other children and, within a short time, was happily rolling a hoop down the hill with a stick, along with the other young peasants.

Don Fernando, as his father and grandfather once did, took pride in the hands-on approach in maintaining a vineyard, and he hoped to encourage Lucía to do the same.

As the weeks passed, Don Fernando each day would interrupt her studies and would show Lucía a different part of the operation to help reinforce her knowledge of the family business that one day she would inherit. Lucía also enjoyed her excursions with her father and, after a while, began to show some knowledge of what needed to be done. Such was the intellect of a bright young lady.

Lucía awakened before dawn and looked forward in going to the vineyard to help her father with the harvest. Most of the vineyard had been picked; only the last quarter remained. Lucía, with the help of Yamina and a couple of servants, got dressed, and then it was off to the chapel for morning prayers, after which downstairs to the great hall for breakfast. Lucía had a simple breakfast of toasted bread with honey, an orange, and her favorite, warm almond milk.

When Lucía arrived at the stables, her father was talking to Captain Gómez and overheard a small part of the conversation about a Moorish raid that had taken place at a small village ten miles to the south of Segoia. "Send out a couple of scouts to the south and see if they can locate the raiding party. Also notify the Grandmaster of the Order of the Christian Knights of Segoia to be prepared for any action that may arise. Be sure to send aid to the village. If you need me, I'll be in the vineyard with Lucía."

Captain Gómez nodded to Don Fernando, turned, and noticed Lucía, to whom he gave a polite bow of his head; he then went back to his room in the stable, where he spent little time due to his responsibilities.

Captain Gómez was the military commander of the army of Segoia. He was in charge of the one hundred soldiers who guarded the city and the palace, which also entailed training men on how to fight in battle in case the need arose, either by order of Don Fernando or the king.

Personality wise, Captain Gómez was always stern and disciplined and not much in the way of socializing; he did not marry, as he had little time for a family and found children to be an annoyance.

"Papa, why doesn't Captain Gómez ever smile? And why is he always so grouchy?" asked Lucía to her father, who was getting ready to mount his horse.

Don Fernando smiled as he mounted his horse and reached down for Lucía.

"He has a lot on his mind. He has a big responsibility to protect not only us but also the rest of the condado."

"Papa?" asked Lucía as they were riding out of the stable. "I have another question."

"No doubt," responded Don Fernando, who snickered.

"Does Captain García own any other garments beside that stinky mess of metal he is always wearing?"

Don Fernando let out with a roar of laughter. "That stinky mess of metal, Lucía, is called a suit of chain mail and is worn as protection in battle. I also have a suit."

"But, Papa, you don't wear it all the time as he does."

"Remember, Lucía, he is a professional soldier, and he has to be prepared to fight at a moment's notice."

"Ah," responded Lucía, who was satisfied with the answer, and then she fell silent for the rest of the ride to the vineyard.

Once at the vineyard, Don Fernando stopped at the winery with Lucía to check on the wine production. There he met Zito, who was examining the newly made oak wine barrels for leakage, and then they were off to the underground chamber, where the wine was stored and where Don Fernando took a count on the number of stored barrels.

Lucía noticed the darkness of the wine cellar if not for torches on the wall, which lit the way. The barrels were three high, and each barrel was carefully rolled in place. Each barrel was tapped with a spigot for tasting, as the wine was aged a month before delivery. Either Don Fernando or Zito would taste the wine to ensure quality of the barrel. When ready for delivery, a barrel would be marked with an x in charcoal. The barrels left over, and usually there were plenty, would be either for the use of the palace or used for gifts. Lucía was given a small sip from a couple of barrels and asked her opinion, under the guidance of her father, and was even allowed to mark several barrels with an x, which were taken out and placed in a horse-driven cart for delivery. Each shipment was accompanied by three soldiers to safeguard delivery and payment.

The sun was now only a few hours old in the sky, as Don Fernando rode around the remainder of the vineyard to inspect the grapes yet to be picked. Then he grabbed a basket and, with Lucía's help, loaded it full with grapes. Lucía became a hit with the working peasants, as she politely engaged in conversation with the people she met in the field and sometimes played with the village children that she encountered. But today it was all business, for the last quarter of the vineyard had to be picked before the weather changed.

The vineyard was running with incessant energy when suddenly Don Fernando thought he heard screams and smelled smoke. He stood straight up and quickly ran out from the row where he had been working and saw about a mile away down the road in front of the vineyard what appeared to be a Moorish raid. His quick movements scared Lucía, who started to tremble in fear.

"Papa!" she yelled. "What's happening?"

Don Fernando rushed back, quickly had Lucía lie on the ground, and covered her with all sorts of debris that he could find. "Lucía, I want you to stay here and not move or make a sound until I come back. Do you understand me?"

"Sí, Papa, but what is going on?" asked Lucía, who was visibly upset.

"It will be all right, I promise, but you must do as I tell you. Do you understand?"

Lucía nodded.

"That's mi pequeño sol," said Don Fernando, and he ran out to the road. To his horror, Don Fernando saw a raiding party of twelve Moorish soldiers, who wore black garments and black turbans wrapped around their necks and covered their faces. With only his white shirt, which was unlaced, a pair of green breeches, and a dagger, he ran toward the commotion. Suddenly, the village church bells rang and sounded the alarm. He could see from a distance that several huts were on fire and several peasants had been cut down and lay strewn across the landscape. Several women and children of the village had been kidnapped and hung over the saddles horns of their captors.

The small army in single file started to leave the premises and headed in Don Fernando's direction, carrying their captives, but the enemy line maintained a good distance between each soldier. The first soldier came by swinging his scimitar. Don Fernando braced himself as he saw a soldier poised for the kill with eyes dark and foreboding. He quickly jumped on the back of his horse, pulled his dagger, and slit his throat. As he threw the dead soldier off this horse, he retrieved his scimitar.

The next soldier rode by, but a young girl who had been kidnapped was so busy trying to fight off her captor he couldn't pull his scimitar. When he saw Don Fernando, he quickly dropped the girl, who ran off, and pulled his sword, but he quickly fell under the blow of Don Fernando's scimitar. Two more arrived and fought Don Fernando on horseback, but they lost the fight with one losing another captive. The eight surviving soldiers rode off with several young women from the village.

A few minutes after the raid, Captain Gómez arrived with a contingent of twelve well-armed men ready for battle. Captain Gómez noticed Don Fernando still on the enemy horse and halted his contingent. "I see that you have been busy, Don Fernando," said Gómez after he perused the bodies of the four dead soldiers, and found Don Fernando apparently unscathed. "Well, thanks be to God that you were not harmed."

"You surprise me, Gómez. I never took you for a man of religion," said Don Fernando with a smile.

"You know me, Don Fernando, always straight in the saddle."

Don Fernando laughed at the comment and then became serious. "Eight escaped, carrying several women, and headed south on the Madrid road."

"Most likely they are heading back to al-Andulus. Well, we'll find them and bring back the women and whatever else they stole. Adiós, my friend." With that parting comment, Captain Gómez led his contingent south toward the direction of the enemy.

"Good hunting as always, Gómez," said Don Fernando as he hurried back for Lucía. "Lucía! Lucía!" cried Don Fernando.

"Over here, Papa!" cried Lucía, who stood up and wiped her garment off from the clinging debris of the ground.

"Are you okay, mi pequeño sol?" asked Don Fernando, holding onto her tightly.

"Sí, Papa, but I was very worried."

"Well, it's all right now." After an embrace, Don Fernando started to walk down the road in front of the vineyard with Lucía. To his surprise, Yamina came riding on a horse. After having heard of the raid, she had hoped to find Lucía.

"You certainly came at the right time, Yamina. Take Lucía back to the palace and have her cleaned up. Avoid the village. It's no place for her right now."

"Of course, Don Fernando," said Yamina.

Don Fernando bent down and told Lucía, "I want you to go back with Yamina. I will be back later."

"Sí, Papa," said Lucía. Don Fernando mounted her on Yamina's saddle, and they both rode back to the palace.

As Yamina rode away with Lucía, Don Fernando traveled to the village to see the devastation. Smoke filled the air and masked the confusion that was taking place. The men of the village had formed a fire brigade with the help of several soldiers to put out the fires. A line extended from the well to the huts that were still ablaze. Another group of men were putting out the fire that had destroyed several rows of the vineyard. Peasants were milling about in confusion and disbelief. Father Piña was already praying over the bodies of the dead.

Zito met Don Fernando as soon as he dismounted.

"How many are dead, Zito?"

"Three here in the village and two more in the vineyard, where the men were cleaning up the debris from the harvest."

Don Fernando stood in stunned silence. The attack had been a complete surprise. This had been the first raid as long as Don Fernando could remember.

Don Fernando turned to Zito after he had examined the area from the spot where he was standing. "I would have thought the Duero Valley to be safe from the Moors, but they seem to be growing bolder. But I never thought they would be so bold as to attack here."

"There was no defense, Don Fernando. They struck in complete surprise from nowhere."

"There is no such place as nowhere, Zito, and that was my first mistake. But I do wonder what happened to the scouts I sent out several days ago. They should have been back by now and could have warned us about a possible attack."

Father Piña interrupted his conversation, "Don Fernando, it's good to see you here. The village people are frightened and need reassurances from you. There are already five dead and several wounded."

"I understand, Padre," said Don Fernando, and he called one of the soldiers who had helped in the fire brigade.

"Mi señor," responded the soldier.

"Go fetch my physician to help with the wounded." With the order, the soldier mounted his horse and rode off quickly to Segoia.

After several hours, Don Fernando was able to access the final damage, and it wasn't pleasant. Five huts had been burned to the ground and several more were damaged, six people had died from the attack, and three more were wounded but not severely. Three young women were missing, and three rows of the vineyard had been burned. Fortunately, the grapes had already been picked from those rows.

Don Fernando was able to assemble all the village occupants in the village church to reassure them that they were safe and that the possibility of the Moors returning was unlikely. He further promised he would get carpenters to rebuild the huts that were destroyed and arrangements would be made for the homeless to have lodging in the city. He would replant the rows of the vineyard that were burned and that Captain Gómez was currently seeking the missing girls. He also would send six well-armed soldiers to guard the village. The village people were pleased with Don Fernando's assurances, which now allowed him to go back to the palace to see to his daughter.

The weeks passed, and Lucía was having nightmares about the events of that dreadful day. Unfortunately, while Lucía was hiding from the Moors during the attack, she had caught a glimpse of one of the saboteurs who had kidnapped a girl about her age and had held her tightly by his side. She was afraid that if he had lost his grip on her, she would have fallen and been trampled by his horse. She had also witnessed a soldier who had been struck down by her father fall to the ground not far from where she was hiding, with his eyes still open in death. Also, between the smell of the smoke, the noise, and confusion of the peasants, all drew images that she could not escape and were seared on her mind forever.

Don Fernando and Yamina tried to comfort Lucía as much as possible and told her that the kidnapped girls were all rescued and returned safe and all personal property stolen returned to its owners. The remaining Moors who had invaded the village would never hurt anyone again. These events were good news to Lucía, who had worried about the girls who were kidnapped.

The events of the past weeks had overshadowed the concerns that Yamina had concerning her future as Lucía's tutor. She was getting on in age and did not feel up to teaching the advanced subject matter that Lucía was capable of learning, but she was willing to stay on for a short while as her nurse.

Don Fernando complimented her for her years of service in teaching Lucía basic subject matter and said that he would speak to the king about a future tutor for Lucía. She would be welcomed to stay on in the capacity of a nurse.

Within days, Don Fernando addressed this issue with the king and queen.

An idea was suggested that Lucía be tutored by Berenguela's instructor at the royal palace. However, it was decided that it would be best that Lucía remain in Segoia. Therefore, a new tutor would have to be found, and only the best in Europe would be considered. The question remained where such a tutor could be found. Perhaps one could be found at the University of Paris or Bologna? It was decided that they would write to His Holiness, Pope Clement, for his ideas on this matter.

Meanwhile, it was Lucía's birthday, and Don Fernando had a special surprise for his daughter. Lucía was told to meet her father in the stable. Lucía ran down to the stable, but when she arrived, there was no one in sight, not even José, the stable keeper.

"Papa, are you here?" asked Lucía, not sure what was happening.

"Over here, mi pequeño sol," said Don Fernando.

Lucía followed her father's voice around a stall. When she found him, he was in another stall with a beautiful white horse, along with

José. "Happy birthday, Lucía," said Don Fernando, who stepped back to let Lucía examine her birthday gift.

"This is my horse?" asked Lucía as she raised both of her hands to her face in an expression of amazement and disbelief.

"Sí, mi pequeño sol, and ride it in good health," responded Don Fernando.

"Gracias, Papa." Lucía went over and embraced her father with tears of joy.

"This is a two-year-old white Arabian stallion, purchased at great expense from a trusted horse dealer who was recommended by your Uncle Alfonso." Lucía approached the horse, petted his face, and then embraced it wholeheartedly.

After a period of time, Don Fernando asked, "What are you going to name him?"

Having had the opportunity to examine him for several minutes, Lucía announced with a big smile, "I shall call him…" After a slight pause, she said, "Rodrigo after El Cid, Papa, from the stories Yamina told me about him and what a great hero he was to Castile."

Fernando smiled. "I could not think of a more appropriate name. I'm sure that Don Rodrigo Díaz de Vivar would be more than pleased." Lucía could now follow her father to the vineyard with her own steed.

While the days passed, Lucía had become accustomed to riding Rodrigo. Then news arrived that Isabella and her entourage were approaching Segoia. Lucía could hardly wait to see her friend again. So much had happened that Lucía could not wait to tell her stories, and yet what about Isabella? She had not heard from Isabella since the first letter sent to her some time ago.

Within a couple of hours, the day that Lucía had been waiting for finally arrived. She and her father awaited for the entourage to arrive on the palace grounds. Upon arrival, Lucía watched carefully as Don Alfonso Coronado stepped out of the wagon first and then helped Isabella out next. Lucía was waiting for Isabella's mother to also disembark, but that was not the case.

After a pause, the two walked over to greet Don Fernando and Lucía. Lucía could tell something was horribly wrong, as Isabella had red eyes and tears were streaming down her face. Lucía escorted Isabella into the antechamber of the great hall, followed by her father and Don Alfonso Coronado. However, Isabella did not stay in the anteroom. She went immediately out to the garden and sat down on a bench in front of the fountain, where she could seek comfort, with Lucía in close pursuit.

Once both were seated next to each other and Isabella had time to quiet down, Lucía asked, "Why are you so sad, Isabella, and where is your mother?"

Isabella started to grieve again and choked back tears in an attempt to speak and be understood. "Mama is dead, Lucía," cried Isabella as she wiped away her tears with a piece of linen.

"Dead! Did you say dead, Isabella?"

Isabella nodded. "Sí."

"But how did she die?"

"Lucía, didn't you receive the second letter I sent you?"

"No, I only received the first," said Lucía as her eyes started to water.

"Well, we never left Coimbra. The day before we were to leave, Mama said that she felt ill and retired to the bedchamber. That night, a court physician came to examine her, bled her, and then administered some sort of herb concoction that she had a hard time drinking. I stayed next to her all night. The next morning, when I awoke, I noticed that Mama was even worse than the night before. Again, the court physician was called. After he examined her, he said that she was in God's hands now. I'll never forget how he said that.

"Shortly, after the physician left, Mama, who was very weak, whispered for me to come close to her. I rose from my chair and put my ear to her lips, and she again softly whispered to me. She told me not to be afraid, that death came to everyone, to be brave for Papa, and to always keep the faith. Then I saw her smile, after which she took her last breath." Isabella could not hold back her tears any longer, but she continued on with her story, barely understood. "Lucía, I wept and wept for several days after her death until I had no tears left."

"And then what happened, Isabella?" asked Lucía, who was also weeping.

"The family had a funeral. My uncle and Papa both agreed to have her buried next to my grandparents in the church crypt at the family estate outside of Coimbra."

"How awful, Isabella. I am so sorry," said Lucía, who wiped away her tears, and they both embraced.

That night, Lucía went to the palace chapel and said a special prayer for the kind and gentle person that Doña Teresa had been and the mother she had never known.

Chapter VI

Several weeks had passed since Isabella arrived home from Portugal, and she continued to spend time with Lucía in Segoia. This proved to be good therapy for Isabella, as she started to accept her loss around people she loved and trusted and who had become an important part of her life.

One day, a priest entered the city, riding a donkey, with two saddlebags draped over its back. The man was simply dressed in a brown robe tied with a hemp belt and sandals and wore a wooden cross around his neck. The guards at the gate laughed at the sight of a tall man riding a donkey. His legs were practically touching the ground, but the priest smiled and kept on riding to the fountain in the city square. Such a sight created interest among the small crowd who had gathered to watch the priest reach into the fountain with his cupped hands to give the donkey a drink of water. With each handful of water, the donkey made a typical braying noise with many hee-haws, which attracted the attention of the children in the crowd. The priest spent time with each child. He asked them their names and allowed them to pet the donkey and then gave each a blessing.

The priest took the reins of the donkey and walked to the palace gates. He told the guards he had urgent business with Don Fernando. Once through the gates, he was led to the anteroom of the great hall, where Don Fernando was at his table on the dais, busily reviewing some documents.

"A Father Baldwin to see you, mi señor," announced a servant.

Don Fernando paused from his reading and rose from his chair to examine the priest who entered the anteroom, carrying his leather saddlebags. His eyes, although gray, sparkled with a smile. His face was smooth and wrinkled and gave the appearance of intellect and wisdom. His mane, which protruded from his tonsure, was a mop of gray thinning hair, and his robe was more gray than brown from the dusty road traveled.

"Do I know you, Padre?" asked Don Fernando.

"No," said Father Baldwin.

"Please have a seat, Padre. Perhaps some refreshments?"

"No, thank you. I assure you, I'm fine," said Father Baldwin with a smile.

"What can I do for you then?" asked Don Fernando, quite interested in the priest who sat before him.

"It's what I can do for you. Let me explain," said the priest with a smile and a voice that put Don Fernando at ease. "My name is Hugh Baldwin, and I have been sent from Rome in answer to your letter to His Holiness, which concerned a tutor for your daughter, Doña Lucía. Here are my credentials and a letter of introduction sent by His Holiness."

Don Fernando rose from his chair and walked off the dais to examine the documents handed to him. Don Fernando noticed the official lead seal of the pope, the heads of St. Peter and St. Paul, with a cross, which separated the two saintly heads attached to the letter with a white cord at the bottom of the document. He read the rather lengthy verbose introduction written in Latin and then turned to Father Baldwin.

"This is a rather grandiloquent introduction, more like a sermon than a letter."

"Sí, His Holiness does tend to get carried away in his use of the Latin language," said Father Baldwin with a subtle laugh. Don Fernando could not help but laugh along with his guest, caught in his infectious humor.

Don Fernando took a seat next to Father Baldwin below the dais, and he listened with interest to his conversation regarding his background. Don Fernando discovered that his guest was a mixture of Norman and English noble stock. In his early years, he was trained as a warrior by his father, but becoming a knight was not in his nature. He also realized that being the youngest of four children, he would also become a poor knight, so he turned his attention to the church and felt very comfortable with his choice of profession. Father Baldwin went on to indicate with humility that he received a classical and advanced education at St. Albans, thanks to his father's support, and was considered a scholar of his day. After further study, he was ordained a priest.

Don Fernando also learned his new tutor could also be quite loquacious in his own right, as he babbled on about being chosen by the English Pope Adrian in his late teens due to his acute intellect and quick-wittedness. The new pope at the time had made him an offer to come to Rome to serve the papacy, which he did in various capacities over the years through succeeding popes.

Don Fernando started to yawn as his new friend continued the conversation by also mentioning his enjoyment of having traveled the world to garner knowledge, especially in the Arab world. Here, he spent time learning and reading original Greek texts about the ancient sciences of medicine, biology, physics, and advanced mathematics.

Finally, Don Fernando had had enough, and he interrupted the conversation, "Well, Padre, I am very impressed with your background and find it to be a good match for my daughter. As you are probably aware, Padre, from my letter to His Holiness, you will be taking over the teaching responsibilities from Yamina, Lucía's nurse and tutor. She is advancing in age and wishes to stay on as nurse only. Oh, by the way, you will also be tutoring my daughter's good friend, Doña Isabella, as well. I hope you will not mind, Padre," said Don Fernando, who returned his papal letter of introduction.

"Not at all," responded Father Baldwin. "And I do hope I have not bored you, Don Fernando. I really do hate talking about myself, but I felt that I had to convince you of my qualifications in order to seek your approval. I owe my entire success from the hand of God and give thanks each day for his many blessings."

"Well, Padre, you have impressed me with your qualifications, and I find you more a university scholar than a simple tutor, for sure. You are a very humble man with a pleasant, outgoing manner and a well-educated man of God. Now, Padre, what about payment?"

"I do not require payment, only simple lodging."

"That I will see to immediately," responded Don Fernando, and he rose from his chair. "Follow me, Padre, and I will show you to your room and introduce you to your new students." Father Baldwin picked up his saddlebags and followed behind his new employer.

While Don Fernando and Father Baldwin were meeting in the antechamber of the great hall, Lucía and Isabella were in their shared boudoir, dancing and whirling around to imaginary music, laughing and giggling to their missteps. The girls were about to have an archery lesson when Don Fernando and Father Baldwin entered the boudoir and found both Lucía and Isabella completely oblivious to their entrance. The girls had left the dance floor and moved to the dressing table, where they were preening and making faces in the oval mirror, which sat on a heavy silver base.

Don Fernando cleared his throat, and the two girls abruptly turned around to see Don Fernando and a cleric standing in the doorway.

"Now that I have your attention, I would like to introduce you to your new tutor," said Don Fernando as he walked over to the girls along with Father Baldwin. "Lucía and Isabella, this is your new tutor, Father Baldwin. He has come all the way from Rome to tutor you."

The girls were wide-eyed as they examined their new sage. "From Rome, where the pope lives?" asked Lucía.

"The very same," responded Father Baldwin.

"Do you know the pope?" asked Isabella.

"As a matter of fact, I do," said Father Baldwin with his kind smile.

The two girls were impressed that they were in the midst of a cleric who actually knew the pope and had traveled so far.

"What are you going to teach us?" inquired Lucía.

With a smile and a twinkle in his eye, Father Baldwin opened his saddle bags and pulled out two heavy thick leather-bound books and placed them on a side table. The girls curious opened them and only found blank parchment.

Lucía laughed along with Isabella. "Is this what you are going to teach us?" asked Lucía.

"Precisely," responded Father Baldwin.

The two girls looked at each other in confusion. "How could blank parchment teach anything?" asked Lucía.

"By itself, nothing," responded Father Baldwin, "but you will be filling the blank pages with the knowledge I will soon be imparting to you on a whole variety of subjects."

The two girls were then put on a daily schedule that was heavy on learning, as well as their continued lessons on manners and etiquette, how to dance and ride, archery, proper dress, and household management. The two girls looked at each other and realized they would have little time for else.

A couple of days later, Lucía and Isabella were working in the vineyard with Don Fernando, who felt that physical labor was as important as mental labor. Also, it was important for Lucía to continue to learn about the family business. While they were busy at their tasks, Lucía heard what sounded like shouting in the peasant village, along with her father and Isabella. Lucía started to panic and thought it was another raid. Don Fernando, after he told Lucía and Isabella to stay quiet, ventured out of the row of grapes, up the incline beyond five more rows of grapes from where the group had been working, and onto vineyard road.

Suddenly, a man turned off the main road by the village and onto the vineyard road and shouted, "Jerusalem has fallen! Jerusalem has fallen!" as he galloped past Don Fernando. He watched the man as he turned down another side road a distance away at the other end of the vineyard and then made another turn and onto the Madrid road, which eventually led to the bridge over the River Duero and beyond. All the time he shouted, "Jerusalem has fallen!"

Lucía and Isabella came running up the incline after the man had passed and were reassured by Don Fernando there was no additional danger.

"Papa, who was that man?"

"I don't know, Lucía," said Don Fernando as his eyes still scrutinized the horizon where the man had just disappeared out of sight.

"Why was he screaming so loud?" interjected Isabella.

"To let us know that the Holy City has fallen," said Don Fernando.

"Papa?"

"Sí, Lucía."

"What does that mean?"

"It means that the Holy City has been captured by the Saracens," said Don Fernando, somewhat lost in thought, "and I fear another crusade."

"What's a crusade, Papa?"

Don Fernando smiled at Lucía's inquisitiveness. "Later, mi pequeño sol, but now it's time to head back to the palace." Both Lucía and Isabella mounted their horses, along with Don Fernando, and they headed home.

At supper, Don Fernando enjoyed much company, as Father Baldwin and Isabella had joined Lucía and Yamina as regulars at the head table on the dais.

Don Fernando turned to his right to speak to Father Baldwin. "I fear another crusade is at hand, Padre."

"I quite agree," said Father Baldwin in a gravelly voice. "I have witnessed and heard about the greed and avarice for the quest of land and power among certain Christian nobles in the Holy Land and the attacks on the caravans heading west by Christian knights. Certainly, this is not the type of behavior that would inspire continued peace in the region," said Father Baldwin with a sly smile.

Within days, Don Fernando's fear was realized, as priests and clerics were crossing Europe to find men to take up the cross and go on crusade to the Holy Land and free it from the Saracens who had captured Jerusalem.

Most people were alarmed at the fall of Jerusalem, except for Don Raimundo, the Conde of Donato. He had been planning for a long time an ambitious move that would propel him to the highest position in the land to become king, and perhaps this event might play into his hands. Don Raimundo had felt for many years that the Reconquista was moving too slowly under King Alfonso and therefore wealth and booty were eluding him. Raids along the border towns of al-Andalus were of little value since most had been well culled over time, and to truly gain any real wealth, a large force would be needed to penetrate the interior where the true treasures were hidden, such as in Seville or the real prize, Cordoba. Without the manpower or authority to do so, it remained, in his opinion, nothing but a dream.

First, he must take the throne before such an ambitious plan could be implemented, yet he should not appear too ambitious and raise any suspicions. Such a plan would require a great deal of gold. He would need to raise an army large enough to take and hold the major cities of the kingdom and to persuade the major noble houses to support him. Where would he find such wealth? Over time, he came to the conclusion the only way to accumulate the additional wealth needed to accomplish his objective was to seize the wealth of one of the wealthiest young nobles in the land—that of Doña Lucía Alvarado. But how would he accomplish this objective? He rationalized there would be only two ways to do so, either by marriage or by death. Unfortunately, the latter would most likely fall into play.

Don Raimundo was a patient man, having waited a long time for events to fall into play, and it was now the time to strike. He had to find a way to rid the king of his most trusted allies, mainly Don Fernando and Don Alfonso Coronado and, eventually, Ávila. The crusades would be this opportunity. The bishop of Segoia would be of help in this matter to convince the two men to take the cross and go to the Holy Land. He knew the bishop to be corruptible from his practice of skimming off the top of the collection plate each Sunday and during weekly services. He had an idea of what to do, which would work out satisfactorily for all involved, but first he had to have a meeting with the bishop, as this was a crucial part of his plan.

"The Bishop of Segoia," said the servant as he announced the arrival of the bishop to Don Raimundo, who was seated at a table in the antechamber of the great hall.

"Ah, my Lord Bishop," said Don Raimundo as he stepped away from the table to greet the bishop and kiss his ring. "Gracias for coming. I trust your short journey from Segoia was a pleasant one?"

"As pleasant as can be expected," said the bishop.

"Some refreshments, my Lord Bishop?" asked Don Raimundo, who motioned to an awaiting servant.

"That would be delightful," voiced the bishop, already smacking his lips.

Don Raimundo nodded to a servant. "Bring tapas, sweet tarts, and wine for the bishop." The servant curtsied and left.

"What is this all about, Don Raimundo? You said it's a matter of urgency."

"Of course. Please sit down, and I will explain myself fully."

The bishop listened patiently as Don Raimundo explained his plan to the bishop. "Now let me understand. You want me to persuade Don Fernando and Don Alfonso Coronado to take the cross and go to the Holy Land and for me to become your ally in a plan to take the crown?"

The conversation suddenly stopped, as the servant came in with tapas of olives, cheese, strips of sliced cured ham, sweet tarts, and wine. The servant poured two goblets of wine, curtsied, and left the room. It didn't take the bishop long to help himself. As he took a piece of ham, the bishop said sarcastically with a slight laugh, "This separates us from our Jewish brethren."

Don Raimundo did not think the remark humorous and was not in the mood for amusement as he tried to continue the conversation with the bishop, who kept feeding his chubby face. His face was so rotund that it appeared to turn his dark eyes into slits, which didn't miss a crumb of the sweet tarts he quickly devoured. He had already stained his red garment with olive oil.

"My Lord Bishop, with all due respect," said Don Raimundo, who was becoming irritated at the bishop's eating habits.

"Of course, Don Raimundo. You must forgive me, but this is the first meal I have had all day," said the bishop as he tried to talk while he drank his goblet of wine, which caused wine to spill from his mouth onto his garments, further staining it.

"Sí, I wish for you to be my ally in my pursuit of the crown," continued Don Raimundo.

"What's in it for me for taking certain risks mainly that of committing treason?" asked the bishop.

"If I am king, I will appoint you the archbishop of Toledo, a very powerful and rich office. Imagine, you will have jurisdictional authority over all the bishops under your domain, and I will overlook you pilfering the pockets of your flock," said Don Raimundo with a smile of contempt.

The bishop sat up straight in his chair, as Don Raimundo hit a nerve. "What do you mean by such an accusation?" protested the bishop.

"Come now, Bishop. Don't pull the look of innocence on me. I know that you steal from the collection plate after every service to live in a vainglorious manner. Remember, I've been to your palace and seen your silver candleholders, gold goblets, and expensive tapestries. In many respects, you live better than the king," said an angry Don Raimundo, who attempted to quickly put an end to any misconceptions that the bishop might have in not backing his plan. He continued, "Don't ever underestimate my abilities, Bishop, as it might be your last."

The bishop sat back in his chair, took a drink of wine, and said with a smile as he put his goblet down, "Relax, Don Raimundo, what cleric would turn down an offer of being made the archbishop of Toledo? Just one more thing, since I am taking a great risk in helping you, I would expect to be paid a small percentage of the booty gained in your raids into the interior, as you have so boldly stated."

Don Raimundo took a deep breath. "How much of a percentage?" he snapped.

"Oh, I'm not really a greedy person, Don Raimundo—say, fifty percent."

Don Raimundo laughed. "Fifty percent? That's outrageous! And you call yourself a cleric, a man of God."

The bishop took a final gulp of wine, stood up, and said, "Everyone has his price, Don Raimundo, and that is mine. After all, without me to put the crown on your head, you will have no real legitimacy among the people. Also, once king, you will need my continued support, especially in clearing your name with His Holiness if he should decide not to recognize you as a legitimate king, even though your claim to royalty goes back to the Visigoths."

Don Raimundo laughed. "Congratulations, my Lord Bishop, I have clearly underestimated you. All right, fifty percent. Just make sure that you turn out to be the ally who warrants such a fat price. Remember, I have spies in Segoia."

The bishop laughed again. "So do I in Donato." With that, the bishop walked to the door, turned back to Don Raimundo, who was eying him suspiciously as he walked out of the antechamber to leave, and said, "Until we meet again. Buenos días, señor."

Don Raimundo was furious that he had been exploited by a cleric of all people, but the plan must go forth, and if it was costly, well, so be it.

Again thinking to himself, Don Raimundo realized that the amount of gold to pay for the size of the army needed to meet his objective would be more than he could currently put his hands on, but Doña Lucía's wealth added to his own would make the difference. He must first obtain her wealth and her royal bloodline. This would take time. After all, she was only six years old, and to ask for her hand in marriage at such a young age, without the arrangement of a parent, would seem odd, if not suspicious. He must wait until she is at least twelve years old, the legal age of consent, and then make his move. Meanwhile, he would, over time, plan a strategy and find mercenaries to carry out his objectives when needed. Above all else, he must appear above suspicion at all times.

Both Don Fernando and Don Alfonso Coronado were convinced by the bishop to take the cross and go to the Holy Land for the greater good of Christianity despite the fact that much was still needed to be done to rid the peninsula of the Moors. Don Raimundo, to avoid suspicion, also agreed to take the cross as well and, most importantly, to ensure that his plan to have both of the above captured, which he had put into play, would be successful.

The king hated to lose his most trusted advisers and reluctantly gave his blessing but realized that he would still have Ávila by his side. The king was thankful that only a few thousand men had agreed to take the cross to go abroad to fight the Saracen, as the rest was needed to fight the Moors at home. The king appointed Don Fernando, Don Alfonso Coronado, and Don Raimundo to lead their country-men to the Holy Land, and now plans were underway to organize the expedition.

Don Fernando decided to have Father Baldwin, whom he had come to trust, as Lucía's regent, along with the king and queen, Lucía's uncle and aunt. Avraham ben Shmuel, a Sephardic Jew from the royal court at Burgos, would assume the role of financial minister and ensure that all contracts were properly carried out until Lucía reached the age of consent. Zito would be in charge of the peasants in the vineyard, and Captain Gómez would remain in charge of the army of Segoia.

Don Alfonso Coronado decided to allow Isabella to stay in Segoia, to the glee of both Lucía and Isabella, as the two were now inseparable. Both would be under the tutelage of Father Baldwin. The Condado of Gustavo would be put under the direction of an alcaide appointed by the king.

The time to say goodbye was getting closer, as the camp of cru-saders had been building outside the city walls for weeks. Tents of all sizes, shapes, and colors could be seen for miles. The scent of cooking food could be smelled throughout the city, along with the scent of rather nasty-smelling latrines.

Each day, Lucía and Isabella, when not doing their studies or other duties, went to the highest tower of the palace to watch as knights and soldiers, priests and bishops, along with an entourage of pages, squires, and servants from all over Castile, came to Segoia to make camp outside the city before they left for the Holy Land. In total, there would be five thousand souls to journey to the Holy Land, and for those who fought, the promise of penance and booty awaited. Many of the knights and soldiers wore a white surcoat over their chain mail embroidered with a bright-red cross.

The night before Don Fernando left for the Holy Land, the great hall was filled with barons and knights from all across the king-dom for a banquet. Lucía and Isabella, who were each seated next to each other and next to their fathers on the dais at the head table, engaged in their own conversation.

After the bishop gave a long-winded blessing, all partook in the feast. Father Baldwin, who was seated next to both Don Fernando and Don Alfonso Coronado, attempted to explain some of the conditions they could expect to find while in the Holy land, as to geography and climate, which could be quite unsuitable for some Europeans not accustomed to a hot, dry climate full of dust and sand flees. The king and queen were busy speaking to the bishop, and the Infanta, Doña Berenguela, was joining in the conversations with Lucía and Isabella. Everyone was having an eventful time, trying to forget their coming departure and whether or not they would ever see their homeland again.

The next day, Lucía went to the stable to say goodbye to her father. Don Fernando hoisted his daughter on top of a barrel. "Now remember what I told you, mi pequeño sol."

"Sí, Papa, to obey, study, do my duties, and be good and not to cause any trouble, especially with Yamina, as she is getting up in age and can't swing the spoon as hard as she was once able to do."

Don Fernando laughed at her response.

"Papa, when will you be back?"

"Just as soon as I can, but in the meantime, I want you to be brave. Can you do that, Lucía, no matter what happens?"

"Sí, Papa. I promise." She gave her father a final embrace. "Adiós, Papa," said a tearful Lucía.

"Adiós, mi pequeño sol."

Don Fernando took his daughter off the barrel, put her down, and mounted his horse with his barrel helmet tied to his saddle horn. Lucía used this time to study her father one more time to make sure that he was engraved in her mind so as to never forget his face. Don Fernando also paused for a couple of seconds and took one last look at his daughter, and then he rode off to join the very long column of men, along with supply wagons and various sundry varieties of animals, servants, and household staff who followed behind.

Everyone patiently waited for their leader to give the order to advance. Lucía waved as he left, and she wiped away her tears and joined King Alfonso, Queen Leonor, who was pregnant again, the nine-year-old Infanta Berenguela, the three-year-old Infanta Urraca, and the baby Infanta Blanca, along with the Bishop of Segoia, Father Baldwin, Father Piña, Captain Gómez, Yamina, Isabella, and the entire household staff, to say goodbye in the courtyard. Isabella started to become emotional, afraid she would never see her father again.

Comforted by Father Baldwin and Lucía, Isabella started to feel better and joined Lucía on the high tower to see the army march off to a strange land that was little understood. Lucía moved an empty wooden box to the opening in the curtain wall so both could stand and see the vast army lined up for miles, with their fathers in the lead, disappear from view over the horizon.

"'Do you know where they are going, Lucía?"

"Papa told me first to Toledo to be blessed by the archbishop. He said that it had to do with an ancient Visigothic tradition before going into battle," said Lucía in an assured tone.

"Wisagopic?"

"No, Isabella, *vis-i-goth-ic*," responded Lucía, trying very hard to sound out the word.

"Visagopic," repeated Isabella one more time.

"Oh, never mind, Isabella."

"Then where do they go?" asked Isabella, who began to fidget with her head resting on one elbow on the curtain wall and her other hand tapping on the cold stone wall of the tower.

"I think Papa said to Barcelona, where they will board ships to the Holy Land," said Lucía, as she stretched out and rested her head on her elbows. Both girls stood there until the entire army departed over the horizon.

After a while, Father Baldwin joined the girls. Lucía turned to Father Baldwin and asked, "Papa said that the army was headed to Toledo for a blessing from the archbishop. Is that correct, Padre?"

"Sí, Lucía, and from there to Barcelona, where they will join the rest of the army from other parts of Spain to board ships to Tyre in the Holy Land."

As it was late, the two girls and Father Baldwin adjoined to the great hall for supper.

Chapter VII

Several months had passed since Don Fernando left for the Holy Land, and Lucía and Isabella, after predawn prayers in the small palace chapel, were busy with their studies. Father Baldwin taught a variety of subjects, such as grammar, logic, rhetoric, arithmetic, and music, along with languages such as Latin, French, and English, with a strong dose of Greek and Arabic mixed in. Since Lucía owned property in England, the English language would prove very beneficial to her. Father Baldwin knew that time was short but had great ambitions for both girls, as they were both very bright and he was a fountain of knowledge. Since girls were not allowed in the major universities, he would bring the knowledge of the universities to them. He would speak, and the girls would write their daily lessons in their large leather-bound book, thus creating their own texts.

After Father Baldwin was through with the lesson of the day, the two girls would have to recite the lesson and keep reciting it until they got it right, especially languages, where Father Baldwin emphasized the importance of diction and the practice of repeating phrases over and over until the girls sounded like natives to a particular language. Lucía over time became so precise in her English diction that she sounded like a native girl. Father Baldwin went a step further, where each night at supper a different language would grace the table conversation on the dais. He also enriched their studies by teaching practical subjects that would affect their lives, such as the knowledge of basic medicine and the use of medicinal herbs.

On certain days, Captain Gómez, to his horror and dismay, tried to teach the girls the basics of weaponry, such as how to shoot a bow and how to use a sword. One day, Lucía asked Captain Gómez, as they entered the armory to practice their bow skills, why the soldiers who were there all ran out in a hurry each time they entered the armory. Captain Gómez did not say a word but shook his head in frustration.

Lucía and Isabella could never shoot straight; perhaps it was the weight of the bow or poor eyesight. However, Captain Gómez didn't care except to proceed as quickly as he could with the lesson and hope no one, including himself, got hurt. Each day was long and began before dawn and ended at supper.

On Sunday, it was Bible stories, and every night, Yamina would tell a story in Arabic about tales of her native land before the girls went to sleep. Life was busy and, at times, intense, as Lucía had no time for anything else, including the vineyard, which she missed. Saturday was the day both girls enjoyed. It was the day of dance lessons, proper etiquette, embroidery, and riding.

In the early evening after supper, before being told to go to bed by Yamina, the girls would go to their favorite spot in the high tower, where they could look out onto the horizon, scout the peasant village far below, and just talk and giggle about the day's events. Here, they felt safe and uninhibited and to speak as they chose.

One day, Father Baldwin was lecturing on a particular subject matter involving rhetoric when Infanta Berenguela joined Lucía and Isabella to learn more about the subject. It was a warm day, and the sun was shining through the double arcade window. Lucía was having a difficult time concentrating on the subject matter and started to daydream. She rested her head on her elbow and became completely mesmerized by the mountains on the horizon. The girls were seated at a table, with Lucía on the end of the bench next to the window. Father Baldwin was standing at the front of the table as a professor would at a university, lecturing, and was oblivious to Lucía's lack of attention. At some point, Father Baldwin called Lucía to answer a question but could not attract her attention, as Lucía was completely absorbed in her daydream. Berenguela was seated next to Lucía, and she wiggled her arm to get her attention.

"Lucía, are you listening to the lecture?" inquired Father Baldwin, who did not appear to be upset by Lucía's bout with mindlessness.

"Well," said Lucía, startled by the sudden interruption from her daydream. "I guess… No no. I'm sorry, Father Baldwin. I guess I just withered in the warm sun."

Father Baldwin thought for a second and put his finger to his lips as in deep thought. "I would like to speak to Lucía alone." He glanced over to Isabella and Berenguela and then, with a smile, said, "Why don't both of you go out into the courtyard and enjoy the warm sunshine?" It didn't require much prodding to get the two girls out the door and into the warm air outside.

"Am I in trouble?" asked Lucía with a worried look on her face.

"No, Lucía, but I am interested what you were dreaming about."

"Well, it's a little personal, Padre."

"Didn't you know I am the master of all things personal?" said Father Baldwin with an infectious smile that quickly put Lucía at ease and brought a smile to her face.

"I don't know. It is rather silly, I fear."

"It's all right. Everyone has silly thoughts on occasion. Even I have silly thoughts."

"Really?"

"Really," responded Father Baldwin.

"Well, maybe it's okay then," uttered Lucía. "I was thinking about Mama riding over the mountains, coming home to stay with me."

"I see." Father Baldwin suddenly found himself in a pensive mood. "You must really miss your mother," he said in his perfect English accent. Then after a pause, he continued, "Lucía, I want to tell you something important you should know. I have been waiting for the right time, and I believe you are old enough to understand."

Lucía looked at Father Baldwin, curious as to what he was about to say.

"I was at the court in Poitiers when your mother was born, as a priest and papal legate assigned there by His Holiness."

"What?" said Lucía, who was in complete shock and surprise.

Father Baldwin went on to explain the situations surrounding Lady Margaret's birth, why she was adopted by Sir Charles and Lady Jeanne de Crécy, and that Lucía was really an Anjou with distant but possible claims to the English crown. Also, she was the granddaughter of King Henry and Queen Eleanor of England, and that was why her mother was sister to Queen Leonor.

Lucía was dumbfounded, as her father told her none of this except that the king and queen were her uncle and aunt.

"Why didn't Papa tell me this?"

"Because he thought you too young at the time to understand, Lucía," shot back Father Baldwin.

"I don't think I understand why a mother would want to give her baby away unless it was unloved," said Lucía sadly.

"Lucía, your grandmother felt your mother would be in real danger if she was raised at court. Her adopted parents could give her a life without worry or concern. As a result, your mother's short life was one of happiness and fulfillment."

"Mama died because I was born," said Lucía, wiping away her tears.

"Lucía, that is not true. What happened to your mother at birth was God's will and had nothing to do with you. Do you understand, Lucía?"

"All I know is that Mama is dead and would still be alive if I wasn't born, and I will never forgive myself for that. I wish not to talk about this anymore." Lucía rose from the bench and started for the door to leave when she heard Father Baldwin say, "Lucía, you should not feel guilty about your mother's death. It was not your fault. You should never feel that way."

Lucía turned her head quickly to listen to Father Baldwin and then just as quickly opened the door and left to play with Berenguela and Isabella in the courtyard. Father Baldwin was left in deep thought to mull over the conversation he had just had with Lucía.

Don Fernando and the army of crusaders finally arrived at Tyre in the Holy Land after having spent some time in Sicily to resupply and to conduct repairs from a bad storm. Unfortunately, events did not improve in the crossing from Sicily to Tyre, as once again bad weather took its toll with the loss of several hundred men and many horses. By the time Don Fernando reached the Christian port city, less than four thousand fighting men were left and about half of the followers who had accompanied the army. The combination of drowning and disease had taken its toll; as a result, they became part of the French army.

The forces marched along the shoreline to Acre, where heavy fighting against the Saracens was taking place to capture the city. It was after a day of heavy fighting that Don Fernando and Don Alfonso Coronado could finally relax after a successful repulse of the attacking Saracens. They found a spot under a palm tree to relax and to drink a skin of French wine, kindly offered to them by a French soldier who had fought bravely by their side that day. While they were relaxing, a servant came to them and said in Castilian that a messenger from Burgos was waiting to speak to them over the rise, which he pointed out.

"Why doesn't the messenger come to us?" asked Don Fernando.

"It is a message meant for the both of you only and not to be overheard by anyone else," said the messenger in an emphatic tone.

The two looked at each other, rose from their spot, and ventured in the direction that the messenger had pointed out to them. It was dark with only enough light from a half crescent moon for them to see their way. After having walked about a half mile, they slid down a steep sandy embankment. After having gained their footing, they were surprised to see no one there. Suddenly, in the dark of the night, they were seized upon by a half dozen Saracens. Don Alfonso Coronado drew his sword but was quickly cut down. Don Fernando had no time to act, as he was jumped upon first and quickly restrained.

It didn't take long for Don Raimundo to show himself.

"Well, Don Fernando, how nice of you to come after my messenger's biding. I was afraid that you might not have been so easily persuaded."

"You sent the messenger?" asked Don Fernando, still somewhat in a state of shock after having been subdued so quickly.

"He must have been quite convincing," said Don Raimundo as he motioned for one of the Saracens to check on Don Alfonso Coronado. The Saracen bent down over the body of Don Alfonso

Coronado and, after having examined him, looked up and shook his head.

"Too bad, I rather liked Don Alfonso. He never gave me any trouble and was a pleasant fellow as well."

At this point, Don Fernando came out of his momentary shock and disbelief and started to struggle. "Wait till I get my hands on you. I will kill you with my bare hands."

"I don't think so," said Don Raimundo confidently, "not where you are going. You see, I had you tracked very carefully since you arrived in the Holy Land through my contacts. You will be spending the rest of your days in Baghdad as a prisoner. I hear that the city is a cultural center, so maybe it won't be so bad after all."

"Meanwhile, with both you and Don Alfonso Coronado out of the way, I can start a real strategy on taking the throne. But first, somehow I must rid myself of Ávila, and of course, let's not forget your daughter, who holds the key to my rise to power with her fortune. Oh, so much to plan and so much to do. I guess I should get started," said Don Raimundo in such an arrogant manner that it took four Saracens to hold Don Fernando down, even though his hands and feet were shackled. "Take him away," said Don Raimundo as he motioned to the Saracens. "Enjoy the trip across the desert, señor. Adiós!"

"Leave my daughter alone! So help me, Raimundo, I swear, somehow I will make you pay!" exclaimed Don Fernando as he was in the process of being gagged.

While Don Fernando was being gagged and final preparations were being made for his departure, Don Raimundo took Don Fernando's sword and sword belt to take back with him to Castile as the two other Saracens were busy preparing to bury Don Alfonso Coronado in an unmarked grave.

Although upset by her conversation with Father Baldwin, both Berenguela and Isabella were able to cheer up Lucía, as they all played in the warm sun. However, after having been outside for a while, Lucía ran in screaming in panic, followed by two guards who thought her in danger. Lucía had run back to Father Baldwin with small red spots on her face and thought it to be the plague.

Father Baldwin examined the spots and smiled. He glanced over at the guards who had followed her. "It's all right," said Father Baldwin. "You may leave us." The two guards exited the room, mumbling something and then laughing as they went down the hall.

"It's the plague! Quickly, call the physician!" cried Lucía in a panic.

Yamina came hurrying into the room. "What is the matter with Lucía?" she asked, trying to catch her breath. "I heard that she was in some type of danger."

"No danger at all," said Father Baldwin calmly. "Now calm down, Lucía," exhorted Father Baldwin in his typical gravely English accent. "Those red spots are not the plague. They are called freckles, which is typical of fair-skinned people like you who get too much sun without wearing a hat." Father Baldwin tickled her chin, which caused Lucía to giggle. "They most likely will go away after a while."

"Freckles?" repeated Lucía. "I have never heard of freckles before. Well, I guess I should wear a hat then."

Yamina had listened to the conversation. "My word! Freckles of all things? And I thought she was being murdered." With that comment, Yamina left the room.

"Gracias, Padre," said Lucía, who felt both embarrassed and ashamed at the same time.

"It's all right, Lucía. Don't look so ashamed. You didn't know." Lucía nodded her head and then went to get her hat.

Chapter VIII

On occasion, the girls would get a day off from their studies, usually on certain saint days after Mass or after having had performed their household duties. They would spend their time giggling and generally acting foolish, to the chagrin of Yamina, who felt that the devil was always lurking and ready to leap on those who were engaged in idle time.

On one particular saint day, after their merriment, they ventured up to their favorite perch on the high tower and looked down on the people below, who were going about their business. Since her father had never taken Lucía to the city, except to pass through the city gate to get back and forth from the vineyard, Lucía always had a curiosity as to what lay on the many streets that branched off the city square.

While both were looking down from the curtain wall, Lucía engaged in a conversation with Isabella. "Isabella, did you ever wonder who those people are and what they do all day long?"

"Nooooo. Yamina told me that you should mind your own business. That was the best way to stay out of trouble."

Lucía retorted, "Where is your curiosity, Isabella?" Suddenly, Lucía had an idea, and she grabbed Isabella's hand. "Why not disguise ourselves as members of the local citizenry and see first-hand what people do? We could sneak out of the palace through a hole I discovered while playing in the courtyard, which would put us outside of the city walls and then walk back into the city. We would be back in the palace before anyone knew we were missing."

"I don't think it's a good idea. I know we will get into trouble, and I for one do not want to feel Yamina's wooden spoon."

"Papa always told me that sometimes you have to take risks in order to accomplish your objectives. Besides, Yamina is old, and if she hits too hard, her arm is apt to fall off."

"Huh?" frowned Isabella.

"Never mind, Isabella," said Lucía as she continued to think and paced back and forth.

"What are you doing, Lucía?" asked a bemused Isabella, who stood with her back to the curtain wall and watched as Lucía was wearing a path on the stone floor of the tower.

Lucía put her hand in the air, which meant that she was thinking and did not want to be disturbed. Within a minute, Lucía came to a complete stop. "I have a great idea. We will dress in old tattered clothes and rub charcoal on our face. I will rub some in my hair to darken it. What do you think, Isabella?"

"What do I think? I see trouble, and I also see myself doing a lot of standing when I could be sitting because of a sore backside. Count me out."

"Come on, Isabella. It will be a lot of fun, I promise, and besides, Papa always said that is important to know your subjects."

"Your subjects, not mine," shot back Isabella.

"Maybe, but people are people."

Lucía decided to add an additional incentive to her plan. "Isabella, you know those special lemon sweet tarts you like so much that can only be found at the city bakery?"

"So?"

"If you come with me, I will treat you to one. So what do you say? Come on. Come on. You know you want one," teased Lucía.

Isabella was already smacking her lips at the thought of eating one. "Ohhhhhh, all right, I guess."

"Great!" cried Lucía. "Now I know that we both have old garments that we can wear, because I have seen them. Isabella you can wear that old green garment, and I will put on a blue one. Once we put them on, we will take ashes from the fireplace and rub them into our garments to make them appear dirty so we can blend in with the peasant crowd," said Lucía, fully confident in her ability to pull off this little venture to the outside world.

"But, Lucía, people are sure to recognize you," said a worried Isabella.

"Not really, Isabella. I have not been out of the courtyard for a long time, way before Papa left."

"It's your red hair, Lucía."

"I know. We will both put on old cloaks, and I will rub ashes on the front of my hair to darken it. The only thing I need is to find an old cloak. All of mine are new," said Lucía, in deep thought.

After a short time, she announced loudly, "I have another idea. I will borrow Captain Gómez's old cloak. He won't miss it. That big old thing will more than cover me up. Better still, I will exchange it for one of my new ones," voiced Lucía, excited by the prospects.

Isabella shook her head. "We are going to get caught."

"Don't be so nay, Isabella."

"All right then. I know we are going to get caught!" exclaimed Isabella.

Lucía ignored her comment.

However, since Isabella tended to be a follower, she agreed to go along with Lucía's crazy scheme and looked forward to biting into a lemon sweet tart.

It was early afternoon when the girls carried out their plans. Lucía tiptoed into Captain Gómez's room in the stable and found his old cloak, which she exchanged for one of her new ones. They both put on old garments and rubbed the ashes from the fireplace into the cloth to appear dirty. Lucía, with Isabella's help, wrapped her very long hair into all sorts of contortions to get it to fit in a coif under Captain Gómez's hood and rubbed the front of her hair with ashes.

They were now ready to leave and, despite Isabella's concerns, sneaked out of the palace. Lucía found the hole behind a bush, which went down and then up in front of a boulder on the other side.

Lucía had already crawled out of the hole and hid behind the boulder as she waited for Isabella.

"Come on, Isabella," whispered Lucía into the hole.

"I'm stuck on something. I think it's the bush." Suddenly, Isabella heard a tear behind her. "Never mind," whispered Isabella as she exited through the hole.

The girls were out and remarkably were able to escape detection from the guards at both the gate and in the towers. Lucía felt proud of herself as they both walked through the city gates as free peasants, free to go anywhere they wanted.

"Remember your promise, Lucía." Isabella mouth was already watering at the prospect of a lemon tart. "You did bring some gold coin with you, did you?" inquired Isabella.

"Of course," said Lucía as they headed over to the bakery and purchased two lemon tarts. Isabella wanted one for each hand.

The girls ventured up several side streets that wound around one side street after another. On each street, they found apartments where fragrant flower plants, such as roses, lavender, and other aromatic flowers, which spiced the air, either hung over balconies or on windowsills.

"Such a pleasant smell," said Isabella, who appeared to enjoy her outing.

As the afternoon progressed, black clouds started to move in, and the girls found themselves lost.

"Where are we, Lucía?" inquired Isabella, who started to get concerned. "It's becoming late, and those clouds look rather ominous."

"Relax, Isabella, I know where we are. It's not that difficult to find your way around the city."

"All right. I want to go back now before this storm lets loose." Already thunder could be heard rumbling in the far distance.

"Just follow me, Isabella. Honestly, where would you be without me?"

"Back home, out of trouble, and sitting in front of a fire, warming myself from the cold breeze I just felt."

Without a word, Lucía rolled her eyes and continued on with Isabella blindly in tow.

After another hour of walking around aimlessly, Lucía had to admit they were lost. The girls were caught in a maze of dead ends and winding streets that circled around. Not only were they lost, but the thunder was becoming much louder, and Isabella felt a few sprinkles.

"I knew this was not going to work out well," exclaimed Isabella. "I'm tired, and my feet are sore."

"Anything else, Isabella, to add to your litany of complaints?" snapped Lucía, who was both angry and embarrassed at having to admit she was hopelessly lost.

"When I think of any more, you'll be the first to know," said Isabella angrily.

The girls were becoming unhinged and in the process of panicking when they heard a crack of thunder, which was so loud it caused both girls to jump. They turned a corner and went down another narrow, winding street and were nowhere closer to knowing where they were than before. It started to pour, and they were getting soaked; however, they did manage to find shelter in a doorway that was large enough for both of them to fit. Tired from their ordeal, the two girls dozed off, comforted only by the fact that they were no longer getting wet.

Lucía felt the sensation of being poked, which caused her to stir and open her eyes. Once her eyes were completely opened, she noticed a woman and a boy who stood over her. The woman appeared haggard and old beyond her years. The boy, who Lucía guessed to be about twelve or thirteen, was both tall and handsome.

"Well, what do we have here?" asked the woman, who turned to her son. "Who are you, and why are you sleeping on my doorsill?"

The conversation had finally awakened Isabella, who had been lying with her head resting on Lucía's shoulder, with both of her legs bent and touching the doorframe of the apartment.

"Please, señora, we meant no harm," said Lucía. "We are lost, and we were only seeking shelter from the storm."

"I see," said the woman, who now had a more sympathetic tone to her voice. "You say that you are lost?"

"Sí."

The woman noticed that both girls were shivering.

"Well, come on in before you catch a death of cold," said the woman as she opened the door. After a short time spent unraveling themselves from the awkward positions of their bodies, they moved inside, while the boy, the young gentleman that he was, took up the rear.

Once inside the two-room apartment, the woman said something undistinguishable to the boy, who went to start a fire. After a few minutes, the fire was ablaze, and the two girls moved in front of the fireplace to warm themselves. While the girls were standing by the fire, the woman picked up a black kettle and put it in on the table and said, "My name is Niña, and the boy's name is Pino."

While Niña was busy with the kettle, Lucía whispered in Isabella's ear that she would do the talking. Isabella nodded.

While Pino was busy on the other side of the fireplace, cutting wood, and Niña was busy mixing peas and cutting sausage for the pot, Lucía had an opportunity to study the conditions of the apartment. On the left side of the fireplace was a wood pile, where Pino was working. On the right side was a hay pile with a blanket tossed on top. In the middle of the room was a trestle table, where Niña was working on supper, with two long benches on either side of the table. On the other side of the apartment hung a curtain that led into another room, which Lucía thought to be the bedroom.

After Niña finished mixing the peas and sausage, she took the heavy black pot and placed it on a hook that was suspended from a chimney bar, which ran the length of the fireplace. Niña started to stir the pot and invited the girls to spend the night.

"Gracias, señora," said Lucía and was seconded by Isabella.

"Girls, please take a seat on the bench," said Niña as Pino, who had finished cutting wood and having added it to the fire, came over and pulled out the bench for the girls to sit.

Lucía could not help but to think how Pino's manners were better than some of the so-called knights and gentlemen of the court.

After a period of uneasy quietness of what seemed an eternity, Niña took two wooden bowls from the fireplace mantel and filled them with soup and brought them to the table. Lucía noticed that Niña had given them the largest share of the sausage meat. Niña also served a few crusts of hard rye bread for the girls to dip into their thick pea soup.

"I'm sorry, girls. I only have two bowls. We don't usually have company, so you will have to share," said Niña.

"This is the best soup I've ever tasted, señora," said Lucía and was seconded by Isabella.

"Well, gracias for your kind compliment. I am not used to hearing such a kind admiration for my cooking," said Niña, delighted with their response.

After a slight pause, Niña asked, "Oh, by the way, I don't believe that I caught your names."

Lucía looked up at Niña in shock at the question and happened to glance at Pino, seated across from her, who smiled at Lucía, something they both had done to each other throughout the meal. Lucía had been caught off guard and totally unprepared for the question. She had to think and quickly.

"Don't tell me you have forgotten your names?" asked Niña with a smile.

Lucía laughed. "Oh no, my name is Margarita, and this is Estefanía. We are both sisters."

"I see," said Niña. "And where are you from?"

Lucía yelled, "Donato!" while Isabella yelled, "Barcelona!" at the same time, and then immediately Lucía yelled, "Barcelona!" and Isabella yelled "Donato!" At this point, Lucía gave Isabella a kick under the table.

"Ouch!"

"What did you say, my dear?" asked Niña, who turned to Isabella.

"Oh, nothing. I just sneezed. I must be catching a cold."

"Well, there does seem to be a slight disagreement," responded Niña, who was becoming very interested in the girls' responses.

Lucía gave a nervous laugh and said, "My sister is a little confused, as we are originally from Barcelona and moved to Donato. Isn't that right, Estefanía?" asked Lucía, who gave Isabella a threatening look.

"Oh, sí, that's right. How foolish of me," said Isabella as she returned Lucía's look.

Niña indicated that she wanted to help the girls find their parents in the morning. The girls looked at each other in panic. Lucía pretended to suddenly remember where her parents were supposed to be and said that it was no bother and that they only would have to know how to get back to the city square. With that remark, Niña suddenly showed indifference.

"Well, suit yourself," snapped Niña, who left her place at the table to clean up after the meal. "Something to drink perhaps? I'm afraid either water or beer."

The girls responded with water, and Niña poured a wooden tumbler for both to share. Lucía, after having smiled again at Pino across the table, thanked Niña for her hospitality and asked her what she did to earn a living.

Niña laughed and stated that she really didn't want to know the answer to her question, but Lucía insisted. Niña stated that she was orphaned at a young age and had to make her way through life the best she could. She became a barmaid and cook at one of the taverns in the city. Pino worked in the kitchen, washed the dishes, and cleaned the floor, plus performed other duties as needed.

Once asked, Niña was a fountain of information and revealed that they received five maravedis a week. They paid out three a week for rent and the rest on food, but despite all that, they felt lucky and thankful, as their home was warm, had two rooms and, once in a while, they saved enough maravedis to change the hay on the cold stone floor.

At this point, Niña rolled up her sleeves to revealed bruises received from men who grabbed her at the tavern. Also, the tavern owner mistreated her as well. Once Pino came to her aid and was pushed aside so hard by the owner that his head hit the side of a table and was knocked out; she had thought him dead. Pino, who had remained very quiet throughout the evening, shook his head in agreement. Both Lucía and Isabella smiled at Pino and told him how brave he was.

For the first time, both Lucía and Isabella learned what real suffering was all about.

After hearing Niña's story, Lucía said, "You have a good heart, and I could tell that by the hospitality you showed both of us tonight. God rewards those who are good."

Niña laughed. "I'm afraid God abandoned me years ago."

Lucía thought a second and asked Niña a peculiar question, "If you could go anywhere or do anything you wanted to do, what would it be? And imagine that you are very wealthy."

Niña laughed at such a question, but Lucía had a certain way about her, such as a warm smile, a pleasant caring manner, and a form of persistence that made people want to answer her questions.

"All right," said Niña. "For the sake of argument, I'd love to go to Paris, buy new clothes for both me and Pino, start anew in a brand-new city, and get a job working as a servant for a great lord and lady who live in a castle. Oh, but this is sheer folly." Niña laughed. She went over to a bucket of water by the door and brought it to the table. Lucía interrupted her routine and insisted on doing the dishes; she pulled up her sleeves and washed them.

After Niña and Pino retired to their bedroom beyond the curtain, Lucía and Isabella spread out the pile of hay, bedded down, and covered themselves with the blanket, which was on top of the pile.

Before going to sleep, Lucía asked Isabella, who lay next to her, "Why Barcelona?"

"That was the only name I could think of at the time," responded Isabella with a yawn and stretch. She added, "I'm worried. I know that Father Baldwin and Yamina must know that we are missing by this time, and we are going to be in big trouble. I can feel Yamina's spoon on my backside now."

"Everything will be all right, Isabella. Time to go to sleep," said Lucía, and the two girls huddled together and closed their eyes.

The next morning arrived, and right before dawn, Lucía and Isabella tried to sneak out. Lucía already reached into her purse, well hidden under her garment, and pulled out several gold coins and buried them in the hay. As they were quietly leaving, they heard a whisper. It was Pino, who wanted to know where they were going.

"We are going to look for our parents," said Lucía.

"How about something to eat first?" offered Pino.

"No, gracias," insisted Lucía. "We must be on our way. But gracias, once again, for your hospitality."

Pino walked out the door with the two girls and gave them directions on how to get back to the city square.

However, Pino was suspicious of Lucía and Isabella and took the opportunity to ask them who they really were. They did not act like peasant girls, and their skin was pure, with no redness that came from working in the sun or hard labor. Pino grabbed Lucía's hand and saw no calluses on them.

Lucía once again had to think fast. "We are just ordinary people who had an easier life than most because our father is a merchant and travels a lot."

The explanation seemed to satisfy Pino somewhat, but not completely. The girls left under his watchful eye. Lucía seemed to be strangely attracted to Pino, as she ran back to him, pushed him against the wall, and gave him a big kiss adult style.

Pino gulped and said nervously, "Perhaps I can do something for you again someday."

"Perhaps," said Lucía, and she backed slowly away with a big smile, turned, and ran back to a completely stunned Isabella, who was frozen in her tracks of disbelief, dismayed by Lucía's behavior.

"What was that all about?" inquired Isabella.

"Oh, nothing," responded Lucía, with a glimmer of mischievousness in her eyes.

Pino, on the other hand, was left completely dumbfounded and stood against the wall for several minutes after the girls had left.

The girls, still in disguise, made their way out of the maze of streets and stopped before they proceeded back to the palace amid the hustle and bustle of people, who were going about their business. They both noticed the guards in the tower and in front of the palace gate.

"How do plan to get back inside the palace?" inquired Isabella.

Lucía turned to Isabella and said, "Shhh! Keep your voice down, Isabella, and let me think." Lucía thought for a moment and quickly turned to Isabella. "We say we are servant girls coming to work. We certainly look like servant girls. It should work."

"All right. Then what?" asked Isabella in a soft voice.

"We will sneak through the courtyard to the stable and back to our chamber," said Lucía in a soft voice with a smile of confidence.

"I don't know, Lucía. Why not go directly to Father Baldwin and plead for mercy? They know we are missing by now and are probably looking for us."

"Let's follow my plan, Isabella."

"All right, but I think my plan is better," said Isabella, much in doubt Lucía's plan would work.

The girls went to the gate and were immediately shooed away.

"Well, now what?" asked Isabella.

"We'll have to go through the wall to get back in," said Lucía.

The two girls sneaked through the rocks on the side of the outside wall that had hidden the hole and made sure the coast was clear before they attempted to climb back through to the other side.

"I'll go first, Isabella, and you follow behind me."

Isabella nodded, anxious to end their venture and to soak in a nice, warm bath. Lucía started up the hole and quickly vanished from sight, which startled Isabella.

"Lucía," whispered Isabella, "are you okay?"

There was no answer to her response. Isabella shrugged her shoulders and started up through the hole, only to feel two hands come down and pull her up through.

"And there is Isabella," said a familiar voice. It was Father Baldwin.

Isabella looked around after having been pulled up from the hole, and she saw a rather subdued Lucía standing next to the padre.

"How did you find us?" asked Lucía.

Father Baldwin reached into his satchel, which hung from his hemp belt, and pulled out a piece of green material, which had been torn from Isabella's garment when it had become entangled on the bush in front of the hole. "I happened to stumble on this early this morning, and when I saw you two trying to get past the guards a short time ago, I knew that you would be coming back through the hole. I waited and sure enough…," said Father Baldwin in his gravely English accent with a slight smirk on his face.

"Why didn't you come for us at the gate?" asked Lucía.

"I was curious as to how your little venture was going to play out."

Father Baldwin said nothing else, and he took the girls by the hand and started to walk through the courtyard.

"It's a beautiful day, Padre, wouldn't you say?" asked Lucía, who tried to be cunning by changing the subject

"Sí, it is, Lucía."

A couple of guards came by and said, "I see you found them, Padre."

Father Baldwin turned and nodded with a smile.

"Are you taking us somewhere, Padre?" asked Lucía, who started to get concerned.

Father Baldwin continued to say nothing as he turned and entered the stable and headed for Captain Gómez's room, which was at the other end of the stable. Captain Gómez happened to be in his room when the padre arrived with the girls in tow. He was both worried and angry. When they entered, he approached the two girls but was quick to notice his cloak being worn by Lucía.

"My cloak! I have looked all over for it. I hope no harm has come to it."

Lucía sounded dejected and, with her typical nervous smile that she revealed when she was in trouble, said, "I'm sorry. I only meant to borrow it. I didn't think you would miss it. It's so old and everything. I did trade mine for yours."

"Sí, and about that," said Captain Gómez as he tried on Lucía's cloak, which was much too small and looked so ridiculous on him everyone broke out in laughter.

Lucía handed Gómez his cloak, and after a thorough examination of the garment, he said, "This garment may look old and worn to you, but it means a lot to me. You see, I was adopted by a professional soldier and his wife, and when my father died in battle, he left me his armor, his sword, and his cloak. I have worn and cherished it ever since. So I was very distressed when I found it missing."

"I'm sorry," said Lucía, who looked down at the floor with a forlorn expression on her face.

"Well, no harm done, but where have you been? I have been searching high and low for you girls and was about to do a complete search of the city. I even sent a group of soldiers to scour the countryside to look for the both of you."

Lucía explained the purpose of their venture beyond the gates of the city, where they had been, the nice woman who had given them shelter, and how they wanted to look like normal everyday people so they disguised themselves as such.

"Well, your little venture has caused a lot of trouble and concern. I do hope that you will not do this again. If you want to go somewhere, you are to tell me so I can arrange for your security. Until you come of age, I am responsible for your comings and goings. I do hope I have made myself clear to the both of you."

Both girls chimed in at the same time, "Sí."

"Good, now go. I have business to attend to," snapped Gómez.

"Come on, girls," said Father Baldwin, directing the girls out of Gómez's quarters.

As the girls walked from the stable, up the stairs, and to the living quarters of the palace, Lucía asked Father Baldwin, "Why is Captain Gómez so grouchy all the time?"

"Well, because he has much responsibility training soldiers and keeping the city safe."

When Father Baldwin entered Lucía's chambers with the girls, they found Yamina busy at work on embroidery.

"Where have you girls been?" yelled Yamina.

Once again, Lucía nervously told her story, but Yamina, who was a strict disciplinarian, was not impressed. She went for her spoon as Father Baldwin left the room. As he shut the door, he could hear the cries of "Ouch, ouch, ouch, ouch!" and then another round of "Ouch, ouch, ouch, ouch!" Father Baldwin squinted as if he was feeling their pain. Yamina then told the girls to get ready for supper and left the room.

"I thought you said that Yamina's arm would fall off if she spanked us," said Isabella as the two girls walked around their apartment rubbing their backside. "I told you that we would get into trouble," added Isabella in an angry tone.

Lucía looked at Isabella. "Not now, Isabella." The girls prepared for a bath and a change of garments before supper.

Chapter IX

Several weeks passed before Father Baldwin received a message from the king to bring Lucía and Isabella to Burgos. Both the girls speculated that they were to be punished for their recent behavior. Upon arrival at the palace, the party was escorted into the throne room, where they awaited for the monarchs to arrive. While they were waiting, the girls could not help but to speculate what their punishment might be.

Suddenly, Isabella turned to Lucía as they were standing in the throne room. "Do you suppose we could be beheaded, Lucía?" thought Isabella.

Lucía did not respond to such a ridiculous question but rolled her eyes and shook her head in disbelief.

Finally, the royal couple arrived, along with Infanta Berenguela. As the royal family took their seats on the dais, the girls gave a deep curtsy. Lucía thought that some type of punishment was forthcoming. However, she noticed that it appeared as if both Queen Leonor and Berenguela had been sobbing, as their eyes were red and puffy and both were clutching a piece of linen. Even King Alfonso looked sad and withdrawn. Lucía thought to herself that something dreadful must have happened.

A herald appeared at the doorway and announced, "Don Raimundo, Your Highnesses." The girls and Father Baldwin moved to the left of the dais, as Don Raimundo walked in and stopped at the bottom of the staging in front of the royal family and bowed. Lucía's heart skipped a beat, as she had always been fearful of this man due to his slitlike, piercing eyes, which she found so perturbing. What was also strange was, he was cradling a sword in his arms. Suddenly, a feeling of complete paralyzing shock overtook Lucía, as she recognized the sword as having belonged to her father. Tears started to well up in her eyes, and she started to weep, to the surprise of Isabella and Father Baldwin, who stood by her side.

"No, it can't be," said Lucía, who was now completely weeping.

"Lucía, Don Raimundo wishes to speak to you and Isabella," said the queen.

Don Raimundo turned his attention to the three who were standing off to the side. "Sadly, I have to report both Don Fernando and Don Alfonso Coronado have succumbed while fighting the Saracens in Acre."

Both girls wept at the horrific news. Father Baldwin, along with Berenguela, who came down from the dais, tried to comfort the girls. Don Raimundo backed away and showed no emotion, and when the girls had finally calmed down, he gave Lucía her father's sword. Sniffling, Lucía asked Don Raimundo how they had succumbed in battle.

"We were laying siege to the city of Acre, and there was much hand-to-hand fighting. Unfortunately, I saw both of your fathers go down, outside the city walls, after being overrun by reinforcements sent in by Saladin. I happened to be in a spot on the edge of the battle as the Saracen forces charged to the center of the fray. After the encounter, I did manage to find your father's sword and brought it back with me."

"Gracias," said a sobering Lucía.

"Two skilled warriors such as Don Fernando and Don Alfonso Coronado are dead? It's hard to believe. They will surely be missed," said the king sadly.

"Well, if there are no more inquiries, with your permission, Your Highnesses, I shall take my leave," said Don Raimundo, who seemed completely aloof to the sadness that was so pervasive throughout the room.

"By all means, Don Raimundo, and gracias for your forthcoming," said the king.

Don Raimundo bowed to the royal family on the dais, and then he glanced over to the left, in the direction of the two girls, made a slight bow, and left the room.

"I am very sorry for your losses," said the queen to both Lucía and Isabella. "We will help you in any way we can. Isabella will now become a ward of the court, under our protection, until such time as a suitable guardian or husband can been found. However, she will remain for the time being in Segoia," explained the queen. "You have our permission to leave unless there is something else we can do for you."

Berenguela, still with Lucía and Isabella, gave them one last embrace as she wiped away her tears. "I have to go now, but I will pray that the Holy Mother will be with you in this time of suffering." As Berenguela left, the girls curtsied and, along with Father Baldwin, traveled back to Segoia.

As Lucía left the palace, still sniffling and carrying her father's sword, she could not help but think that her father was still alive. Somehow, she knew that someday he would return to her. However, Isabella felt that she was now all alone in life, but she was reassured by Lucía that she still had her, and they would always be family.

It was Easter Sunday, and Father Baldwin had just finished having assisted Father Piña with Mass at the peasant village church. After Mass, they went to Father Piña's apartment for some cheese, bread, and wine. They were enjoying the afternoon when a discussion turned to the Bishop of Segoia.

"Something I must tell you regarding our bishop that displeases me greatly," said Father Piña with a look of concern.

"You can tell me, and I promise I will keep my silence."

"I'm afraid that our bishop is feathering his own nest at the expense of our Holy Mother Church."

"In what regard?"

"I have seen him steal from the collection plate at the peasant church and when assisting at Mass at the cathedral in Segoia."

"How so?"

"On three occasions, twice here at the village church, and once at the cathedral, I saw him dump the church offering on a table, count it, and put about three quarters of the coins back in the collection plate and pocket the rest. He is also falsifying records to cover up his thievery with two sets of books."

"Intriguing," responded Father Baldwin. "But what solid proof do you have to verify your accusation?"

Father Piña continued, "One evening, when the bishop was away, I sneaked into his office unnoticed, and I found to my surprise two sets of accounting books for the diocese. I compared the book that showed what was actually taken in during the service with the one that showed what was actually sent to Rome, along with made-up expenses, such as disbursements for nonexistent clerics and alms for the poor, which he pays little or no attention to. I then went back several months of church offerings, compared the two, and found the same misdeeds that corroborated his treachery. He was taking about a quarter of the money for himself. I also noticed that he had been charging fat fees for confession, and when I confronted him about this, he said that the fees were used to help finance the crusades, but I know he pocketed the coins as a testament to his own greed.

"He also treats people with horrible disdain. A trusted witness from the village, a servant in the bishop's household, saw him severely beat a young servant for having given some household food to a poor man who had come begging at the door. The bishop said that he was an unworthy vagabond looking for mercy for his stomach instead of his soul. It was also witnessed that he had forced a young attractive peasant girl into his quarters to rape her on threat of excommunication. If the situation couldn't get any worse, he had the hand of a servant girl cut off for picking flowers in his garden to cheer up her sick mother. The bishop has also been seen visiting Don Raimundo on many occasions in Donato, and there is a rumor of some sort of plot going on between them, but no real details have been forthcoming. So they're all my displeasures concerning this man."

"Why haven't you reported your accusations to the Bishop of Toledo?"

"The Bishop of Toledo has been out of the country, trying to seek support for the war against the Moors. I know, based upon our previous conversations, that you have some pull in Rome. If only His

Holiness knew what this man was doing to his people, I know action would be taken."

Father Baldwin thought for a minute, putting his finger to his mouth, and said, "I will find proof of his treachery and, in due time, bring it to the attention of His Holiness. Meanwhile, when possible, have the witnesses sign a prepared document on the bishop's misconduct and malfeasance, witness their signatures, and I will be sure to have His Holiness investigate this matter to a successful conclusion."

The years passed, and Lucía was becoming a young woman at the age of twelve. One day after being tutored, Lucía came to Father Baldwin to confess a sin. Embarrassed, she wanted to whisper it in his ear. Father Baldwin listened carefully and broke out laughing. Apologizing, he told her that her feelings were not a sin but only human nature. It was normal for both sexes to feel that way about each other. When asked who the boy was, Lucía told Father Baldwin she had seen a handsome young squire accompany his master to the Order of Christian Knights of Segoia and she'd had a dream about him.

On another occasion, Lucía was screaming that she was bleeding for no reason. Father Baldwin and Yamina came running. Once Father Baldwin determined the problem, he let Yamina deal with that particular biological issue with both girls.

Yamina said to her, "Congratulations, Lucía. You have now become a young woman." Lucía seemed confused at first but, after further explanation, sort of understood.

As the year passed, Father Baldwin allowed Lucía to handle the affairs of her condado more and more, under his guidance. She found that managing her household staff was far easier than reviewing and deciding claims made by landowners, but Lucía was not your typical twelve-year-old. She had been well educated and was quite an astute young lady, although she did, on occasion, have a propensity to get into trouble and to revert to childhood behavior when seriousness was not at issue. Yamina had retired her wooden spoon, and all were involved in bringing Lucía into maturity.

However, little did Lucía know what was about to happen, which would test both her maturity and resolve. It was a month that Lucía would never forget—July 1195. Lucía knew that her uncle, King Alfonso, was at war against the Moors, as she had received a mandate from him for the Condado of Segoia to provide one thousand men as well as five hundred knights from the Order of the Christian Knights of Segoia, a monastic warrior order, to gather in Toledo to bar the Almohad Caliph Abu Yusuf Yakub al-Mansur from advancing northward from Cordoba. She did not know, however, that he had marched his army to Alarcos, the southern boundary of Castile, and had fought the Moorish army there, to disastrous consequences.

Never would she have expected what was to happen near the end of that fateful month. Lucía was busy working on paperwork with Father Baldwin in the anteroom of the great hall when a messenger sent from the king was announced. The soldier handed Lucía a message signed and sealed by the king, which both Lucía and Father Baldwin read. It requested that Segoia be turned into a hospital for a great many wounded men returning to the area. Lucía signed an order for as many tents as could be found to be set up in the city square and also to use the cathedral, the bishop's house, and the palace to address the number of the wounded.

Fortunately, Father Baldwin knew the use of herbs, which he had taught to Lucía. She, in turn, ordered her household servants to collect all the yarrow and mandrake and to prepare the yarrow mixed with goose grease to form a poultice to dress wounds and to prepare the mandrake for any surgeries and amputations. Meanwhile, yards of linen was being cut to cover wounds.

Within days, the wounded started to arrive. Father Baldwin and Lucía were visited by the king's surgeon and given instructions as to where to place the wounded. The worst of the wounded were put in the cathedral, where they could receive final blessing of the church before death and to receive comfort that they were being watched by the Holy Mother. Next, attention turned to the bishop's house across from the cathedral and to the city square. The bishop was not happy and tried to shoo away the wounded but was overrun. Finally, came the palace, where more wounded could stay. The rest of the wounded and those requiring surgery or amputations would be stationed in tents in the city square. The king's surgeon who was in charge of the operation directed traffic. The servants who made the yarrow poultices brought them to the tents that housed the medical supplies. The mandrake was given to the surgeons to be used as anesthesia or used as they saw fit.

It was a very hot day, as Lucía and Isabella, along with their assemblage of servants who were now to be nurses, stood by the fountain in the town square and watched as the incoming wounded entered the city. There were the wounded who were walkers; there were knights bent over in their saddles, barely able to ride. There were men being dragged in litters, and there were men who were completely out of their minds and walked around aimlessly, talking to themselves, having had suffered from the intense heat and exhaustion of the day.

When the need arose, Lucía and Isabella, along with her servants, pulled up their sleeves to help the wounded. While Lucía was sponging off a wounded soldier, Isabella came with a waterskin to give him a drink and suddenly pointed to the city gate, where several wagonloads of nuns from the Cistercian convent in Valladolid had come to help the wounded. Along with them was a wagon loaded with medicinal herbs and other various additional medical supplies. Although the arrival of the nuns helped to take the pressure off Lucía's limited resources, both Lucía and Isabella still gave whatever aid and comfort they could to the wounded. One soldier in delirium thought she was an angel.

By the second day, the wounded were still coming until finally only a few stragglers were left. The stench of the dead and wounded, along with the intense summer heat, permeated the air with such a foul odor that many caregivers were getting sick or collapsing of exhaustion. Both Lucía and Isabella had never seen such carnage, with men screaming in pain, blood inches deep in some places, and everywhere flies en masse. Lucía thought that hell could be no worse. Isabella happened to look at the pile of amputated arms and legs that were left to be burned in a pit outside the city, and she immediately ran to a corner and vomited heavily. Lucía was becoming dizzy, and she held on to her stomach. Finally, as a result of being affected by the heat, loud screaming, and confusion, Lucía collapsed.

Father Baldwin, along with Father Piña, were both visiting the wounded and offering them spiritual comfort when both heard a loud voice yell. "Padre! Padre!" said a servant who was in panic and running at full speed, holding her gown with both hands so as not to trip. "It's Doña Lucía. She has collapsed. Please come and hurry!" Father Baldwin was just inside the city gate, and he ran to the city square, where Lucía lay face down on the hot cobblestone in front of the water fountain.

Father Baldwin picked her up and, along with a concerned and weak Isabella, who was following behind, made the long trek from the city square, through the palace gates, and to her boudoir. Once they arrived, he put Lucía on her bed and then had to attend to Isabella, who had just fainted. He picked her up as well and placed her alongside Lucía. Yamina, who had stayed in the palace to help the wounded, had seen Father Baldwin carry in her charge.

"Ah, Yamina, there you are," said Father Baldwin with a smile.

"My gracious!" said Yamina after seeing the girls lying next to each other on the bed.

"It would seem that too much sun, along with the hard work of caring and comforting the wounded, has taken its toll," said Father Baldwin. "I do need a pitcher of water, a cup, a sponge, and a cool bath for each of them."

"I shall see to it immediately," said Yamina, and she ran out of the room.

Within minutes, Yamina returned with the pitcher, cup, and sponge. "I ordered the bath for each of them, and it will be brought up immediately."

"Excellent," responded Father Baldwin, who was dabbing a wet sponge of cold water on both Lucía's and Isabella's heads.

When the girls became conscious, Father Baldwin left them to their cool bath with instructions for Yamina to make sure they drank plenty of water, ate some food, and got some rest.

The next day, both Lucía and Isabella were in better spirits and were once again out caring for the wounded. It was about midday when Lucía saw her uncle, the king, arrive, still dressed in his armor, to visit the wounded. Lucía had never seen her uncle appear so sad and defeated. Both she and Father Baldwin approached the king to speak to him.

"Ah, there is my little Lucía, although you are not so little anymore," said the king with a forced smile as he was dismounting. "I want to thank you for allowing Segoia to be used to take care of the wounded. My god, such a horrible sight!" said the king as he perused the city and saw the extent of the carnage.

Lucía smiled. "Perhaps you should come to the palace and get some rest yourself."

The king glanced over to Lucía, who stood along with Father Baldwin slightly off to his left. "Gracias for your kind offer, Lucía, but I won't be staying very long," said the king.

"How bad is it?" inquired Father Baldwin.

"Castile has suffered a terrible defeat at the hands of the Almohad Caliph Yaqub al-Mansur and his treasonous ally, Don Pedro Fernández de Castro. The Castilian army has been completely destroyed. Several of the kingdom's bishops are dead, and many castles have fallen into the hands of our enemy. I'm afraid the Moors are at the very gates of Toledo itself. Segoia is out of the reach of our enemy, at least for the time being," responded the king.

"Perhaps I should take Lucía and Isabella to England or France, to one of Lucía's properties there," suggested Father Baldwin.

"I don't think that would be necessary. The Moors have also lost many men as well and don't have the strength to advance, but be vigilant," said the king as he moved on with a couple of his knights to visit the sick and wounded.

Lucía walked over to Isabella, who had been caring for a wounded knight with a terrible leg wound. A piece of chain mail had penetrated into his wound and was protruding from it.

"Well, what did he say?" asked Isabella.

"Who?"

"The king, your uncle, of course," snapped Isabella, who had become tired and frustrated at attempting to help someone she could not really help. Suddenly, she noticed the knight she had spent so much time with had abruptly succumbed from his wound. Isabella, upon seeing his death, started to weep.

"Isabella, there was nothing you could have done. Infection has set in, and the resulting fever took him."

"It's just…it's just…," said Isabella, who wept so heavily that she couldn't get her words out.

Lucía embraced her friend and then reached for a clean piece of linen she had been carrying on her belt and gave it to her to wipe away her tears.

"I'm sorry, Lucía," said Isabella, who was trying to control herself but still bleeding tears. "You must think me a baby for such an outburst."

"No, Isabella. I understand. And you're no baby. Besides, you're much too big to breastfeed," said Lucía with an infectious smile.

Isabella started to laugh behind her tears.

The king, accompanied by Father Baldwin, after several hours of having had visited the wounded and having had given what comfort he could, prepared to leave, along with his contingent of knights. He mounted his horse and, with the responsibility of defeat still fresh on his mind, said to Father Baldwin, who had helped him mount his horse, "I must go now to champion some sort of southern defense to protect our kingdom. Adiós, Padre, and watch over my little Lucía and Isabella."

The months passed, and fall arrived. The last of the wounded had gone. The dead bodies, the amputated body parts, and used bandages had been burned outside the city to prevent infection. The city square had been cleaned and was back to normal.

It was at this point that Father Baldwin once again agreed to meet with Father Piña at his apartment above the village church. Father Piña had managed to obtain the bishop's accounting books from a trusted friend, a servant in the bishop's household, while the bishop was currently away attending a council meeting in Toledo. The books clearly revealed that the bishop was stealing from the church and lining his pockets. He was taking a quarter of the offerings from Sunday Mass and charging outrages fees for confessions, depending on the severity of the nature of the sin.

"Remarkable," said Father Baldwin as he reviewed the accounting books with Father Piña and studied each entry very carefully.

"I also sent a letter to the Archbishop of Toledo that expressed my concerns about the bishop," said Father Piña, who got up from the table, walked over to a chest of draws, pulled out a drawer, reached in, took out a piece of parchment, and handed it to Father Baldwin.

Father Baldwin read the letter and grinned. "I like the part where the archbishop states that this matter does not concern a simple village priest."

"The letter made me wonder if in some way the archbishop is involved in this scheme as well," said Father Piña.

"I know the archbishop to be a good man and not one to become involved in such a scandal," replied Father Baldwin in a serious manner while taking a sip of water from a wooden cup.

Father Baldwin arose from his chair at the table. "I will soon be going back to Rome, as my work here is coming to an end. When I return there, I shall make His Holiness aware of the situation here in Segoia. When you study in Rome, you get to meet and know many influential people in the church. Make sure that you have the accounting books returned as quickly as possible to his lordship."

"You'll be missed my friend, especially our friendly discussions and chats," said Father Piña while walking Father Baldwin to the door.

"And remember, the situation here will change, I promise," said Father Baldwin, who put his hand on Father Piña's shoulder.

After leaving the village church, Father Baldwin contemplated his next step while giving his donkey some exercise riding in the countryside. He became so immersed in thought and prayer he did not give much attention to where he was going and soon discovered that he was on the road to Soria. The forest was still, except for a slight cool breeze on a warm fall afternoon. The beauty of the forest was all around him with the brilliant hues of red and yellow and the radiant rays of sunlight, which poured through the trees from a cloudless cerulean sky.

As he was riding along, his thoughts became interrupted by a sobbing sound, which was faint at first but became louder as he approached. When he arrived at the place where the sound had originated, he found a young girl dressed in the black habit, wearing the white veil of a novice. She was kneeling by the roadside, weeping and praying at a shrine of the Holy Mother. Father Baldwin could see that the girl was deeply distressed. She was so deep in prayer and on such a high emotional binge that she did not hear Father Baldwin's approach. Father Baldwin stopped and listened for a while. The girl was asking the Virgin for guidance. She was lost in a strange country and did not know where to turn. She was hungry and tired and begged the Virgin for help.

Father Baldwin had listened to her sad commentary and knew she needed assistance. Maybe he having wandered to this place in time was no accident.

"Help has arrived," said Father Baldwin in his gravely English accent, which so startled the girl she quickly turned around in astonishment and huddled in the corner of the shrine, next to a fallen tree trunk in fear.

"You have nothing to fear, my dear," said Father Baldwin. "I am here to help you in any way I can." Father Baldwin dismounted from his donkey and sat on the fallen tree trunk.

"Come, sit here with me, and tell me what's wrong," said Father Baldwin.

The girl was still huddled in the corner of the shrine but slowly rose and nervously took a seat next to the padre.

Father Baldwin turned to her, and he watched her sit down next to him. He reiterated again, "Now you have nothing to fear. Can you tell me what's bothering you?"

The girl was still sobbing, and Father Baldwin took her into his arms to comfort her until she calmed down. After a while, the girl calmed down enough and was able to talk.

"My name is Gabriella," sobbed the girl as she sniffled and wiped away her tears.

"What a pretty name," said Father Baldwin with a kind smile that engaged her in conversation. "Where are you from, my dear?"

"Originally, I am from Pavia, Padre," said Gabriella, who was no longer sobbing.

"Pavia. That's a long way from here. How did you get here?" inquired Father Baldwin.

Gabriella began, "My family owned a farm and earned enough income to live on. We were not wealthy people, but we were born free. My mother died when I was quite young. Between my mother's death and a bad drought, my father decided to sell the farm. He said he could no longer take care of me. So with the money from the sale of the farm, he put me in a convent outside of Milan for a better life that he said he could not give me. I never saw him again."

"How did you happen to come here?" asked Father Baldwin.

She continued, "Even though I received an education and became a novice, I hated the life of a nun in a convent. The convent in Milan sent me to a sister convent in Castrojeriz to see if they could change my behavior, as I was too much of a discipline problem for the abbess in Milan. I tried to obey, but the abbess said that I was incorrigible and would have me whipped, so I ran away and ended up here."

"Have you taken your final vows yet, my dear?"

Gabriella shook her head no.

"Do you want to go back?"

"Never!" responded Gabriella.

Father Baldwin thought for a minute and said, "I have an idea. Will you trust me?"

Gabriella was slow to respond but eventually nodded and said, "Sí."

"I will visit the convent and have you discharged from your duties. That I promise," said Father Baldwin. "Meanwhile, you'll need a place to stay, and I know the perfect place of refuge for you."

Father Baldwin placed her on the donkey and ventured back to Segoia. When he arrived at the palace, Gabriella was totally mystified at the splendor of both the city and the palace and was taken aback.

"Don't be afraid, my dear. You are among friends here."

He immediately took her to Lucía and Isabella's shared boudoir, only to find that they were both in the high tower, where they spent most of their free time and enjoyed the bird's eye view of the countryside.

Father Baldwin, along with Gabriella, climbed the winding stairs of the tower and opened the oak door, only to be met by a burst of wind, which caused Gabriella to hold her white veil to her head.

As they walked onto the tower, Father Baldwin saw the girls talking and looking out over the countryside. The girls sensed a presence and quickly turned around, and they watched Father Baldwin walk toward them with a stranger in tow.

Father Baldwin introduced Gabriella to the girls, "Gabriella, this is Doña Lucía, the Condesa of Segoia, and this is Doña Isabella, the Condesa of Gustavo."

Surprised by being surrounded by nobility, Gabriella did not know what to do, and she curtsied, looking surprised. She thought Father Baldwin would leave her at a church or perhaps with an acquaintance in the country, but to be left in a palace was something Gabriella had difficulty comprehending.

After Father Baldwin explained Gabriella's circumstances to both Lucía and Isabella and what a nice companion she would make, both Lucía and Isabella took her down to their boudoir, where Gabriella huddled in a corner in fear.

"Don't be afraid," said Lucía, who offered her hand in friendship and gave Gabriella's hand a slight squeeze. "We are not going to hurt you but offer you friendship." Gabriella smiled and finally felt comfortable enough to embrace both Lucía and Isabella.

Within a short time, Gabriella was beginning to fit into her new environment, and her ability to read and write both Latin and French, plus other knowledge gained during her time of wearing the habit, would make her a valuable asset to Lucía's future court. But now the time had come to rid Gabriella from the habit of a nun and dress her in the garments of a woman of rank. Both Lucía and Isabella gave Gabriella several garments for her to wear. Never had Gabriella ever seen such beauty and smoothness of texture, never mind that she would actually own and wear one.

Once Gabriella had removed her habit and veil, a new person came to life, and her personal nature was revealed. She was much thinner than the two girls had originally thought her to be. Her short brown hair had grown to shoulder length. Even though she was plain looking, her brown eyes added a glimmer to her round face. Unfortunately, the scars on her back were all too real and exposed the real suffering encountered in the convent and the reason for her rather stiff demeanor and the holy attitude she demonstrated on occasion.

However, the time had come for Father Baldwin to leave Segoia. The girls were about to turn thirteen years of age and had had finished their formal education. The girls had learned in a span of seven years all that Father Baldwin could teach them. The parchment pages of their leather-bound book were filled with the knowledge gleaned from subjects in both the liberal arts and the sciences. Lucía and Isabella had purchased many copies of classical works from local monasteries and bookstores in the city. They now had the makings of a library worthy of a king.

Chapter X

One night in early November, Father Baldwin left Segoia without having said goodbye. Father Baldwin did not like farewells, as they tended to impede one's ability to leave a place without a heavy heart. When Lucía, Isabella, and Gabriella woke up the next morning, they found that Father Baldwin had left during the night. They were all shocked and confused.

It wasn't long after when a there was a knock on the door of the boudoir.

"Enter!" yelled Lucía.

It was a servant. "A messenger from the king awaits you in the hallway, mi señora."

"Gracias," said Lucía.

"What do you suppose that is about?" asked Isabella as Gabriella looked on with concerned interest.

"I don't know, but it may have to do with Father Baldwin leaving so abruptly," said Lucía, and she told the servant to have the messenger enter.

The messenger gave a bow to Lucía and said, "Mi señora, the king and queen wish your presence in Burgos immediately. I have been given instruction to accompany you there personally."

"I shall change first and be with you shortly," said Lucía, and the messenger gave a bow. She then proceeded back into her bedroom, followed by Isabella and Gabriella.

Lucía, with the help of Isabella and Gabriella, quickly changed into a plain dark-blue slender-shaped garment that was made of satin and a gold ring belt to complement the double gold necklace chain, which Isabella picked out for the occasion. Gabriella combed her long reddish-blond hair until it glistened in the morning light.

Lucía looked into the small mirror on her dressing table, and after she primped and preened for several minutes to make sure that every hair was in place and everything else was as exactly as it should be, she was ready.

"Well, how do I look?" asked Lucía, who rubbed her garment with her hands as if it needed smoothing.

"You will be the envy of the court," said Isabella.

Gabriella, due to years in the convent, maintained a more austere attitude toward vanity and did not voice an opinion.

"I'll be back as soon as I can," said Lucía.

When Lucía arrived at the palace, she was immediately brought to the entrance of the throne room, where she was told to wait. After a few minutes, Lucía was announced, and she walked into the room, where she noticed the king and queen seated on their thrones and Infanta Berenguela standing next to her mother.

Lucía made a deep curtsy as her aunt and uncle looked her over very closely.

"Ah, Lucía, how you have grown, and what a pretty gown," said the queen.

"Gracias, ma'am. It was kind of you to notice," responded Lucía with a smile.

"Perhaps you're wondering, Lucía, why Father Baldwin left so suddenly?" asked the queen.

"Sí, ma'am, that did cross my mind."

"Unfortunately, he was called back to Rome. He said that it concerned a papal matter of some kind. I don't know, as he was here for a very short time and did not go into any detail. Besides, he said his work here was done and that you were ready to assume your inheritance and govern your condado. What do you think of that?" inquired the queen.

Lucía was taken completely off guard.

"You mean really govern my condado?" said Lucía in complete surprise.

"Sí," said the queen. "Really govern. In his judgment, he feels that you are intelligent enough to be fully capable of running your condado as well as your lands in England and France. However, I have my reservations with someone as young as you, but both your uncle and I are willing to allow you to do this with certain stipulations. Remember, you are still a ward of the court until you reach the age of eighteen or become married, and as a result, you are to come to us if any serious problems should arise. Captain Gómez will be in charge of your safety and well-being, a de facto guardian to watch over you. Also, whatever Captain Gómez tells you to do, you are to obey."

"You mean he will be like a father to me?" asked Lucía with a slight frown.

"Sí, he will be in a manner of speaking, as we cannot be with you all the time. Also, he will report your behavior back to us. Just remember, Lucía, usually someone in your situation would have a guardian to run their condado until, as I said before, you come of age or you marry. Now do you think that you can take on this responsibility?" asked the queen.

"Sí, ma'am," said Lucía. "But how about Isabella?"

"Isabella will stay in Segoia until a guardian is found. Due to her quiet, soft-spoken, and rather shy nature, Father Baldwin did not feel that she was qualified yet to control her condado. She will continue being a ward of the court until age eighteen or marriage."

"The House of Castro is legally Isabella's family. However, they have banished Isabella's branch of the family over some silly dispute going back several generations," said the queen. "The Castros have always turned their back on the Coronados, even at court. So a guardian has to be found. Is this all clear to you, Lucía?"

"Sí, ma'am," said Lucía, excited about the prospects of what her new life would hold.

"Oh, and please tell Isabella about her fate, if you would?" asked the queen.

"Sí, ma'am," said Lucía.

The king invited Captain Gómez to Burgos to discuss his new duties regarding Doña Lucía. King Alfonso, who was seated at a table to the left of his dais in this throne room, was contemplating what to say to Gómez, who he knew did not particularly like children, when his thoughts were interrupted by a court herald.

"Captain Gómez of Segoia to see you, Sire," said the herald.

"Have him enter," said the king to the herald.

As Gómez entered the throne room, the king rose from the table and walked over to greet him. "Gómez, welcome."

Gómez made a polite bow to the king and said, "You are looking well, Sire."

"Gracias, and you too," said the king in a cheerful mood.

A servant entered with a pitcher of wine, along with two silver goblets and tapas of bread, cheese, and sausage. She placed it on the table and immediately poured the two goblets with wine up to the brim.

"Some refreshments, Gómez?"

"Gracias, Sire." As Gómez reached for a goblet of wine, he looked around the room and studied the wall hangings. "I have always admired the colorful tapestry that so eloquently graces the walls of this room," said Gómez.

"I didn't realize that you had an eye for such things," added the king.

"Maybe it has to do with the hunting theme. I've always enjoyed the hunt, whether it was animal or man," he said with tongue-in-cheek.

The king smiled at Gómez's comment and took a swallow of wine while Gómez drained his goblet dry.

"Do you wish to sit, my friend?" asked the king as he put his goblet on the table.

"If you don't mind, I would rather stand, Your Highness," responded Gómez.

"Very well, I'm hoping you can help me. As you are aware, Father Baldwin has left his duties as regent. Unfortunately, he was called back to Rome, which leaves us with a decision as to the future status of Doña Lucía and Doña Isabella. Upon the recommendation of Father Baldwin, we have decided to give Lucía full power to govern her condado as well as her other lands in England and France. However, she is still young and will be in need of guidance on occasion. I need for you to be her de facto guardian on location and to report back to us on her behavior. You will be in charge of her safety and well-being. The queen and I will still look in on her from time to time when we are in the area, and we will handle discipline when necessary, based on your recommendation. However, if need be, you will be empowered to do so yourself. Oh, and regarding Doña Isabella. We are in the process of finding a guardian for her, but she will stay in Segoia until the proper time. So what do you say, Gómez?" asked the king.

Gómez laughed. "With all due respect, Sire, you expect me to be a nurse to Doña Lucía and Doña Isabella? I'm a warrior, not a nurse. Also, I have a great many other responsibilities that can keep me away from Segoia for several days at a time. Besides, I do not like children, and they do not like me. I do not even know how to get along with them. I'm afraid that you have the wrong man."

Now it was the king's turn to laugh, and laugh he did. "Give Gómez a sword, and he will fight one hundred Moors to the death, but give him a young girl, and he will melt like butter in the hot summer sun."

"That's not true, Sire. I am not afraid of anyone, never mind a young girl," responded Gómez.

"Well then, I guess I have found my man. Besides, Lucía has respect and admiration for you. I have both seen and heard this. You have a better relationship with her than some fathers have with their own daughters."

"I do?" uttered Gómez, mystified by the king's comment.

"Sí, you do. Oh, by the way, Doña Lucía has been advised concerning our conversation. Well, I guess that finishes our business. Good luck, Gómez. I shall look forward to your reports."

Still somewhat mystified as to what he had agreed to, Captain Gómez politely bowed and took his leave.

Don Raimundo had heard at the council meeting the king was looking for a guardian for Doña Isabella. He happened to know the man who would be her undisputed guardian. There was no one better for such a task than an uncle. In this case, that would be Don Ramón.

Unfortunately, Don Ramón had a serious personality flaw. He was no good. Ramón had been disinherited by his father, Don García, many years before, as he was not only a complete embarrassment to his family but also incorrigible. He had beaten and raped several young peasant girls in the village. Such conduct was unbecoming of a member of the noble Coronado family. As a result of his ongoing behavior, he was banished by his family, and his name was never mentioned again. His younger brother, Don Alfonso Coronado, became the sole inheritor of the Condado of Gustavo.

While Don Ramón's escapades were ongoing, the young King Alfonso was very early in his reign and was fighting the various noble houses to bring peace back to a country, which had been racked by warfare for many years after the death of his father, King Sancho. As a result, he had no knowledge of Don Ramón, who, for Don Raimundo, the opportunist that he was, would play very nicely in his plans. But first, he had to find Don Ramón.

He thought to himself, *Where would you find a man who had been gone for so many years and was both despicable and as much of an opportunist as you?* Then he remembered that Don Ramón had visited him years ago and said he was on his way to the Holy Land to seek his fortune. Sí, that was where he would look, but since Don Raimundo had not seen him when he was there, he bet that Don Ramón would be in Jerusalem. He sent his henchman, Scarface, and a couple of men to meet with his contacts there, locate him, and bring him back to Donato.

Within three months, Don Ramón had been coerced to return to Castile to meet with Don Raimundo. Don Ramón, along with Scarface, entered the anteroom of the great hall, where Don Raimundo was waiting. As he entered the room, Don Raimundo noticed that Don Ramón was in shackles.

"What's the meaning of this, Raimundo, and what right do you have to interrupt my life?"

Don Raimundo glanced over at Scarface. "I'm sorry, mi señor, but he did not come willingly. Restraint was necessary."

"I see. Remove the restraints," demanded Don Raimundo.

As Scarface removed the shackles, Don Raimundo studied Ramón carefully, as he had not seen him for many years. His short but unkempt beard and hair surrounded a long face, which had become dark and withered from years of being under the hot desert sun. As he looked into Ramón's dark eyes, he could not help but realize he was staring into a dark and evil soul.

"What's the meaning of this Raimundo?" demanded Ramón, who displayed a belligerent attitude.

"Easy. Take it easy, my friend. It's been a long time. Wouldn't you agree?"

"Not long enough, Raimundo. When I left here all those years ago, I made a vow never to return. Now you have forced me to break that vow. For what?"

"How would you like to get your inheritance back?"

"What are you talking about?"

"Very simply. I plan to overthrow the king and need your aid to do so. Please sit, and I will explain."

Ramón started to laugh and then blurted out, "You're mad."

Don Raimundo went to sit on the edge of the table on the dais, and he nodded at Scarface, who forcibly, with the aid of a guard, made Ramón sit in a chair in front of him.

"Now that we're cozy, I will explain further. The king, since the disaster at Alarcos, has lost a great deal of respect from the nobles of the realm. His army has virtually been destroyed. His only real trusted friends are the Conde of Ávila and me."

"My plan is to raise an army of mercenaries through my contacts. To pay for such an army needed to take the throne and Castile, I plan to take the fortune belonging to Doña Lucía Alvarado either through marriage or death."

"This is all very interesting, but tell me, señor, how does that affect me?"

"The king is looking for a guardian for Doña Isabella. As you are well aware, the House of Castro has turned their back on your family for several generations. Here is your opportunity to step in and retrieve your inheritance by simply becoming your niece's guardian."

"How am I to prove that I am her uncle? The king doesn't know me."

Don Raimundo got up from corner of the table and unlocked an old gray wooden cabinet behind him and pulled out a tattered piece of parchment. "That is why I managed to obtain this document, which records your birth from the church in Gustavo, to prove who you are."

Don Ramón stroked his chin under his dark unkempt beard. "It appears as if you have thought of everything, señor."

"Not everything," said Don Raimundo. "I have to be prepared for the unexpected, and that is where you come in. I may need Doña Isabella in the future. She is from royal lineage, and if I become king, she could help to add some legitimacy to my claim to the throne since my claim goes back many centuries to the Visigoths. All you have to do is control her and rule the condado as you see fit. Isabella is a rather shy and weak girl and certainly should not present a problem to someone who robs caravans and fights defending Saracens. Once I become king, you will have a high office in my reign and lots of riches."

"How did you find out about my misdeeds?" snapped Don Ramón.

"I have my contacts in many places, enough to know both the Saracen and Christian armies have established an alliance to hunt you and your army of cutthroats down and eliminate you once and for all to keep the peace."

"Well, a person has to make a living, right, señor?" added Ramón with a sly grin.

"Now you can make a very nice living for yourself without being hunted down like a dog."

Ramón had finally calmed down and started to think of his future prospects. "Perhaps it was a good time to leave the Holy Land after all," said Ramón with a sarcastic smile.

"Perhaps, but now the next step is to present yourself to the royal court, and with me by your side to vouch for you, there will be no problem. Just remember one thing: no harm is to come to Doña Isabella. All you have to do is to control her, and with your power over her as guardian, you can control both her future as well as ours. Now you will need to clean up and put on new clothes to present yourself to our king and queen."

Isabella was soon called to Burgos at the behest of the king. Both Yamina and Lucía made sure that Isabella was properly dressed. Isabella wore a red garment with an embroidered gold rose and leaf pattern with a gold girdle belt and red slippers. Lucía wore a plain blue garment with a silver girdle belt and silver slippers.

Isabella, accompanied Lucía, was heralded into the throne room of the royal palace. Once there, Lucía noticed Don Raimundo and a stranger standing off to the left of the dais where both the king, queen, and Infanta Berenguela were seated on their thrones. They had already been involved in an audience with Don Ramón and his claims to guardianship.

"You are looking well, Isabella," said the queen.

Isabella was trembling, as she made a deep curtsy, "Gracias, Your Highness."

The queen could tell that Isabella was very nervous. "Don't be fearful, my dear. There is nothing to be afraid of."

Isabella nodded.

"We are here to discuss your future, Isabella. Your uncle, Don Ramón, has traveled a long way to be your guardian."

"My uncle? I didn't know I had an uncle," declared Isabella, who appeared perplexed at such an acknowledgment.

"Sí, Don Ramón is definitely your uncle and is here to take you back to Gustavo, where, under his direction, you will be able to govern your own condado. He will remain your guardian until you reach the age of eighteen or should you marry."

Isabella was frightened about the prospects of leaving Segoia, where she had felt comfortable for so many years. But to leave with a stranger?

"May I say something to Isabella, Your Highness? It may help to relieve some of her anxiety," said Don Ramón, who turned on his charm.

"You may by all means, Don Ramón."

"Gracias, Your Highness," he said, and he walked over to Isabella, who was holding tightly onto Lucía's hand. As Ramón approached her, Isabella backed away slightly. "There is nothing to fear from me. I realize that we don't know each other, but that will soon be rectified," said Ramón in a very gentle manner. Then Ramón looked over to Lucía. "Is this your friend?"

Isabella nodded.

"She will be allowed to visit you at any time, or you can visit her."

Lucía then looked at Isabella with a smile of approval. "It will be all right, Isabella. I know you will be fine. Go with your uncle."

With reassurance from Lucía, Isabella felt more confident and agreed.

"Then it is all set. If it is agreeable with Your Highnesses, I shall stop at Segoia, have Isabella pack her things, and be off to Gustavo."

"Permission granted," said the queen, relieved that a guardian had finally been found for Isabella.

Ramón smiled in agreement, and then he looked over to his friend, Don Raimundo, and gave him a sly nod.

Chapter XI

At thirteen years of age, Lucía was now in control of her own condado and received several young ladies-in-waiting who were to make up her court. The Lady Constance Hillaire de Beauville was the oldest. She was mature beyond her fourteen years and had a very attractive oval face, complete with blue eyes and long light-brown hair, which she wore down to her lower back. Lady Constance was from an old Norman family whose father, Count de Beauville, owned lands in both Normandy and England.

Adele María di Buttaro was from the landed nobility of Sicily. Her family roots were originally Norman who had fought with Roger de Hauteville in his conquest of the island. The family eventually obtained a large tract of land in Syracuse. At the age of twelve, Adele was maturing into a fine lady and would be an attractive catch by an able high-ranking nobleman or a prince at some point in the future. The dimples on either side of her small mouth were evident in her smile, and her long dark hair and brown eyes completed the pleasant appearance of a young Sicilian woman.

Doña Geralla Anglesa de Cardona, another beauty, was a cousin of King Alfonso II of Aragon, who was also known as Count Alfons I, Count of Barcelona. Her family was of Catalonian/Aragonese background and were wealthy landowners whose property lay outside Barcelona. Geralla had large brown eyes on a small oval face crowned by long curly dark knee-length hair. At twelve years of age, she was not as mature as Adele but was still worthy of attention by a future noble suitor.

Finally, there was Beatrix from the House of Hohenstaufen, a thirteen-year-old who was from the noble Hohenstaufen family. She was the opposite of the others, as she was a slow learner and related poorly to people. Her round face and fat cheeks, framed by her rather short red hair worn down to her shoulders, gave her the appearance of being fat and unattractive.

Such were the girls, along with Gabriella, who composed Lucía's court. Constance, who was the oldest and who had a completed education, was put in charge of the ladies to ensure that they did their duties and were on time for their lessons, especially archery, which already was driving Captain Gómez crazy. By putting Constance in charge of the ladies and Gabriella in charge of the day-to-day operations of the palace, Lucía could handle the vineyard and other important affairs that would develop from time to time.

A few days after Adele's arrival to Segoia, Lucía was walking from the palace along the arcade to the anteroom of the great hall when she noticed Adele seated on a bench inside the garden. Lucía stopped and went to sit with her, which startled Adele, since the noise of the water fountain had muffled Lucía's footsteps. She noticed that her young charge had been weeping.

"I'm sorry if I startled you, Adele."

Adele sniffled. "Oh, that's all right. I was just admiring the garden. It is truly beautiful. Unfortunately, I became homesick since it reminded me of the palace garden my family has." Then Adele smiled. "It used to anger Father Bertrand, my tutor, to have to look for me in the garden. As I spent so much time there, it made me late for my lessons. How I miss the palm trees swaying in a gentle breeze, the smell of orange blossoms in the spring, and the medley of sweet smells from flowers, which tickled the nose with such delight. Then there were the colorful aloe plants and the cacti and, most of all, the view of the sea from the high cliff. On a clear day, you could see the sailing ships in the distance filled with crusaders off to the Holy Land." Then she paused and said, "I'm sorry, Doña Lucía. Papa always said I talked too much."

Lucía put her arm around Adele's slender shoulder. "You don't have to apologize. It must be hard to leave your family and what is familiar to you to take a long journey to an unknown part of the world. I understand, and I know, like you, I would find it difficult to do myself. I want you to feel comfortable here, and if the garden gives you comfort, I want you to know that you are welcome here any time. However, don't be late for your lessons," injected Lucía with a big smile and a giggle.

Adele smiled. "I promise I won't, and gracias. I feel so much better now."

Lucía gave Adele a squeeze. "Remember, anytime you want to talk, I will always be available."

Adele nodded, and Lucía rose from the bench and walked back through the arcade.

As Lucía was about to enter the anteroom of the great hall, she was stopped by Gabriella, who was completely out of breath. "Oh, mi señora, I've been looking all over for you."

Lucía smiled and waited patiently as Gabriella got her breath back. "What happened? Are you all right, Gabriella?"

Finally, having calmed down and breathing normally, she responded, "Mi señora, you have a visitor who was quite insistent on seeing you. I put him in the anteroom of the great hall."

"Do you know who it is?"

"He said to tell you that his name is Don Fernando Núñez de Lara and that he had some business to discuss with you."

Lucía thought for a moment before going in to attend to her guest. *What business would a Lara have to discuss with me?*

Then she looked at Gabriella and said, "Gracias, Gabriella, you did well."

"Is there anything else I can do for you, mi señora?"

"No. I'll be fine."

Lucía was feeling a little ill at ease to be visited by a member of one of the most powerful noble houses in Spain. Lucía took a deep breath and entered the anteroom.

When she entered, Lucía noticed that Don Fernando had taken a seat at the polished oak table and patiently awaited her entrance. As she entered the room, Don Fernando rose as Lucía went to greet him. He was dressed in his armor, and with the cowl over his head, only his face was visible. There was nothing striking about him except for a full beard.

Don Fernando reached for her hand and kissed it. "Mi señora, it is a pleasure to meet the beautiful and charming daughter of my very dear friend, Don Fernando. I know he would be very proud."

"Gracias for your kind words, Don Fernando. May I offer you some refreshments?"

"Gracias, but no."

"Then how may I help you?"

"First, I want to say that I knew your father. He was not only a dear friend but also someone I respected and admired greatly. I was so sorry to have heard of his loss. He will be dearly missed by many. His death is a real blow to Castile. Now the reason for my visit is, your father has a large tract of land in the south that borders mine in the area of Madrid. I was wondering if you would be willing to sell it. I will offer you a fair price for it."

"I'm sure you would, señor, but this tract of land belongs to my father and is not mine to sell. Perhaps you should take this matter up with him when he returns."

Don Fernando was shocked and confused by her statement. "But he has been declared dead, and this land is part of your patrimony and now belongs to you."

"True, he has been declared dead, but I know he is still alive and will return someday. Until then, señor, I plan to keep everything as is." Lucía, with a pleasant smile, then added, "Gracias for your offer, Don Fernando, and I am sorry that you made this trip for nothing."

"Is there any way I can convince you to sell, mi señora?" Don Fernando was eager to buy it.

"Nothing you could say, nor any amount you were to offer, would change my mind," said Lucía.

"Hmm, then I shall take my leave, condesa, but if you should decide to sell in the future, please allow me the privilege of first offer."

"I will give you that privilege if I am the one, and not my father, who sells this land."

"I understand," said Don Fernando. He walked over to Lucía, who had stood during the conversation, took her hand, and kissed it again. "It has been a pleasure to have had a conversation with someone as beautiful as you, mi señora. Until the next time. Adiós."

Lucía breathed a sigh of relief as Don Fernando left.

Lucía had made arrangements to meet with her chancellor, Avraham ben Shmuel, in the anteroom of the great hall regarding the condition of the vineyard and to review the accounting books of the income it produced. Father Baldwin, during his tenure at Segoia, did not have Lucía involved in the winery business due to the intensive nature of her studies. Thus, her chancellor handled all the business affairs for the period.

Avraham ben Shmuel was a Sephardic Jew who as chancellor and secretary had the responsibility of not only collecting the income derived from the vineyard but also the collection of taxes, fees, tolls, and all tribute due to the condado as well. In addition, he also had the responsibility of ensuring the collection of the same from Lucía's holdings in England and France. This was a grave responsibility for one man who was also in charge, as secretary, of a staff of scribes and assistants.

Lucía, as a young child, had been fearful of her chancellor; she reasoned it was most likely due to his appearance and mode of dress. He had an old weathered face with dark eyes and a long white beard, and he was dressed in a long flowing black robe with white stripes on its wide sleeves and a black cloak, which covered a white head turban. His appearance was both diabolical and frightening to one so young.

Avraham had been waiting patiently with his accounting books in the anteroom when Lucía entered.

"Buenos días, mi señora."

"Buenos días, Avraham," responded Lucía as she went to sit in the high-back chair, which was much too large for her slender body, to the right of the dais. She managed to wiggle her way to a comfortable position by sitting sideways with her hands in her lap.

"Before we begin, mi señora, let me say that your green garment suits you well this day."

With a smile, Lucía responded, "Gracias for your compliment, Avraham." And then she continued, "I plan to go work in the vineyard, much as my father did, but before I do, I need to know if all is ready for the harvest. Are there any problems that need my attention?"

"I am aware of none, mi señora."

"Has all the income from my condado and my holdings in England and France been collected to date?"

"Sí, except for the usual delay from England due to your uncle Prince John, as he apparently spends much time scrupulously reviewing his books to make sure he extracts every pound due him."

Lucía laughed. "That sounds like my uncle."

"But have no fear, mi señora. He eventually sends the full amount due you by a trusted courier."

"Thank God for that," responded Lucía.

"Let me review the accounting books with you, mi señora, until you get a grasp of my accounting methods. However, I would suggest sitting at the table together, so I may show you better."

Lucía agreed; she wiggled her way off the chair and took a seat next to Avraham at the polished oak table at the center of the anteroom.

As Avraham spoke, Lucía was impressed on how quickly he rattled off figures and statistics, and on several occasions, she had to slow him down, as he was going much too fast for her to comprehend.

"As you can see, mi señora, a nice profit has been made since your father has been gone, and all contracts have remained current. Well, that's about it, unless you have any further questions," said Avraham after about an hour of droning on. Lucía had yawned her way through the presentation.

Lucía yawned again and laughed at her own boredom. "I'm sorry, Avraham."

"Not at all, mi señora. I realize that for the average layman, accounting is not at all interesting."

Finally, something they could both agree upon, and Lucía thanked Avraham again and prepared to go to work in the vineyard the next day.

The next day, before dawn, Lucía was awakened by her ladies, with Gabriella in the lead. They helped her pick out the appropriate attire to work in the vineyard, which consisted of a long white sleeve undergarment covered by an old green sleeveless overgarment and a hemp belt. An old pair of leather work boots rounded out her wardrobe. Her long reddish-blond hair was wrapped in a long braid and slung over her left shoulder. A white coif covered her head and tied under her chin. After a prayer in the palace chapel with her entourage and a quick bite to eat, she had Rodrigo saddled. She put on a straw hat and galloped off to the vineyard.

It was sunrise when she arrived at the vineyard across from the peasant village about one mile down the road from the city. Lucía looked back toward the horizon from which she had just come and saw the many tall towers of Segoia, which rose proudly into the early morning sky. She quickly dismounted and slapped Rodrigo on the rear, and he quickly galloped off down the road where he had spotted a patch of grass.

The peasants were beginning to stir in the village, as they walked slowly across the road to begin work. Being there brought back memories to Lucía when she had come with her father many years before. A cart came around and dropped off three baskets for each row to place the grapes in once picked. Fortunately, Lucía had remembered her pruning knife to cut off the grape clusters from the vines and to inspect them for ripeness before picking them. She was the first one busy at work and could not wait to reacquaint herself with the village peasants.

Lucía blended in so well with her mode of dress that the workers thought she was new help from the city and were suspicious of her eagerness to engage in conversation. Lucía attempted to converse with a peasant worker, but she was interrupted by an old woman who warned Lucía not to talk or rest or she would suffer unpleasant consequences. She was told that Doña Lucía had ordered anyone not working hard enough to be whipped. Lucía was greatly appalled at her statement and shook her head in disbelief.

Suddenly, Lucía heard a crack of the whip in the row behind her and heard someone who cried out in pain. Lucía stood in place, motionless and in total shock, speechless as to what was going on around her. Her lack of motion was enough to attract the attention of the man with the whip.

"Get busy!" cried the man as he cracked his whip so close to Lucía that the energy of the motion caused a slight wind, which caused the bottom of her green garment to slightly rise.

Lucía was so angry at such uncalled-for aggression that she found her tongue and commanded, "Put down that whip and leave the premises, or I will have you whipped!"

The man was so taken back by such an act of disobedience that for a second, he did not know what to do. Here was a young girl who had just challenged his authority; he could not let this act go unpunished. But first, he was curious, "Who are you to question my authority?"

"I am Doña Lucía Alvarado, the Condesa of Segoia, and you, señor, are a bully and a miscreant whom I have already told once to leave the premises."

Her identity, revealed for the first time, caused the people around her to gasp with the sound of astonishment. The raucous caught the attention of many of the peasants who worked in the vineyard and caused them to gather around the furor.

The big burley man laughed. "Yeah, and I am the King of Castile."

"Who are you to be so blatant against someone from the nobility?" asked Lucía, who had become very angry.

"I am a caretaker, and you are a peasant. Now get busy."

At this point, Lucía asked a peasant worker to run and get help.

"All right, you asked for it." The caretaker cracked his whip, which cut through Lucía's shoulder, tore her garment, and emitted a small stream of blood from her wound.

"Rodrigo!" cried Lucía. As the horse had heard his master's voice, he started to gallop through the vineyard and through the crowd to come to her rescue. Upon arrival, Lucía reached for her father's sword in its scabbard, which was attached to her saddle.

The commotion caused several other caretakers to venture over to see what was happening. "What is going on here?" exclaimed another caretaker.

"This girl said that she is the Condesa of Segoia."

"What is she doing with a sword?"

'She stole it from this horse."

"A thief as well!" said the other caretaker, who Lucía figured must have been the leader of this band of scoundrels. "She is no condesa. How many women of the nobility do you know would come dressed like this and pick grapes?"

The other caretaker shrugged his shoulders.

"Well, teach her a lesson, and let the other peasants watch to see what will happen to them if they are disobedient."

The crowd around Lucía gasped in fear as she raised her sword. "I'm warning you, señor. Don't do this."

As the caretaker cracked his whip, Lucía swung her sword and cut a piece from it and did it each time until there was little left of the whip to the glee of the watchful crowd.

Finally, to the relief of Lucía, Captain Gómez arrived with a dozen men and immediately took the caretakers in custody. Everyone in the vineyard was told to report to the winery. Once there, the dozen caretakers that had caused such pain and grief to the villagers were lined up in front of them.

Captain Gómez saw Lucía's wound, and she explained what had happened. Her explanation so angered Gómez that he asked Lucía to identify the man who had whipped her, and she immediately pointed him out. Gómez immediately went over to the man, pulled his sword from his scabbard, and ran the caretaker through, which caused him to fall dead to the ground, to the cheers of the crowd.

"Let this be a lesson to everyone," said Gómez. "Anyone who lays a hand on any woman of the nobility, especially Doña Lucía, will be treated as such."

Lucía then approached the other caretakers and asked who hired them.

"We were told by Don Raimundo that the Condesa of Segoia was looking for help to supervise the vineyard to ensure the peasants worked and were hired for that purpose," said the leader of the group.

A peasant walked up to Lucía and gave a polite bow. "Do you remember me, mi señora?"

"Sí, I think I do. You are Zito, the peasant village leader. Am I correct, señor?"

"Sí, I am him. Let me try to explain what happened. After Father Baldwin left, these men came into the village and told us they had been hired by you, señora, and were now in charge. They took over several of our village huts, forcing those families to seek shelter elsewhere. Each day we were expected to be in the vineyard at dawn. Those who were not would be whipped, which caused the death of several of the elderly too sick to work. We were not allowed to go to the city and were told not to complain to anyone about our treatment for fear of death and retribution."

Both Lucía and Gómez were totally aghast that such a situation was allowed to occur, unbeknownst to them or any other official in Segoia. Zito also added that every one of the caretakers were responsible for harming the villagers.

Lucía, like her father, was a firm believer in justice and would now decide the fate of the men who had harmed her people.

Lucía turned to address the peasants of the village, who stood before her. "I am truly sorry for the pain these men caused you. Believe me when I say that I had no knowledge of what was happening here due to attentions paid elsewhere. I will promise you that this will never happen again and people here will be treated with kindness and respect, regardless of their station in life."

A cheer went up from the crowd when she was finished.

"Now for my judgment, each of the guilty men standing before you will be publicly whipped twelve times and then turned over to the king for further justice."

Another cheer went up for Lucía, who had now won the villagers admiration and loyalty by her proven ability to act competently on her own.

Lucía returned to the palace and had her wound attended to by Yamina. Her ladies meandered about and sputtered, discussing what they would do under similar circumstances.

During the harvest, Lucía found that she could easily enter into conversation with the village peasants and found out much that was happening in their daily lives. She listened to their rumors, laughed at their jokes, found out who was getting married in order to give her blessing and who was sick and needed help. As a result, Lucía became very much beloved and trusted by the populace as a person who was known to be very approachable.

One day, she noticed a lost child in the middle of the cart path with tears in her eyes. Lucía had just placed a cluster of grapes in the woven basket when she heard a mournful cry. As she looked around to see where the sound had come from, she noticed a young child who stood in the middle of the cart path, weeping for her mother. Lucía took off her gloves and walked over to the child, bent down, and very gently held both of her little arms.

"What is your name? asked Lucía with her infectious smile.

"I want my mama," sobbed the child.

"Well, let's see if we can find her."

Lucía turned to the people who were working in her row and asked if anyone knew who the little girl was.

"Oh, that's little Ana," responded a woman in the row. "Is she lost again?"

"Do you know where her mother is?"

"I don't know what part of the vineyard she is working in today, mi señora. However, the child likes to venture off on her own and tends to get lost."

Lucía thought for a minute. The cute little brown-haired girl, who Lucía guessed to be about four years old, stood next to her and sobbed. Lucía then cried out, "Rodrigo! Rodrigo!"

Where is that horse? thought Lucía to herself.

Finally, the horse galloped up the pathway, and Lucía knelt down in front of Ana, who had started to calm down. "This is Rodrigo, Ana. Would you like to pet him?" Ana wiped away her tears and nodded. Lucía lifted her up so she could pet him gently on the side of his head. "Would you like to ride with me as we look for your mother?" Lucía asked. Ana started to smile, and she nodded again. Lucía took the child and put her on the saddle and then mounted Rodrigo and lightly galloped up one path and down another, asking for the little girl's mother.

After a period of time, some distance away, Lucía came upon a row and a woman who met them in the cart path, quite distraught. Ana smiled and pointed to her, and Lucía handed Ana down to her mother. After they both had a laugh as to how quickly little legs could move, they both went back to work.

Chapter XII

Several weeks later, Lucía was awakened by Gabriella, now her trusted assistant. "Mi señora, there has been a raid on the peasant village. Come, you need to get dressed."

Lucía was tired from working hard in the vineyard and had overslept. She quickly rose from her bed but was still drowsy from being abruptly awakened from a deep sleep.

"When did this happen?"

"Not too long ago, mi señora. Apparently, the bell from the village church had sounded the alarm, and smoke could be seen from the palace rising from the village. I was told by a page that Captain Gómez was on his way there with some men."

Lucía's ladies-in-waiting quickly helped Lucía get dressed.

"Adele, please have Rodrigo saddled, and arrange an escort for me."

"Sí, mi señora," said Adele as she curtsied and then quickly ran out of Lucía's bedchambers.

Lucía, having been hurriedly dressed, quickly ran to the stable. Her usual escort of four guards was waiting for her when she arrived. Along with her escort, Lucía galloped out of the palace, through the city, out the gate, and onto the village road.

Upon arrival at the village, Lucía was stunned by what she saw. Several huts were on fire, and several people were lying dead face down on the ground. This event brought back haunting memories of that dreadful day when she was so young when a Moorish raid had burned several huts and killed several of the villagers. She also noticed that several rows of grape vines closest to the road had been trampled. Fortunately, they had already been picked. Some village people, along with several soldiers, were helping to put out the fires that had spread to several huts; other people milled about, dazed by what had happened. Yet a few more were mourning the dead and taking care of the wounded.

Captain Gómez, along with a contingent of a dozen well-armed men, had already arrived, and seven of the soldiers, who were not helping to fight the fires, had spread out into the vineyard on horseback with crossbows to ensure the enemy was not hiding there, ready to inflict another grave wound on the village.

As Lucía dismounted along with her escort, she heard a familiar voice. "Doña Lucía, what are you doing here? This is not the place for you."

"Am I not the condesa?" asked Lucía, who looked Gómez straight in the eye, a bit peeved that he would even think to challenge her right to be there.

Gómez sighed, as the last thing he wanted was a meddling child to interfere with his investigation. "Of course, you are, but you may be in danger. Remember what the queen told you—I am responsible for your safety and well-being, and what I say is final in such matters."

Lucía only heard half of Gómez's typical paternal babble. As the smoke started to clear, she became distracted by what she saw lying dead on the ground. Gómez was still speaking to Lucía as she walked away toward a burned-out hut, and not far from it was the body of a little girl lying face down on the ground. She knelt down next to the small body and slowly turned it over to reveal that the dead child was none other than Ana, the little girl that she had helped to find her mother several weeks before.

A crowd of villagers and soldiers started to gather around Lucía, who was still kneeling. She carefully picked up the body and held it in her arms and started to weep with such a mournful sound that even the strong battle-experienced soldiers were seen wiping away a tear or two. Not far from Ana, Lucía recognized the little girl's mother, who was also lying dead. Lucía, still weeping, stood up and held the little girl close to her bosom and carefully placed her next to her mother.

After a couple of minutes, Lucía was able to compose herself and wiped away her tears. With red eyes, she turned to the crowd, which had become so quiet that the only sound heard was the crackling of flames yet to be extinguished. She asked, "Who did this, and what happened to this little girl and her mother?"

"Lucía, I can see that you are visibly upset. Let me get to the bottom of this," said Gómez as he put his hand on her shoulder.

Lucía jerked away from his touch and barked so loudly it caused him to back away. "This is my condado. I will ask the questions, and if I catch the ones responsible for this atrocity, I swear to God that they will pay with their lives!" screamed Lucía. "Now what happened here? Did anyone see anything at all? Please, someone must have seen something. All I want is information no matter how insignificant it may be to bring justice to little Ana, her mother, and the rest of the dead."

A woman from the crowd, who had remained very quiet to this point, stepped out from the throng. "I happened to be in my hut, getting ready to work in the vineyard just at sunrise, when I heard the thundering sound of horses coming closer and closer to the village from the south. I am fortunate enough to live far enough away from the attack yet close enough to have seen some of the attack in progress from my door. There were about twelve of the enemy."

"By enemy, you mean the Moors?" interrupted Lucía.

"Sí, they were dressed as Moors. They all carried torches, which they threw on several of the huts. I saw little Ana run out of her hut, only…" The woman was overcome with emotion. "I'm sorry," she apologized, wiping away her tears.

"That's all right. I understand fully well. Please take your time, and when you are ready, you may continue," said Lucía.

The woman was able to compose herself, and she continued, "I saw Little Ana run out of her hut, only to be trampled by a horse, and when her mother went out after her, she was cut down by those savages."

An older man from the crowd also stepped forth. "I am a freeman who works the fields not far from here. I was at the village church to see Father Piña, who was not there. I happened to be walking down the steps of the church when I saw the Moors come into the village. I managed to take shelter, but I saw something very interesting concerning one of the supposed Moors. I was hiding behind a hut. He did not see me, but I saw him very clearly. The man had a scar on his left cheek that went from the bottom of his left ear to his mouth. A couple of years ago, I was in Donato, in the palace of Don Raimundo, on a business matter, and I noticed the same man coming out of Don Raimundo's private chambers. I could never forget that face."

Lucía started to cringe at the name of Don Raimundo. The very thought he might have something to do with the raid made Lucía so fearful that a chill came over her, and without saying a word, she mounted Rodrigo and galloped back to Segoia, to the complete surprise and utter shock of the crowd, especially Captain Gómez.

Lucía had always been frightened of Don Raimundo since she was a small child. His demeanor had always struck her as being evil. But the possibility of his involvement in the raid and all that had happened in the village earlier had become too much for Lucía.

With a sigh, Captain Gómez left a few men at the village to guard against any further intrusion, and after reassuring the peasants that their huts would be rebuilt, he mounted his horse and rode back to the palace.

Once back at the palace, Lucía, still upset from what she had seen and heard in the village, went directly to her mother's sarcophagus in the crypt of the palace chapel. Before she proceeded down the shadowy stairs, she paused to bless herself with holy water in the chapel and then proceeded to her mother's burial site.

The dimly lit chamber gave way to a sarcophagus with an effigy carved from stone of Lady Margaret. Lucía was weeping as she touched the image of her mother and started to cry out and beg for her mother's help. Lucía had been challenged by a real foe and lacked the wisdom of dealing with the possible threat it presented.

"Mama, I need you. Please, I need your help. I beg of you." Lucía then bent over her mother's image and wept uncontrollably. "Don't you see I can't go to Captain Gómez for help in this matter, or I will lose all credibility with him? He still thinks of me as a child.

If I am the condesa, then it is up to me to make the decisions. That is what Papa did, and he's gone. It's up to me to protect my people. Help me, Mama. Please help me." Lucía then continued to weep loudly.

Finally, she was able to compose herself, took a seat on the bench, and realized she had allowed her emotions to get away from her. She began to feel foolish in having allowed that to happen.

How am I ever going to be a good condesa if I allow myself to get so emotional? Lucía thought to herself, still sniffling. *Papa would never have acted this way.*

Lucía then wiped away her tears, knelt in prayer, and prayed that the Holy Mother would help shed some light on her dilemma.

That night, Lucía fell asleep but was awakened by someone who called out her name. At first, it sounded like a soft whisper, which became louder and louder. Then a strong breeze occurred, which pushed aside the curtains surrounding her canopy, and a foggy image appeared at the foot of her bed. Lucía was frightened at first, but there was certain warmth about the image that made her feel safe.

"Lucía! Lucía!" whispered the image, which slowly took shape. Finally, the shape materialized in full form and revealed a young girl about the same age as Lucía. She had very long blond hair and had a strong scent of roses about her. Lucía could not believe what her eyes had just affirmed. Still in shock, she closed her eyes for several seconds and then opened them to ensure that she was fully awake.

The spirit walked up the stairs of the dais to Lucía's bed, where Lucía was about to pull the covers over her head in disbelief of what she had just witnessed.

"Don't be afraid, Lucía," said the spirit who stood over her with a smile. "Do you know who I am?"

"I think so," said Lucía nervously. "Mama, is that you?"

"Sí, I am Margaret, your mother," said the spirit, who gazed affectionately at Lucía.

Lucía felt rather awkward at having called a girl practically the same age as herself her mother.

The spirit could sense what Lucía was feeling. "I know you were expecting someone older, perhaps someone with gray hair and maybe a few wrinkles," said the spirit with an infectious laugh. Lucía now felt relaxed and at ease, and she nodded her head.

"Come, Lucía, and sit with me," said the spirit as she sat down on the edge of the bed.

Lucía pulled back the bed covers and wiggled her way to her mother and sat next to her.

"You're so real." Lucía touched her and felt her warmth.

Lady Margaret responded, "I am real and only have a short time here with you. I'm here because of a miracle. I actually heard your plea and seen you so overcome by your sorrow that I had to come and try to comfort you as best I could. Can you tell me what is bothering you, Lucía?"

"I'm afraid, Mama. I do not know what to do. Someone attacked the village, and I believe that somehow Don Raimundo might be involved."

"What do your instincts tell you to do, Lucía?"

"Perhaps to confront my foe and tell him that such an act will not go unnoticed and that if he continues, he will feel my full wrath. That's what Papa would do."

"Well, that sounds like the daughter of Don Fernando. It sounds that you have already decided what to do."

"But I don't know if it is the right thing to do, and I don't want to bother my uncle and aunt about this, because I feel that I need to handle this on my own."

"Then do so, if you feel it best."

"How would you handle it, Mama?"

"I don't know, Lucía. This is a problem for you to work out on your own. All I can say is to follow your instincts. There will be times in life when you are right and other times when you are wrong. No one is perfect, Lucía, but you have to believe in yourself. If you can do that, then you will always feel confident in what you do and be able to accept any outcome that might occur."

Lucía thought about her mother's advice for a moment. "I never thought about trusting my instincts before. It certainly makes sense. Gracias, Mama."

"You don't have to thank me, Lucía. You worked out your problem before I arrived. Now let me take a look at you." Lucía stood up in front of her mother. "How you have grown into such a beautiful young lady. I am so proud of you."

Tears came back into Lucía's eyes. "I'm sorry, Mama, that I was the cause of your death."

"Lucía, you must not think that way. I had a choice, and I, like you, had to make a decision. I wanted you to live, as any other mother would want for their child. You see, I felt confident in my decision, as you feel about yours. Now I don't want to ever hear you say that again. I made a choice, and I am happy with that choice. Don't diminish it with guilt."

Lucía then embraced her mother and noticed that on her right shoulder was a mold of a small cluster of red dots.

"Are you happy where you are, Mama?"

"Very happy, as you will also see for yourself someday."

"Is Papa still alive, Mama?"

Lady Margaret smiled. "What does your heart tell you, Lucía?"

"I believe that he is still alive and will come home again someday."

"Then so be it. Keep having faith, Lucía, and you will see miracles abound. I must go now."

"Will I see you again, Mama?"

"Someday we will all be together again, and I will see you at that time, but that is a long time away, as you will lead a long and fruitful life, Lucía."

Lady Margaret then put Lucía back to bed, tucked her in, put her doll next to her, and gave her a kiss. "Just remember, Lucía, I will always love you and be with you, trying to guide you, especially when you feel a little prod to your conscience."

"Mama?"

"Sí, Lucía."

"Is this a dream?"

As Lady Margaret walked away, she said, "It is what you want it to be, Lucía." And with that final remark, she slowly vanished into a heavy mist.

Suddenly, Lucía awakened and yelled out for her mother to an empty dark room. *It must have been a dream*, Lucía thought to herself, but then she noticed that her doll was next to her, which she remembered had been lying on the chest at the foot of her bed before she went to sleep just hours before. She shrugged her shoulders and felt a lot better about herself and her future, as she fell back to sleep.

The next morning, Lucía was awakened by Gabriella and her ladies, whom she immediately dismissed, except for Gabriella, whom she immediately appointed as her majordomo due to her intellect, quick learning skills, and most importantly, her trust in her. Lucía now started to have more confidence in her instincts and felt that this was the right decision to make. Gabriella, on the other hand, felt unworthy of such an honor; however, after a little coaxing, a little pleading, and a little persuasiveness, Gabriella finally acquiesced.

While Gabriella helped Lucía put on a dark-blue garment, Lucía told her about her dream, which Gabriella interpreted as a gift from God, and she said that such gifts should not be analyzed but should be given thanks for.

Spoken like a true nun, thought Lucía to herself.

Lucía completed her wardrobe with a silver chain link belt and a pair of brown leather boots. Her hair was brushed and braided. Lucía decided to add her father's chain of office two long silver chains linked together by rectangular silver plates, which rested on her shoulders and reached down to her bosom.

"If I may ask, mi señora, why you are so formally dressed?" asked Gabriella.

"I have some official business to take care of, Gabriella, and I want to dress the part."

After Lucía announced to her ladies-in-waiting that Gabriella was her majordomo and would be in charge when she was not at the palace, Lucía sent a servant to find Captain Gómez.

After a while, a servant appeared at the door of her boudoir, where Lucía was busy working at a table on some documents. "Captain Gómez is here to see you, mi señora."

"Enter," said Lucía.

Gómez entered the anteroom. "Do you wish to see me, Doña Lucía?"

"Sí. There is a matter I wish to discuss with you pertaining to the attack on the village yesterday."

"And what might that be?"

"I have a suspicion that Don Raimundo might have been involved in the attack," said Lucía, who was busy signing a document.

"There is no proof that he was involved," responded Gómez.

"Enough proof that I feel I need to take action."

"What kind of action?"

"I feel that I must confront him."

"Before you do something you might regret, may I suggest that this matter be discussed with the king?" warned Gómez.

"I am the Condesa of Segoia, and I am going to do what I feel is right for my condado. I am not going to run to my uncle every time a matter such as this occurs. All I want to do is to approach him and give him a warning that such an incident will not be tolerated and that if it continues, then I will have to take action."

"I still think that the king needs to be advised," insisted Gómez.

Lucía banged her fist on the table and screamed, "By the bones of St. James, Gómez, I am not a child and will not be treated as such!"

Gómez snapped back, "And your aunt and uncle appointed me responsible for your safety and well-being, and I also promised your father that I would look after you. This is not the path to take."

Lucía finally calmed down and sighed. "Gómez, I need your help. This is a matter of appearances. I do not want to be thought of as young girl who is so easily frightened of her own shadow that she runs and hides under her bed whenever she is confronted by a hostile action. If I do not do something, then I will be putting my condado in a constant stream of danger to anyone who would be willing to take advantage. Surely you can understand that."

Gómez was silent as he gave Lucía's request some thought. "Something tells me that I am going to regret this, but what did you have in mind?"

Lucía smiled. "First, I plan to go to the village to see if I can gather more evidence and then to travel to Donato and confront Don Raimundo. I need for you to back me since I am a little frightened of the man."

Reluctantly, Gómez said, "I'll provide an escort of twelve men and have your horse saddled."

Lucía walked over to Gómez. "Gracias for your understanding."

"Is that all?" asked Gómez.

Lucía nodded. "You may go about your duty."

With pursed lips, Gómez left her boudoir. *She is just as stubborn as her father*, Gómez thought to himself as he walked down the staircase to the stable.

Lucía led her small army to the village, and the peasants were somewhat stunned to see their condesa so formally dressed. She had her soldiers once again look around for any evidence that might strengthen her suspicions. She asked Zito to find any witnesses who might have seen the raid.

After having taken time to examine the area where the raid had taken place and having taken the time to once again cross-examine witnesses, there was no new evidence to be found. The only evidence Lucía had was a man with a scar who possibly worked for Don Raimundo. Lucía was now in a quandary as to what to do next.

After some time of having witnessed Lucía pacing up and down, waving her arms around, and talking to herself, Captain Gómez decided to intervene.

"Doña Lucía, is there a problem that I may be able to help you with?"

Lucía seemed confused. "I just don't understand why I can't find any more evidence. There must be something I missed."

"Lucía, maybe there is no more evidence to find. You may have to make a decision based on what evidence you have. Once again, I implore you to discuss this matter with the king."

Lucía knew deep down she had to take action on her own to save face. After all, she was an Alvarado, and she knew that her father would be drawn to the same conclusion and also be forced to confront Don Raimundo. This gave Lucía the strength she needed.

"Captain Gómez, I have made my decision. We will ride to Donato and confront Don Raimundo. However, I need you and a few soldiers to accompany me when I confront him."

"Have no fear. I will be with you," said Gómez, who was reluctant but relieved that at least she had made a decision and was ready to move on.

The crowd that had gathered now watched as Lucía mounted her horse and led her small well-armed force of men down the road to Donato.

An attendant, who happened to have been standing near the entrance of the door to the palace, saw Lucía approaching and immediately warned Don Raimundo of her coming. The bishop of Segoia, who happened to be there, did not want to be seen, and he hid behind the heavy curtains behind the dais in back of Don Raimundo.

Lucía dismounted at the stairs leading to the entrance to the palace and, along with Captain Gómez and four soldiers, walked up the stairs through the hallway to the anteroom of the great hall and charged through the door. She found Don Raimundo patiently working.

Don Raimundo remained calm as he looked up and saw Lucía standing below the dais, along with Captain Gómez and the four guards who accompanied them.

Don Raimundo rose from his chair and, with a smile, said, "Ah, how nice to see your lovely presence here in Donato, mi señora, and what a lovely lady you have grown up to be. What brings you to my palace?"

She confronted Don Raimundo in a soft but commanding voice; however, she appeared somewhat nervous in her accusation. "I have reason to believe that you were behind a raid on the peasant village in Segoia yesterday, and I have come to warn you—"

Lucía was interrupted by Don Raimundo, who scowled at her with his piercing eyes. "A raid, you say, on your village, and you believe me to be responsible? That is a serious accusation, mi señora, even by someone like you. Why would I raid your land? Do you have any proof of this accusation? I can assure that I had no part to play in this, but if you can tell me if there was anyone from Donato who participated in this occurrence, I will make sure he is severely punished."

"I understand there is a man who has a scar on his left cheek in your employ, and it was he who was seen participating in the raid."

Don Raimundo laughed. "That is preposterous. There are a lot of men who have scars on their cheeks. Is that the only evidence you have?" asked Don Raimundo, who now raised his voice. "I employ a lot of people directly and indirectly, and I don't know of anyone who fits that description."

"Maybe so, but let me warn you and others who may want to do Segoia harm. Any aggression on Segoia or its people will not be tolerated. If I find out who committed such an act, I can promise you they will have a war on their hands, and I will win it; I've got the resources to do so. That is all of got to say on the matter. Adiós, señor."

Lucía and her contingent left as quickly as they had come. Don Raimundo let them leave without saying a word. As Lucía left, the bishop appeared from behind the curtain. "I'm surprised you let that brat talk to you in such a manner."

Raimundo walked over to the window, and he watched Lucía ride off with her men. "I must admit that I was both surprised and shocked by her boldness. I have to be careful in the future. She is more astute then I realized."

"But still to come here and accuse you of such a thing. How do you suppose she found out?"

Suddenly, Raimundo turned to the bishop. "Apparently, Scarface was not careful enough to cover his face during the raid. Well, no matter. I will keep him out of sight for a while."

"Won't this situation delay your grand plan for a while?" asked the bishop.

Raimundo walked back to the bishop and said with both calm and confidence, "You see, my fat friend, everything comes with time and patience, but I will never underestimate her again. The next time, one way or another, it will play to my advantage." And then Raimundo mused out loud, "She is, indeed, very wealthy and powerful in her own right, and she could indeed raise a substantial army. She also has the ear of both the king and queen. I must be very careful in the future. Apparently, intimidation will not work well in this case."

"Then what are your plans? That's if you have any," asked the bishop in an arrogant manner.

Don Raimundo, annoyed at the bishop's attitude, said, "My fat friend, that is really none of your concern at the moment. Just remember, all you have to do is to keep your ears open as to what is happening in Segoia and, at the appropriate time, put the crown of Castile on my head, as the Archbishop of Toledo. Meanwhile, you can continue fleecing your flock. Do we have an understanding?"

"Of course, Don Raimundo. You know I am loyal to you and will remain so to the end. If our business is concluded, I will take leave now."

As the bishop took his leave, Don Raimundo again walked toward the window and began to muse about a possible future plan.

Lucía had just received a letter from Isabella and was happy that she was all right and in no apparent danger from a Moorish raid. Lucía quickly dashed off a response and sent a letter back with the messenger. Isabella was a true friend, and she would always care for her. Now it was time to give Rodrigo some exercise and to have her ladies accompany her to improve their riding skills.

With instructions from Lucía, Constance found the ladies-in-waiting and directed them to the stable, where they each prepared for their journey by saddling their horses that were assigned to them. Both José, the stable keeper, and Gómez helped the ladies with their saddles.

When Lucía entered the stable, she noticed that Gómez was attempting to teach Beatrix how to saddle a horse but was having a communication problem. He would tell her what to do, and she would only mumble something in German and shrug her shoulders. Gómez was becoming rather perturbed.

Lucía went over to Gómez, as the rest of her ladies were in their saddles and were patiently waiting.

"Gómez, what seems to be the matter?"

Gómez threw his hand in the air. "I've been here for some time, trying to help her with her saddle, but she doesn't seem to understand what I am saying. She just keeps mumbling in a tongue I don't understand."

Lucía looked at Adele and Geralla, who were already in their saddles. "Has anyone seen Constance?"

"She told us to come to the stable, and that was the last I saw of her," said Adele.

With a sigh, Lucía quickly saddled Rodrigo. Then Constance arrived. "I'm sorry, mi señora, but I had to find the chef to tell him the ladies were going horseback riding and would not be back to help with tonight's supper preparations."

"What did the chef say?"

"He just grumbled and continued with his work."

"Constance, I need your help since you understand some German. Can you please try to teach Beatrix how to saddle her horse?"

"I'll try, but she is a slow learner."

"I know, but see what you can do."

Meanwhile, Beatrix, who had been standing in the stall with her arms folded and her lips pursed, was glad to see Constance, who entered the stall, took a bridle off the wall, and explained in German what to do. As Constance explained what to do, Beatrix followed her instructions very carefully and then had a brief conversation with her in German.

Constance smiled and walked over to Lucía as Beatrix mounted her steed.

"What did she say?" asked Lucía.

"She thanked me and said she does not wish to be any trouble but is having a hard time understanding Castilian," said Constance.

"Gracias, Constance."

It must be the language barrier that makes her appear as a slow leaner, Lucía thought to herself.

Lucía mounted Rodrigo and looked over to Beatrix, who smiled with approval and said, "Danke."

Once Constance had quickly saddled her horse, Lucía and her ladies, with an escort of four household guards, were on their way out of the city, and they galloped their way out into the countryside with the sound of laughter and merriment.

Chapter XIII

Early the next morning, a messenger arrived at the palace with an accompaniment of several armed soldiers who wore the royal colors and said that he had been sent by the king to bring Lucía to Burgos. While the messenger waited, Lucía, with the help of her ladies, quickly changed into a new dark-green garment, a brown leather ring belt, and brown boots; she then quickly left to board the wagon that was waiting to bring her to the royal residence.

Gabriella due to her ex officio position was now in charge of the palace. Lucía's ladies, along with Gabriella, came to the courtyard to see her off on her journey. Once Lucía boarded the wagon, the contingent left Segoia for Burgos.

Don Raimundo realized that in order to make his ambitions come true and to sustain them, he needed to be vigilant in his pursuit, as one misstep could lead to a fatal blow. First, he decided to try a less truculent approach, and that approach was soon forthcoming. Second, he needed an ally, where mutual trust and self-ambition would be respected. He thought of the countries that surrounded Castile, many of which were potential enemies of the king. However, they might not readily recognize his claims to the throne, and this could lead to a further depletion of wealth and men.

Don Raimundo was not a man to wallow in self-defeat, and an idea suddenly entered his mind. Why not turn to a man who shared his ideals down to its very core? Don Raimundo had heard of the ambitions of Prince John many times at court, where Queen Leonor often spoke of his misguided principles and her disgust of a brother who would turn against his own family to meet his own ambitions. A man such as this would have respect for ambition, and

Don Raimundo might also be able to offer something he could not refuse. He now had to wait and see how his first approach of a more pleasant demeanor would work on Lucía. However, he would send an envoy to Rouen to find Prince John and to explore a possible alliance.

Lucía had been traveling only a short time when she realized that she was not on the road to Burgos. Unfortunately, she was trapped and unable to escape. The guards on horseback were too close to the wagon for her to jump out, and she could not get their attention. Lucía now felt very vulnerable to whatever was planned for her at the end of her destination.

After a while, the wagon arrived in the palace courtyard of Don Raimundo, who was waiting for her in the anteroom of the great hall. Since Lucía was reluctant to leave the wagon. The guards had to drag her out kicking and struggling to get loose. When she arrived in the anteroom, the guards had both her arms in restraint, and they forcibly placed her in a chair in front of Don Raimundo.

"Get your hands off me!" said Lucía, who pulled her arms away from the soldiers.

Lucía quickly looked around for a potential avenue of escape if the opportunity should present itself. She had noticed there were two doors in the anteroom. One door in the back led to the corridor, from which she had just come, and it led to the courtyard. The other was to the right of her, and it led to the great hall, but guards were at each exit. In front of her, on the dais, was Don Raimundo, who was now standing to greet her, in front of a giant curtain, which Lucía figured covered a wall. In the back of the room was a fireplace, which, along with two braziers on either side of the dais, provided warmth during the winter months. She was definitely trapped with no place to escape.

"I guess I'm your prisoner," said Lucía with a look of disdain.

"On the contrary, you are free to go. I merely brought you here to discuss a matter with you," said Don Raimundo, who was exercising a pleasant demeanor of sociability.

"Forcibly!" exclaimed Lucía. "And using a ruse to get me here."

"Would you have come otherwise, mi señora?" asked Don Raimundo as he took his seat in front of his worktable.

Lucía did not respond.

"I thought as much. Now perhaps you would enjoy some refreshments after your travel, mi señora?"

"Why don't you just get to the point?"

"Very well. I brought you here to discuss your future."

Lucía laughed. "My future? How could my future possibly interest you?"

"Perhaps a great deal, depending on your response. I would like to ask for your hand in marriage."

Lucía expression changed quickly from laughter to seriousness. "You must be joking! I would never marry you under any circumstances. Now may I go?"

"Not yet. I have not finished with my proposal. If you were to marry me, I would make you my queen."

"What are you talking about?"

"Very simply, my dear. You possess certain resources I need to accomplish my main objective."

Lucía reluctantly asked, "And what might that be?"

"To be king of Castile."

"Castile already has a king—my uncle. Or have you forgotten, señor?"

"I would simply displace him. As a result, you and I could share in all the riches that such a position could offer."

Lucía promptly rose from her seat. "You're absolutely mad. Moreover, this sounds like treason, which I could never be a part of. I'm leaving now, and you can be assured my uncle will hear of your treachery."

As Lucía turned from her chair to walk out, she quickly bumped into the stomach of the most grotesque creature she had ever seen and was slowly pushed back into her chair with a plop. The creature was very badly deformed with large ears that were bent away from his head and came to a point. He had a very large and wide noise, along with a deformed mouth, where two of his bottom teeth were sticking out over his bottom lip. He was about seven feet tall with massive arms and legs with no neck. As he stood in front of Lucía, he portrayed a very strong and muscular beast.

"Let me introduce you to García, my residence ogre. As you notice, he can be very persuasive. I only use him on special occasions such as this. You should feel honored. I met García when he was still a young boy wandering the streets of Soria. He was living on the streets, hiding wherever he could find shelter from the abuse and cruelty that followed him, existing on whatever he could find to eat, mostly garbage. Amazing, even the church, much like his parents, turned him away and said that he was the devil's child. Isn't that right, García?"

García grunted and nodded his head.

"I brought him here to live in the palace. I fed him, clothed him, and gave him shelter. He in return does my bidding."

Lucía at first felt fear, but that quickly turned to pity, as she studied him more carefully. As Don Raimundo spoke, Lucía glanced over to García, who stood to the right of the dais, and wondered how God could be so cruel as to make a monster out of a man who would have to suffer a lifetime of abuse and unspeakable loneliness.

"What can I do to persuade you otherwise, my dear condesa?"

"Absolutely nothing. Even if I consented to such an arrangement, I would soon be disposed of once you controlled my wealth to your treacherous ends."

Don Raimundo could tell his conversation was leading nowhere. "Ah, too bad, my dear condesa. You would have given me both the wealth and the legitimacy I would need to accomplish my objective. You may go, but if you should change your mind, I will be here. Oh, by the way, this conversation never happened. Think of the embarrassment this would cause you if you were accused of having had participated in an act of treason," said Don Raimundo, who rose from his chair and instructed García to see Lucía back to the wagon.

"Don't worry, señor. I would not think of hurting my uncle with the specter of treason coming from a man whom he reveres so as a trusted friend or from a loving niece."

"Wonderful. Then we are in agreement," said Don Raimundo, who poured a cup of wine for himself and appeared relieved that she was committed to silence.

As Lucía walked back to the courtyard with García, she noticed that he had a bad limp as a result of two deformed feet, which caused him to walk slowly and bowlegged. Lucía again could sense the misery, the loneliness, and the sense of hopelessness that he was feeling, which no human being should have to suffer. She also felt sorry that he was trapped in a life of slavery, doing the bidding of an evil and treacherous man.

With tears in her eyes, she looked up to him when no one was around. "You must have had a horrible childhood, García, but somehow you miraculously survived it."

Suddenly, García stopped dead in his tracks and looked down at her and gave a grunt.

With tears running down her cheeks, Lucía had pieced together what must have been a horrifying cruel life and continued, "The cruelty you must have suffered, as people either ran away from you in total fear or threw things at you. With nowhere to go, shelter must have been a problem as you lived in fear, especially at such a young age, and the feeling of loneliness must have been so dark and foreboding."

As García listened, he had never seen anyone display such pity or emotion to his life before. He stood beside Lucía, speechless, and could only respond to her with a grunt.

As they arrived in the courtyard, Lucía boarded the wagon, with the help of García, whom she noticed had a gentle touch. She then pulled a large ruby ring from her gloved finger and placed it in García's hand. "This ring is yours. You don't need to work for Don Raimundo any longer. I would like to employ you into my service. If you decide to work for me, simply give this ring to a Captain Gómez, and he will direct you to me. I will advise him of such. If not, then you may keep it as a gift. You certainly deserve at least that much. However, remember that God loves you. You are not alone, and neither are you evil. So believe." Lucía then gave García a kiss on his cheek and went to sit down in the wagon. As it slowly left the courtyard on its way back to Segoia, García was left standing in the courtyard, not knowing how to respond to such an act of kindness.

Chapter XIV

As a result of being the niece of King Alfonso and Queen Leonor of Castile, Lucía became very close to her cousins—in particular, Mafalda, the youngest of the infantas. Mafalda was very fond of Lucía and considered her a big sister whom she admired and deeply respected. Mafalda would often beg her mother to stay with Lucía in Segoia. The queen finally relented and allowed her daughter to do so, accompanied by a very long list of instructions for her proper care.

Lucía was busy at work in her boudoir, reviewing the figures from her monthly income, when a herald entered the room. "Infanta Doña Mafalda to see you, mi señora."

Lucía rose from her chair and, after a deep curtsy, went to greet her young guest. Lucía kneeled down and gave her young guest a warm embrace and then rose to her feet. "Mafalda, how beautiful you look today. Your green garment with the gold trim is truly exceptional," said Lucía with a warm smile.

"Gracias," Mafalda responded in a little girl's voice.

"Are you ready for some fun?" asked Lucía to her small charge.

Before Mafalda could answer, a trusted court official entered the boudoir, followed by a bevy of royal servants. Lucía quickly had to dodge several servants who entered the boudoir and through the door to Lucía's bedchamber, with several trunks of clothes and various sundry of other items. As Lucía was about to repeat her question again, an old woman quickly ran through the boudoir to the bedroom to give last-minute instructions to the servants.

"Whooo?" asked Lucía, who pointed to the strange woman.

"Oh, that's my nurse," said Mafalda, who quickly responded before Lucía could finish her question.

"Oh, your nurse. Well, I guess you have officially moved in," said Lucía with a nervous smile.

"Ah ha," said Mafalda with a sly smile.

After all trunks were unpacked from the wagon in the courtyard, the court official returned to speak to Lucía and to give her a scroll that contained a rather long list of instructions on the infanta's complete care.

Lucía took the scroll from the official to read it, but as she was about to peruse it, her eye happened to catch the nurse who had already made herself at home in Lucía's bedchamber and was busy working on her embroidery.

"Well, I must admit that your people are very fast and efficient," added Lucía.

"We try to be," responded the royal official. "Before I leave, is all satisfactory, mi señora?"

Again, Lucía's eyes were drawn through the door to Mafalda's nurse, who interrupted her embroidery to give Lucía a toothless smile, which caused Lucía to do a double take.

"Sí, I believe so.'"

"I shall take my leave then, mi señora," said the royal official, who bowed and left.

Lucía read through the rather lengthy list of dos and don'ts. "Doesn't your mother allow you to have any fun at all?"

Mafalda just shrugged her shoulders. "She believes that study and learning how to be a proper queen is more important."

"But there is one item on the list that I agree with. I can help you with your Latin lessons."

"Bueno!" replied Mafalda.

Again, Lucía was drawn to Mafalda's nurse. "What about her?"

"Oh, don't worry about her. She won't bother you with whatever plans you have for us," said Mafalda with a sly smile.

Lucía decided to make Mafalda's visit as much fun as possible and make enough time in her busy schedule to accomplish it.

Over the weeks that Mafalda was at Segoia, she danced to make-believe music with Lucía's ladies by taking a partner by the hand and frolicking around the great hall. They experimented with makeup, made weird faces in the mirror, and practiced archery. At the young age of six, she was a better shot than Lucía. They also enjoyed horseback riding, read poetry, and went shopping.

One day toward the end of Mafalda's visit, Lucía decided to take her on a picnic in the forest some distance from the palace in order to be alone together and without an escort. A picnic combined with study would be the order of the day in a tranquil setting. Mafalda enjoyed riding in the countryside, especially with the person she most admired and respected.

Lucía found a beautiful spot under a tree in an old ravine, away from the rocky ground and completely surrounded by forest. The ravine had a gentle rise on both sides and was easily accessible. After an hour of learning Latin versus and playing hide-and-seek, it was time to eat. Lucía had packed bread, sausage, cheese, grapes, and a skin of grape juice.

After a heavy lunch, it was time for more Latin verses, where Mafalda would repeat each verse and learn what each word meant. Before long, they both began to feel drowsy. Lucía had repeated the simple Latin phase *veni mecum* ("come with me") over and over again until they both fell asleep, leaning on each other, with their backs resting on the side of the ravine.

After a while, Lucía was awakened by a noise. She happened to gaze beyond the slope to the surrounding forest beyond, and not seventy yards away were several Moors on horseback. Startled, she carefully looked behind her and found several more about the same distance away. Fortunately, they had not yet noticed her in the ravine.

"Mafalda, wake up," whispered Lucía and gave her a slight nudge.

Mafalda slowly awakened and wiped her eyes.

Lucía continued to whisper, "Don't say a word, and listen to me carefully."

Suddenly, Mafalda noticed the Moorish warriors and gave a muffled sound of surprise. Lucía could see the expression of fear on her face. She said, "Mafalda, I want you to listen to me carefully. Can you do that?"

Mafalda nodded without having said a word, but her face was filled with great fear.

"Good," whispered Lucía. "As soon as I tell you, I want you to very slowly and carefully mount your horse and gallop away as quickly as possible without looking back. I will be right behind you. Can you do that?"

Again Mafalda nodded.

"All right, go mount your horse without making a sound," instructed Lucía.

Mafalda mounted her horse, and a Moorish warrior was quickly alerted to their presence and signaled to his comrades on the other side of the ravine. Mafalda quickly galloped away as Lucía was mounting Rodrigo. However, Lucía's face became filled with terror by what she saw next. Down the road, which had led into the ravine and not eighty yards away, Mafalda had been intercepted by a dozen Moorish warriors, who had gathered around her. Crippling fear overtook Lucía as she could hear the loud laughter of the Moors and saw them touching Mafalda's face and hair, and then she heard Mafalda's screams.

Lucía was terrified and started to panic, but she quickly got control of herself when she fully realized Mafalda was in real danger and she was her only hope. Fortunately, the Moors had focused all their attention on their captured prize and didn't pay any heed to Lucía. This gave Lucía time to think, as it appeared the Moors were not in any rush to escape with Mafalda.

An idea came to her mind, and she spread out her long reddish-blond hair so it would blow in the wind. She also took her father's sword out of the scabbard, which was on her saddle. Both Lucía's arms and legs were shaking, as she knew that the possibility of her death was real, but she had to protect the infanta. Then she thought of her father's bravery that day in the vineyard when he had rescued several kidnapped villagers from the Moorish raiders. Now it was her turn to show the same kind of bravery. She started to say to herself and kept on repeating, "I am an Alvarado. I can do this. I am an Alvarado. I can do this." This gave her the shot of bravery she needed.

The time had come to engage the enemy, and Lucía started by giving Rodrigo such a kick with her boot that the horse gave a long loud neighing sound and reared up on his two hind legs. Lucía then screamed a loud cry of foreboding. Finally, the Moors had taken notice and between Lucía's hair that was flowing in the wind, her continued loud cry, and her brandished sword held high in the air, the warriors thought her a witch. They started to panic. Several horses reared at the sight and threw their riders to the ground and trampled them in panic. A couple even fled in fright, as Lucía had become very convincing.

Once on the scene, she started to swing her sword as she screamed for Mafalda to run. To her surprise, she actually struck a warrior and caused him the fall to the ground. Lucía continued to hold her own but barely. Lucía realized she would quickly be overcome but was willing to die to give Mafalda time to escape. To her credit, Lucía kept swinging her sword until she noticed that she had been drawn out of the fight. When she looked around, she noticed that another group of Moors had come to join the fight, but these men had come to her defense.

Mafalda had taken refuge on the clearing on the high-steep forested hill above the skirmish below. Lucía galloped up the clearing on the side of the hill at breakneck speed and dismounted Rodrigo before he had come to a full stop. She ran over to Mafalda and, with tears of joy in her eyes, quickly embraced her. "Are you all right? Are you hurt?" asked Lucía as she carefully examined her for any wounds. Mafalda shook her head and embraced Lucía.

After the skirmish, a man dressed as a Moor cantered up the hill on a dark horse. Lucía watched the man carefully while she still held onto Mafalda. He was wearing a black tunic that reached down to his knees and a white undergarment that reached down to his ankles. His head was covered by a long white winding cloth that covered both his head and neck. Around his waist was a black leather belt with a small curved dagger tucked in it, along with a scimitar, which hung from it.

Once the stranger had reached the top of the hill, Lucía held Mafalda close to her side. The stranger was very polite and mannerly.

He greeted them and said, "Peace be upon you," accompanied by the sweeping of his hand over his heart. "Allow me to introduce myself. I am Yusuf Abd al-Rashid ibn Mosa. Are both of you all right?"

Lucía looked into his dark eyes and viewed his strong and muscular Middle Eastern physique. Lucía could tell he was a leader by the way he presented himself. "We are both well. Gracias," responded Lucía. Mafalda didn't say a word and was still in some shock from her earlier experience.

"I am happy to hear that, Doña Lucía and Your Highness, Doña Mafalda. If you would allow me to make a suggestion, the next time you venture off into the woods, you should bring an armed escort. These woods can be dangerous, as you no doubt found out. Roving bands of Moors have been known to frequent this area. You are in no danger now, and my men will watch over you until you reach Segoia, but you will not see them unless necessary. Adiós, mi amigos." The stranger turned his horse and cantered back down the hill, leaving Lucía with many questions she was unable to ask.

Mafalda had overcome her shock, became more talkative, and wanted to ride with Lucía. Lucía tied Mafalda's mount to her saddle horn and had Mafalda ride in front of it. As it became dusk and cooler, Mafalda enjoyed the ride back to Segoia while hidden under Lucía's cloak for both warmth and a sense of security.

"Gracias for saving my life, Lucía," said this tiny voice under Lucía's cloak.

"You don't have to thank me, Mafalda. I got you into that horrible situation, and I just had to get you out of it. Instead let's both of us give thanks to the stranger who came along and saved both of our lives. Also, let's keep what happened today our own little secret. There is no point in upsetting your mother needlessly."

"Sí," responded the little voice again, and the two traveled along the road back home.

Don Raimundo sat in the anteroom of the great hall and came to the realization that the only way to obtain Lucía's wealth was to have her dispatched quickly and efficiently. The time was right, as much of the Castilian army had been destroyed at Alarcos and the king's popularity was at a low both in Castile and among several of the other surrounding kingdoms as well. His quandary was how and when to strike. An idea came to mind. *La Fiesta de Santiago* ("the Festival of Saint James") has been celebrated in Segoia each year for centuries.

His musing was suddenly interrupted by a servant. "The Bishop of Segoia to see you, mi señor," said the servant at the door of the anteroom.

"Come in, dear Bishop," said Don Raimundo, who motioned to a servant awaiting instruction. "Bring some refreshments for my hungry guest."

The servant curtsied and left the room, and Don Raimundo went to greet his guest.

"Please sit here and tell me what has happened in Segoia."

"Nothing to report of any real news, except Doña Lucía has been entertaining Infanta Mafalda for the past several weeks," said the bishop, who sat down in the chair in front of the dais while Don Raimundo walked up the two stairs of the platform and proceeded to sit down at his worktable.

"Come, Bishop, you must have more vital news to report than whom Doña Lucía is entertaining."

"It's been quiet in Segoia, Don Raimundo."

Suddenly, an idea that Raimundo had been thinking about came to fruition, as he gave the bishop a sly smile. "Then perhaps it's time to stir the pot?"

"What do you mean, Don Raimundo?"

"Recently, I invited Doña Lucía to Donato, and we had a rather contentious conversation about her future, in which I asked her hand in marriage and told her about my desire to make her my queen."

"Your queen! You mean you told her of your plot?" said the bishop, aghast.

Suddenly, the servant walked in with a tray of sausage, cheese, bread, and grapes, and another servant followed with a pitcher of wine and two cups. The tray was quickly placed on the table, and the wine was poured. "Will that be all, mi señor?" asked the servant as he placed the pitcher of wine on the table.

Don Raimundo nodded, and both servants curtsied and left the room.

"Come, Bishop, and join me on the dais and enjoy a small repast," said Don Raimundo, who pointed to the vacant seat at the end of the table.

The bishop walked up the stairs, sat in the chair, and quickly drained the cup of wine down to the last drop.

"I can't believe that you told the condesa about your plot. Now she will go tell the king, and we will both hang."

"Not so fast, dear Bishop. You forget that she is still very young, and I found her to be quite naïve in her belligerence toward me and my proposal. I was able to convince her that even being a participant in talking about committing treason is in reality the act of committing treason. She told me that she does not wish to hurt her uncle by being accused of such a crime and would not say a word about our conversation. Love is a strong bond that is hard to break. Don't you agree, Bishop?"

"Perhaps," said the bishop, who was busy chewing on a piece of sausage and pouring more wine in his cup. Raimundo stroked his chin as he looked toward the guest. "There is only one way to handle this situation, and that is to have her killed. I believe that the upcoming la Fiesta de Santiago would offer a proper setting for such a plan. An assassin could easily get lost in the crowd, and if he was concealed, why, even better!"

"Aren't you forgetting that she is royalty and the king will most likely turn this kingdom inside out to find the assassin? No one would be safe from questioning or suspicion," added the bishop.

"But big dreams require big risks, unless, of course, you wish to remain just the Bishop of Segoia. Think of the power that you would have in the church if you became the Archbishop of Toledo," said Raimundo, who poured himself a cup of wine with a sly smile.

After Lucía and her ladies said their goodbyes to Infanta Mafalda and saw her leave the gates of the palace under heavy guard, Lucía hurried back to the anteroom of the great hall for a meeting with

Avraham ben Shmuel, who, among his duties as chancellor and secretary, was also Lucía's finance minister.

When she arrived, her chancellor was waiting for her, along with a contractor who brought plans to replace a bridge that was in poor shape and deemed unsafe in the town of San Marcos on the River Tajo, a day's journey from Toledo. The town had been in Lucía's family since the days of King Alfonso VI, who had captured it from the Muslims in 1085.

Both the contractor and Shmuel were seated at the table, drinking wine and discussing financial matters regarding the bridge, when Lucía entered. Both of them arose from their chairs when Lucía walked in. The contractor immediately walked over to Lucía and made a slight bow of his head. "Mi señora, my name is Maffeo, and it is a pleasure to meet you in person, and what a beautiful presence you make."

Lucía smiled. "Gracias, I'm sorry. Did you say Maffeo?"

"Sí, mi señora. My family is originally from Tuscany."

"You're Italian?" inquired Lucía as she carefully scrutinized the short stocky man who stood before her.

"Sí, mi señora."

"And your family is in the bridge-building business?"

My family has been contractors for bridges, roads, castles and has even helped with the building of several cathedrals over the centuries. I come from a long line of builders."

"How interesting. My family—"

Shmuel, who had been patient, started to grow impatient at the growing length of the conversation; he cleared his throat quite loudly and interrupted Lucía in midsentence.

"I'm sorry. We should get down to business," said Lucía in a more serious tone.

"Sí, of course," said Maffeo, and everyone took a seat at the table. Maffeo unrolled his plans for the new bridge for everyone at the table to inspect. "The old bridge is no good. Too many worms live in the wood and over time have destroyed its basic framework. I propose a new bridge in the same style as the old one. As I told

Shmuel, mi señora, I can do this for 1,500 maravedis, which includes dismantling the old bridge once the new one is completed."

"That sounds rather steep," said Lucía.

Shmuel raised his hand and interrupted, "Gracias for your time, señor, but we can't make a deal at 1,500 maravedis. Adiós, señor."

Just as Shmuel started to rise from his seat, Maffeo chimed in, "Well, maybe I can do for 1,200 maravedis."

"Good day, señor," repeated Maffeo.

"All right, I do for 1,000 maravedis. You drive a hard bargain, señor," said Maffeo, who suddenly cracked a smile. "However, I would be more than honored to do this for the beautiful condesa," Maffeo said in an affectionate tone, and he turned to Lucía. "Of course, if that meets with your approval, mi señora?"

Lucía had listened to the conversation with her head resting on her elbow. She raised her head and looked at Shmuel for guidance, and he nodded in the affirmative.

"Well, that sounds fine with me. When can you start?" asked Lucía.

"Just as soon as I can acquire the necessary materials, but first, I need your hand on the original and a copy of the contract that I had written by a scribe. I will fill in the amount of 1,000 maravedis on both," said Maffeo as he dipped a feather in the ink well provided, filled in the amount on both contracts, and then pushed the contracts on the well-polished table in front of Lucía to sign.

"Oh, by the way, I will need some soldiers to stand guard in case of an attack by the Moors. Maffeo does good work and does not want to be interrupted by having to rebuild what has been destroyed."

"I believe I can arrange a suitable number of soldiers to protect you and your men as you work," said Lucía as she carefully read the contracts and then handed them to Shmuel for his perusal. Once Shmuel read them over, he gave the contracts back to Lucía for her to sign.

Lucía scratched her signature to the bottom of both contracts, followed by Maffeo, and then they had them witnessed by Shmuel, who kept the copy and gave the original back to Maffeo.

Lucía rose from her chair. "Well, it's been a pleasure, señor. I wish you luck in this endeavor."

Maffeo grabbed her hand and gave it a kiss. "The pleasure has been all mine, mi señora, to meet such a beautiful flower of womanhood and to be in her employment."

"Well then, if you will excuse me, I must attend to other duties," said Lucía with a nervous laugh and embarrassed by the rather intimate attention she had been given by Maffeo.

Chapter XV

It was time now for Lucía to turn her attention to the Festival of St. James, which the City of Segoia celebrated each year. St. James, a mythical Christian warrior and known throughout Spain as Santiago Matamoros (St. James the Moor Slayer), had been a hero to the Christian people of the peninsula for centuries due to a legend that went back to the ninth century. A Christian king had a dream of the saint on horseback, trampling the enemy to death during a battle against the Moors. The City of Segoia did not wish to compete or take away from the pilgrimages of people to Santiago de Compostela or from the festivities there. Furthermore, La Catedral de Santa María de Las Montañas, the cathedral in Segoia, named for the mountains seen from the city, did not contain any religious relics belonging to the saint; but the people were in deep admiration of Saint James and would pray to him after their men left the city to take to the battle-fields to fight the enemy, who had overrun their peninsula over four hundred years before.

The festival in Segoia consisted of a fortnight of festivities, which Lucía had fond memories of as a child. There were merchants from near and far who would display their wares inside the large area just inside the city gates. There were all kinds of goods for sale, such as leather goods, beautiful fabrics from different parts of the world, jewelry, and various and sundry of other items to open the purses of the people at large. Lucía especially enjoyed both the shopping and the various food stands that sold various meats, pies, and all kinds of sweets.

Entertainment abounded with wandering troubadours, jugglers, games to be played, archery, and mystery plays taken from Bible stories. Two sports that Lucía outlawed were jousting and bullfighting.

For Lucía, this was the time for merriment in celebration of a beloved saint, not for the injury or death that jousting or bullfighting caused.

The city had been decorated for the fortnight long festivities. Tents and booths filled the large empty area just inside the gates of the city. Scallop shells, the symbol of St. James, abounded everywhere.

On the first day of the festivities, Lucía was awakened before dawn by her ladies, along with Gabriella, who aided her in dressing for the ceremonies that were to take place. It was decided that Lucía would wear a beautiful yellow bliaut with gray geometric symbols around her neckline and around her sleeves, as well as a matching gray linen ring belt. The ladies, however, to Lucía's amusement, did have a brief argument as to the footwear that she should wear. Once again an important decision was reached that Lucía would wear matching yellow slippers instead of leather boots. It was Lucía who picked out a beautiful gold necklace fashioned with rubies between two gold chains, as it once belonged to her mother.

Once satisfied that every hair was in place, she put on a hooded cloak and prepared to walk to the cathedral for mass in a procession, along with her ladies and a dozen guards to meet the Bishop of Segoia on the steps of the cathedral.

"How beautiful you look, mi señora," said Geralla.

"Absolutely," responded Gabriella.

As the ladies were admiring Lucía, a household servant in panic and out of breath came running into Lucía's boudoir. Once he was able to breathe normally, he gave a chilling message to Lucía. "Mi señora, the man who portrays Santiago Matamoros is too drunk to get on a horse and ride from the back of the cathedral through the main streets of Segoia to open the festivities."

His message sent Lucía in a panic, as this was a vital part of the ceremony to open the annual fortnight event. "What am I to do. This can't be." Lucía dismissed the messenger and started to think. All the careful planning had come to fruition, except for the most vital part of the ceremony. She had carefully written her speech, which was tailored to announce the arrival of Santiago Matamoros after his Mass on the top step of the cathedral.

Lucía paced the floor of her boudoir while her ladies watched. She would have to find a substitute. After a couple of minutes of thought, an idea came to her. "I have a solution," Lucía proudly announced to her ladies, to their pleasure and cheers, and quickly ran out of her boudoir, down the hall, and down the long spiral staircase to the stable below, quickly followed by her entourage.

Once in the stable, Lucía dressed in all her splendor asked a stable hand, "Have you seen Captain Gómez?"

"He is in his room, mi señora," answered the surprised stable hand with a bow.

"Gracias." And Lucía ran to his room with the ladies on her heels.

The door to Captain Gómez's room was closed. Lucía knocked on the door and heard a loud "Enter!"

Lucía walked into his room, while her ladies waited outside, to a rather surprised Captain Gómez, who rose from his chair to greet his unexpected guest. "Doña Lucía, I thought that you would be on your way to the cathedral by this time in all your finery."

"I still have time before I have to go, but I need to talk to you. It's rather urgent," said Lucía with a nervous smile and while wringing her hands.

"It must be," said Gómez with a look of apprehension of what was to come next.

In a pleading voice, Lucía said, "I need to ask a big favor of you."

"I know that I will regret asking, but what is it?"

"Well, I am sure that you know that each year we have a man to play the part of Santiago Matamoros to start the festivities of our fortnight celebration."

"You mean the poor fool who has played the part for many years?"

"Well, I never thought of him as a poor fool," said Lucía in a reflective tone.

"It doesn't matter. What do you want?" inquired Gómez in a brusque manner.

Lucía, still wringing her hands nervously, asked, "Unfortunately, I guess the man started the celebration early, as he is too drunk to ride a horse and be our revered saint. I need someone to fill in and be our saint after I give the cue from my speech."

Gómez laughed as Lucía smiled nervously. "Poor fool. I don't blame him for getting drunk. I probably would too if I had to do that every year and wear that stupid ceramic head. I suppose you want me to take his place?"

"Well, please, please? I promise that I will do anything you ask, and I promise not to give you a hard time anymore. It's that important to me and for the people who come each year to see the spectacle."

"Now let me understand. You promise to do anything that I ask of you at any time and at any place?"

"Sí, I promise," said Lucía, with her hands cupped together.

"Once again, I feel that I am going to regret this," said Gómez reluctantly.

"Oh, gracias," said Lucía, and she went over to where Gómez was standing and embraced him.

The conversation continued as Lucía explained to Gómez what he had to do; she then prepared to leave for the cathedral, but before she did, she took a good look at Gómez's room.

Captain Gómez lived in Spartan quarters of about two hundred square feet, which consisted of a bed, a table with several chairs, and an old gray wooden cabinet with a lock. On either side of the cabinet were several pegs nailed into the wall to hang his armor, clothes, and weapons, which consisted of his sword, dagger, crossbow, and quiver of crossbow bolts. Lucía also noticed a pitcher of wine and a simple wooden cup half full on the table.

"Are you comfortable here, Gómez?" asked Lucía in a concerned tone. "I could arrange better quarters for you in the palace."

"What, and become soft like many of your attendants? No, I like here well enough. Besides, here I'm closer to my men."

Lucía just smiled and realized that it was no use to argue with a stubborn man. She left as Gómez prepared for his grand entrance.

Gómez rode to the back of the cathedral dressed in his armor. A member of the city council met him there with a ceramic head in the likeness of Santiago. It was a hot day in July, and the ceramic head did not provide any ventilation except for the two eyeholes. Gómez easily put the ceramic head of the saint over his head, as it was quite large and tended to roll around and not stay in place for good eyesight; however, with a slight adjustment, he was ready for his performance.

At dawn, Lucía, with her ladies, walked from the palace, past the city square, to the cathedral, along with twelve of her guards and, as customary, met the Bishop of Segoia on the steps of the cathedral. Lucía kneeled before him and kissed his ring. From the steps, Lucía could hear a choir of monks as the procession, led by the crucifer and bishop, marched into the cathedral among the nobles of her condado, and other various guests, to the choir, where Lucía and her ladies took a seat on a bench.

After mass, Lucía gave a short speech on the steps of the cathedral to open the festivities and, at the end of her dialogue, introduced the coming of Santiago Matamoros to open and watch over the festival. This was Gómez's cue, but he did not hear her, so Lucía repeated the introduction again, along with a nervous smile and laugh. Finally, before she could finish her introduction, Gómez came bolting from the side of the cathedral to the city square, reared his horse high, brandished his sword, and proceeded to ride around the city square three times, all the while screamed loudly, "I am Santiago Matamoros, and I will watch over this festival and trample any Moors who try to upset my celebration!"

All was going according to plan when the ceramic head of Santiago turned around on Gómez's head until he was completely blind and unable to maintain his sense of direction. His lack of sight caused him to divert into a low-hanging rope of scallop shells between two venues and he toppled over backward from his horse onto a table of sweets.

Lucía was in shock, and she quickly picked up the hem of her garment with both hands and ran over to Gómez as he slowly climbed off the table.

"Are you all right, Gómez?"

Gómez, with his ceramic head still turned backward, was able to remove it, and he quickly discovered the crowd around him and that he was covered from head to toe in different assorted squashed pastries.

Lucía could tell that he was not happy. Some people's shock suddenly turned into laughter.

Gómez handed the ceramic head to a soldier who had come running over to the table. "Get this thing out of my sight."

Lucía tried hard not to laugh, but the sight of Gómez covered with squashed pastries was too overpowering for her not to laugh.

"All right, laugh as hard as you want," said Gómez to Lucía in an angry tone, which caused her to recoil. "It's going to take me days to clean this mess off my chain mail, and remember your promise to do anything that I ask. You owe me."

Lucía did not have a chance to respond as Gómez, to the roar of the crowd, walked back to the palace, grumbling. Lucía's ladies giggled and talked among themselves.

Lucía saw Gómez show his displeasure on two soldiers who happened to walk by and stared at their captain, who was a mess from head to toe. "How would you like extra duty?" yelled Gómez at the men, who quickly turned their stares elsewhere.

Lucía turned to her ladies, who were still giggling as they watched Gómez walk back to the palace. "I guess that I shall have to avoid Captain Gómez for a couple of days," said Lucía, who could not help but giggle as well.

"It might be a good idea that we all do," said Gabriella to the ladies, who nodded in agreement.

After Lucía paid the poor vendor handsomely for his destroyed venue, she and her ladies perused the various other venues and were delighted at what they saw. There were unique items, such as beautiful ceramics from Cordoba, silver and gold jewelry, beautiful leather goods, and spices from exotic places. And despite Gómez's attack on a sweet table, there were several venues of sweets still available.

As Lucía's ladies headed back to the palace to help prepare for the formal banquet that evening for the nobles of the realm and other invited guests, Lucía joined the bishop for breakfast.

After breakfast with the bishop, Lucía rode Rodrigo to the village church for another mass. Lucía enjoyed the company of the village people, and they all adored her. However, the day was moving along quickly, as Lucía chatted with Father Piña and joined her village friends for a simple banquet in front of the church. During this time, she engaged in conversation with various members of the community and, after the repast, joined the children of the village to play games to the cheer of the adult spectators. After several hours, the time had come for Lucía to say goodbye and to head back to the palace to get ready for an evening banquet and festivities.

Several days later, Lucía and Gabriella made plans to visit the various venues and have fun shopping. Lucía wanted to disguise herself to fit in with the general populace and not attract any undue attention. The morning of their shopping spree, Lucía's ladies awakened her just before dawn. The ladies scurried around and tried to find an appropriate garment for her to wear as Beatrix busily combed her hair at the dressing table.

"That old dark-gray thing," responded Lucía as she looked up from her mirror, "not really my favorite. It lacks—well, it's just drab. Maybe find something else that has a little more color."

After having spent time to find a garment that was not quite so elegant and yet colorful as to make Lucía appear like a commoner, Constance became frustrated. "I'm sorry, Doña Lucía, but Adele, Geralla, and I have gone through all your garments, and this gray garment is the only one that is ordinary enough not to attract attention."

Lucía was still staring in the mirror, primping, and became frustrated when a hair or two would pop up and not be properly held down. "By the bones!" said Lucía angrily, but she stopped before she continued on and embarrassed herself by taking the saint's name in vain.

Gabriella entered the room in time to hear Lucía's remark. "What's wrong Beatrix?" asked Gabriella.

"Mi señora can't comb down several pieces of hair."

"Hmm, let me try, Beatrix." Gabriella took the comb away from her, reached over, and took a small finger full of cream from the dressing table, applied it to the stubborn areas of hair, and combed them down successfully. Finally, she combed in some rose water to complete the grooming.

Lucía again primped. "Wonderful. Gracias, Gabriella. Is that the cream that you gave me?"

"Sí, it is," said Gabriella, who was still behind her with the comb.

"What is it made out of?"

Gabriella smiled. "You don't want to know."

Suddenly, Lucía was interrupted by Constance. "As I said before, mi señora, this is the only garment that we could find that is ordinary enough to make you fit in with the crowd."

Lucía rose from her chair and went over to Constance, who held the garment, and she examined it. "Well, I guess it will have to do. All right, I will wear it."

Constance and the other ladies breathed a sigh of relief to be done with an exhaustive search through several trunks of apparel.

As Lucía and Gabriella walked from the palace across the city to the venues, little did they know that an assassin lurked around the site and waited for the opportunity to strike. Scarface, disguised as a cloth merchant, had entered the city and set up a tent among the many as he patiently waited for Lucía to appear. Once he had identified her, he would use his crossbow and fire a fatal shot from a small opening in the entrance of his tent. Once successful, he would quickly leave the city in the confusion, atop a horse-drawn cart that carried several bolts of fabric to complete the ruse.

Scarface, so as not to be identified, had carefully covered up his scar with a large patch over his left eye and wore a hooded cloak. He had cleverly asked several people whom he had identified as servants from the palace as to when Doña Lucía might be at the venues for him to be able to interest her in some fine fabric. He had received his answer and patiently waited for her to appear as he slowly pretended to set up a venue to sell his wares.

Lucía and Gabriella walked through the many booths and were tempted by the many items for sale, especially the fine jewelry hand-crafted in Cordoba. Lucía turned to Gabriella, holding a beautiful double-chain necklace made from silver linked together with silver inlaid turquoise. "This is exquisite, Gabriella, such fine workman-ship and detail."

The merchant, an Arab, had been watching Lucía and Gabriella's interest in the fine piece of expensive jewelry. "For such a beautiful lady, I will make a fine offer. For you only twenty-five maravedis. Anyone else, I would sell it for twice as much."

"Oh, it is so beautiful, Lucía!" Gabriella was so entranced by it that Lucía decided to purchase it. It truly was a fine piece. As quickly as she purchased it and left the venue, she placed it in Gabriella's hand. "What are you doing?" inquired Gabriella.

"This piece is for you so you don't have to keep borrowing mine during formal court occasions," said Lucía with a big smile.

"Oh, I can't possibly—"

Gabriella was quickly interrupted by Lucía, "Sí, you can, and I will not take no for an answer." Lucía had a big heart, and it felt good to give this to someone who had had such a difficult time in her life.

Gabriella embraced Lucía. "Gracias, Lucía. I will treasure it always."

Scarface had spotted Lucía in the crowd from his venue. He entered the tent and closed it behind him and slowly loaded his crossbow, which he had sneaked in, in a large leather bag. As he care-fully placed the head of the arrow outside a small opening, he took careful aim at his target and delicately squeezed the trigger, launching the projectile.

Meanwhile, a young man who happened to be close to Lucía had seen the head of the projectile aimed at its intended victim. He yelled at the last second, "Look out, mi señora!" He quickly stepped in front of Lucía, and the arrow pierced his stomach; he quickly fell to the ground in front of the condesa, to the screams and confusion of the crowd.

Lucía, for what seemed like an eternity, stood in back of the young man, who lay at her feet, frozen in complete shock. Scarface cursed as he realized he had missed his victim, and he knew by the large crowd that had gathered around Lucía that another clean shot would be impossible. He quickly left the city in the confusion that followed while he cursed himself for such a careless blunder.

The crowd now had become conscious as to Lucía's identity, as she had lowered the hood on her cloak. She heard someone say loudly, "That's Doña Lucía!" Yet another said, "That's the condesa! I hope she is okay."

"Someone call the guards and find both a physician and a priest. Quickly!" screamed Lucía, while several people from the crowd scattered in different directions. Lucía knelt down to see if her savior was still alive. He looked familiar to her and then realized that her savior was none other than Pino, whose mother had taken Isabella and her into their home that stormy night many years before.

"Pino?" asked Lucía.

"Sí, mi señora," responded Pino, holding his stomach.

"But how did you know?"

"I saw the projectile protruded through the opening of the tent over there." Pino pointed out with his bloody finger.

Several guards who were alerted by the noisy crowd that had gathered around Lucía arrived to find her knelt over her wounded hero. They were immediately directed by Lucía to check the tent and do a formal search of the premises.

Suddenly, Pino smiled and said, "Do you remember that night when my mother and I rescued you and your friend from that bad storm?"

"Sí, I remember," said Lucía as she wiped away her tears.

Pino, in pain, continued, "Although you were dressed as waifs, I had my suspicions as to who you were. I didn't say anything to expose your identity, as I was not completely sure, but after my mother found the gold pieces in the hay that you had slept on, my suspicions were confirmed. She thought it a miracle, and I let her think so."

Pino winced in pain but continued, "Your story about your parents sounded strange and not knowing where you were from sounded even stranger. Also, your skin is pure and soft, not that of a peasant."

Lucía knelt down and placed his head carefully on her lap and tried her best to comfort him as he started to twitch and then went lifeless. Lucía was weeping. Gabriella, who had been nearby in the crowd, came over and tried to comfort her. The crowd that surrounded Lucía and Gabriella was becoming larger.

Lucía was still on her knees when Captain Gómez galloped to the scene with a dozen men, a physician, and Father Piña, who had happened to be at the cathedral during the assassination attempt.

"Disperse the crowd" said Gómez to several of his men who were still on horseback. "You two close the gates of the city. No one is allowed to leave." After he gave his orders, he went over to Lucía. "Are you all right, Lucía?" Lucía wiped away her tears and tried to control her weeping and nodded, while Father Piña administered the last rites to Pino.

Sobbing, Lucía shouted to Gómez, "Have someone get my transport! I want to take this man home."

"Lucía, come with me now." said Gómez in a determined voice.

Then Lucía looked up a Gómez with tears running down her face and screamed, "I told you what I want! Do it!"

Gómez sighed and turned to another soldier who had stood by and said, "Go get Doña Lucía's transport and bring it here."

Gabriella was quiet but stood by Lucía and offered comfort as Lucía held Pino's bleeding body close to her.

Lucía, still on her knees and weeping, looked up at Gómez. "He saved my life. I can at least do that for him."

Gómez stood by and nodded without saying a word.

Within a short time, the wagon arrived, along with Constance, who had come to offer whatever assistance she could. After Lucía, Gabriella, and Constance were seated in the wagon, Pino's body was carefully placed on the floor. Gómez, upon inquiry of several people in the crowd, had learned that Pino lived with his mother and where she could be located. The wagon ventured up several small narrow streets. Upon arrival at Pino's apartment, Lucía carefully climbed out of the wagon.

"Gabriella, you and Constance stay in the wagon. Gómez, I want time to prepare his mother before we bring in the body. I will tell you when."

Gómez nodded without saying a word.

Lucía entered the house with two guards, to the surprise of Niña, who had fallen asleep in front of the fireplace and was suddenly awakened. "What is going on? And who are you to enter my home in such a manner?" asked Niña in an angry tone. However, after having had a chance to wipe her eyes from the blurriness of sleep, she carefully examined the lady who had entered her home.

"Do you remember me, Niña?" inquired Lucía.

Niña got up from the chair, still focused on her surprise visitor, and walked over to Lucía, who still stood in front of the doorway. "I'm afraid that my eyes are not too good," explained Niña, who had lessened her former anger.

Niña squinted her eyes that revealed a face of wrinkles further worn by time and appeared even older than what Lucía had remembered. "Am I supposed to know you?"

Lucía smiled. "Do you remember the two little girls who appeared in your doorway many years ago?"

Niña started to think and scratched her head. After a minute of silence, she then turned to Lucía with a look of astonishment. "Sí, I remember now. Two little girls whose heads were covered in shawls and, from what I can recall, had become lost."

"You remembered," said Lucía with a teary smile. She was still thinking of how to tell this poor old lady, who had known nothing but hardship her entire life, that her son was dead.

Niña turned to Lucía. "Apparently, you found your parents. Are you lost again?"

"No," said Lucía with a bit of a teary laugh. "I was not honest with you when we first meant."

"In what way?" inquired Niña.

"I am really Lucía, the Condesa of Segoia, and the other little girl was Isabella, Condesa of Gustavo. I had never forgotten that act of kindness that you showed us that evening and had always remembered you and your son." Suddenly, Lucía burst into tears. "It troubles me deeply to tell you that your son was killed by an assassin's arrow as he saved my life."

Niña was confused. "That can't be. He told me that he was going to the venues and would be back before dark."

Lucía, with tears that ran down her face, grabbed the old lady by the shoulders and said, "An assassin was waiting in ambush for me in the marketplace. Your son saw the attempt on my life and jumped in front of me and took the assassin's arrow instead. He is a hero."

The old lady became emotional as Lucía had Pino's body brought in and placed on a liter in front of the fireplace. "No no no, this can't be," said the old lady, who wept as she bent over the body of Pino and held him in her arms. After a while, Niña put her son down and turned to Lucía, who embraced her as they both wept.

Lucía turned to her guards, who had been at the door, and said to them, "Leave us." With that, the two guards walked out of the home and shut the door. After a while, both Lucía and Niña could weep no more. Lucía shared what little memory she had of Pino, to the enjoyment of his mother.

The subject then turned to Niña. "I want you to know that I will pay for all his funeral expenses, including his burial spot, which I would like to be in the palace cemetery. I also want you to know that you will no longer have to work, as I will make sure that you are well taken care of, and upon your death, you may be buried next to your son."

"I don't know what to say." Niña was very grateful for Lucía's act of kindness.

Luca took Niña by the shoulders again. "Please say that you will accept my offer of an annual allowance of six hundred maravedis payable in monthly installments to last the rest of your life. Because your son gave his life for another, his mother should not have to suffer."

Niña nodded with a big smile, which reflected both grief and relief that she would no longer have to worry about paying the rent or buying food. Lucía then sat down at the table with Niña and planned a funeral fit for a don.

Chapter XVI

Don Raimundo was outraged Scarface had failed to assassinate the condesa. However, once Scarface reported the circumstances concerning his failure, Don Raimundo agreed that there was little that could have been done that would not have jeopardized his treachery. Both Don Raimundo and Scarface agreed that it would be beneficial if he went into hiding for a period of time until another plan could be hatched.

As Scarface left the anteroom of the great hall, a servant entered and walked to the dais where Don Raimundo was seated. "An emissary from Prince John to see you, mi señor."

Don Raimundo smiled with glee and full of expectation that perhaps an ally was found who shared his same ambitious, desires, and goals.

Don Raimundo stood up and walked down from the dais and prepared to meet his potential ally. "Have him enter."

"Sir Edmund Laurence, the Earl of Stonington," announced the servant.

Sir Edmund entered the anteroom and was immediately greeted by Don Raimundo, who quickly perused the nobleman who stood before him. He was of a muscular build that filled his armor well. As he removed his chain mail cowl, Don Raimundo noticed his short curly dark hair intermixed with a small amount of gray that revealed a man, perhaps, in his late thirties. He had a long face, complete with dark beard and moustache and dark eyes that cast an ominous look of dread.

"Sir Edmund, welcome to Castile. I trust that you had a pleasant journey."

"If you can say that being attacked by a band of highwaymen and breathing in the dust of your drab countryside with heat so intense that your body becomes languid is any indication of a pleasant journey, so be it."

Don Raimundo was taken back, not expecting to hear a diatribe concerning his countryside. "I'm sorry that your journey was unpleasant. It does tend to become very hot during the summer months on the open plain. Perhaps I might interest you in some refreshments, Sir Edmund."

Sir Edmund sat down in his appointed chair. "That would be satisfactory."

Raimundo yelled to an awaiting servant as he took his seat on the dais, "Some wine and refreshments for our weary traveler."

Don Raimundo noticed that there was no interaction between them and no friendly banter. Sir Laurence appeared as if he was on a mission and wanted to be done with it as quickly as possible. He reminded him of his henchman, Scarface.

Finally, Don Raimundo grew impatient with the silence and decided to get down to the business at hand. "What news of Prince John?"

Sir Edmund looked up at Don Raimundo on the dais. "The prince is doing well and is currently in Normandy, fighting alongside his brother against King Philip. I came from Normandy at his behest to investigate a possible alliance. The prince, however, is only modestly interested in such an arrangement and is more concerned about his niece by birth. Such a person with close ties in both England and France offers a possible threat to the prince and his reach for the throne. His desire is to annihilate his competition, including his niece."

Don Raimundo listened intently to the conversation in an attempt to try to win the full support of Prince John. "You mean Doña Lucía," he interrupted.

"Who else?" exclaimed Sir Edmund. "He finds her to be rather a troublesome sort, especially with her vast wealth, as she could easily raise an army and fight for the throne as a claimant to the crown."

Don Raimundo laughed at such a prospect. "Apparently, the prince doesn't know Doña Lucía as well as I do. She has no desire for any throne, including that of Castile, which I offered to her alongside of mine when I am victorious. She is very loyal and not one to commit treason to serve her own ends. This is not the temperament of someone who has a treacherous eye on a crown. I don't believe that Doña Lucía poses any threat to the prince, either now or in the future. However, her wealth is my main objective. Once I have secured that, it will give me the basis for all the resources I will need to take Castile. If, by chance, it means her demise, so be it."

Sir Edmund smiled. "Then we are in agreement. Prince John will be very happy."

The conversation was interrupted by a servant who brought in wine and a plate of olives, bread, and cheese.

"Ah, Sir Edmund, you must try some of our local wine, spiced for the summer with orange and lemon, along with our local goat cheese," said Don Raimundo as he sat back in his chair while the servant poured the wine.

Sir Edmund took a long drink that almost emptied his cup. "Excellent! I have never tasted such ambrosia as this before," he said as the servant refilled it again to the brim.

Don Raimundo looked at the servant. "Leave us."

Once the servant left, Don Raimundo was eager to engage the emissary in the most important question yet to be asked: "Will the prince consider sending an army on my behalf?"

Sir Edmund swallowed the final drops of wine in his cup and gave him a most distant look of disdain, as if he was a common peasant begging for a few scrapes off this master's table.

"At this point, I am afraid your question is a bit premature. Tell me, as we have discussed your ambition throughout this conversation, what royalty has existed in your family that would allow you to be considered worthy of the throne?"

Don Raimundo had now become angry, and he felt he was purposely being humiliated by this arrogant fool, but he realized that he had to continue the conversation with full restraint if he was to ever to win his support.

"My line goes back to the Visigothic kings who once ruled this land before the Moors invaded," he said very carefully to control his temper.

A moment of silence ensued.

"I see. Very well then, I shall give you Prince John's terms if he should decide to help you in your cause. First, you must dispatch Lucía, his niece. Second, you must raise an army and take Burgos, Toledo, and of course, Segoia. Once captured, King Alfonso is to be imprisoned. Queen Leonor, along with her children, is to be sent to Normandy, unharmed, where they will be taken to England. Once the terms are completed, the prince will send as many men as he can spare. After all, he is still at war with the king of France."

Don Raimundo was at the boiling point, but once again, he held back in order to gain favor. "Under those conditions, I might as well fight on my own."

"Oh, I'm sorry. I forgot to add one more item," said Sir Edmund. "And that is the prince also expects to receive one-half of any booty received during your conflict with his brother-in-law, the king. Are you in favor of these terms?"

"I guess I have no choice," added Don Raimundo with a look of disdain.

"Good," said Sir Edmund as he rose from his chair followed by Don Raimundo.

"Oh, one more thing before I leave. Prince John wishes to establish a line of communication between you and the happenings in Segoia regarding his niece in order to keep an eye on her and to be able to communicate with you if necessary. This will be done with a spy who will be stationed in the palace and will report to you any meaningful news of significance regarding her, such as her travels, which might work to your benefit to have her dispatched. The mysterious stranger will appear at your door dressed in monk's garb and will give you written correspondence about anything significant. The spy will not talk and will keep his identity a secret, which you must do also. No one is to know who the spy is, and if any harm comes to him, any possible alliance with the prince is finished. Before I leave, are there any questions, Don Raimundo?"

"No!" said Raimundo abruptly.

"Then I shall venture back to Normandy and report on our meeting to the prince. Good day."

Don Raimundo watched Sir Edmund as he left his chambers. Once Sir Edmund had left, he angrily pounded his hand on the table. "Of all the arrogance! If he had not been in his position as emissary to a possible ally, I would have taught him a lesson that he would not have easily forgotten."

After his outburst of anger, Don Raimundo mused on another plot to end Lucía's life. He also sent for Ramón, Isabella's uncle and guardian, to discuss a marriage proposal with him.

Several days later, Ramón entered Don Raimundo's chamber in a drunken state while Raimundo was fencing with Scarface. Raimundo finished the duel by a strong blow with his sword, and Scarface's sword went flying out of his hand. Immediately, Raimundo turned and pointed his sword at Ramón's throat. "How dare you come staggering into my chambers drunk."

Ramón carefully pushed the point of the sword blade away from his throat. "I got your message. Did you send for me to kill me or to talk to me?"

"Don't tempt me, señor. Look at you. You look like a common criminal from the streets of Madrid with an unkempt beard, ragged clothing, and eyes that give the appearance of someone ready to steal a purse."

"Your message didn't say to come neatly dressed," added Ramón with a slight slur of his words.

Don Raimundo pointed to the chair in front of his dais. "Come here and sit before you fall down." Don Raimundo then climbed the steps of the dais and sat back in his chair.

Suddenly, Don Raimundo blurted out, "What of Isabella these days?"

Ramón slouched down in the chair and held onto the arms to keep from falling onto the floor. "Isabella, the lovely Isabella," Ramón repeated sarcastically. "She does my biding or else."

"Or else what?" interjected Raimundo.

"She feels my hand," said Ramón with a laugh.

Raimundo immediately left the dais with a sprint and grabbed ahold of Ramón by his throat. Suddenly, Ramón's face turned to fear. "If you harm that girl in any way, I will kill you. Do you understand?"

Ramón, in panic, shook his head. "Sí, señor."

"Now sit down and listen," said Don Raimundo. He pushed Ramón back into his chair. "I plan to marry Doña Isabella, who is a cousin to the King of Portugal. Her pedigree will complement my royal Visigothic roots nicely. This marriage will hopefully legitimatize my claim to the throne to the nobles of Castile, along with a promise to aggressively move to conquer al-Andalus."

"So what does that have to do with me?" asked Ramón arrogantly.

"What does that have to do with you? You fool. Why do you think I had you dragged out of that wasteland that you were in? Perhaps I even saved your life in the process," exclaimed Raimundo. "Maybe I should spell it out for you once again. If all goes well, you shall have your inheritance and become a wealthy, trusted courtier of mine. All you have to do is to control her. Allow her to make some decisions in her condado with your guidance, of course, and make sure that she doesn't become engaged to someone else. At the time I ask for her hand in marriage, you graciously approve. Is that so hard to do?"

"How should I handle Doña Lucía?" asked Ramón. "Isabella keeps asking to visit her."

"Limit her visits with the condesa. I don't want her to influence Isabella. I'll handle Doña Lucía in good time. Just remember not to mention my pending nuptial with Isabella until the right time, and in the name of the saints, stay sober! Now get back to Gustavo and protect my bride-to-be."

Chapter XVII

It was a hot day, and Lucía sent the village peasants who worked in the vineyard home, as they had made considerable progress in preparing for the upcoming fall harvest. Lucía decided to take a ride to a lagoon that she had discovered on one of her ventures with her ladies. It was complete with a cooling waterfall and surrounded by tall trees and grasses.

Such a godsend on a hot day, Lucía thought to herself. She had carefully packed a long piece of linen to dry off after a swim; she didn't have to worry about being interrupted, as the lagoon was in the middle of nowhere. There were no villages within miles, and it was far away from any traveled roads.

Once she arrived at the lagoon, she directed Rodrigo to the surrounding tall grasses to graze. The waterfall was very noisy, and there were rocks in the water near the shore to be wary of, but deeper water lay farther out. All around the thirty foot waterfall were overhanging shade trees, which made the area feel even cooler.

The water was inviting, and Lucía couldn't wait to go for her swim. She quickly undressed and carefully laid her garments on a large rock near the water. She carefully picked her way around the rocks and stones and found an area deep enough for a swim and jumped in. After swimming to the surface, she enjoyed the cool breeze from the trees that were gently swaying in the light wind.

Suddenly, to her chagrin, she heard a voice cry out, "Bonjour, mademoiselle!"

Aghast, Lucía looked to the shore in shock and panic and quickly covered her breasts with her arms. "Who's there?" she cried.

"It's only me," was the response.

Lucía followed the voice to the thickly covered grassy area along the right bank of the lagoon and saw from what she could make out in the tall grass to be a crusader, as he wore a red cross emblazoned on his soiled white surcoat over his chain mail. She carefully swam closer but kept a respectable distance away from the stranger.

"Who exactly is 'It's only me'? A name, señor!" shouted Lucía in an angry tone of voice.

"I am Sir Guillaume Gilbert de Champville at your service, Mademoiselle," he said loudly enough to be understood through the noise of the waterfall.

"Well, Sir Guillaume, did you come to rob, rape, or murder me?"

"No, I just came here to get some sleep along with my friends after a long journey," responded Sir Guillaume.

"Friends?" shouted Lucía, as her eyes widened. "How many friends?"

Sir Guillaume responded, "Two others: Gaston and Étienne."

"How long have you been here?" inquired Lucía.

"Long enough to have seen you arrive, Mademoiselle."

Lucía hesitated at the next question she was about to ask. She really didn't want to know the answer, but she had to satisfy her curiosity. "How much have you seen, señor?"

"Enough," said Sir Guillaume, spellbound by her beauty.

Humiliated and embarrassed, Lucía swam closer to shore, still in deep enough water to hide her body but close enough to get a better view of the stranger through the tall grass at the edge of the lagoon. She stared for several seconds at him; her eyes then followed the contour of his lean body up to and including his clean-shaven face, blue eyes, and his short-cropped dirty-blond hair. Suddenly, Lucía began to feel something in her she had never experienced before, but she dismissed it as nothing more than a chill.

"Why are you here, señor?" asked Lucía. She again focused on Sir Guillaume's blue eyes as she kicked her legs and tried to stay afloat.

"I am a French knight, along with my friends, in the service of King Philip of France. My friends and I thought that we had booked passage from the Holy Land to Nice. However, once aboard, we were duped, as it turned out to be a pirate ship. We were robbed of all our possessions, including our weapons, our purses, and our horses. Worst of all, we were forced to jump overboard off the coast of Cadiz. At first, we did not know where we were until we realized, once we swam ashore, that we were in unfriendly territory and carefully traveled at night, stealing food along the way, until we crossed over to the Christian north. We have been walking fortnights, some of it in the heat of the day. We are exhausted, tired, and require rest."

Lucía burst out with laughter.

"What humor is this?" inquired Sir Guillaume.

Lucía finally controlled her laughter long enough to respond, "Sir Guillaume, you claim to be a knight, yet what a fool to be so duped by pirates as to lose your possessions and become virtually helpless in defending your honor and the honor of others."

"Your remark strikes like a dagger in the heart of my misfortune, mademoiselle," said Sir Guillaume in a strong tone.

"In any case, my arms are getting tired, and my legs feel as if they are about to fall off, so I must now ask for you and your friends to leave."

"Leave? But we just got here. We have no plans to leave, and who are you to say that we have to go?" responded Sir Guillaume, somewhat perturbed.

"You certainly don't expect me to leave the lagoon naked for your enjoyment, do you?"

"Well, it didn't stop you from going into the lagoon."

"Grrrrr! Just who do you think that you are talking to, señor!"

"To an unruly peasant girl," Sir Guillaume replied with a smirk.

Sir Guillaume could see by Lucía's face that she was becoming angrier by the moment.

"An unruly peasant girl! Hmm!" retorted Lucía. "What makes you think me a peasant? Not that there is anything wrong with being a peasant and not a member of the nobility!"

Sir Guillaume laughed. "You, a member of the nobility?"

"Grrrrr! Well then, how to you explain my horse?"

"Easy. Perhaps you either stole it from your master or he allowed you to borrow it in return for certain favors."

"Oh, now you think me either a thief or a whore! Where is your chivalry as a knight? Oh, I forgot you lost that, too, when you allowed pirates to rob and throw you overboard."

Sir Guillaume decided to use a different approach on this unmitigated shrew. "Well, if you say you are a member of the nobility, would you allow food and comfort to a poor, homeless knight who came to your door?"

"Of course, you fool."

"Then I have proved my point," said Sir Guillaume, and he bowed before Lucía, who was trying to stay afloat.

"What point is that?"

"You just offered hospitality to me, a homeless knight, of course."

Lucía shook her head in disbelief. "What? I gave no such offer," said Lucía emphatically.

"*Oui*, you did."

"No, I didn't."

"Oui, you did."

"No, I didn't."

"Oui, you did."

"No, I didn't."

"Well! Well! We just had our first argument," said Sir Guillaume with a big smile of victory.

Lucía, at the boiling point, turned red with anger. "I asked you nicely to leave."

"To leave, oui. Nicely, *non*," responded Sir Guillaume.

"If you don't leave, I will call my guards, and they will gladly remove you. So there, hmm!"

"I don't think they will hear you, but I will do you a favor," said Sir Guillaume, and he screamed at the top of his lungs. "Guards!"

His scream awoke Gaston, who lay under a tree near the embankment but could not hear the conversation between Sir Guillaume and Lucía, as the noise of the waterfall drowned out Lucía's responses. So it appeared as if Sir Guillaume carried on a dialogue with himself.

"Sir Guillaume, whom are you talking to? I fear you have gone mad. Why don't you get some sleep while you can and stop your madness?"

"I can't. She won't let me."

"She? Who is she?" asked Gaston.

"The lady in the lagoon. Who else?"

"What lady in the lagoon?" inquired Gaston again.

Lucía was in disbelief that Sir Guillaume did what he had just done.

After a minute of silence, Sir Guillaume remarked, "See? No guards. *Bon soir*, mademoiselle."

"You are the most pertinacious, inconsiderate, and disrespectful fool I have ever met," said Lucía, who was becoming as frustrated as she was angry.

"And you are the most arrogant shrew I have ever met. So there," responded Sir Guillaume.

"Get out now, or I will come over and scratch your eyes out. And don't think that I can't!"

"I would be happy to oblige. Do I come into the lagoon, or do you come on shore to scratch my eyes out?"

"Grrrrr! I'm going to turn my back, and you had better be gone before I turn around again, or so help me."

After a couple of minutes, Lucía turned back around and saw that Sir Guillaume was no longer there. Thinking he must have gone, she decided to check to make sure, as she swam closer to the tall grass at the edge of the lagoon.

"Are you still here, señor?" she then repeated the question again.

Finally, Sir Guillaume stood up, which caught Lucía by surprise and caused her to back away to give her some distance from the knight.

"Look, you appear to be a smart enough to take a hint. Go away so my friends and I can get some sleep."

Lucía had finally reached her boiling point, her legs were weakening from trying to stay afloat, and her disposition was devoid of any feeling of charity. Lucía picked up a stone and threw it toward her nemesis. She continued to throw stones until one inadvertently hit Gaston in the stomach.

"Hey, cut that out, or I will come in there and take you over my knee," said Sir Guillaume. "You're acting like an enfant terrible."

Lucía broke down and started to cry. "I can't stay afloat anymore. I'm tired and want to go home, but you are still here, and I refuse to show myself for your pleasure. Some knight you are. Now get out!" she screamed, wiping away her tears with her hand and sniffling.

Gaston was now wide awake. "Who is throwing stones?"

"Why don't you ask the enfant terrible in the lagoon?"

Gaston turned over, parted the thick tall grass on the embankment, and saw Lucía staring him in the face with a furrowed brow, which startled him. "Sir Guillaume, there is a lady in the lagoon, and she doesn't appear very friendly."

Sir Guillaume looked at Gaston. "Did you know that you are a champion of the obvious?"

"No, Mother, not now," said Lucía, who had felt a twinge of guilt for being so inhospitable.

Gaston looked at Lucía again. "Mon Dieu! She is talking to her mother. How many other people are living in the lagoon? Maybe she's a witch. Perhaps, Sir Guillaume, we should go before she casts a spell on us."

Gaston stood up and went over to wake Étienne, who had been asleep during the entire time, but he could not raise him. "Sir Guillaume, I need your help to pick up Étienne. I cannot wake him. I have never met anyone who could sleep as much as Étienne."

Sir Guillaume conceded and, along with Gaston, carried Étienne from the lagoon back on the trail for home.

"I hope you're happy. We are leaving now. You can go back to your master. *Merci* for your hospitality," said Sir Guillaume sarcastically to Lucía, who was still kicking her legs to stay afloat.

The three left the lagoon with Étienne in the middle, propped up by Guillaume and Gaston.

"She looked like a wild one, Sir Guillaume. I could see it in her eyes," said Gaston.

Sir Guillaume smiled. "She was the most beautiful girl I have ever met from her blondish-red her to her white skin and blue eyes. Perhaps someday I will come back and marry her."

"You have gone mad, Sir Guillaume, or she has already cast a spell on you," said Gaston, who walked along with one arm of Étienne over his shoulder.

Once they had left, Lucía waited a few minutes to be sure they had gone and then started to make to land at the edge of the lagoon, only to be interrupted by Sir Guillaume, who had returned.

Lucía was livid as she quickly got back into deep water, covered her breasts, and started to tread water again. "I thought you and your band of miscreants had left. What are you doing back here?"

"If you will excuse me, I came back to ask for directions. I need to know where I can find the road to Santiago and the road to the Pyrenees."

Lucía carefully controlled her anger and gave directions, but Sir Guillaume acted dumb. In desperation, Lucía let her arms loose from her breasts and pointed to the direction of the road to Santiago to the interested eye of Sir Guillaume, which caused Lucía to slip back underwater.

"Oooooh!" exclaimed Lucía in surprise. As she came back to the surface, Lucía asked Sir Guillaume, "Are you sure that you are not involved in some plot to have me drowned through needless chatter!"

"Non. Remember, I am a knight who protects ladies in distress."

Lucía laughed sarcastically, and Sir Guillaume started anew on his way again. Again, Lucía waited several minutes to ensure that Sir Guillaume had gone before she made her way to shore.

Well, finally, Lucía said to herself, but as she was about to swim to the edge of the lagoon, Sir Guillaume appeared once again.

"I don't believe what is happening," said Lucía. "You are like a nightmare that doesn't go away. Now what!" Lucía shouted.

"I am sorry to bother you again, but my friends and I wanted to know if you knew of anyone who might be generous enough to spare some food for three knights of the cross," asked Sir Guillaume with a sly smile.

"No! Not for someone like you," screamed Lucía.

"Now that is no way to treat someone who has fought for your religion," responded Sir Guillaume in a strong tone as he left.

"Get out!" shouted Lucía.

Lucía waited for several more minutes, and once convinced that Sir Guillaume had really left, she bounded for the edge of the lagoon and walked to the rock where her dry linen laid. Luca was shivering, and her legs felt wobbly as she rested them against the rock and quickly wrapped the linen around her.

Meanwhile, Rodrigo had turned from his grazing to watch Lucía.

Lucía shouted over to her horse, "Well, what are you looking at? And by the way, where were you when I needed help from that miscreant who called himself a chivalrous knight?"

Rodrigo just snorted, neighed, and then went back to graze in the tall grasses with his back turned away from her. Lucía then jumped upon the rock and lay there to enjoy the warmth of the sun.

An hour later, Lucía dressed, mounted Rodrigo, and headed back to the palace while in deep thought about her disastrous afternoon. Lucía soon realized that she was more angry at herself for having had allowed the events to have happened in the first place. The air was dry and dusty from a breeze that had developed when she finally reached the road to Segoia. After having had traveled a short distance, she could not believe what she was seeing along the road ahead. There on the road, among other passing pedestrians, were Sir Guillaume and Gaston still carrying Étienne.

Lucía came up with a devilish idea. She quickly put the hood of her cloak on her head so as not to be recognized and, after having had picked up speed, sped quickly past the three, kicking up much dust. Lucía looked back and laughed, as the knights, still carrying their friend, danced around in circles to avoid the dusty air. She also heard them say something inaudible and probably not worth repeating.

Suddenly, she felt another twinge of conscience. "Sí, Mama, I know that wasn't very nice," Lucía said to herself.

Once back at the palace, Lucía happened to meet Geralla, her Aragonese lady-in-waiting, in her boudoir, packing away several of her garments, which had been newly washed and dried into a trunk.

Geralla turned as Lucía entered her boudoir, surprised by her sudden entrance.

"I'm sorry to have startled you," Lucía said with a smile.

"Oh, that's all right. I was just putting away a couple of your garments that I had a servant scrub to remove the candle wax. You will be pleased to know that it was done without doing any damage to the garments whatsoever."

Lucía was very pleased to know that something had gone right in a day that had gone so wrong. With a big smile, she went to Geralla and embraced her. "Gracias for taking such good care of my garments, but I do need to ask a favor of you, if you would be so kind?" asked Lucía, holding onto Geralla's shoulders.

"Anything you ask, mi señora. What do you wish?"

"On the way back to the palace this afternoon, I saw three crusader knights who appeared to be in need on the road to Santiago. I want you to go to the kitchen and procure three cooked chickens, three rounds of cheese, and six loaves of bread and put them in a sack, along with a skin of wine and a skin of water. After, I want you to see Shmuel and request a purse of thirty gold maravedis, and then go to the armory and obtain three swords, along with belts and scabbards and finally to the stable for three saddled horses. Take a guard to accompany you, and deliver these items to the three knights along the road. You will identify them by their white surcoat emblazoned with a large red cross and most likely carrying the third knight between them. However, do not reveal my name to them. After all, Geralla, a person of the nobility should show hospitality to a homeless knight. Always remember that."

"Sí, mi señora, and I want to say that you are being extremely generous."

Lucía smiled. "I think they are worth the consideration."

Within twenty minutes, both Gómez followed by Shmuel came to Lucía's boudoir. "May I ask what is going on that you want to give three strangers three horses and three sets of swords?" asked Gómez.

"And a large purse," added Shmuel.

"This afternoon, while I was out for a ride, I saw three knights whom I felt were worthy of some kindness. They were wearing the crusader cross and were carrying neither a purse nor weapons. I just knew that they were in need. Now don't you think that someone who has fought for our religion should be treated with respect and kindness?" asked Lucía with her charming smile, which produced two dimples as she delivered a convincing argument.

Gómez, a military man, could understand Lucía's argument and was hard-pressed to countermand it. He left her boudoir, shaking his head, along with Shmuel.

"Does that mean that I should grant Lucía's request for the purse?"

"Do what she wishes," responded Gómez.

Within an hour, Geralla was on a horse with all the items Lucía had requested and on the road to Santiago, accompanied by a guard. When Geralla met the three knights, she stopped her horse in front of them, to their complete surprise. Fortunately, they were the only ones who wore the surcoat of a crusader and were easily identified.

Geralla dropped the sack of food, the skins of water and wine, and the swords and purse on the ground in front of the completely startled knights, while her armed escort handed the reins of the three horses to Sir Guillaume.

"Señores, a kind benefactor has seen your plight and given you supplies to continue your journey home. Adiós," said Geralla, and she quickly left before being interrogated as to whom this benefactor might be.

Sir Guillaume, along with Gaston and Étienne, stood on the road in total disbelief and amazement as to what just happened as Geralla and her escort disappeared into the distance.

"Pinch me, Sir Guillaume, as I must be dreaming," said Gaston.

Sir Guillaume picked up the sack and saw the food. He announced to the other two, "Chicken, bread, and cheese, along with a skin of wine and a skin of water." He tasted both. Then he picked up the purse and counted out the thirty pieces of gold maravedis. The other two looked on and still could not believe the good fortune they had come into. As it became dusk, no one else was on the road, and the knights examined the strong Spanish steel of their new swords, buckled on their sword belts, and mounted their horses to make camp further up the road to enjoy a feast, all thanks to a very kind and generous benefactor.

After telling her story of that afternoon to Gabriella and her ladies-in-waiting at supper, Lucía went to the highest tower in the palace. In the darkness of the night, she looked out to the north and wondered if she might catch a glimpse of the three knights, especially Sir Guillaume, on the road to Santiago and then onto the road over the Pyrenees back to France. She imagined them carrying torches to light their way in the darkness. She might even catch a glimpse of a small dot of light on the far horizon. Lucía thought of Sir Guillaume's blue eyes and dirty-blond hair and sighed.

Suddenly, a dose of reality hit Lucía, and she quickly shook her head and asked herself, "Why am I thinking of him?" After all, she was still miffed at the thought of him having had seen her in a compromising position. She promised if she ever saw him again, she would seek her retribution at a time and place that seemed appropriate.

Chapter XVIII

Lucía awakened to a beautiful November day, most welcoming for a ride in the countryside. With the grape harvest over, this would be an ideal time to take Rodrigo out for some exercise. Lucía decided to take a ride in the forest, but first she attended prayer in the chapel and then a simple breakfast of bead, cheeses, and grape juice. She then went to the stable to saddle Rodrigo and finally ventured off with an escort of four household guards. All of Lucía's guards wore the coat of arms of her family, a yellow surcoat over their chain mail emblazoned with a cluster of purple grapes and two silver swords pointed upward on either side of the cluster. In addition, each soldier carried a lance with a yellow pennant also emblazoned with the same colors.

Lucía also felt colorful on this morning, as she wore an orange garment over her white undergarment, along with a black belt, black gloves, and black leather boots. Her long hair was carefully braided and worn as one long braid over her right shoulder. Her cloak was black with a hood worn as protection from the cool breeze.

As Lucía rode through the thick deciduous forest, she noticed the leaves on the trees were a colorful mix of orange, reds, and yellows, and the ground presented a carpet of the most colorful array of rainbow colors. Not having had set out in the forest with a particular direction in mind, Lucía suddenly found herself in an area on the edge of her condado very rarely traveled. The old road began to shrink until it became a path with overhanging trees through rocky terrain and a combination of rocky forested hills and flat clearings. As she kept riding, she found a road that went perpendicular from the main road. On her left side was a six-foot rocky outcrop of rocks, with the rocky forest beyond, and to her right was a road leading to what seemed to be a village of some type. Lucía gave instructions for her escort to stay in front of the rocky outcrop while she traveled down the road to the forest village, about fifty yards from the turnoff.

Lucía proceeded carefully down the road and saw no one around. The huts that dotted the area were made from adobe brick with a white wash of stucco and thatched roofs. They appeared to be simply built but sturdy. The first hut she passed was different, as it was larger than the others, twice as high, and at least six times as long and wide, with a horseshoe arch at its entrance.

Lucía, cautious but curious, yelled, "Is there anyone here?" There was no answer. She repeated again but louder, "Is there anyone here? Who are you people? Who's in charge? Someone please answer me."

Suddenly, a small boy of Syrian origin appeared from one of the huts to her right. As the child came closer, Lucía noticed that he was wearing a dark garment and a white cap on his head and appeared to be badly malnourished.

Lucía dismounted Rodrigo, not feeling threatened but feeling that she was being watched. She went over to the boy and knelt down in front of him while pushing away the hood of her cloak.

The young boy did not back away and was clearly not frightened of Lucía, as she, with a big smile and in Arabic, asked him, "Can you tell me your name?"

"Hisham," responded the boy without a smile.

"Are you hungry, Hisham?"

The boy nodded yes.

Lucía then went to her saddlebag and took out some food wrapped in linen: some bread, a small round of cheese, a round of sausage, and a couple of apples and grapes. Lucía placed the food on a large stump, of which many dotted the area around the village, reached into her boot, pulled out her dagger, and started to cut the items into small bite-size pieces. As she was about to hand a piece of apple to the boy, a stream of other children came out to join the feast. Lucía, surprised to see such a rush of about fifty children, made them line up and kept handing out small pieces of food until there was none left.

The children who had not been fed had a look of disappointment on their faces, and one little girl looked at her with tears in her eyes.

"Oh, don't cry," said Lucía, saddened by her tears. "I have an idea."

She turned and yelled to one of her escorts to have him bring all the food in each of their saddlebags to her. Within a couple of minutes, Lucía was able to share more of the same food with the rest of the children, handing out to each small amounts of food until that was gone as well. In the end, Lucía was able to bring a smile to all their little faces.

One little girl came up to Lucía as she wiped off her dagger with a piece of linen and asked, "Are you an angel?"

Lucía knelt down in front of her, laughed, and said in Arabic, "I'm afraid that I am far from one."

The little girl had never seen blondish-red hair before, and she touched it and then carefully touched Lucía's nose, backed away, and ran off with a smile.

Suddenly, a voice rang out in back of her, "I extend my thanks for your generosity, Doña Lucía."

Lucía, startled by the voice and by having had her name called out, quickly turned around and saw a man that she recognized. "I know you," said Lucía. "You're the man who saved Mafalda and me from the Moorish raiding party."

"Sí, and let me introduce myself again. My name is Yusuf Abd al-Rashid ibn Musa. I am the sheik of this village."

"Are you the king?" inquired Lucía.

Yusuf laughed. "Not really a king, more like an elder leader of the village. However, I did inherit this position from my father. It would be my pleasure to give you a tour of the village, mi señora."

"I would be most interested."

Suddenly, one of Lucía's escorts appeared on horseback. "Mi señora, are you all right?"

"Quite. We have nothing to fear from these people. Go back to your post, and I will let you know when I am ready to leave."

190

"Sí, mi señora," said the escort, and he turned his horse around and proceeded back to the others in wait at the end of the road.

Lucía continued her conversation in Arabic with Yusuf as they started a tour of the village. "You speak my language well, mi señora. May I ask how you learned?" inquired Yusuf.

"My nurse, a Mozarab from Cordoba, taught me the language, along with my tutor. Papa always said that learning Arabic would be helpful someday."

"It sounds as if Don Fernando was a wise man."

Lucía stopped in her tracks. "Did you know my father?"

"I make it a point to know who everyone is and what is happening on the peninsula. Our lives depend on this knowledge. Who is friend and who is foe is very important to our existence," said Yusuf in a more serious tone. Lucía listened carefully to Yusuf as they continued their walk. "We have a population of about five hundred men, women, and children, and we raise our own chickens, sheep, and goats to maintain our own food supply," explained Yusuf.

They continued to the back of the forested village to a very large clearing of ten acres surrounded by trees on all sides. Across the clearing was another group of farm huts. The entire village on both sides lined the clearing, where as Yusuf pointed out, all the farming took place.

Lucía carefully perused the large area, which had been cut from the forest. "Remarkable," said Lucía in complete awe of all she had seen.

"The fields, as you can see, mi señora, are now empty due to the seasonal harvest. We grow barley, carrots, lentils, and other vegetables as well. Our meat consists of chicken, sheep, and goats, all prepared according to our religious customs. Goat cheese is very popular among my people. Unfortunately, mi señora, we usually have more than enough food, but due to the famine, we had barely enough food and had to ration the amount for each family. That is why the children were so hungry. In good times, we have a surplus of food to trade with our friends in the south for olive oil, dates, oranges, and other citrus. By working together and sharing the fruits of our labor, we are able to survive well," added Yusuf.

"You and your people ought to be commended for what you have carved out of the forest, but how long have you been here? I don't remember Papa saying anything about your village," asked Lucía.

"Perhaps it's best if I start from the beginning and give you a brief history of who and what we are," said Yusuf as they both turned and headed back to the main compound. "We are a mixture of both Syrian and Berber descent. My family was originally from Cordoba. About fifty years ago, the south was invaded by a new wave of conquering Moors called the Almohads. They were very oppressive in their treatment of their newly conquered lands to the point that my grandfather, along with family and friends, decided to escape northward from their oppression. As they traveled along, as the story goes, more people joined with them, including the dark-skinned Berbers. They were all looking for a new place to live together, peacefully, along with their Christian brothers."

As the conversation continued, Lucía could not help but notice that Yusuf had a strong but gentle nature about him. She learned of his strong desire to live in peace and that at the age of thirty, he had never married, as the responsibilities in governing his people greatly affected his personal life.

"May I ask a question, señor? I've seen several soldiers during our tour. Do you have an army?" asked Lucía out of curiosity.

"The village has a standing army of one hundred and fifty men and used only for self-defense purposes. All the young men of the village have a turn in the military and have been professionally trained by former soldiers who pass on their skills and techniques. It is important for my people to have the peace and security that a strong defense offers."

While they were walking back to the main compound, by coincidence, a soldier politely interrupted to speak to their sheik about a matter of importance. Lucía paid particular attention to his dress: a conical pointed metal helmet, which was wrapped in black winding cloth to cover neck and face; a shirt and sleeves of chain mail worn over a white tunic, which reached down to his knees; black leather boots over white leggings; a black leather belt, from which hung a scimitar and a curved dagger. All the soldiers carried a bow, a quiver of arrows, and a lance.

"Many pardons for the interruption, mi señora. Now where was I? Ah, sí, but before I continue, I hope that I am not boring you with useless details," asked Yusuf as they found themselves back from where they had started their tour.

"Not at all," said Lucía. "I've been told I am a good listener."

Yusuf gave a smile to Lucía as a father would to a child who was engaged in a conversation and wanted to learn more. "Very well then, I'll continue. For a generation, my grandfather's colony traveled from one landowner to another until they settled on land belonging to Don Raimundo, under my father, Musa, and my uncle Malik.

"Don Raimundo had agreed to give title to the land on which the colony had settled out of friendship. An outdoor ceremony and a banquet were to take place to celebrate the union between the two peoples. For a small sum, title was to be given to the colony for the land that we had already worked. I remember how I begged my father to attend the ceremony, but I was too young. However, I followed secretly through the woods without being seen. How excited I was to see both my father and uncle in their best dress on horseback, along with an escort of many of our fine knights, at the ceremony to accept title for our very own land. I'll never forget having seen Don Raimundo seated on a dais among the many tents around the area and the smell of food being cooked on the open firepits."

Yusuf paused for a second to clear his throat. "Don Raimundo arose from his chair to greet his visitors and to give words of welcome. It was a short time later that Don Raimundo signaled for the signing of the document to begin. Both my father and uncle approached the dais to witness the signing, but before Don Raimundo started to sign the document, he yelled, 'Now!' At the sound of his voice, many soldiers ran out of those tents and cut down my father and uncle and slaughtered all our knights in attendance. I could not believe my eyes when I saw what had happened, how a perceived compliment of having invited one to visit and share in a celebration of friendship could turn into such an act of betrayal.

"To have witnessed such treachery was more than I could bear, and I ran back to the village and told the council what had happened. I became the new sheik and governed, along with the council, which became regent until I reached the age of consent. We quickly packed away our tents and settled here, away from civilization and on the lands of another condado, far enough away from Don Raimundo to remain safe. I promised myself that someday he will pay for his treachery. I will personally kill him myself," said Yusuf, whose face had turned red with anger.

"I am so sorry you have lost your loved ones and suffered so, señor. But please remember, all my people are not like Don Raimundo," added Lucía sadly.

Yusuf smiled. "You have proven that by your very act of kindness toward the children of my village, mi señora. However, if you wish us to leave, we will do so."

Lucía was adamant when she responded, "Not at all! You and your people have worked hard here. I want you to stay under my protection."

"You are very gracious to extend that offer to people whom you have just met, condesa. However, we are willing, of course, to pay rent for the use of your land."

"That will not be necessary. You have more than proven to me that you deserve to be here," said Lucía as she mounted Rodrigo.

"On behalf of my people, I want you to know that you have made a friend and an ally," uttered Yusuf. "We shall always be in your debt."

"I believe that everyone deserves a chance, amigo. Buenos días, señor," said Lucía, and she turned Rodrigo around and left the village to join her escort and to head for home.

On her way home, Lucía had an idea to help Yusuf and his people get through the winter. Once home, she sent for her chef, who quickly responded to Lucía's request and came to her residence in the palace.

"You requested to see me, condesa?"

Lucía was sitting in a chair next to the fireplace, sipping a cup of grape juice, and reading a book of poems, one of which reminded her of a song that she once heard sung by a French troubadour at the royal court.

"My dear chef, gracias for your quick response."

"It is my pleasure, mi señora."

Lucía put the book on her lap. "How much food do we have to get us through the winter?"

"More than enough, mi señora," said the chef, who was standing before Lucía, puzzled by the question.

"Good. Then I want you to prepare several carts and wagons of food, enough to feed a population of five hundred people through the winter and through the spring planting season. Do not include in your preparation pork of any kind or wine. Is that clear?"

The chef was surprised at her request. "May I ask the condesa the nature of your request?"

"Simply fill the necessary number of wagons and carts and advise me when it is done."

"Well, mi señora, if I honor your request, we may not have enough food to see us through the winter."

"It seems to me that we could all do with less to help those without. That is part of my responsibilities as condesa to help my people in the time of need. Don't you agree?" asked Lucía, who was resolute in her request.

"Of course, mi señora." The chef left but not before sputtering expletives on his way out the door.

Lucía, who knew the chef, could only laugh. She yelled to him, "For those remarks, you had better see a priest."

It didn't take long before Captain Gómez paid a visit to Lucía. A servant announced his entrance. "Captain Gómez to see you, mi señora."

"Tell him to come back later. I'm busy," said Lucía, who had continued reading her book of poems as she planned in her mind a trip to Paris.

"You will see me now!" exclaimed Gómez, who rushed in past the servant.

"Gómez, you always have the habit of barging in at a bad time. What is it this time?" asked Lucía, irritated at his constant attempt to interfere with her plans.

"Doña Lucía, as you know, I have been put in charge of your safety and well-being. I did not volunteer for this position, but due to the respect and love that I have for your uncle and aunt, I agreed to—reluctantly, I might add."

Lucía sighed. "Sí, Gómez, you have made that point very clear on many occasions. Now what can I do for you?"

"I just spoke to the chef, as he put in a request for several wagons and carts to load a large supply of our food that we have stored away for the winter months. He stated that he was not told where the food and the many sacks of grain for bread were headed. Can you explain further, my dear, condesa?"

"It will be given to people who need it more. I will divulge at the right time."

"Oh, I can see that this is trouble in the making. For your sake, I will not honor your request until I know where this food is going," uttered Gómez angrily.

"You have no right to question me so," shot back Lucía.

"Oh, I have every right, and the king will definitely back me on this."

Lucía thought for a moment and realized that Gómez was within his bounds to ask. "All right then, I found a colony of Arabs living on the edge of my condado who are starving. I gave them permission to stay, and now I want to share our food so they don't starve over the winter. Any other questions?" asked Lucía in an angry voice.

Gómez was surprised at the unexpected reply and stood there for a short time without saying a word. And then he pointed his finger at Lucía, which caused her to sit back in her chair with a look of surprise. "You mean we have a camp of Moors living within our border, and you want to feed them? Have you lost that little mind of yours?"

Lucía replied in a softer tone, with her usual nervous smile, when she realized that she might not win the argument. "They are a mix of Syrian and Berbers. They are a peaceful people with children who are starving. I know, as I had a tour of their village. They are our friends and allies, and I feel a sense of responsibility and Christian generosity toward them. I know that Papa would do the same. Don't you understand, Gómez?"

Gómez stopped, thought for a moment, raised his hands in the air, and left, to the glee of Lucía, who knew that she had won the argument.

Within a couple of days, the shipment of food was loaded and ready to take to the village. Lucía gave careful directions to Gómez, who would lead the caravan with a minimal amount of armed soldiers to the village.

Lucía also visited the village a short time after the shipment of food had been delivered to ensure all had been transported as per her request. The people of the village were so grateful and hungry at the same time they put on a feast in her honor in the sheik's palace.

Chapter XIX

Lucía was excited to have received a letter from King Philip of France to come visit him in Paris and her duchy in Pomeroi. Lucía also envisioned a visit to Toulouse on her way to Paris to see her Aunt Joan, the Countess of Toulouse, who had sent letters of encouragement to Lucía during her younger years. But first, Lucía had to pay a visit to Isabella to invite her along on her lengthy journey north.

Lucía took the road to Gustavo up to the castle which rested on a small rise that loomed above on a dry dusty plain. About a mile down the rise to the left lay the village of Gustavo. As she approached the fortification with her escort of four guards, a guard on the only tower of the castle on the left wall hailed Lucía and inquired as to her visit.

"What is the nature of your visit?" asked the guard, who did not recognize Lucía. To Lucía, this was unusual, as all of Isabella's guards knew her and she'd had free access to the castle. "I am Doña Lucía Alvarado, Condesa of Segoia, to see Doña Isabella, Condesa of Gustavo."

"Go away!" said the guard, who waved his hand and spoke in a belligerent manner. "She doesn't see anyone. Now move."

Lucía was both very concerned and angry over such treatment. "I demand to see Isabella or her uncle at once, or I will go back to Segoia and bring enough men to storm this castle. Do you understand me?"

The guard hesitated for a short time and then yelled down to another guard in the courtyard, "A Doña Lucía to see Doña Isabella. You had better get Ramón to come to the tower."

Lucía and her escort waited patiently. Several minutes went by but still no Ramón. More time went by before Ramón finally appeared.

"What do you want?" asked Ramón.

"I want to see Isabella. I did not know that I needed an appointment to visit her."

"Very well, but only for a few minutes," uttered her uncle, and he signaled for the guard below to open the door to the entrance to the small courtyard. Once it was opened, Lucía and her escort continued under the watchful eye of Ramón.

Once Lucía dismounted Rodrigo, her escort followed her into the castle to the third floor to Isabella's residence, which was down a long hallway lined to the right, halfway down, with a solid wall and the other half with horseshoe arches. Above the arches was a string course of individual white blocks of stone with alternating carvings of a bird and a cluster of grapes, a pattern of Visigothic design. The arches held up a fifteen-foot ceiling, and beyond the arches was a huge open area, where Lucía found Isabella seated in a chair in front of a table on a dais with a horseshoe double-arch window to her back and a dry riverbed below.

Isabella was surprised to see Lucía as she walked down the dais to greet her longtime friend. After they both embraced, Isabella took Lucía to her boudoir across the hall for more privacy, still under the watchful eye of Ramón. Before she entered, Lucía had her escort wait for her at the stairwell entrance.

Once they entered her boudoir, Isabella gave Lucía another deep embrace. "It is so good to see you, Lucía. To what do I owe the pleasure of your visit?"

"First, I want to know if you are all right, Isabella."

"I'm fine. Why do you ask?"

"Because the reception I received by the guard in the tower was not a pleasant one. It was so unlike the friendly reception I used to receive years ago. Did you know I had to threaten to storm the castle if they didn't allow me to see you?" said Lucía with a smile.

Suddenly, Isabella's mood changed, and she turned away from Lucía and walked to the window in her boudoir. "I wish you had not done that, Lucía," said Isabella with her back turned to her longtime friend as she looked out the window to the vast dry plain and the forest area several miles away in the distance.

What Isabella had just said and the manner in which she spoke was eerie and caused a chill to run down Lucía's back.

"But I wanted very much to see you, Isabella. It's been a long time, and I had to make sure you were all right."

Isabella quickly turned to Lucía with a big smile and another change of mood. "But I am fine, as you can see. Now what brings you here?"

"I'm planning to go to Paris and wish for you to come. We would have a most enjoyable time together. Not only will we see Paris, but you will be able to meet King Philip and perhaps my Aunt Joan in Toulouse, as well as to accompany me to Pomeroi in northern France, where my mother was raised."

After a brief hesitation, and without a smile or any sign of enthusiasm, Isabella responded, "It sounds very nice, Lucía, but I doubt I can come."

"But it would be a good experience for you."

"My uncle will not allow it. Things have changed, Lucía. My uncle is now in charge of my life until I reach the age of eighteen or get married, and he is very strict. I have to ask permission to do anything. I simply don't have your freedom, Lucía."

"Then I will ask him myself and see what he has to say," said Lucía, determined in her quest to seek out Ramón.

"Lucía, I beg you. Please don't."

Lucía stopped at Isabella's mournful plea and turned back toward her.

"Please don't make trouble," Isabella cried out.

"Of course not, Isabella," said Lucía as she embraced her. "You have always been like a sister to me. I never want you to forget it. *Bueno?*"

"Bueno," responded Isabella.

"If you ever need anything or if you ever need help, you let me know. Bueno?"

"Bueno," responded Isabella.

Suddenly, the door burst open, and Ramón walked over to Lucía. "The visit is over. Isabella has other things to do besides talking to you. Now leave."

Lucía, not accustomed to such a display of rudeness, did not respond, but she looked over at poor Isabella, who looked down at the stone floor in shame. Lucía decided to leave so as not to cause any further embarrassment.

She gave Ramón a scowl and then turned to Isabella for a final embrace. "Adiós, Isabella. I will talk with you later, and remember, I will always love you as a sister."

Isabella gave Lucía a nod and a forced smile, and Lucía scowled at Ramón again and left for home.

Within a couple of days, after Lucía's visit to see Isabella, Gabriella received a message from the palace and gave it to Lucía, who was seated in the anteroom of the great hall as she reviewed the accounting books of the income from the recent wine sales.

"A message from the palace, mi señora," said Gabriella as she handed the message to Lucía.

Lucía smiled and was in a happy mood as she took the message. "Gracias, Gabriella, but please call me Lucía, not 'mi señora.' That form of address makes me feel like an old lady. Besides, you are both my majordomo as well as a dear friend, so addressing me by my first name is more than appropriate."

"Of course," responded Gabriella.

Lucía turned her attention to the message. "My aunt wants to see me. Now what have I done?"

"Is everything all right, Lucía?" asked Gabriella.

"I think so. But with my aunt, it is difficult to tell. I must leave immediately, or I will hear a lecture on being prompt."

Lucía proceeded to walk out of the anteroom and to the stable to make arrangements with Captain Gómez for an immediate escort to the palace at Burgos.

Once at the palace, Lucía was escorted into the throne room, where a servant announced Lucía's presence. "Doña Lucía to see you, Your Highness."

"Have her enter," responded Queen Leonor.

Lucía entered the throne room and noticed her aunt was seated on her throne, wearing the three gold lions of the Plantagenet emblazoned on her white garment.

Lucía made a deep curtsy. "You sent for me, ma'am?"

"Sí, I did. But first, how are you getting along, Lucía?"

"I am well. Gracias," said Lucía.

"I do worry about you, Lucía, as I don't see you that often. However, I shall have to remedy that with more frequent visits. I wish to stay in contact with all my children, as my mother does with me and my siblings."

The last thing that Lucía wanted to hear was frequent visits by a controlling aunt meddling in her affairs. "Oh, but you don't have to worry about me, Aunt Leonor. I am doing quite well, have no problems, and stay out of trouble."

"Really? Then how do you explain the complaint I received from Isabella's Uncle Ramón, who said that you were insolent and provocative in your visit to see Doña Isabella?"

"Oh, that. Well, I felt she was in danger and might need protection."

"By threatening to storm the castle!"

"Well, maybe a little extreme. But the surly guard on the tower was not going to let me in, and I wanted to make sure that she was well," said Lucía with a nervous smile.

"Lucía, I know that you have a strong friendship with Isabella, but Ramón is Isabella's guardian, and his decisions are to be followed without your interference. I hope that I have made myself clear."

"But—" Lucía was interrupted very sternly by the queen.

"There are no buts regarding this matter, Lucía! Do we understand each other? Need I say more regarding this incident?"

"No, ma'am," said Lucía with a sigh.

"Good! Now what about this visit to Paris that Ramón told me about?"

"Ah. Oh, that," said Lucía, whose eyes were darting left and then right and whose facial expression appeared as a child who had been caught doing wrong. "Well, I was thinking about going to Paris and visiting with King Philip."

"King Philip?" repeated the queen.

"Sí, you see, I received a letter from the king, inviting me to visit Paris and to see Pomeroi, my duchy, where my mother was raised," said Lucía, excited at the prospect.

"I see. Were you planning to tell me about this letter and your planned trip or just leave without notifying me and without my permission?"

"Wellll…"

"Well, what, Lucía? It's a simple answer."

There was a moment of silence until the queen said, "It is obvious to me that the answer is no."

"No no no!" responded Lucía, who looked down at the floor with a guilty look. "Well, maybe now," Lucía added with a guilty smile.

"I blame myself," said the queen. "I must find more time to meet with you and find out about such matters. Remember, Lucía, the king and I are your guardians. We must be told about such things in order for us to properly look out for your welfare. You are not allowed to go wildly off on your own without consulting us first. Is that clear?"

"Sí, ma'am."

"Now do you have the letter from King Philip?"

"Sí, ma'am. I did bring it with me," said Lucía, and she handed the letter to the queen.

Queen Leonor took the letter and read it, "Well, I see that we must prepare for your trip to Paris, forthwith, under one condition: it is done my way. Unfortunately, it will not be until the early spring. It is very dangerous to travel through the mountains during the winter. Besides, it will give us ample time to properly plan for your departure."

"I was also hoping to see Aunt Joan in Toulouse. I have written to her but have received no response," added Lucía.

"Not a good idea, Lucía. Unfortunately, your aunt is involved with her own problems, from what I have been told by your grandmother. Now run along, Lucía. I will be in touch."

Lucía, excited when she returned to Segoia, told her ladies the news about their upcoming trip to Paris in the spring. This news, indeed, excited the ladies with much enthusiasm, and they ran about and examined their garments to determine which to pack.

Within days, a stranger, dressed as a monk wearing a large brown hood so as not to be identified, entered Don Raimundo's chambers. A servant announced the presence of the stranger to Don Raimundo.

"Have the stranger enter," he ordered as he busily worked at the table in the anteroom of the great hall.

Don Raimundo stopped what he was doing and looked at the stranger who was so completely covered with the monk's garb it was impossible to know the identity of his visitor. "What do you have for me?" asked Don Raimundo.

The stranger handed Raimundo a note, which he took and read, "Ah, so Doña Lucía is making plans to go to Paris, is she?" The stranger nodded in the affirmative. "Very well. Good job, and gracias," Raimundo said with a smile as he watched the strange visitor leave.

Don Raimundo didn't waste any time in having Scarface come to his chamber to discuss a possible plan. Scarface sat in a chair in front of the dais, where Don Raimundo was seated, relaxed and cheerful. "I have news regarding Doña Lucía. I received a message not long ago from our mysterious spy from Segoia. The message states that Doña Lucía is making plans to travel to Paris. This provides a good opportunity to have her annihilated once and for all. She is not going until the early spring, which gives us time to plan an unexpected reception for her in the Pyrenees.

"Scarface, see if you can form a small army of about a hundred men who know the mountains and be able to stage an ambush. Meanwhile, I will keep my eyes and ears open to find out more information."

"Sí, mi señor," said Scarface, and he rose from his chair and left the palace to start his mission.

Chapter XX

The queen helped Lucía plan for her journey to France. As a matter of fact, Queen Leonor was very emphatic that Lucía would act as an ambassador of goodwill to represent Castile at the French court. As a result, the entourage should be one of splendor and magnificence, where all carts and wagons displayed the yellow castle of Castile. In addition, all soldiers who accompanied Lucía and her entourage would wear a red surcoat with the yellow castle of Castile emblazoned on the front of their blouse over their chain mail, and each soldier would carry a lance with a red pennant emblazoned with the yellow castle proudly displayed on them.

However, Lucía, not one for such display, would have been happy with a much smaller, less colorful entourage. Also, there were expensive gifts secretly packed in one of the supply wagons, which would be carefully guarded, along with three white Arabian stallions—all for the king and queen of France.

Spring had blossomed, and the long-awaited day of departure had arrived with anticipated excitement. King Alfonso and Queen Leonor, with the entire royal family, along with the bishop and other notables, including household servants who stayed at the palace, were on hand to say goodbye to Lucía and her company.

Lucía had been at prayer at her mother's sarcophagus and was the last to enter the courtyard, accompanied by Gabriella and Constance. She saw the large number of wagons and carts. In her mind, this was bad enough, but then she saw the small army of armed soldiers that were to accompany her all lined up and awaiting departure.

She had to voice her opinion. "In the name of…!" said Lucía, turning to her aunt and uncle, who were both seated on a dais. After a curtsy, she looked at them and said, "I want to thank both of you for your help and support to have made this journey possible, but," said Lucía softly to the king and queen, "this looks more like an invading army. What will the rulers of the countries that we will be crossing think of this entourage, which is more than we originally discussed?"

"Don't worry, my dear. I have written to all concerned, and they have given permission for you to cross their lands," said the queen confidently. "Never forget, Lucía, that a person of your status deserves such pomp and ceremony, and don't worry about matters here. We will handle your affairs while you are gone. Also, Captain Gómez is in charge, and what he says must be obeyed. Now, have a good journey, and we will be looking forward to your correspondence and safe return."

"Sí, ma'am," said Lucía, and she made a final curtsy and was immediately escorted to her wagon, where Gabriella was already seated.

The king then turned to Captain Gómez, who had been standing next to the dais. "Gómez, although permission has been granted by the king of Navarre for you to travel through his lands, I still want this expedition to stay off the main roads whenever possible so as not to attract attention. Our relationship with Navarre has been tenuous at best as of late. Try to appear as innocuous as possible."

"Of course, Sire," responded Gómez.

Once seated, Lucía and her entourage of her ladies-in-waiting, servants, soldiers, and a priest began their journey to Paris. Lucía was happy the two wooden benches, which faced each other for easy conversation, were covered with a pillow made from goose feathers and wrapped in red velvet. The high wooden back allowed for additional pillows for added comfort. The rounded wagon top was covered with a canvas and red curtain material, which hung from the top under the canvas on rods and could be pushed back and forth as needed to view the countryside.

King Alfonso heard a rumor about a possible plot to have Lucía murdered somewhere in the mountains. The news came from a witness, a trusted servant from the royal palace, who happened to be in a tavern in Burgos and overheard a man talking to his friends in an attempt to recruit them for an ambush. He only heard the name of Nájera. However, he did not hear where or whom was to be attacked. The servant had brought this information immediately to King Alfonso.

"You did well, reporting this information to me," responded the king to the servant. "I will make sure that you are rewarded. Also, take heart that you might have saved the life of my dear niece."

With that, the servant bowed and left the king's chambers.

The king paced up and down his chamber and wondered how best to handle the situation, as he did not wish to worry the queen with this matter. Suddenly, an idea came to mind, and he prepared for immediate travel to see the Count of Ávila. As he was about to leave, he was interrupted by his two young daughters, Urraca, age ten, and Blanca, age eight, who wanted their father to settle a dispute.

"Papa, will you please tell my sister that I am the oldest and she is to listen and obey me?" asked Urraca, who had turned to Blanca with a scowl on her face and her arms folded.

The king bent down and put one hand on each of their shoulders. "Hmm, I have a situation that demands my immediate attention that I have to attend to. Perhaps it best that you see your mother regarding this matter."

The two girls stormed out of the room. The king shook his head in disbelief and then headed to the stable for both a horse and a suitable escort.

When he arrived in Ávila to see the count, the latter was already waiting for him in the courtyard and went to greet him. "How are you, old friend?" asked the king, who had dismounted his horse.

"Greetings to you, Sire. It is great to see you, but what brings you to Ávila?"

"I have a favor to ask you."

"We can discuss this matter over some wine," said Ávila as the two men walked to his chambers.

Once both were seated in a chair, an awaiting servant came along and poured wine in both silver cups. Ávila could sense that the king was anxious to address the business at hand. "Now what can I do for you, Sire?" inquired Ávila.

The king took a gulp of wine and carefully swallowed it. "Ávila, you and I have been friends for a long time, and I trust you with my life."

Ávila nodded in agreement.

"Something has developed rather quickly. My niece, Doña Lucía, is at this hour on the road to Paris with a large entourage of ladies-in-waiting, servants, cooks, and a force of sixty men-at-arms. I believe that certain forces are planning to attack my niece in the Pyrenees, somewhere near Nájera. I'm asking you to take one hundred well-armed men in pursuit of her entourage and follow at a safe distance so as to not arouse any undue suspicion from the perpetrators. Such a force should be adequate to outnumber any foe," said the king, who gave great thought as he spoke to make clear the danger involved and what was at stake. "I would do this myself, but I have a pressing matter in Toledo that simply cannot wait."

"Don't worry, Sire. I will be more than happy to take care of this matter for you. The safety of Doña Lucía will be my top priority. I will make arrangements to set off immediately and ride day and night to catch up to them and to follow discreetly behind, of course," said Ávila, who attempted to reassure the king.

"You have my gratitude, Ávila. Also, no one must know about our conversation to alert any spies who might be in our midst," uttered the king, who emptied his cup.

"Of course," said Ávila in a reassuring voice.

"Now I feel much better," said the king, who arose from his chair and left the palace, accompanied by Ávila, to his own contingent of twelve men. As he mounted his horse, the king waved goodbye to his friend. "Adiós, mi amigo."

"Buenos días," responded Ávila, and he set off to prepare for the hard ride to catch up to Lucía and her contingent.

Several days had passed, and the entourage had made its way slowly to the Pyrenees. Lucía lifted the curtain in her wagon, and from the hills, she saw the vast flat yellow, green, and brown plains of Burgos behind her and the mountains in front of her. She would soon be entering the hills and valleys of the Pyrenees. Lucía asked the driver to stop, which halted the entire column of soldiers, wagons, and carts. Lucía and Gabriella exited their wagon, with Lucía rubbing her back and rear.

"Is there anything wrong, Lucía?" asked Captain Gómez, who had galloped back from the front of the contingent.

"Except for a sore back," responded Lucía, who anxiously rubbed it as best she could.

The other ladies started to exit their wagon as well, to the chagrin of Captain Gómez, who was hoping to make at least a few more miles before resting the horses. Gómez looked around. "Well, I guess this is as good of a place as any."

He gave the order, and the soldiers dismounted and stretched. There was no danger now, as they were in the open, to the relief of the captain, who had left a forested area a few days back without incident but realized that shortly, not far ahead, the road would again climb with embankments, more woods, and the ever-present possibility of danger.

It was late in the afternoon before the contingent reached La Calazada. Gómez found a suitable spot to make camp for the night on the plain outside the town, on the Oja River, which flowed through the area and was a good source of water to replenish their supply before they moved on with their journey the next day. The soldiers and servants quickly started the task of unloading the various carts and wagons of tents and supplies for the evening.

As tents were being pitched and supper being prepared, Lucía wandered off to see the river and to hear the rushing water of the Oja first-hand, which had overflowed its banks. Lucía plodded her way carefully through the watery muck at the edge of the rapidly flowing river and stood under a tree at the edge of the bank. Across from the river, on the opposite bank, was a similar line of trees followed by the plain leading up to the bluish-green mountains beyond.

She was joined by Gabriella, who brought Lucía her cloak. "I thought that you might need this, Lucía," said Gabriella, who handed her the black cloak.

"Gracias, Gabriella. Isn't this beautiful?" asked Lucía, who put on her cloak as she stared at the distant snowcapped mountains that were being brought to life by the setting sun.

"Very peaceful," responded Gabriella.

They were joined by the ladies, who carefully picked up the hem of their garments and walked through the mud to also stare at the peaceful scenery. Adele started to shiver and held her folded arms close to her chest.

Constance, who stood next to Adele, saw that she was cold. "Adele, where is your cloak?"

"I think it was packed somewhere in my trunk," responded Adele. Constance removed her cloak and, with a smile gave it to Adele. "Gracias," responded Adele.

"See if you can find your cloak and warmer clothing before you go to bed tonight. You are going to need them as we climb higher into the mountains," explained Constance, who went back to warm herself from one of the several fires that had been started.

Lucía and her ladies walked back to camp and stood in front of a fire. They could smell the ever-present aroma of fresh tarts being made by the cook, along with a large pot of mutton stew, with carrots, cabbage, and lentil beans.

As Lucía looked around the camp, she saw the colorful array of many of the tents around her. Lucía had a large striped yellow and white one with a large red shield with a yellow castle emblazoned on both flaps to the entrance of her tent. Inside was a table, which could seat six people, with six chairs, and two table-size candelabras made out of silver, which held six candles each. A brazier on a stand stood at the foot of Lucía's full feather bed, heated with hot coals for warmth. Lucía's trunks were placed at the foot of her bed in front of the brazier. On the walls of the tent were small colorful tapestries of hunting scenes. Lucía wanted something less luxurious, but the queen insisted that this was expected for a girl of her position. There was no sense in arguing with the queen, as Lucía had always lost the argument.

Lucía would sometimes eat in her tent, along with Gabriella and her ladies. Many times she would invite Gómez, who often declined, since he did not wish to hear the constant idle chatter of girls. She also invited the padre to give them his blessings. Other times, she would sit on the ground with her soldiers and share a meal while she engaged them in conversation. At night, guards were posted to protect the inhabitants of the camp.

On this night, several pilgrims on their way to Santiago came to camp to ask for food and lodging. Lucía graciously welcomed them under the watchful eye of Gómez and his guards. The pilgrims wore simple garments, carried walking sticks, and spoke of their experiences while traveling on foot from Paris to visit the tomb of the blessed St. James in Santiago. They spoke of their hard travel up steep roads and the cold wind and snow. Lucía listened intently to every word of the pilgrims and shared information about the road that lay ahead. The next day, they were gone by dawn before anyone arose in the camp.

Before dawn, the camp was broken down, with all tents and other supplies placed carefully in the accompanying carts and wagons, and the expedition was ready to embark on the day's journey by sunrise.

Meanwhile, after having had ridden day and night with only a little rest, Ávila had finally caught up to Lucía. He stayed far enough behind to remain out of sight but kept an eye on the expedition, which continued its travels in Nájera, as it approached a steep wooded road with an embankment covered with trees on either side. Gómez continued slowly up the steep trek until all the wagons and carts had passed beyond the steepest part of the road and could move at a faster pace.

During the slow pace of the uphill climb, both Lucía and Gabriella enjoyed reading a book of poems that Lucía had brought with her to entertain themselves during the long ride. Suddenly, as they were quietly reading, they heard a loud cry, which startled both of them. As the cries multiplied and became louder and louder, both Lucía and Gabriella pushed aside their curtains and saw to their horror a large number of men dressed in ordinary garments, running down both embankments carrying all sorts of weapons: swords, axes, maces, and clubs.

"Gabriella, get down on the floor now!" cried Lucía, who quickly closed both curtains, pulled a dagger from her boot, and lay across Gabriella on the floor of the wagon. Lucía heard the screams of the girls in the other wagons but was helpless to do anything. One of the servant girls jumped out of a wagon and started to run in panic up the embankment but was quickly dispatched by a crossbow. Suddenly, the curtain opened and revealed one of the marauders. He had a smile on his face as he tried to enter the wagon. Lucía arose from her prone position. She had one hand holding her dagger, pointing it at the perpetrator, and the other hand pushed against the floor next to Gabriella to maintain her balance. She was ready to strike, if he should enter. Fortunately, he was quickly cut down by a soldier, and Lucía resumed her position atop Gabriella.

As the battle continued on, Lucía had a worried look on her face. She was deeply concerned about what was happening outside and what fate awaited her people if the battle was lost. Lucía was still lying prone on top of Gabriella among the cries of confusion and death. Then came unnerving silence, followed by cheers. The curtain was pushed aside to reveal Ávila, who had finally arrived and put an end to the siege.

"Are both of you all right, Lucía?" asked Gómez, who had a look of concern on his face.

"We are both okay," replied Lucía as she arose from atop Gabriella and sheathed her dagger back in her boot.

Gómez helped both Lucía and Gabriella out of the wagon, and Lucía wasted no time in going to each wagon to check on her ladies and servants, only to find to her dismay that a young servant girl had been killed in the action. She found the girl lying on the side of the embankment with an arrow in her back, face down, in a pool of blood.

The priest joined Lucía, and he knelt down over the young girl's body and gave her the final blessing of the church. Then he left to attend to the other dead. Lucía, who was holding back tears, also knelt down over the dead girl and was now joined by her ladies and the other servants, who stood over her. Lucía had remembered seeing her working in the palace kitchen and was upset at herself for not knowing her name.

"What was her name?" asked Lucía as she wiped away her tears; she was now joined by Gómez and Ávila.

One of the servants uttered, "Ana."

"We tried to stop her, but she jumped out of the wagon before we could grab her," said another.

"She could not have been more than twelve or thirteen," said Gómez sadly.

"We have to give her a proper burial. I will not hear a word against it," said a determined Lucía.

"Unfortunately, you will have to add several more to the list," interjected Gómez.

"How many did we lose?"

"We lost two of our men, and Ávila lost five of his."

Lucía turned to Ávila. "Gracias for coming. You saved our lives, and I will always be grateful to you. Now you will have to excuse me," said Lucía, who wept as she ran up the embankment, dodged several dead bodies on the way, and ran deeper into the forest.

She finally came to a tree, and she fell to the ground and wept uncontrollably on her arm against the bark. "Why? Why? Why!" screamed Lucía, beating her fist against the tree. Several minutes later, Gómez appeared and picked her up and embraced her. "It is my entire fault," cried Lucía, whose voice was muffled on Gómez's shoulder.

"No, it was not," responded Captain Gómez, who was a military man and used to seeing death but not used to comforting young ladies.

"Tell me, Gómez, why did they have to die?" asked Lucía, sniffling.

"I don't know, Lucía. No one can answer that question. Unfortunately, conflicts happen, and sometimes death is the outcome."

"They died because of me and my selfish desire to see Paris," added Lucía.

Gómez pulled away from Lucía and held her by her shoulders. "Lucía, you are a condesa and a French duchess. There will always be people who will die in your service. You must accept that and live with it. For you, it must be a fact of life. It is important, however, that despite death, you remain strong for your people, who will always look to you for strength."

Lucía looked at Gómez and wiped away her tears. "You are right, Gómez, and gracias for waking me up to reality. I am ready to head back now."

Gómez smiled. They both walked back through the forest to the entourage and discussed the outcome of the battle. "What of the attacking army?" asked Lucía.

"They were not much of an army, more like rabble. Although they took us by surprise, we managed to fend them off, as they were no match for us. That is why our casualties were so light. Once Ávila appeared, they started to scatter to the wind. I doubt we will see them again."

"How many of the enemy was there, Gómez?" questioned Lucía.

"I figure about one hundred men, give or take—a few here, a few there."

As both Lucía and Gómez walked down the embankment, they were greeted by Ávila in his chain mail and blue surcoat emblazoned with a red lion rampant. He had a barrel helmet held under his arm.

He reached for Lucía's gloved hand, kissed it, and then said, "It has been a long time since I have seen you. You were only a little girl at the time and with your father, Don Fernando, whom I miss very much."

"I too miss him very much," said Lucía, and she smiled at both Gómez and Ávila. She asked, "Will you both join my ladies and me for supper tonight in my tent?"

Gómez nodded, and Ávila responded, "It would be an honor."

It was midafternoon by the time the burial ceremony had been completed, and the contingent moved on further up the road and found a clearing to make camp. Ávila's soldiers also joined the encampment. At supper, there was friendly chatter about different topics and finally a discussion of the day's events, which led to a poignant question.

"Doña Lucía, do you know of anyone who would want to harm you?" asked Ávila, who reached for a chicken leg from the silver platter on the table.

"Not that I know of," answered Lucía.

Ávila looked across the table at Lucía as he tore into a round of bread. "I don't mean to alarm you, my dear, but you should know that the king asked me to follow you discreetly, as he became aware of a plot to have you killed."

Lucía sat back in her chair with a look of fear on her face and didn't utter a word. Her ladies also looked fearful, and Lucía politely asked them to leave so as to not upset them further. As the ladies left, both Gómez and Ávila stood until the ladies were gone.

After the ladies left, Lucía looked Ávila in the eye. "With all due respect and gratitude that I have for you, señor, such remarks should only be addressed to me and Captain Gómez and not to anyone else. My ladies as well as I have all been shaken by today's events, and I see no need to upset them further."

Ávila looked at Gómez, who had also been taken aback by his remark, and then turned back to Lucía. "I apologize. I did not mean to upset you and your ladies, but you should be aware that you have a spy in your midst."

Lucía finally accepted the reality of Ávila's remark and remembered what Gómez said about being a strong leader. She looked over to Gómez and asked, "Are we still in danger?"

"I don't believe so," said Gómez in a reassuring tone.

Lucía then turned to Ávila as he voiced, "I agree. My army pursued what was left of the marauders and killed quite a few of them. I firmly believe they will not be back."

Within several days, it was apparent that the marauders would not return, and Ávila made plans to return home. It was just before dawn that Lucía, her ladies, Gabriella, Captain Gómez, and the priest stood in line to say goodbye to their friend.

With Ávila's soldiers on their horses, ready to leave, Ávila went up to Lucía at the head of the departure line, bowed his head, took her hand, and kissed it to say farewell. "It has been an honor and a privilege to have been in your company, mi señora. Your father would have been very proud of you. God rest his soul."

"Gracias for what you did for us, señor. I will always be in your debt. Have a safe journey back, and also please give my uncle my thanks for having had sent you on such a long journey of rescue."

Ávila then went up to Gómez. "Adiós, amigo, until the next time," said Ávila as they both embraced.

"You have a safe journey back, amigo. Until the next time," replied Gómez.

Ávila then made an extended bow of acknowledgment to the ladies, who all stood tall and proud as he walked to his horse.

"Oh, I'm also leaving two of my men to replace the two that you lost in battle. They shall now always be in your service and wear your colors. Have a safe journey," said Ávila, and he mounted his horse and waved farewell while the others waved back. They all watched until the final soldier passed, and then they proceeded on their journey.

Chapter XXI

It was a beautiful spring day, and Lucía opened the curtain of her wagon to enjoy the bright sunshine and the open fields, vineyards, hills, and flats of Logrono. She also waved to several groups of pilgrims who were heading for Santiago.

"How friendly the pilgrims are," said Lucía to Gabriella, who was busy reading her book of poems.

Gabriella looked up from her book to look at Lucía. "Did you say something?"

Lucía smiled and giggled. "Gabriella, you should be more attentive to this beautiful countryside. It is truly charming and welcoming."

Gabriella smiled and pushed back her hair, which had blown in her face from a cool breeze that had suddenly appeared. "Perhaps you're right," she said, and she pulled back her curtain to enjoy the fresh air.

As time passed, the fresh air caused both Lucía and Gabriella to fall asleep. When they awoke, it was late afternoon, and Gómez had stopped to make camp.

That night, a group of Knight Templars, on their way to the Templar church at Torres del Rio, stopped by for food and drink and to spend the night. Lucía found the Templars fascinating and entertaining with their stories of their fight for Christendom in lands beyond. However, they were gone before dawn.

On the road again, the entourage was headed for Pamplona, where Lucía saw many sheep on the rolling hills. Suddenly, the sky darkened and started to pour, and it rained all night. Early in the morning the next day, it still rained hard, and everything was completely soaked. The tents, clothing, and even the bedding did not escape the unrelenting fury of the spring rain. Lucía and her company of ladies were all shivering in the wet cold air. Unfortunately, having made camp in a wooded area off the rolling plain outside Pamplona did not help. There was plenty of wood to be had for a fire, and several of the soldiers had made many attempts to start one, but the wet wood proved it impossible.

Due to the bad conditions, Gómez decided for Lucía and her ladies to go into the city and find rooms at an inn to stay warm. For the most part, he had been lucky at this point to have had stayed off the main roads to avoid detection. However, these conditions were just impossible. Gómez sent a soldier disguised as a traveler to find an inn or a place of refuge for the ladies.

Lucía and her ladies shivered and huddled together in the middle of her tent and covered up with as many cloaks and heavy clothing that could be found. Even the charcoal for the brazier was so damp that it was impossible to light. Gómez pushed aside the flaps that covered the entrance of Lucía's tent and found Lucía and her ladies packed so close together that a wedge could not pry them apart.

"Lucía, may I have a word, please?"

Lucía pried herself from her ladies, who quickly closed the gap, and went over to Gómez, who stood at the closed entrance of the tent, which kept out the burst of wind that would occasionally blow.

"Lucía, I must find shelter and warmth for all of you in Pamplona. I only wish that the relationship with the King of Navarre was on friendlier terms so you could perhaps seek shelter with him at his palace. However, be it as it may, I have sent a soldier disguised as a traveler to find shelter for you and your ladies in town."

"Did not my aunt say the King of Navarre had given permission to cross his territory? Would not shelter be included?" inquired Lucía in a trembling voice due to the cold.

"Not necessarily. If that was the case, the king would have invited you to visit with him at his castle, and your uncle was very emphatic on being discreet in crossing his territory. No, this must be handled in a furtive manner. Fortunately, we are hidden far enough in the woods that no one can see our camp. I do not want the king to know we are here," said Gómez in a calm, soft voice.

Lucía, concerned, asked Gómez in a soft voice, "What would happen if we were caught?"

"Perhaps nothing, or perhaps he could hold either you or one of your ladies for ransom. I don't know. I am not going to chance anything that could possibly harm either you or your ladies."

Lucía thought for a moment and had an idea. "How about a church or monastery for shelter?"

"Not with Cathar heretics around. I would not trust a church or monastery, unless I knew that it was a true follower of Christ and not heretical. I had a conversation with our priest, and he agreed with me on this issue."

Gómez was interrupted by the soldier who came back from Pamplona.

"Captain, there is one room available at an inn in town. I had to pay for it in advance, as I did not want to risk losing it," said the soldier softly so as not to upset or panic the ladies who were too busy huddling, shivering, and talking among themselves to have overheard the conversation.

"Good work. However, there is one more thing I want you to do," said Gómez, who paused for a second. "Wait here. I will be back shortly."

Gómez disappeared for a couple of minutes and then came back with another soldier, who was soaked and whose garment was dripping water. Gómez turned to Lucía. "This is the plan. These two men will serve as your guards, but they will be dressed as pilgrims, and so will you and your ladies. Find old clothes, and change into them."

Gómez then turned to the two soldiers and said softly, "You are my best men whom I trust more than anyone else, as you have been with me for many years. I want both of you to accompany the ladies to the inn in Pamplona. Tell the innkeeper that you are pilgrims on the way to Santiago and you are thankful to have found shelter at his inn."

Gómez gave the soldier who had found the inn a purse to be used to pay for food, and then he turned to Lucía. "Lucía, these men will keep their swords hidden under their cloaks. I trust these men dearly and know they will behave as gentlemen. You are to go with them, and you and your ladies are to stay in your room at all times and not leave until I come for you. This is for your protection and the protection of your ladies. Do you understand?" asked Gómez sternly.

Lucía nodded. "Sí, I understand."

"Good, now advise the other ladies of our plan," said Gómez, who left the tent.

Within a couple of shivering hours, the ladies, led by Lucía and their escorts, left the tent in the blowing rain and mounted horses to take them to town, along with another disguised soldier to take the horses back to camp. The group galloped several miles through mud and deep pools of water. Before they entered Pamplona, they dismounted and walked across the stone bridge over the Arga River and took a longer walk through the city gates, up narrow and stone-covered streets, to the inn located in the middle of town.

When they entered the inn, the innkeeper, a fat man with dark eyes and balding head, laughed when he noticed the number of people in the party. "Eight people in such a small room—two men and six women. You are lucky men, señores!" he said to the guards.

"Well, as you can see, we are desperate to find shelter from such a nasty storm. It may take a day or two to dry out, so we may require the room for more than one night. I am willing to pay five maravedis more than I gave you earlier if you promise to deliver food for tonight and tomorrow to our room. Also, we don't wish to be disturbed. We have come a distance in foul weather, and the ladies need their sleep. Do you understand, señor?" said Lucía's escort in charge as the second escort looked on. Lucía and her ladies went to the fireplace to warm themselves.

Again the innkeeper laughed. "With this, señor, I will provide a banquet and give you my best room with a fireplace. However, I have never seen a traveler as wealthy as you."

"Let's say that I have been lucky in life," said the escort in charge as he glanced over to Lucía and her ladies by the fire and then turned his head back to the innkeeper.

With a sly laugh, the innkeeper responded, "I think I know what you mean, señor. Maybe I join you later, eh?"

"That will not be necessary. Just provide the food and wine, and I will be happy," said the escort, and he went to fetch Lucía and her ladies to follow the innkeeper up the open stairs to their room on the second floor.

As they entered their room, the ladies quickly gravitated to the fireplace. Lucía looked around. There was a table with two chairs in the middle of the room with two candelabras covered with wax, which had leaked out onto the table. To her left were two beds, each covered with a blanket and positioned straight ahead of the fireplace, along with a pile of wood. However, there was no rush matting on the wooden-plank floors.

The innkeeper remarked, "You see, señor? Just as I said, the best room in the house, complete with fireplace, firewood for the fire, and two beds. For two more maravedis, I will have someone bring you straw to sleep on."

The escort looked at Lucía, who nodded her head. He then reached into his purse on his belt and gave the innkeeper two more maravedis. The innkeeper looked at the ladies, shook his head, and gave another sly laugh as he left the room.

"I never thought that he would ever leave us alone," said the escort.

"You did well, señor, but where is the other escort?" asked Lucía as she and her ladies took off their wet cloaks.

"He is downstairs, sitting at a table, drinking a cup of wine, mi señora, in order to blend in as he watches who enters and who goes up the stairs."

"May I ask your name, señor, and the name of your confederate? I just hate to keep calling you my escort."

"Please, mi señora, I know that this may sound awkward, but our names are not important. We are your humble servants sworn to protect you to our deaths."

Lucía, with a puzzled look on her face, was interrupted by a knock on the door. Two servants entered, carrying two baskets full of straw for the room.

"Gracias," said the escort, and the maids left.

"Well, a little tight but warm. I will let you work out the sleeping arrangements," said the escort. Then he was again interrupted by two other servants, who brought in a wooden plate of cooked chicken accompanied by two large loaves of bread, a round of cheese, another smaller plate of grapes, and a large pitcher of wine and water, along with three cups, which was placed on the table.

"Will this be enough food to sustain you, mi señora, before I go?" asked the escort.

"More than enough, but where are you going?" asked Lucía with a worried look on her face.

"Not far. I can promise you, if needed, we will be here, mi señora," said the escort as he left the room.

"Where is he going?" asked Gabriella, who had been talking to the other ladies in front of the fire.

Lucía shrugged her shoulders. "He said if we needed them, they would be near. Outside of that, I don't know."

"Strange," added Constance.

"I imagine that he would feel or make us feel uncomfortable by staying in the room with us," said Gabriella.

"Maybe he is watching the room for anyone who tries to break in," uttered Geralla.

"Well, ladies, whatever the reason may be, it's time to eat and then go to bed. We will see what tomorrow brings," said Lucía as she started to cut the chicken. Gabriella poured the wine diluted with water, and the girls sat around the fire to enjoy the feast.

When it came time to retire for the evening, Lucía went over to the beds and pulled down the blankets on each. Then she started to laugh. "You will never believe what I am seeing!" said Lucía, who was standing between the two beds. Gabriella came over, followed by the other ladies, and saw to their abhorrence filthy straw mattresses with no pillows.

"Perhaps we should sleep on the straw tonight to avoid the fleas and other vermin that may be lurking in the mattresses," said Lucía. All the ladies agreed and presented no argument to the contrary, as they busily made one long bed of straw to sleep six.

Two days later the weather had turned warm and sunny. After all the items in camp had dried out, Gómez came and fetched Lucía and her ladies, and they started on their journey anew. Several miles outside Pamplona, Lucía opened the curtain to let in the fresh air and sunshine and saw a bishop who wore his bright-red garments on horseback, riding alongside a lady of prominence, who was also elegantly dressed, with an entourage of servants walking behind at a steady pace. They both took an interest in Lucía's retinue. The bishop gave his blessing while still riding on horseback, and Lucía and her company all crossed themselves.

A couple of days later, the entourage was slowly climbing higher into the mountains, and the flat plains and easy rolling brown hills were giving way to fast-flowing streams and steep rolling green hills, while a multitude of sheep grazed on the high pastureland.

Due to the rain and the flooding streams, the roads were turning very muddy in spots, which made the wagons hard to maneuver. As the entourage progressed slowly ever forward, the wagons started to become bogged down in mud until they became stuck and couldn't move any farther. Gómez, who made remarks that didn't bear repeating, ordered everyone out of the wagons. Lucía, her ladies, and servants slowly left their wagons, carrying the hem of their garments in their hands, and carefully plodded their way through the mud until they found more-solid ground on which to stand.

Gómez gave an order and left, and several soldiers dismounted and started to push the first wagon out of the mud. Lucía decided to help, followed by her ladies and servants. They slowly plodded their way back through the muck, which was well over Lucía's ankles, and started to push the wagon. The soldiers who had been pushed out of the way by the ladies were crowded to the side of the road and watched.

Gabriella was standing next to Lucía and saw her slip into the mud.

"Oooooh!" shouted Lucía as she fell head first into the muck. When she pulled herself up, she was covered from head to toe in mud. Gabriella started to laugh at Lucía's face, which showed her white eyes and white teeth under a cake of mud. Lucía started to push and slipped again, laughed at herself, and then looked at Gabriella.

"You look too clean," said Lucía, who continued to laugh. Then she threw mud on Gabriella's garment.

"Oooooh!" cried Gabriella, and she bent down, made a mud ball, and threw it at Lucía.

Suddenly, a mud fight began, with everyone laughing and throwing mud as the soldiers watched and enjoyed the spectacle.

Gómez, who had left the scene with a couple of soldiers to find a place to camp for the night, came back to find utter chaos. He dismounted and stood on the side of the road. At this time, Gabriella went to throw mud at Lucía, but she ducked, and the mud hit Gómez in the face.

Suddenly, the laughter stopped, and Lucía, whose back was turned away from Gómez, asked, "Why is everyone so quiet?"

"Perhaps it's because I have returned," said Gómez, who tried very hard to keep his composure. Lucía turned slowly and faced Gómez with a nervous smile and knew his anger was building.

"Doña Lucía Alvarado, a word, if you don't mind!" he shouted.

Lucía knew that she was in trouble when he said her last name. Then he turned to the soldiers, who stood on the side of the road, and barked, "You men, back to your duties!"

The ladies carefully plodded their way back to the side of the road, while the soldiers attempted to push the wagons out of the muck. Lucía, with the facial expression of a child who had done wrong and was awaiting punishment, walked over to Gómez on the side of the road and nervously asked, "You wanted a word with me?"

Gómez motioned for her to follow him deeper behind the tree line on the side of the road. "Lucía, King Philip is expecting us within a couple of fortnights. The rainstorm and your antics of today have put us behind schedule. Now exactly, what do you propose we do: keep His Highness waiting while you spend your time fooling around on this journey? I'm a military man, and with me, everything runs according to a plan and a schedule. I don't like being behind schedule if I can help it. I am responsible for you and your ladies, and I have to wonder sometimes what the intelligence level is among all of you."

Lucía squinted as she received the scolding, and when she thought it was over, it only continued.

"Now what have you got to say for yourself?" asked Gómez angrily.

Lucía thought for a moment and said softly with a nervous smile, "Not to fool around anymore and not to act childish?"

"Is that a question for me to respond to or a resolve by you to change your behavior?" Gómez asked angrily.

"Ah, I guess to resolve to be more mature," said Lucía with a nervous smile.

"Good answer," snapped Gómez. "Now I found a place to camp tonight about a mile or so up the road. Have your ladies ready as soon as the wagons are ready to go."

"Ah, I am afraid that we are going to have to clean up since we are all muddy and wish not to dirty the wagons. Is that all right?" Lucía meekly asked.

"You ladies are going to be the end of me yet, I swear, and no, it's not all right. More time wasted," barked Gómez. "I'm going to send the wagons ahead, which means that while we are making camp for the night, you and your ladies will have to walk and then clean up once you reach camp."

"But…but…but…," said Lucía.

"No buts. That's my order. Now obey it! And you had better start walking now before it gets dark," shouted Gómez, which caused Lucía to wince. With the scolding over, Gómez went back to join his men and move ahead. Lucía, her ladies, and her servants took to the rear and followed along on foot.

Once at camp, all the girls took baths. The two wooden tubs were taken from one of the supply carts and filled with heated water from the nearby river. One tub was placed in Lucía's tent and the other in the servants' tent.

The tent flaps were closed by a servant, who helped Lucía undress and to help her into the tub. Gabriella stood by to render additional assistance if necessary. "Thank the Blessed Virgin we did not forget to pack the linen liners for each of the tubs," said Lucía with a smile of delight, and her eyes closed. She slowly drifted down into the scented rose water and rested her head on the high back of the tub. Once the servant had assisted Lucía safely in the tub, she took Lucía's muddy garments and went to the river to wash them.

Lucía opened her eyes and looked at Gabriella. "Ah, this is so relaxing. I dare say I do not want to get out." Then Lucía laughed at Gabriella, who still stood by the tub. "You look like a mud doll standing there."

Gabriella said with a smile, "Maybe I should jump into the tub and muddy the water a bit."

Lucía was still laughing. "You wouldn't dare!"

Gabriella acted silly and pretended to climb in.

"No!" cried Lucía with a laugh. Suddenly, there was a voice at the entrance of the closed tent. "Who is there?" inquired Lucía.

"Who do you think?" asked Gómez, who was still angry about the earlier events of the day.

Lucía said with a nervous smile, "I'm bathing. Is there a problem?"

"How long is it going to take for everyone to bathe and clean up? I want to leave way before dawn tomorrow to make up for lost time."

"I promise we will hurry along as quickly as possible."

Gómez growled and shook his head. Then he turned and left to look after another matter.

"By the bones," said Lucía, and then she stopped herself before she went any further. "He is in an awful mood, I swear. I have never seen a man always in such a snit. He doesn't seem to enjoy anything. It is always duty, duty, duty."

Lucía then went into a deep voice and tried to imitate Gómez. "How long is it going to take for you ladies to bathe and clean up? I want to leave way before dawn tomorrow to make up for lost time." Both Lucía and Gabriella laughed at her imitation of the captain.

After a while, a servant was called and entered the tent to help Lucía dress into warm garments. Gabriella took her turn in the bath.

Within several hours, all the ladies and servants had bathed, and all the muddy garments had been cleaned.

It was still very dark as Lucía made sure that all the ladies and servants were ready to leave on time so as to not upset Gómez. As the entourage pushed on, the road was becoming somewhat steeper and rockier. When the cart hit a bump in the road, Lucía slid onto the floor in a fit of giggles.

"Are you all right, Lucía?" asked Gabriella, concerned.

Lucía continued to giggle and nodded. Another bump, and Lucía slid to the floor again. This time, both of them giggled. "It must be the silk garment that I am wearing," said Lucía, who giggled so hard she had a hard time vocalizing her words.

Suddenly, the wagon stopped to the screams of the servant girls. Lucía opened the curtain and looked back to see that the servants' wagon had a broken wheel. Gómez trotted over, dismounted from his horse, and studied the damage. The wagon wheel had split in two, which caused it lean to the left, and resulted with the ladies sliding on top of each other in complete disarray.

"Are you girls all right?" asked Gómez, who, with another soldier, helped them from the wagon on the very narrow road.

Lucía and Gabriella exited their wagon and squeezed their way between the wagon and the high green embankment next to them to assess the damage. The four girls were all right, except one girl who had a bloody arm, as she had fallen from the wagon and tried to brace herself.

"Let me take a look at that arm," said Lucía as the rest of the servant girls walked to the front of the contingent to get out of the way.

"Gabriella, I need the waterskin in our wagon."

As Gabriella went to fetch the waterskin, Lucía and the servant girl moved to join the others at the front of the contingent. Lucía carefully examined the arm and, to her relief, found it was not broken.

"Are you in pain?" asked Lucía. The girl shook her head and uttered a quiet no. Gabriella came with the waterskin, followed by the priest. Lucía asked him, "Padre, can you find the yarrow and maybe a couple of clean rags in the supply cart?"

The priest went immediately and, within a short time, returned with the requested items. Lucía gently moved back the torn part of the sleeve and gently washed away the blood and dirt from the wound with a clean rag; the servant girl winced. Fortunately, the wound was not very deep, and Lucía carefully sprinkled some ground-up yarrow on the wound and tied a clean rag around it to hold it in place.

"Gracias, mi señora," said the girl as she curtsied.

Since Lucía knew her parents from the village, she embraced her and said, "Your parents, I know, would be very proud of you." The servant girl smiled and joined the others, and Lucía squeezed her way back to where Gómez was discussing the broken wheel with a former wheelwright turned soldier.

Lucía observed how the solid wheel had splintered when it had hit a rock on the road and how the metal band around the wheel had become badly twisted and mangled.

The soldier studied the wheel. "This must have been an old wheel, Captain. Look, you can see that the wood on this part of the wheel that splintered had rotted away."

Fortunately, Gómez had the foresight to bring a couple of extra wheels on the journey. While most of the soldiers stood around, a couple of men climbed the steep embankment with axes to find a long branch strong enough to lift the wagon, while several others were hunting for rocks heavy enough and flat enough to build a fulcrum.

While the ladies waited, a couple of men doing penance came along and engaged in conversation with Lucía. The two men were dressed in sackcloth, had long stringy hair, and were covered from head toe in dirt. Both walked barefoot with only a staff to help them on their pilgrimage to Santiago to visit the tomb of St. James. They had come from England to Normandy and, from Normandy, followed the road to their current destination. Lucía could now practice her English, which she spoke so elegantly, without an accent, the two travelers thought they were speaking to a fellow countryman.

The conversation lasted for quite some time. The men talked about life in England, the trials on their journey, and the importance of Roncesvalles to refresh both body and spirit before continuing on one's travels. Lucía marveled at their spiritualism and strength of resolve to have traveled so far with black, blistered, and bleeding feet. At the end of the visit, Lucía called upon her priest to give the men his blessing, which they received gladly, and then she sent them on their way with a sack of bread and cheese to see them through.

Not long after the two pilgrims left, the wheel on the wagon was repaired, and the entourage was again on its journey. They were now on the road to Roncesvalles. The snow-covered mountains that dominated the horizon lay ahead, and the pastureland with its roaming sheep were about to be left behind.

Within several miles, they soon found themselves back in the forest. Gabriella gazed out the left side of the wagon and saw the road as it became steeper and narrower with deep ravines. Lucía opened her curtain and saw rushing water in a swollen stream many feet below that gave rise to a forested hill, which was steep and rocky.

As the narrow road climbed to a higher elevation, Lucía was focused on the scenery, determined not to miss anything that could possibly come into view: deer, wild goats, vultures, or perhaps a brown bear or wolves, which could all be lurking anywhere in the forest area either above or below.

They had finally reached the snowline and the winter snows, which had not yet melted. The snow became deeper and deeper as they continued to ascend the steep mountain pass until it almost, in some spots, covered the wheels of the wagon.

Suddenly, the clouds moved in, and the wind started to blow, and a mixture of snow and rain fell. Both Lucía and Gabriella were freezing in the wagon, as their heavy clothing was in a trunk somewhere in a supply cart. Neither thought that it would be as cold as it was for the springtime. Both Lucía and Gabriella's hands were freezing, and they both blew on them to try to warm them. Finally, both huddled together for the warmth, which had eluded them.

A cheer by the soldiers brought Lucía scurrying to open the curtain. "Gabriella, Roncesvalles!" cried Lucía, which sparked attention. From the opening in the curtain, they looked down the side of the mountain and, through the snow and the foggy outline of trees, saw a church and a monastery.

"Do you know what this means, Gabriella?" The two girls looked at each other in joy.

"Hopefully, a fire, food, and lodging," answered Gabriella with excitement.

"And for a couple of nights, not to have to sleep in a tent," they both said in unison with a giggle.

"My back could surely use a rest," said Lucía with a big smile as she sat up straight to stretch. "Maybe even the grouch might be able to relax and be less authoritative."

Gabriella giggled. "Do you really think he might?"

"I've known him my entire life and sadly no. He really needs a wife to look after him, but he will say"—Lucía deepened her voice and again tried to imitate Gómez—"I'm a military man and military men don't marry or have children."

Both girls laughed and were in a merry mood when they realized they would soon be at the monastery and lodging, feeling the warm breath of a fire.

Upon arrival at the monastery, which was nestled at the base of a steep tree-covered hill, they were met by a monk, who welcomed the ladies as they were slowly helped from their wagons by several soldiers. They picked their way carefully over the icy walkway to a building. When the ladies entered the building, they were immediately drawn to a warm, welcoming fire and joined several other pilgrims of different classes who were either going to or from Santiago. Lucía stayed behind and stood on the walkway along with Gabriella, as they shivered, admiring the beautiful view of the rain-and-snow mix that had changed to all snow and frosted the trees a thick coat of white.

As Lucía stood in the cold and shivered with her arms held to her chest to keep warm, she could not help but muse, while she viewed the wintry scene around her, that after a little more than a fortnight and a half, the contingent had safely arrived at the monastery of Roncesvalles, a well-known place of refuge for all weary travelers, whether healthy and well, rich or poor, sick or destitute, Jew or pagan. Whether they were on their way to or from Santiago, all were welcome. Best of all, they were only a day's journey from St.-Jean-Pied-de-Port on the other side of the Pyrenees and the beginning of the French road to Paris.

Lucía soon joined her ladies around the fire, and that night, they enjoyed a tasty stew and fresh bread while she chatted with several pilgrims who were all anxious to share their experiences on the road to Santiago. After two days of quiet reflection and prayer at the chapel and a warm meal and fire at night, Lucía made a point to see the abbot to make a contribution for his hospitality and for the furtherance of the good works of the monastery for all future pilgrims.

The contingent left Roncesvalles before dawn, on the third day of their stay, and continued their journey to St.-Jean-Pied-de-Port in the foothills of the Pyrenees. Despite being early April, it was windy and cold, with quite a bit of snowfall still on the ground, but it melted when the warm April sun touched a patch of unsuspecting snow. They crisscrossed mountain streams and small ravines filled with icy water that flowed from the mountains down the streams to the rivers below. When not watching or enjoying the alpine scenery, Lucía and Gabriella spent the time talking about a young handsome knight they met at the monastery.

Finally, just before nightfall, as both girls looked down from the mountain, they could see the village of St.-Jean-Pied-de-Port. They arrived in the early evening and made camp on the outskirts of town. Beyond St.-Jean-Pied-de-Port lay the green hilly countryside of Gascony and Aquitaine, the home of Lucía's grandmother, Queen Eleanor, whom she wanted nothing to do with, due to how she had treated her mother, a princess. She'd been erased from history by adoption, which, in Lucía's mind, in essence, was akin to throwing her away, unwanted and unloved. Lucía would always regard herself as a de Crécy, not a d'Anjou, which her aunt insisted she included in her name.

As the wagons rolled into Gascony, Lucía was excited to have the mountains behind them and the beautiful rolling hills of the Gascon countryside ahead of them. The weather had turned warm, and both Lucía and Gabriella opened their curtains to view the green hills and to let in the warm air, which felt good after the cold, damp air of the mountains. They passed small villages and saw several Roman ruins as they traveled along the base of the often barren and sometimes forested hillsides of the province.

Due to the good weather, they were able to make up for some of the lost time, which had occurred in the mountains, until they hit the outskirts of the town of Dax, where the contingent came to a halt.

"Why have we stopped?" asked Gabriella as she put down her book of poetry and looked over to Lucía for an answer.

"I don't know. It seems strange," responded Lucía. She put her book aside, opened a flap of the curtain, and peered out onto a large open stretch about a mile wide and a mile long, which divided a heavily wooded area and then made a sharp turn to the left and continued on from there.

"All I see is a large open field next to me, dividing the forest," said Lucía.

Gabriella responded as she peered out her side of the wagon, "And all I see are thick woods."

Captain Gómez came over to the wagon as Lucía again opened the flap. "It appears as if there will be a slight delay. We have hit an English road block, and they will not let us by until they are satisfied we are not carrying weapons for the Basque rebels, who are apparently around here somewhere."

"That's ridiculous!" cried Lucía. "Didn't you tell them we are a peaceful envoy to the French court, and who I am?"

"Of course, but we are going to have to wait anyways," said Gómez, disgusted due to losing more time.

"Well, do something!" snapped Lucía, who was becoming testy at the nature of the delay.

"What exactly would you have me do? Start a war?" responded Gómez.

"N-no! I mean… Never mind," exclaimed Lucía, and she shut her flap, angry at the inconvenience.

"Can you imagine, Gabriella, accusing us of being a supplier of weapons to a rebel group, all the while we are traveling under the coat of arms of Castile! Of all the…! Grrrrr." Lucía sat back in the middle of the bench with her arms folded as Gabriella looked on. As Lucía sat in the wagon and brooded, the flap was opened from the outside, which gave both girls a scare.

"Well, what do we have here?" asked an English soldier, who was dressed in chain mail on horseback and wore a red surcoat emblazoned with three yellow lions and a nasal helmet. Lucía recognized the coat of arms as that belonging to her aunt's family.

"I beg your pardon," said Lucía in perfect English.

The soldier, who was slightly cross-eyed, quickly responded, "Sorry, me ladies, but I have to check every wagon and cart." Then he shut the flap.

The expression on the soldier's face caused Lucía and Gabriella to laugh and giggle. They tried to control themselves, but the humor of the moment led to uncontrollable silliness, which was hard to stop, until they both found themselves laughing and giggling about nothing. Lucía developed the hiccups and tried to be serious, but every time she hiccupped, she laughed even harder.

"I have to stop." Lucía laughed. She ceased for several seconds but burst out again after she made a loud hiccup, and then she put her hand to her mouth. She tried to stop once more, but one look at Gabriella, who was also in the fit of the moment, caused another round of hysterics.

After having been stopped on the road for quite some time, Lucía said, still in a fit of laughter, "I guess that I shall have to do something, or we may be here indefinitely," she hiccupped as she put her hand to her mouth again. "But first I've got to stop laughing."

"Think of some sad event," suggested Gabriella, who tried to be serious but was still under the control of the relentless urge to giggle.

Lucía thought for a short time. Then she concentrated on the death of her mother and started to slowly recover from her fits with an idea. "I think I have a plan to get us out of here, Gabriella, but first, I need a wimple, which I dare say I dislike. But it will help me look more official and more mature. Now where did I pack it? I know I did because my aunt insisted on it."

"I believe I know where it is," said Gabriella. "I will be right back." Fortunately, the soldiers were too occupied in other matters to notice Gabriella as she left the wagon.

Lucía opened the flap of the curtain just enough to peek at Gabriella as she hastened a servant from the wagon next in line to accompany her to the cart that carried Lucía's wardrobe. Once at the cart, the servant very carefully opened the trunk and took out the cloth that would serve as a wimple and gave it to Gabriella, who quickly returned to the wagon.

Lucía sat sideways on the bench, and Gabriella sat in back of her and carefully tied her long hair into two buns on each side of her head. Then she tailored the white cloth around Lucía's visage until it covered her head, neck, chin, and the sides of her face. A head band of thin gold cord was placed around her forehead to help hold the wimple in place. The remaining cloth dropped down her back to complete her headwear.

"There, all done," said Gabriella as she moved back to the bench across from Lucía.

"Outside of looking like a nun, how do I look?" asked Lucía with a nervous smile.

"You look very official, and the white wimple, with your green garment, does make you look more mature," added Gabriella.

Lucía nodded her head with a smile.

"Are you ready to make your appearance?" inquired Gabriella.

"I think so. Gabriella, please say a prayer for me that this plan will work."

"I promise," said Gabriella as she smiled and watched Lucía leave the wagon.

Lucía left the wagon and walked to the front of the thirty soldiers, two abreast, who were the front line of her entourage. There, she saw Captain Gómez talking to the English soldier who was in command. All attention now turned to Lucía as she walked up to the men. Gómez did a double take when he realized this was Lucía, who was acting very differently than the young girl he knew.

Lucía walked directly in front of the commander of the English soldiers in a very mature manner, which pushed Gómez out of the way. He stood back in complete surprise and disbelief at Lucía's change in dress and behavior.

"Is there a problem, señor? Why have we been stranded here for such a long time? I am the Condesa of Segoia, niece to your King Richard and to King Alfonso, the King of Castile. I am headed to Paris, where King Philip is expecting me within a fortnight, and if I don't make it in time, there will be a search and questions, and I am sure that you will not want to be responsible for my delay. I know that it will not go well with King Philip or King Alfonso, never mind King Richard, who will not take kindly to the fact that his niece was treated as a common criminal at the hands of his own men. Now I demand that we be allowed to leave immediately, or I will take this as an act of war, and any bloodshed will be on your head," shouted Lucía to the commander.

"My lady, I meant no harm, but—" said the commander, who was interrupted in midsentence by Gómez.

"Will you excuse us, señor?" said Gómez, who now felt he had to intervene before Lucía started a real battle. He took Lucía's arm, and both scuffled off into the field away from curious ears to have a talk with his overzealous charge.

"What do you think you are doing?" asked Gómez, upset at Lucía's sudden involvement in the situation at hand.

"Doing something! More than what you are doing to get us out of here," said Lucía angrily.

"Now you listen to me," said Gómez, peeved at Lucía's interference. "The commander has sent word concerning this situation to the earl in charge of this area. We should be free to go shortly. I don't need you barging in with threats of warfare. Now go back to your wagon, and stay there until I tell you otherwise. Is that clear!"

"But—"

"No buts! Do what I tell you to do! Do you understand!"

Suddenly, in the distance, a faint cry was heard, and coming around the bend with an escort of eight soldiers was the earl, who waved his hands and shouted, "Let them go! Let them go!" They galloped at such a speed that when the horses stopped, they slid on the grassy area of the field in front of Lucía and Gómez.

"My profound apologies," said the earl as he dismounted and tried to catch his breath. "I am the Earl of Woolsey, the garrison commander for the area. I have just received correspondence from Queen Leonor that your entourage would be coming through here. I have been away, and when the correspondence originally arrived, it was put in a place that I just discovered. Please except my apologies.

"In order for you to proceed without any further delay, I will send a soldier ahead to alert the other garrisons along the way to have a path cleared for you to speed along through Bordeaux and Portiers as well as provide you with an escort to the French border. I would also consider it an honor for you to take supper with me and my court and to lodge at the garrison," said the earl, who presented himself in a kind manner.

Lucía responded to the earl's kind gesture in perfect English with a smile, "Gracias for your kind invitation, señor, but we must be going, as to not to cause any further delay."

"I understand. Perhaps another time then," replied the earl. The earl then arranged for an escort with four soldiers in the front and two at the rear of the contingent and waited for them to leave before he returned to his garrison.

After several hours of waiting, the contingent finally advanced forward and, over the next week, sped through the cities, towns, and villages of the warm Aquitanian countryside. In each case, armed guards on either side of the road held back people and commerce until the contingent passed.

They sped through Bordeaux and Poitiers and, a little more than a fortnight later, reached the French domain. Outside Orléans, the contingent was met by an escort of twelve French knights. Lucía thought the young French knights were dashing dressed in their chain mail covered with a blue surcoat emblazoned with the gold fleur-de-lis of the French court. Lucía was now only a little more than two days from Paris.

Chapter XXII

"Gabriella, I see Paris!" shouted Lucía in excitement as she peered out the curtain and marveled at the massive outside walls and towers of the city. The contingent was following the French knights, and they entered the city through the Left Bank.

As they continued their journey to the Palais de La Cite, the royal residence, Lucía opened the flap on her curtain and carefully eyed a group of handsome young students attending one of the several schools of learning that composed the University of Paris who were actively engaged in conversation.

Most likely these are theology students discussing some boring discourse on current dogma or some other philosophical debate, Lucía thought to herself.

Lucía had remembered that Father Baldwin had had told her about the schools of learning in Paris, located on the Left Bank, in one of his stories about his travels. As they traveled deeper into the city, Lucía and Gabriella enjoyed the sights and sounds of the one of the busiest cities in Europe.

The entourage traveled over a bridge between the Left Bank and the Ile-de-Cite, the island in the Seine where the royal palace was located. Lucía could hear the clip-clop of the horse's hooves on the stone pavement as they entered the palace grounds, where they stopped and were met by Queen Agnes, who was surrounded by her attendants and four royal guards, all in uniform with blue surcoats emblazoned with gold fleur-de-lis over their chain mail and nasal helmets. Each guard carried a spear and was fully armed.

With Gómez's help, Lucía, Gabriella, and her ladies-in-waiting disembarked from their wagons and found themselves in front of the queen. Lucía and her ladies all made a deep curtsy.

"Welcome to Paris," said Queen Agnes. She went over to Lucía, helped her rise from her curtsy, and kissed her on both cheeks to welcome her.

"Merci, Your Highness," said Lucía as she curtsied again.

"All of you, please rise," said the queen with a welcoming smile.

As Lucía rose from her curtsy, she took a good look at the queen and noticed, despite her wimple, she was indeed beautiful with a kind face and engaging smile.

"If Your Highness would not mind, I would like to introduce you to my ladies."

"Of course, I would love to meet them," said the queen.

As she introduced each of her ladies, each of them curtsied. "And finally this is my guardian, Captain Gómez."

"Your Highness," replied Captain Gómez. Queen Agnes put out her hand, and with a bow, Gómez kissed it.

"I do hope that your long journey here was a pleasant one?" asked the queen.

"As well as can be expected, but it did have its perils," said Lucía.

"I don't doubt. You will have to tell me later all about your journey and your wonderful country of Castile."

"I shall look forward to it," replied Lucía.

"Now you should get your rest after your long journey. Tomorrow, we are going to have a banquet in your honor. Unfortunately, the king could not be here to greet you personally, as he was called away on an affair of state. He wanted me to convey his apologies. He wanted me to make sure that you were well taken care of and had the opportunity for rest. He will be back later tonight for tomorrow's banquet and will meet you then. And now if you follow me, I will show you to your quarters."

Lucía looked toward Gómez. "Go ahead, Lucía. I'll join you later as soon as I set up camp outside the city."

With a smile, Lucía followed the queen and her attendants up the ceremonial staircase to the inside of the palace, up three flights of stairs, and to the several rooms on that floor: one room for Lucía and Gabriella and one room for her ladies. Her servants would share the great hall at night with the other palace servants. Almost immediately, household attendants delivered trunks and other sundry items from the courtyard to her room.

"I shall leave you now to give you the opportunity to get settled and rest. My servants will be available to see to whatever needs that you might have. Also, I shall have supper sent to both rooms."

"Merci for your welcome and hospitality, Your Highness," responded Lucía as she and Gabriella made a final curtsy.

With a smile, the queen left, and a royal guard closed the door behind her.

Excited, Lucía explored her elegant room. It was quite large and contained a canopied platform bed with two tall braziers, which stood at either side of the bed for additional warmth. In the middle of the room was a table covered with a dark-blue cloth with two candelabras and four chairs. A beautiful tapestry with a hunting scene covered the walls from floor to ceiling. A red Arabic carpet with deep blues, browns, and yellows, which conveyed a geometric theme, covered the stone floor. A candelabra hung down from the ceiling, and a fireplace with plenty of wood was in the center wall.

Lucía was happy to finally be in Paris, and she opened the window shutters and looked down on the courtyard below and parts of the city in the distance. She only wished Isabella could have been there to share this experience with her; she then remembered to write a letter to Isabella about her journey, before she retired.

The next morning, Lucía and Gabriella were awakened by the ladies, with Constance in the lead, followed by several servants who brought in a light breakfast: a small loaf of bread, a small round of cheese, and a pitcher of warm mulled wine. The shutters were opened, offering a view of a spectacular sunrise, which was seen as a good omen. The ladies helped both Lucía and Gabriella dress for the morning.

Once they were dressed, there was a knock at the door. It was a palace servant who came into the room and, with a deep curtsy, said, "Her Highness has sent me to ask Doña Lucía and her ladies-in-waiting if they would like to join her in prayer in the oratory."

Lucía, honored to be asked by the Queen of France to join her in prayer, graciously accepted. The servant waited as Beatrix busily wrapped Lucía's long hair into side buns to fit her white wimple, which would contrast very well with her red garment and make her appear more mature. When the final touches were done, Lucía looked into the mirror on a side table to make sure that no lock of hair was out of place. When she was satisfied with her appearance, Adele fastened the wimple to her head and added a gold cord to hold it in place.

Lucía turned to Adele with an impish smile. "Well, do I look presentable?"

"Très bien," responded Adele.

As Lucía and her ladies followed the servant to the oratory in the palace, several servants remained behind to lay out Lucía's wardrobe for the banquet. Once at the oratory, Lucía blessed herself with holy water from the font before entering the chapel. As she entered the small chapel, she saw the queen dressed in a white garment and wimple, kneeling in prayer along with two attendants who were praying behind her. The servant escorted the ladies to the benches behind the queen and Lucía next to the queen.

After a time of quiet prayer and reflection, the queen, joined by Lucía, sat upon the bench while the ladies and the queen's attendants were escorted out of the chapel. A quiet conversation ensued.

"How was your evening?" asked the queen with her engaging smile.

"It went well, as I feel well-rested from my journey. I especially enjoyed the bed and found it to be comfortable and warm as opposed to the tent and the cold air of the outdoors, which I had become accustomed to," said Lucía with her own engaging smile.

"Unfortunately, my husband returned late last night and was anxious to know all about your arrival, the rooms in the palace where you are staying, and your treatment upon arrival, and sundry other questions. I swear he kept me up half the night," the queen said with a slight laugh. "I finally had to tell him to stop the chatter, as I needed my rest."

"Did he?" asked Lucía.

"Well," replied the queen with modest laughter.

Lucía was impressed with how easy Queen Agnes was to talk to and yet carried herself with modesty and grace.

"Now, I must get ready for the banquet," said the queen to Lucía.

"So too must I," replied Lucía, and they both rose from the bench and left the chapel. The servant had waited for Lucía outside the door of the chapel and escorted her back to her room.

When Lucía entered her room, a wooden tub with a linen liner was waiting for her. Lucía quickly undressed behind a screen and stepped into the tub with the assistance of Gabriella. Lucía eased down into the tub of rose water; lavender petals were sprinkled on top.

She looked at Gabriella. "How I wish I could stay and rest here all day in this heavenly bath."

"Well, you won't get much sympathy from me," added Gabriella, busy obtaining Lucía's garments from which she could choose which one to wear to the banquet. After a while, Gabriella said, "Time to get out and get dressed."

"Well, if I must," responded Lucía, and she stepped out of the bath and dried off with a piece of linen.

As Lucía was helped into a short-sleeved undergarment, Constance held up a yellow garment. "Is this to your liking, mi señora?"

"Hmm, let me see the white garment and the brown one."

Beatrix brought in the white garment, while Geralla brought in the brown one. Meanwhile, Adele was busy laying out all Lucía's jewelry.

Lucía made the mistake of asking her ladies what they thought she should wear to the banquet; it provoked a lively discussion as Lucía stood in the middle of the room with only an undergarment. After a while, a consensus was reached, and the ladies all agreed that the new yellow bliaut with red trim around the low neckline, the hem, and the end of the long sleeves the best choice. A red ring belt, red slippers, and yellow wimple with a red headband topped off her accessories. Next, Adele laid out Lucía's jewelry on the bed for her to choose. Lucía chose the necklace of four large rubies fashioned between two gold chains, which had belonged to her mother.

Once the wardrobe had been picked out, Lucía sat in the chair at the dressing table in front of the mirror with only her short-sleeved undergarment on as Beatrix combed Lucía's hair until it was silky smooth. Beatrix next made two perfect side buns, first wrapping a braid around her forehead. Once her hair was complete, Gabriella and Constance helped her dress.

Once dressed, Lucía stood in front of the mirror on the dressing table, bent down, and started to preen her hair. After several minutes of constant preening, she turned to her ladies and servants and said with a nervous smile, "How do I look?"

Everyone commented on how beautiful and elegant she looked. "You'll be the talk of Paris," said Constance. After she was satisfied with her appearance, Adele did the final honors by fixing Lucía's wimple to her head.

"Oh, before I forget," said Lucía. She hurried to the table in the middle of the room and gave a sealed letter to Gabriella. "Please make sure this letter to Isabella is delivered to a messenger before day's end."

"Of course," said Gabriella with a smile of approval.

Lucía then stood in the middle of the floor by the table and waved her arms in the air. "Well, I guess this is it."

Her ladies and servants all gathered around her to wish her luck, and Lucía thanked them for their assistance on such an auspicious occasion. With a combination of both nerves and excitement, Lucía's thoughts suddenly turned to Isabella as she waited to be escorted to the great hall. Lucía was definitely concerned for her friend and how she was being treated by her uncle. Lucía loved Isabella as a sister, and to think she was being mistreated was heart breaking.

A loud knock on the door awakened Lucía from her thoughts. Gabriella opened the door, and there stood Gómez and a handsome court page. They would serve as her escort, along with four Castilian soldiers, to meet the king and the French royal court. It was now time to walk to the great hall. Lucía wrung her hands in nervousness.

"Are you ready, Lucía?" asked Gómez, whose eyes lit up to see the mature, very attractive young woman who stood before him.

Lucía nodded with a nervous smile.

"You'll be fine, and by your appearance, you will definitely dazzle the royal court," added Gómez. "And remember, I will be by your side."

Gabriella, the ladies, and the servants all curtsied as Lucía left the room. In the hallway were the four Castilian soldiers, who stood at attention, armed with spears. Each spear carried a red pennant emblazoned with a yellow castle, the coat of arms of Castile. With the page in front, Lucía and her party walked to the great hall.

"I find it remarkable, Lucía, how you can act like a child one day and a mature woman of high rank the next," said Gómez with a smile as they walked along the hallway.

"And how you can be a grouch one day and acceptable the next," added Lucía with a sly smile as she turned to her escort neatly dressed in his armor.

Her remark prompted a slight laugh and big smile from Gómez.

"Your father would be very proud of you."

"I hope so," added Lucía. They continued down the stairs and the long walk to the great hall with the court page in the lead.

"Are the gifts ready to be presented?" asked Lucía with concern.

"Sí. Don't worry, Lucía. All has been taken care of. The court will be in complete awe."

Upon arrival at the great hall, Luca and Gómez waited to be announced, as the king was still conducting business with the royal court. Lucía waited patiently by the door and leaned against the wall. Although she could not see, Lucía could hear the king speaking on some affair of state.

After a while, which seemed an eternity to Lucía, a herald came and told her she was about to be announced; Lucía gulped.

Then the trumpeters blew their horns, and the herald announced, "I present to Your Royal Highnesses and to the royal court in session this day an ambassador from the royal court of Castile, Doña Lucía María Margarita Diega Alvarado de Crécy de Anjou, Duchess of Pomeroi, Condesa of Segoia, and Countess of Bickford."

Lucía, escorted by Gómez and his four soldiers, walked along the carpeted aisle toward the dais, where Lucía caught sight of both King Philip and Queen Agnes, seated on their thrones, each wearing a gold crown. Lucía walked between the many courtiers and nobles of the royal court who stood on both sides of the aisle and studied her carefully as she passed by.

Lucía now stood before the king and queen and, with a deep curtsy, said, "Your Highnesses, merci for your warm welcome and hospitality upon our arrival by the queen. I bring greetings from King Alfonso and Queen Leonor of Castile and to the friendly relations between our two countries. As a token of friendship, I bring gifts. The first gift is three barrels filled with wine from my vineyard in Segoia."

At the given signal, a servant pushed the three barrels of wine down the aisle in front of the king, at which time he walked down from the dais and inspected them.

"The second gift is to Her Highness, the queen."

Upon a given signal, another servant brought in a jewelry box carved from bone and ivory with a geometric theme in bas relief; it was from Cordoba and was filled with jewels. Lucía handed the box to the queen with a deep curtsy. The queen, in turn, admired the craftsmanship of the item, opened the box, and lifted it high for all to see its contents: necklaces and broaches made from gold and silver, each embedded with diamonds, emeralds, and rubies, to the amazement of the court, which could be heard throughout the hall.

"The third gift is to His Highness, the king," cried Lucía loudly for all to hear.

This time, the stable keeper brought in three white Arabian stallions and another servant, a new sword crafted from Spanish steel. It had a cross guard made from solid gold with three dark-blue emeralds embedded deep within it, as well as a solid gold pommel with another dark-blue emerald in its center. Again, Lucía could hear the loud cry of amazement from everyone throughout the hall.

The king patted the three stallions after a close look at the animals and greatly admired the sword, which he swung around a couple of times to get the feel of it. He then looked at the court and said loudly with great appreciation, "If these gifts are any example of the friendship between France and Castile, then it should be a long-lasting one."

This brought about a loud expression of agreement by the court, followed by a loud round of applause, which echoed throughout the hall.

King Philip handed the sword to an attendant. "Take this to my chambers and make sure armed guards are placed by the door. I do not want anything to happen to this valuable token of friendship."

King Philip then turned to Lucía and said loudly to the court, "And now my gift to you, our lovely young ambassador from the royal court of Castile, who has traveled so far to visit us." He then turned and motioned to an attendant who stood by the bottom step of the dais.

The attendant carried a blue pillow, which contained a double silver chain necklace, and in between the silver chains were three gold fleurs-de-lis with a dark-blue emerald in the middle of each fleur. He took the necklace from the pillow and tied it around Lucía's neck and whispered, "A beautiful necklace for a beautiful lady."

"It's so beautiful. Merci, Your Highness," said Lucía as she turned to the king and curtsied. Lucía now saw close up how the years had taken away some of the king's former handsomeness, which was apparent due to his tall stature and still-comely but aging appearance. However, the balding head and lameness told another tale of the troublesome illnesses he suffered while on crusade.

"My lady, would you do us the honor of sitting with us here on the dais?" asked the king.

"Merci, I would be delighted, Your Highness."

King Philip took Lucía's hand and escorted her up the steep three steps of the dais and had her sit in a chair between his throne to her right and Queen Agnes's throne to her left. The king was very gentle with Lucía.

As she sat in a high-back chair, she looked down at Gómez, who was standing to the side, in front of the dais, along with her four-soldier escort. He nodded his approval with a comforting smile.

From her vantage point on the dais, Lucía saw the royal court conversing among themselves as the finishing touches of the banquet was being prepared in the next room. Lucía reasoned that the room she was in was a large anteroom of the great hall next door and not the great hall itself. So much was happening so quickly she had no time to put things in perspective.

Lucía was quietly studying the assemblage before her when her concentration was interrupted by Queen Agnes, who wanted to know more about Segoia and Castile. Lucía told her about her city, including the size and population of her demesne and of her several-hundred-year-old family vineyards. Lucía quickly glanced over to the king to see if he had been listening to the conversation, but he had an aloof expression on his face, deep in thought with a distant look.

Suddenly, the king awakened from his thoughts and interrupted Lucía, who was engaged in conversation with the queen, "Did you know your grandmother sat in the very spot where the queen is now sitting?"

Lucía was surprised by such an unexpected question. "No, I did not know. It must have been a long time ago."

This brought up another matter close to Lucía's heart concerning her mother. "Did you know my mother?" asked Lucía.

King Philip smiled gently, sat back in his chair, and turned to Lucía. "I was very young then. I remember seeing her at court on several occasions. She, like you, was very attractive and loved to engage in conversation even at such a young age. Then one day, she was whisked away to Castile and married your father. I never saw her again. Unfortunately, I never had the pleasure to have met your father, and I am truly sorry to hear of his demise."

The conversation was suddenly interrupted by a herald, who came to advise the court that the banquet was ready to begin. Lucía noticed how everyone rushed out the door with apparently ravenous appetites.

"I guess we should go before the food is completely gone," said the king to Lucía with his usual sense of humor.

The king and queen came down from the dais. "Since you are the honored guest, we would like you to join us on the dais, along with your captain," said Queen Agnes.

To everyone's surprise, protocol was changed, and King Philip did the honor of escorting Lucía to the great hall, and Captain Gómez, to his shock, was asked to escort the queen. Lucía could not help but look behind her and, with a slight giggle, saw Gómez with the queen, who fired all sorts of questions at the poor captain.

"Once in a while, I like to completely surprise my royal court by doing the completely unexpected," whispered King Philip to Lucía with a mischievous look.

Once everyone had been seated, King Philip stood up from his throne on the dais, looked at Lucía seated next to him, again welcomed her to his court as an ambassador of goodwill, and proclaimed the banquet to be in her honor. After the king's speech, there was a loud round of applause. When the king sat down, the Bishop of Paris arose and gave the blessing. After a long-winded litany by the bishop, out came the servers, and the banquet began at full haste.

During the banquet, Lucía noticed how taciturn King Philip was and how unkempt his dress was, but he did love to eat and drink. He never missed an opportunity to fill his plate or to leave a drop of wine untouched. He was mainly aloof and engrossed with his servings, and most of the conversation was with Queen Agnes.

"You'll have to forgive the king. He doesn't usually say much, unless he wants something, and then he tends to be very vocal," said the queen quietly to Lucía. However, Lucía did notice that the king was conversing with Gómez concerning the ongoing war with the Moors in Spain. Lucía even had the queen engrossed as she relayed her story of her near demise at the hands of the Moors when she had picnicked with Mafalda.

After King Philip finished his conversation with Gómez, he turned his attention to Lucía. She was busy eating a tart, but she managed to gulp it down quickly in order to speak with the king. "I must apologized, my lady. I thought your escort for the remainder of your time in France would be here by now. I had sent him on a mission a fortnight ago and expected him back by this time. I will introduce him to you as soon as he arrives. He will be in charge of your safety and well-being while you are in France and will ably guide you to Pomeroi," said the king, who motioned to the steward for more wine.

"By the way, your wine is excellent," added the king as he drained his cup and asked for more. "I did notice, however, that you don't drink wine. Curious—a winemaker who doesn't drink wine," said Philip with a smile, on the brink of feeling no pain.

"I do, on occasion, drink, but it has to be diluted with water, or I get sick."

Suddenly, the conversation was interrupted by the bishop. "Maybe the duchess can tell us if the heresy of Catharism has reached Castile."

Lucía was about to enter the dangerous ground of a topic hot with controversy and intermixed with political and military overtones. She realized her response had to be decisive so as not to be drawn into the controversial issue any further. "No, it has not. Besides, we are busy fighting our own war with the Moors. We are the vanguard of Europe. Many lives, señor, have been lost in Spain in the pursuit of preventing the Moors of furthering their reach into the continent, with little or no help from the north."

The king decided to change the subject and did so quickly, in a rage of temper that brought all conversation in the hall to a halt. He stood up from his throne, looked at the bishop and shouted, "This topic will not be discussed any further at this table, not now and not ever! I want to enjoy a meal, especially with guests, without being entangled in a discussion of the heresy of Catharism. Perhaps, dear bishop, instead of getting our invited guest involved in this issue, you should invite Doña Lucía and her escort to see the construction of the new cathedral before she leaves Paris."

The bishop, looking down at the table, cleared his throat and responded, "Oui, by all means. You and your escort are invited to visit anytime you wish."

Lucía, still in shock at the outburst by the king, looked over to the bishop and nodded in gratitude.

The king, embarrassed by his behavior, turned to Lucía. "Please forgive my outburst, but I grow weary of this discussion."

"Of course," responded Lucía with a polite smile.

The rest of the banquet was more relaxed: eating delightful desserts of various pastries, tarts, sweet cakes, and dried fruits and listening to the court musicians play with an occasional song from a troubadour. By the time the final course of various aged cheeses arrived, Lucía could not eat another morsel.

Chapter XXIII

The banquet had lasted all day into the evening, and when it was over, Lucía had successfully engaged in conversation with many of the nobles of the realm who were quite taken with the young condesa. Captain Gómez, who had also been engaged in a long conversation with both the bishop and king, excused himself to tend to his men.

After everyone had left the banquet, the king lingered on in a conversation with Lucía in which he both marveled and was enchanted with her young beauty and her intellect. This was unusual for an impatient king of very few words.

Finally, the escort arrived while Lucía and King Philip were engaged in conversation. Lucía's back was turned away from the main entrance to the great hall and did not see the escort when he entered.

"Ah, I see your escort has arrived," said the king. Lucía turned around slowly with a smile to greet him, but before the king had a chance to say his name, Lucía's expression changed, as they both recognized each other.

They said in unison, "You!"

A surprised look appeared on King Philip's face. "You two know each other?"

Lucía's escort was Sir Guillaume. With a sly smile, he said, "You might say that I know more about her than—"

Sir Guillaume's comment was immediately interrupted by a yawn from Lucía, who attempted to conceal her anger at the appearance of this buffoon, now going to be her guide and essentially her guardian while in France.

"Excuse me, Your Highness. If I may ask your leave, as it has been a long day. I fear I am falling asleep."

"Of course, my dear," said the king, surprised and confused at the event that had just unfolded.

Lucía made a deep curtsy and completely avoided Sir Guillaume as she quickly walked from the hall with great celerity. Sir Guillaume stood beside the king and was surprised at the fleet of foot in which his new charge had left in such a hurry.

The king turned to Sir Guillaume. "It must be your effect on the young ladies." The king then cleared his throat and motioned with his head to go after her.

Sir Guillaume responded, "Of course, right away, Sire." He quickly left, to the laughter of the king.

Sir Guillaume, giving chase, called out to Lucía, "Hold on. Why are you walking so fast?"

"Why are you walking so slow?" responded Lucía angrily.

Sir Guillaume was about to catch up to her when she stopped so suddenly he almost ran into her. "You clumsy oaf!" exclaimed Lucía, and she took her hand and slapped his face once on the left cheek and again on the right cheek.

"Hmm, I feel much better. Hmm, much better," uttered Lucía, and she moved on.

"What was that for?" yelled Sir Guillaume, who held his hand on his right cheek.

Lucía quickly picked up the pace. "You're neither a knight nor a gentleman. To think you were going to tell the king of seeing me naked on that most unpleasant day I shall never forget," voiced Lucía loudly, waving her hands around angrily.

Lucía picked up the hem of her bliaut and quickly started up the narrow winding staircase with Sir Guillaume close at hand as he tried to catch up to her, but he was becoming winded at such a fast pace.

"I have to ask you a question."

Lucía ignored her escort. She opened the door to her room and went to shut it, only to find a foot in the door.

"I demand that you move your foot immediately, or I shall take it off."

"I only need to ask as to what time to fetch you in the morning for the tour of the city."

Lucía was determined to continue to ignore him until she gazed into his eyes and felt the same peculiar feeling she had felt when they had first met. She began to stutter, "I need for you to…to…to leave! Now!" she shouted as she kept pushing the door back and forth on Sir Guillaume's foot.

"You're going to take my foot off if you continue slamming the door against my foot."

"A lady's prerogative," responded Lucía angrily.

"I will leave as soon as you tell me what time to fetch you in the morning. Just tell me what time. That's all I ask."

"At dawn!" screamed Lucía, who became both weary and confused by her emotions.

With his question answered, Sir Guillaume pulled his sore foot out of the heavy oak door just as it slammed shut, and he hobbled back with a limp to the king in the great hall, holding his jaw.

The king, who had been talking to his chef, turned around to see his most trusted knight in such bad shape. "What happened to you?"

"I just had a conversation with your honored guest."

The king laughed and said, "That must have been some conversation. Tell me, Sir Guillaume, did you speak with her with your mouth or with your hands?"

"Oh, that is very funny, Sire," said Sir Guillaume, still miffed at the encounter. He squinted in pain when he moved his foot.

"Sir Guillaume, would you mind walking with me to my chambers?"

"Of course not, Sire."

While they walked together, King Philip asked, "I am curious Sir Guillaume, how you and the Doña Lucía met?"

Sir Guillaume relayed the story about his misfortune aboard the pirate ship and his travels through al-Andulus, but when he told the king what had happened at the lagoon, the king let out such a laugh that all of Paris had to have heard it.

The door slammed shut, and Lucía, red with anger, gazed at Gabriella seated at the table in the room.

"What happened?" inquired Gabriella, surprised to see Lucía so upset.

"Do you have any idea who our escort is?"

"No, should I?" she asked as she put down her book of poetry on the table, rose from her chair, and turned to Lucía, who still stood in the doorway.

"Remember the young knight from the lagoon I told you about?"

With a laugh, Gabriella remarked, "You don't mean…?"

"Sí," shouted Lucía. "Grrrrr! Of all the true knights in France who followed the code of chivalry, I have to be escorted by an impertinent, rude, egotistical, and obnoxious buffoon! Grrrrr!"

"That might have been the knight who came to the door earlier."

"Did he have blondish hair cut short, blue eyes, clean shaven, and tall?" asked Lucía, who was slow and deliberate in her description of Sir Guillaume.

"Sí. That's him. He was looking for you. I told him you were probably still in the great hall. I thought him to be very handsome," said Gabriella. "Furthermore, I can tell, despite your ranting, you're fond of him."

Lucía still angry. "How can you say such a thing, Gabriella?"

"I could see it in your eyes and the way you looked at him. I may have been reading a book of poetry, but the real poetry was what I witnessed at the door just now."

"That's utter nonsense!" responded Lucía.

"We'll see if it's nonsense or not," said Gabriella with a smile.

The next morning, Sir Guillaume took a deep breath, not knowing quite what to expect, and knocked on Lucía's door. Gabriella answered the door and saw Sir Guillaume standing there a little befuddled.

"I have come for your lady to escort her around Paris."

Gabriella, with a giggle, replied, "Mi señora is getting dressed and will be out shortly." And she shut the door. Sir Guillaume waited outside the door and started to pace back and forth.

"How do I look?" asked Lucía to her ladies, who had helped her pick out her clothes.

They all agreed she was absolutely beautiful and, once again, would be the talk of Paris. However, Lucía's vanity got the best of her again, as she primed her hair and looked at herself in the mirror to make sure that every hair was in place. Lucía wore a dark-blue garment with tight sleeves, a brown leather ring belt, and brown boots. Beatrix had fixed her hair with two large buns on either side of her head. Finally, after much priming, a white wimple with a gold circle was placed on top of her head to keep her hair in place.

When Lucía was ready, she looked at her ladies and asked, "Are you ready for a tour of Paris and shopping?"

The ladies were excited, and they nodded their heads in agreement. Then all started for the door at once. Since much time had passed that Sir Guillaume had inquired as to Lucía's readiness, he once again approached the door and was about to knock when the door suddenly opened, and out ran the ladies, chattering all the while.

They were so excited about the day's events in Paris that they paid no mind to Sir Guillaume, knocked him to the stone floor of the hallway, and quickly walked to the palace entrance to board their wagons and begin their tour and their shopping expedition.

The last to come out of the room were Lucía and Gabriella, who noticed Sir Guillaume lying on the stone floor. "What are you doing down there, Sir Guillaume?" asked Lucía.

Sir Guillaume shook his head and slowly stood up. "I was trampled by your ladies."

"Really, Sir Guillaume? A brave knight like you overcome by young ladies who all together probably weigh less than you do? Hmm!"

"Well, it was unexpected," said Sir Guillaume, who tried to plead his case.

"Shall we get on with it, Sir Guillaume? The day is growing shorter."

The ladies, already in their transports, waited patiently for both Lucía and Gabriella to arrive, along with six French soldiers assigned to protect their safety. Once they arrived, Sir Guillaume helped both Lucía and Gabriella into the wagon and then, after giving instruction to the driver, joined them. They were finally underway. Sir Guillaume sat on the bench across from Lucía and Gabriella and explained the sights as they moved on.

Sir Guillaume pushed the curtain of the transport aside and pointed out the new cathedral of Notre Dame, across from the palace, which was under construction. As they approached, Lucía could see the magnificence of the structure, although the cathedral was far from being completed. Construction workers were busily working on different sections of the cathedral, and the two wagons pulled up in front of it.

They were greeted by the Bishop of Paris, who gave a tour to Lucía and her ladies. The bishop pointed out, before they entered the completed part of the church, what the massive layout of the church would look like once the building was completed. Once inside, they viewed the apse, the choir, and the high altar, which were all completed. The nave and transepts were under construction.

Once the tour ended, the bishop gave his blessing, and the others left. Lucía stayed for a while in the choir and said a prayer for her mother, father, and Isabella. She then sat for several minutes and reflected in silence on what a magnificent tribute to the Blessed Holy Mother this cathedral would be when finally completed.

When Lucía left the cathedral, she noticed her ladies had already moved on to the Right Bank to shop under the protection of several French soldiers who had accompanied them. Since Lucía had already seen the Left Bank when she entered the city, she was interested in shopping, but Sir Guillaume insisted that there was more to see in the city. Lucía and Gabriella continued with the tour.

After another hour, Lucía and Gabriella had become bored with Sir Guillaume's historical babble. "Sir Guillaume, this is all very interesting," said Lucía with a yawn, "but Gabriella and I are bored to death and falling asleep. We would like to go shopping before day's end."

Sir Guillaume was somewhat befuddled. "Oh, but we haven't come to the interesting part yet."

"Sir Guillaume, shopping. Now!" said Lucía, who was becoming agitated.

"Of course," uttered Sir Guillaume. He yelled, "Driver, the Right Bank!"

"Merci," said Lucía sarcastically.

As the wagon approached the Right Bank, Lucía and Gabriella looked out from the opening of the curtain and saw the narrow and noisy streets filled with many people of all ages and classes busily going into different shops or buying items from the many street vendors. The wagon stopped at the back of the one that had gone ahead as several French soldiers stood guard.

As Sir Guillaume helped Lucía and Gabriella from the wagon, Lucía's ladies came to greet them and to advise them of the many places to shop, to the chagrin of Sir Guillaume, who hated shopping.

Lucía turned to Gabriella. "I have been looking forward to this for a long time. The first item on my lengthy list of purchases is to find a gift for Isabella. The queen told me about a vendor that sold gold and silver jewelry. That will be a good place to start."

Both Lucía and Gabriella started off down the street of market vendors with Sir Guillaume in tow. Along the way, Sir Guillaume met his comrades: Gaston and Étienne. They had met the ladies earlier at the marketplace to assist as both escorts and guards. After a quick greeting and reintroduction to Lucía, both men left Sir Guillaume to chase after the ladies as they went from one vendor to the next in a dizzying pace while the men tried not to lose sight of them in the crowded marketplace.

"Ah great, a couple of more buffoons to add to the growing list," said Lucía softly to herself.

Lucía found the vendor and saw a beautiful expensive double silver chain with gold squares inlayed with a small ruby surrounded by a silver circle. The vendor gave the chain to Lucía for her to inspect. She turned to Gabriella with the chain in hand. "I think that this chain would make a great gift for Isabella. What do you think?"

"It would truly look nice on her," replied Gabriella.

Lucía turned back to the vendor and said, "Then it's settled. I'll take it." As she reached into her purse to pay the vendor, she put the necklace in her leather pouch, which hung from her belt.

As the shopping continued, Lucía could no longer handle her purchases and turned to Sir Guillaume. "Here, make yourself useful." She handed him her packages. They started to pile up in his arms as both Lucía and Gabriella went from one shop to another.

Sir Guillaume could hardly see in front of him and dared not drop any. The girls looked behind and saw Sir Guillaume slowly make his way up the narrow streets of Paris as he tried to look over the pile of purchases. Lucía and Gabriella tried to conceal their giggles at the sight, but that gave way to laughter. Sir Guillaume tried to enlist the aid of his friends, but their hands were also filled with packages from the ladies and could provide no help. Fortunately for Sir Guillaume, he made it back to the wagon without dropping one package. The afternoon light had dimmed, and it was time to go back to the palace.

The days started to go by quickly for Lucía until it was time to prepare to leave Paris for the next round of her journey to Pomeroi and see where her mother had spent her childhood.

The last day in Paris was a memorable one. Sir Guillaume and Lucía walked among the students on the Left Bank and listened to the various philosophical and theological discussions that took place almost daily in both small and large groups.

Sir Guillaume remarked, "This is where the intelligentsia of our city is located: priests, bishops, and theologians, along with political philosophers, and sundry other forms of idealist from all over Europe who come here to study under the protection of the crown."

It was a beautiful spring day, pleasantly warm with a few puffy clouds in the sky, and the surrounding countryside began to turn green with the mixed scent of flowers. Lucía took it all in one last time, as her thoughts again turned to Isabella, who had not responded to the many letters that she had written. She had much to tell her about her final days in Paris, especially concerning Sir Guillaume, whom she found to be an annoying buffoon, and whose assignment as being in charge of her safety and well-being while in France she resented. Perhaps she would receive a letter from her soon, but now was the time to enjoy the marketplace: the crowds of people lining the narrow side streets, the fresh scent of flowers that had just bloomed, and the ships that sailed up and down the Seine from many lands. Her final days in Paris had come to an end.

That night after supper, Lucía decided to take a walk along the Seine. Sir Guillaume warned Lucía that the streets of Paris were dangerous after dark, as they were not lit. "You're not afraid, are you, Sir Guillaume?" asked Lucía.

"Only for you," responded Sir Guillaume.

"With you escorting me, I shall have no fear then," added Lucía.

Sir Guillaume acquiesced, and soon they both walked from the palace to the bridge over the Seine, which connected the Isle de la Cite to the Left Bank. It was a beautiful evening, as the stars burned brightly in the sky. Lucía wore her black cloak over her white garment, as the evening suddenly chilled with a cool breeze. The activity on the Left Bank earlier in the day had now given way to the quiet of the night.

As Lucía looked down upon the dark river below, it appeared as black as the sky above. Only a dull reflection of flickering light could be seen from the candles that lit the many rooms of the buildings of the Isle de La Cite. Lucía gave a sigh and wondered what it would be like to live in Paris. She was still young and impressionable; however, being with Sir Guillaume promoted certain feelings that she had never known before. But she shook them off, as enigmatic as they were.

While on the bridge, Lucía had become more personal as she faced the Seine. "Tell me, Sir Guillaume, as I know so little about you: where are you from, and do you have a family?"

Sir Guillaume thought for a moment and said, "We were land barons from northern France and very loyal to the crown. My older brothers were Henri, Roger, and Giles. My only sister was Geneviève, who was the oldest. When my mother died, she assumed my mother's responsibility in running the castle and was the one who broke up the fights among us brothers. Being the youngest, I was the closest to her. The winter she fell sick, I didn't move from her bedside. By the end of that winter, she was gone. A few years later, my brothers Henri and Roger, along with my father, Sir Edmond Guiscard Guy de Champville, died in battle during one of King Philip's campaigns. Giles, my older brother, inherited everything and kicked me out. Being young, I had a choice of joining the church or becoming a knight. I became a knight and loyal servant to King Philip, with whom I gained favor."

Lucía's curiosity continued, "And your friends?" asked Lucía.

"Gaston was the son of a French knight. We met in the service of the king about five years ago. Despite being loud and boisterous, we became good friends."

Sir Guillaume continued as he turned away from Lucía and faced the Seine with his hands cupped over the railing of the river below, "Étienne. Well, that is a story in itself. I met him while on crusade. He was the son of a freeman, a farmer by trade. As the story goes, as told by Étienne, he had always wanted to be a knight ever since he was a small boy and saw knights pass by on the road by his father's farmhouse on their way to Paris. One day, a knight stopped at the farmhouse and asked for lodging. Étienne's father talked to him, and the kindly knight agreed in return for lodging and the little money his father had saved to help prepare the eight-year-old boy for his future.

"Many years later, Étienne accompanied the knight on crusade. Unfortunately, during a battle, the kindly knight died. In his dying breath, he bequeathed his armor and sword to Étienne. Several days later, I was fighting in a battle and found myself completely surrounded by Saracens. Étienne risked his life, as a true warrior, and fought his way through their lines and rescued me from a certain death. After the battle, he told me his story, and for his valor, I took him to King Philip and convinced him to knight him. At the young age of sixteen, Étienne became a knight. To me, he is more like the younger brother that I never had, more than a friend."

Lucía didn't say a word but reflected on their conversation.

Suddenly, out of the corner of his eye, Sir Guillaume saw three men who were quickly approaching the bridge with weapons in hand. "Ah, stay here and don't move," said Sir Guillaume as he turned to Lucía.

Lucía, taken by surprise at Sir Guillaume's warning, quickly turned and heard one of the men say, "Let's take them!"

As they approached, Sir Guillaume drew his sword. Lucía looked on in fear as she leaned against the railing on the bridge and tried to stay out of view under the cover of darkness.

"Well, what do we have here?" asked Sir Guillaume.

The ruffians stopped, and one of them retorted, "We want that fat purse hanging from your belt and that young lady of yours, or else…"

"Or else what?" asked Sir Guillaume.

"We will have to take them from you," said a voice from one of the three.

Sir Guillaume responded, "Well, it appears as if I will have to teach you some manners."

Quickly, two of the men surrounded Sir Guillaume, and the third man went over to Lucía, grabbed her, and held a knife to her throat as he watched the other two men engage Sir Guillaume. However, the two ruffians were no match for Sir Guillaume as they were armed with clubs and simple knives and were only looking for a quick purse from some unsuspecting stranger.

When the engagement began, Sir Guillaume quickly dispatched one man as he charged Sir Guillaume with his club and received a three-foot piece of steel between his ribs. The other man, who smartly figured out that he was outmanned, ran away, which left the third one still holding a knife to Lucía's throat. The man held Lucía in such a strong grip that she could not move nor dared to.

Sir Guillaume walked slowly toward him with sword drawn and said sternly to the remaining ruffian, "If you hurt her or leave a mark of any kind on her, I promise that I will hunt you down like the animal that you are and slowly dismember you piece by piece."

With that warning, the ruffian started to lose his confidence and quickly withdrew the knife from Lucía's throat and ran away into the night.

Sir Guillaume sheathed his sword as he walked up to Lucía, who was rubbing her throat, and inquired, "Are you all right, Doña Lucía?"

Lucía's feelings turned from fear to anger. "All right? You jest, Sir Guillaume! Of course, I'm not all right. I'm still shaking in my boots."

"I mean, are you hurt?" asked Sir Guillaume, who decided to rephrase the question.

"I don't think so," said Lucía as she checked herself for any obvious signs of injury.

"Good. Then I think we should go back now. They might be back with their friends."

"Perhaps so," said Lucía angrily.

"I did warn you that Paris can be dangerous at night," injected Sir Guillaume with a grin.

"So you did," retorted Lucía brusquely, who was angry to be proven wrong by a man she still regarded as somewhat of a buffoon.

As they left the bridge, Lucía, in a snit, started to walk at a fast pace, getting ahead of Sir Guillaume, which forced him to sprint in order to catch up to his reluctant charge.

"Do you have to walk so fast?" asked Sir Guillaume, who was becoming winded from the fast pace.

"Did you think that maybe you walk too slow, or is all that chain male slowing you down? Perhaps you should try to keep up if you can," said Lucía.

"Why do you have to act like such a brat?"

Lucía responded to his remark by sticking out her tongue at Sir Guillaume.

"Oh, that is really ladylike, more like a child who needs to be taught some manners," said Sir Guillaume, who now was losing his patience with Lucía. "Perhaps I should take you over my knee and tap that royal ass of yours."

"Just try it!" shouted Lucía as she stormed through the palace gates at full speed past Captain Gómez and to her room.

Sir Guillaume stopped in front of Captain Gómez and shouted to Lucía, "Once again, I need to know what time to fetch you in the morning. We should leave early."

"Go away!" shouted Lucía from a distance away.

Captain Gómez laughed at the conversation that had just unfolded. "I see you two are getting along well."

Sir Guillaume shook his head. "Was she always like this?"

With a slight laugh, Captain Gómez responded, "Don't let that pretty face fool you, Sir Guillaume. She can be spirited at times and very stubborn." And then he paused. "However, I have never seen her act quite like this before. She must like you to give you such attention, but does not wish to convey those feelings to you. She is still very young and perhaps does not understand those feelings herself."

Sir Guillaume looked at Gómez with a double take. "Like me! I would hate to think what she would do if she loathed me."

Captain Gómez, with a grin, slapped Sir Guillaume on the shoulder. "You're doing a fine job, my friend, and with a little luck, she will eventually come around."

"I hope you're right, or it is going to be a very long journey indeed," responded Sir Guillaume.

Gómez laughed as he mounted his horse to go back to his men still camped on the outside Paris. Sir Guillaume shook his head and wondered how he was going to handle his troublesome charge in the morning. He knew that he would have to break proper etiquette by calling on her in the early morning before dawn, without advanced warning, as her Castilian guards would not let him disturb her this late at night.

Lucía entered her room in frenzy and waved her arms about. Two servants were pulling down the covers of her bed, while Gabriella and Constance were having a quiet conversation by the fireplace.

"Grrrrr! Of all the arrogance of that pompous buffoon, by the bones of St James, I swear." At this point, Lucía had used the name of St. James in vain and realized her sin. "May God forgive me and

St. James, too, for what I have just said. I haven't uttered St. James's name in such a sinful manner for a long time and thought myself over such a sinful way of expressing my disconcertment over matters of my own intolerance. May God help me over the confused feelings that I now feel within myself," said Lucía in a loud and dramatic fashion.

Both Gabriella and Constance could not help but listen to Lucía's ranting as the two servants politely bowed and left the room.

Lucía ran over to both Gabriella and Constance, who now were standing by their chairs in front of the fireplace. "Please tell me that I am not going crazy!" shouted Lucía in emotional anguish.

"You're in love, Lucía," responded Gabriella, who looked at Constance. They both smiled in agreement.

"How can you love someone you despise?" asked Lucía.

"Perhaps you should look within yourself and see whether you are confusing your disdain for Sir Guillaume with the true love that it might actually be. True love can't be denied," voiced Constance.

"That makes no sense to me," responded Lucía.

"Love never does," added Gabriella.

"However, I do remember a story Yamina once told me of a young maiden who denied the love of a handsome knight because she thought him too arrogant."

"How did the story end?" asked Gabriella.

"She looked within herself and discovered that it was she who was the arrogant, unforgiving one and not the knight," said Lucía slowly as if she had an epiphany.

"But I'm not arrogant. He is definitely the arrogant one and not me," exclaimed Lucía.

"And so the denial continues," added Gabriella. "But perhaps the seed of affirmation has been planted after all. We shall see."

Suddenly, Lucía smiled with a bit of optimism. "I have an idea to teach Sir Knight a lesson in humility." She called for the guards.

"Sí, mi señora?" asked one of the guards.

"I need for you to bring me two heavy pieces of flat stone slate to my boudoir."

"Sí, mi señora," said the guard, and he turned to leave.

"What are you going to do with the slate stones?" asked Constance.

Lucía went over by her trunks and demonstrated to both Gabriella and Constance. "My trunks have a false bottom. I will take out my garments, remove the false bottom, and put in one slate stone in each trunk and then replace the false bottom and garments in each. When he comes to fetch us in the morning, he will want to carry out my trunks to the cart. Of course, with the additional weight, he will have a tough time lifting the trunk and be embarrassed and humiliated!" Lucía laughed.

"Oh, Lucía, you wouldn't," said Gabriella.

Lucía bent over a trunk, turned to Gabriella, and with a smile, nodded and grunted, "Aha!"

"Well, if nothing else, the ruse will be worth the entertainment," added Constance.

As the conversation ensued regarding the stones, there was a knock on the door. Gabriella walked over to open the door, and there stood a young page who wore a blue garment embroidered with the gold fleur-de-lis of the royal court. "The queen has sent me to ask Doña Lucía if she would like to join her for evening vespers at the oratory."

"Please wait here a moment, and I will fetch the condesa," said Gabriella.

Lucía stood by a trunk that she had unpacked to lift out the false bottom. She was interrupted by Gabriella. "The queen sent a page to fetch you for evening vespers in the oratory and is waiting."

Lucía turned to the door and saw the page, who stood at attention and waited for an answer. "Very well, I will go with the page, Gabriella, but when the men arrive with the stone slate, have them place one in each trunk."

Gabriella nodded, and Lucía went off with the page to meet the queen in the oratory.

Once at the oratory, Lucía saw the queen kneeling in prayer in front of the altar, and after having had dipped her fingers in holy water at the font by the oratory door and blessed herself, Lucía joined the queen in prayer. After a period of private prayer and reflection, the queen rose from the kneeler and sat on a bench in back of the kneeler, joined by Lucía.

"Merci for coming," said the queen in a quiet, whispering voice. "I understand that you will be leaving early tomorrow before dawn?"

"That's right, Your Highness," responded Lucía.

"I hope your visit with us has been satisfactory?" inquired the queen.

"More than satisfactory, Your Highness."

The queen smiled. "So what are your future plans, if I may so boldly ask?"

"On to Pomeroi to see where my mother was raised and then back to Segoia, where I need to be, hopefully, by harvest time."

"Oui, that's right, for the grape harvest," responded the queen. Then she continued after a pause, "I understand that you were involved in a provocation this evening while you and Sir Guillaume were on a walk."

"That's right, but how did you find out?" asked Lucía.

Queen Agnes grinned. "News travel fast in the palace. I also understand that Sir Guillaume came to your rescue."

"That's right. I was held by knife point to the throat, and he scared off the perpetrator."

"How terrible! I pray that you are all right."

Lucía nodded.

After a slight pause, the queen continued, "Sir Guillaume is a good man. He has made a name for himself in the French court and is a trusted adviser to my husband in matters of warfare. Someday he will make a lady a good husband."

Lucía was embarrassed by the queen's statement and turned red and thought that maybe Sir Guillaume had put the queen up to such an endorsement.

The queen sensed that she had somehow embarrassed Lucía by her reaction. "Oh, my dear, I apologize. I didn't mean to upset you or cause you any disquietness," said the queen. "I don't know your relationship with Sir Guillaume. I merely wanted to point out that he is a good, loyal subject and friend to both my husband and me and will make a good, trusted escort that you can lean on in case you run into anymore danger, such as what happened this evening."

Lucía turned to the queen and, with a smile, said, "Merci for your endorsement, Your Highness, and believe me, I did not take offense."

The queen smiled. "Good. Both King Philip and I want to maintain a good relationship between France and Castile. What you have told me about your country and people sounds wonderful. I also know that your country is on the vanguard of Europe against the dreaded Moors. I want you to know that you and your country will be in my prayers," said the queen in earnest. "And I do hope, Lucía, that you find what you're looking for in Pomeroi. However, I fear that the time is getting late, and you have to rise early in the morning to start your journey. So I will say my good night to you and retire. I look forward to saying my goodbyes in the morning, along with that of my husband." Both Queen Agnes and Lucía rose from the bench, and after she gave the queen a deep courtesy, Lucía retired back to her boudoir.

As soon as Lucía entered her boudoir, she noticed that her ladies were busy folding and preparing her gowns for packing. Constance met Lucía as she walked into the room. "The stone slates arrived a short time ago and have been placed in your trunks."

"Wonderful. Sir Guillaume will get a big surprise tomorrow when he tries to lift them. Good work," said Lucía with an impish smile on her face.

The next morning, Sir Guillaume knocked on the door before dawn and was surprised to find Lucía and her ladies all packed and ready to go.

Sir Guillaume was invited into the boudoir and addressed Lucía, "Well, this is a pleasant surprise, Doña Lucía. You're actually ready to go and on time. I thought that after last night—" Sir Guillaume was interrupted by Lucía before he could continue.

"After last night what?" asked Lucía.

"Well…," said Sir Guillaume, somewhat embarrassed, as he looked around the boudoir and saw her ladies all staring at him at once.

"Well, what?" asked Lucía again.

"The disagreement that we had," said Sir Guillaume in a soft voice, as he heard the giggles of the ladies around him.

"I don't recall any disagreement, and I don't have time to stand here and try to recount what happened last night. Neither do you. Shall we move on, Sir Guillaume?"

"Ah, oui, I agree," responded Sir Guillaume, a little befuddled.

"These are the last two trunks that need to go on the cart, and they belong to me. Do you want me to find an attendant, or can you take them?"

"I'll carry them," said Sir Guillaume.

Then Lucía turned to her ladies-in-waiting. "Ladies, it's time to proceed down to the courtyard and the wagons that are waiting for us," said Lucía.

The ladies all left, except for Constance, Gabriella, and Lucía, who stayed behind to watch Sir Guillaume attempt to pick up the trunks.

Sir Guillaume bent down and expected to be able to easily lift the first trunk while still moving, but when he reached down while on the go and tried to lift it, he quickly lost his balance, spun around, and landed on the floor.

The girls tried to hold their giggles but couldn't help themselves.

Sir Guillaume rose to his feet and looked at Lucía. "What do you have in these trunks?

"Oh, just garments and ladies wear," responded Lucía.

"They must be made out of armor," quipped Sir Guillaume.

"You mean a strong knight like you can't lift a simple light trunk of ladies garments?"

"I didn't say that. The weight of this trunk took me by surprise. I'll be down shortly," spoke an optimistic Sir Guillaume.

The girls left with an occasional giggle.

Upon reaching the courtyard, King Philip and Queen Agnes had already assembled, along with several members of the court and several royal guards, to see the entourage off to the next part of their journey to Pomeroi. Captain Gómez had already assembled his large escort of soldiers, wagons, and carts all proudly waiting for Lucía and her two other ladies to arrive.

When Lucía arrived at the courtyard, she had to explain to the king that she was waiting for Sir Guillaume to arrive with two more pieces of her luggage and could not leave yet.

"Ah, I see, my dear. We will wait then," said the king.

Some time went by, and still Sir Guillaume had not arrived. Lucía was in an awkward moment, as the queen was busy fanning herself in the warm early morning sun and the king had finished his small talk with the accompanying members of the court. Finally, Sir Guillaume appeared on the landing outside the entrance to the royal palace, and with a great deal of effort, he struggled down the stairs, pulling the trunk in front of him, until it gave way and knocked him down a couple of bottom stairs to the oohs and aahs of the people who observed the poor knight on the ground, defeated by a trunk of ladies garments. The oohs and aahs suddenly turned into giggles, as Sir Guillaume, somewhat embarrassed by his escapade, arose from the ground and continued, first, to try again to lift the trunk that was too heavy, second, to drag the trunk to the awaiting cart.

When Sir Guillaume arrived, the king asked, "Perhaps, Sir Guillaume, some help is needed." And he ordered a guard to have a couple of attendants fetch the final trunk.

The exasperated knight acknowledged, "Merci, Sire."

Sir Guillaume struggled, and after several attempts to lift the trunk onto the cart, Lucía, who had had enough, went over to the dray and remarkably with all her strength and resilience, which included the motivation to make a fool out of Sir Guillaume, managed to lift the trunk to the edge of the cart and slide it on. What followed was a roar of laughter.

In amazement, Sir Guillaume looked at Lucía. "How did you…?" he asked as he pointed his finger from the ground and moved it up to the cart.

"Are you getting weak, Sir Guillaume? A big strong knight like you," said Lucía, again to the roar of the crowd who had already gathered. "It is getting late, Sir Guillaume. Shall we leave before the day is done?"

Sir Guillaume, red-faced and embarrassed, tried to plead his case to an attendant, while Lucía said her final goodbyes to the royal party. Lucía walked over to the king, and after she made a full curtsy, the king inquired, "How did you ever lift that trunk, Lucía?"

"I simply wanted to help a poor knight in distress with his laborious task, which gave me the strength to do it," said Lucía with an impish grin.

"Remarkable," said the king, to the agreement of the queen, who stood next to him. "I can see that King Alfonso must have his hands full with you in his court. Have a safe journey, my dear, and pay us a visit again." The king then quickly went over to the ladies, who made a full curtsy. The king said, "*Adieu*," and turned to leave the courtyard, along with his courtiers.

"I will pray for you, not only for your safe journey, but for Our Blessed Holy Mother to keep you and your people safe in your fight against the Moors," said Queen Agnes, who embraced Lucía. "You have been able to engage the king, which few people have been able to do, and with that, you can take pride. *Au revoir*, my dear. May your journey be rewarding and safe."

After the queen left and the final trunk had been loaded onto the baggage cart, Lucía went by her transport, along with Gabriella, to wait for Sir Guillaume to help them board. However, Sir Guillaume was still talking to an attendant and to Gómez, who had joined the conversation, and paid no attention to Lucía and Gabriella, who were waiting patiently to board the wagon. Her ladies and servants had already boarded their transports and were ready to leave the palace grounds.

Lucía started to clear her throat to get Sir Guillaume's attention, but to no avail. She turned to Gabriella. "Don't tell me he is also deaf," said Lucía, who became annoyed at the wait.

"Maybe he can't take a hint," added Gabriella.

Lucía cleared her throat again, louder this time, still to no avail.

Finally, she again cleared her throat very loudly and added, "Sir Guillaume, by the bones!" Then stopped herself and continued, "Are we leaving today or not?"

After Sir Guillaume gave final directions to Pomeroi for Gómez to follow, he turned to Gómez and said, "This should be an interesting journey. Wish me luck."

With a smile, Gómez slapped Sir Guillaume on the back and mounted his horse to take the lead with the escort of French soldiers.

Sir Guillaume helped Gabriella and Lucía board the wagon and joined them onto their final destination to Pomeroi, where Lucía was hoping to get a better understanding of her mother's childhood and that of her adopted parents.

As they exited the palace gates and traveled through the city, Lucía and Gabriella pulled back the curtains of the wagon to catch a final glimpse of Paris, and when they finally exited the city onto the road that would lead them to Pomeroi, Lucía said her final goodbye, "Adieu, mon cher Paris jusqu'a ce que nous nous retrouvions."

Chapter XXIV

Once on the road from Paris, the entourage headed northeast on their journey to Pomeroi. King Philip had provided an escort of twelve soldiers, all wearing the colors of the royal court, to accompany the entourage on their travels through France. The twelve French soldiers, along with the contingent of Castilians, made for an impressive spectacle, which was viewed by many on the French countryside. People would stop to gaze at the marvel that passed before them. The caravan passed large fields and forests and, on occasion, a castle on a hill.

During this period, Lucía occupied her time by reading several wooden bound books, kept neatly in a leather pouch under her seat, from her library at home. She pulled out the pouch and took a book out to read. It was a Greek tragedy, which had been translated into Latin from its original Greek text. She pulled the curtain aside enough to let in the natural sunlight by which to read by. Gabriella, seated next to her, was reading her favorite book of poems, which were translated from Arabic.

As Lucía read her Greek tragedy, she had an eerie feeling of being stared at across the way by Sir Guillaume, who was seated by himself. "What are you staring at, Sir Guillaume?" asked Lucía slowly while still reading.

"I apologize. I did not mean to stare, but I could not help but to notice how the sunlight seems to dance on your head, highlighting the red color of your hair," said Sir Guillaume, who was thoroughly enchanted.

With that remark, Lucía closed her book shut with such a loud thud that it caused Sir Guillaume to sit back and wince.

"Sir Guillaume, did you not bring something to do on such a long journey?" inquired Lucía, somewhat annoyed at having had lost her concentration by what she considered a rather perverse statement.

"Non, as I usually travel by horseback, so this mode of travel is new to me."

"I also travel by horseback, but at least I had common sense enough to bring something to while away the time and not grow completely bored," exclaimed Lucía, slowly raising her voice and then becoming louder, which caused Sir Guillaume to wince once again.

"Oh," responded Sir Guillaume meekly, to the giggles of Gabriella, who raised her small book of poems to her face to hide her mirth.

With a big sigh, Lucía reached under her seat, pulled out her leather-bound pouch again, reached into the pouch, and pulled out a large book for Sir Guillaume to read. "Here, Sir Guillaume, something for you to read to keep you busy and to stop staring at me," voiced Lucía.

Lucía had handed him a heavy book written in Latin upside down. "What language is this?" asked Sir Guillaume.

"It's written in Latin." Lucía paused and then continued, "Sir Guillaume, you can read, can you not?"

"Of course, I can read, but this doesn't look like any Latin I've ever learned."

Lucía looked at the book. "Well, Sir Guillaume, it would help if you read the book right side up instead of upside down."

"Ah, you're right," said Sir Guillaume, befuddled and embarrassed by his own stupidity. Once again, Gabriella could not help but giggle at the back and forth conversation between the two as she held her book directly in front of her face.

The book was bound in wood and covered in sheepskin. When Sir Guillaume loosened the strap and opened the parchment pages, he was surprised at the title: *The Conquest of Gaul* by Julius Caesar.

"Now what's the problem, Sir Guillaume?"

"Nothing," he responded. "I'm just surprised that you have such a book."

Lucía shot back, "And why is that?"

"Well, books like this are at a great cost and beyond the means of some of the wealthiest nobles, and yet for a girl to be reading this type of book, well…"

"Well, what?" asked Lucía, who was becoming defensive. She looked Sir Guillaume straight in the eye and, after a pause, continued on, "Sir Guillaume, you may think me as being just a silly girl, but you forget that I am a condesa and have the responsibility to protect my people from powers that are hostile from outside of my condado. By studying such a great soldier and general like Julius Caesar, I can learn certain battle strategies that could serve me well in case of a possible encroachment by an enemy," voiced Lucía.

After Lucía's diatribe, Sir Guillaume looked at Lucía, dumbfounded. Lucía made her case very convincingly, yet his charge did not appear to be the warrior type but very much a soft and fragile soul who needed protection from the evils of the outside world. That was why he was there.

After a couple of hours of travel, Lucía had the entourage stop in a wooded area for her and her ladies to relieve themselves. The woods covered a large area on both sides of the road and contained gullies, where the ladies would not be seen.

Sir Guillaume was the first to exit the wagon, and then he helped Lucía, Gabriella, and her ladies climb down from their transports. They immediately went off chattering and cackling mindlessly into the woods. As a natural instinct, Sir Guillaume started to follow Lucía and Gabriella down into the gully but was rebuffed by Lucía, who stopped halfway down the wooded hill, turned around, and addressed Sir Guillaume in no uncertain terms, "Why are you following me, Sir Guillaume? Perhaps you wish to see me relieve myself, or maybe you wish me to strip down again for your pleasure?"

Once again, Lucía had targeted her escort and managed to hit the bulls-eye, which put Sir Guillaume in a defensive state and left him completely flabbergasted and embarrassed, willing to plead his case to whoever would listen. But he lacked the receptive audience, with only the giggles from the ladies in the gully below to serve, to no avail, the quick vindication he so desired.

"Perhaps I will go in this direction," said Sir Guillaume as he pointed to the other side of the road.

"A good choice," said an annoyed Lucía.

As Lucía picked up the corners of her green garment and walked down the wooded hill to the gully below, she turned to Gabriella. "I wish I could get that buffoon out of my mind. He makes me crazy with his idiocy."

Gabriella laughed as she stepped into the gully. "He makes you crazy, because you don't want to admit that you have fallen for him, and you mask your emotions by thinking him a buffoon or dumb and stupid. Believe me, Lucía, I can see it in your eyes when you casually look at him and then quickly turn away, at which point you try to shake off your true feelings through dumbfounding him or trying to convince yourself he is an idiot by making sharp remarks."

"That is completely ridiculous, Gabriella. I would know if I had true feelings for him, and I don't."

"All right then. We shall see."

Adele came over to Lucía and said, "When are you going tell Sir Guillaume your love for him?"

Lucía was surprised at the remark and looked at Gabriella, who raised her eyebrows and gave an expression of "I told you so."

"Humph!" squeaked a frustrated Lucía, and she turned and walked back up the hill.

While the ladies were walking down the hill to the gully, Gómez saw Sir Guillaume walking up the wooded hill in a dejected mood. Along with his mount, Gómez walked over to Sir Guillaume, who had leaned against the wagon, and started a conversation with him. "Ah, how are you making out with the señora?"

"Not well, I'm afraid. Is she always so disagreeable?" asked Sir Guillaume.

"She can be as stubborn as her father ever was," said Gómez.

"A family trait?" uttered Sir Guillaume.

"Perhaps. Her mother was a beautiful woman and her father a stubborn knight. You put the two together, and you get Lucía." With a smile, Gómez added, "It is as simple as that. But let me tell you, even though I can be tough on her, Lucía is kind-hearted and easy to approach compared to other people of her rank. I've seen her generosity first-hand, and believe me when I say it is genuine. Her army is loyal to her because she treats them with dignity and respect. She cares for her peasants and prays with them in their church. She works with them in the fields. She is there to comfort them when they are sick, and she seeks to be friends with her enemies.

"So you see, señor, Lucía is a rather special person, and despite her improper behavior on occasion, you would never know that she is the granddaughter of a king and could easily be a queen in her own right. So cheer up, Sir Guillaume," said Gómez as he mounted his horse. "I like you, and I am very much in favor of you. Believe me, she will come around." He then cantered off to the front of the column.

After Gómez finished with his speech, Sir Guillaume gave him an insipid smile as he rode off and went across the road to relieve himself. He took his time, as he figured the ladies would lag a while longer. After several minutes had passed, Sir Guillaume rejoined the entourage. As he entered the wagon, he was surprised to find Lucía and Gabriella were already seated and were patiently waiting for him to return.

"I thought you got lost, Sir Guillaume," said Lucía.

"How long have you been waiting?"

"Long enough. Shall we be on our way, Sir Guillaume?" responded Lucía as she eyed him askance. "I would like to reach Pomeroi before dark."

"Of course. Driver! Let's go!" he shouted.

The entourage continued on the road and passed small villages, pastureland, and woods. Lucía uncovered a small opening in the curtain and saw a man walking his livestock on the side of the road near an open pasture and also saw a Knight Templar headed for Paris, seated on a beautiful white Arabian, which reminded Lucía of Rodrigo.

As the journey continued, Lucía and Gabriella put their books on their lap and observed the lush environment of the French countryside compared to the rather dry, brown, and yellow countryside of Castile.

Lucía turned to Gabriella. "I'm bored," announced Lucía quietly with a smile as she reached under her seat and put away her Greek classic in her leather pouch.

Gabriella held her book of poems in her lap, and a conversation started in Castilian; the subject was Sir Guillaume. Lucía was attempting to trade insults concerning her brave knight with Gabriella, who wanted no part of the bad behavior. Although Gabriella remained sober during Lucía's rant, Lucía did not take a hint but continued on with her insults. Gabriella tried to change the subject. Unfortunately, Lucía did not wish to change the subject and kept up her bad behavior, as if she wanted Sir Guillaume to do something to stop her.

Sir Guillaume, with his hands in his lap, sat on the bench across from Lucía and stared out the small flap of the closed curtain to the passing countryside while Lucía was on her tirade. Unbeknownst to Lucía, Sir Guillaume understood enough of the language to know he was being singled out, as Lucía would giggle after each insulting barb.

It reached a point that Sir Guillaume had had enough, and he reached over and grabbed Lucía by the arm in midsentence, put her over his knee, and administered a spanking to her royal ass.

"Are you crazy!" shouted Lucía, who struggled to right herself. "Do you know who I am?"

"Oui, a spoiled brat who lacks manners, and if you act like one, I will treat you like one," said Sir Guillaume angrily.

"Just wait!" exclaimed Lucía. "No one has ever treated me as such, not even my father. Ouch!"

"Perhaps he should have, and then you might have the manners to know how to treat people."

Gabriella was completely surprised at Sir Guillaume's quick action, and she raised her book of poems to cover her eyes.

Lucía rose from her embarrassing position, turned, rubbed her buttocks, and raised her hand to strike. Sir Guillaume, who held her arm midair, pulled her face closer to his and locked his lips to hers. Lucía, in a fit of passion, dropped her arm and reached around Sir Guillaume's neck, along with her other arm, while she knelt on the floor of the wagon and continued the raw emotion to a fever pitch, as the hand of romance had finally broken through the tough exterior that Lucía had desperately tried to portray.

As the wagon grew quiet, Gabriella lowered her book smiled and said, "*Amore*. At last, amore."

Lucía heard a rustling sound of the curtain on the opposite side of the wagon. She quickly turned her eyes toward the sound—while still in a lip lock with Sir Guillaume—and saw Gómez looking in while he rode alongside. Lucía quickly released her grip on Sir Guillaume, rose from her knees, and sat back on the bench in an attempt to look innocent.

Lucía acted flustered at the speed of events that had just occurred when she looked at the captain and said, "Sí, Gómez."

"I hope that I am not interrupting anything?" asked Gómez.

"Ha, what could you possibly be interrupted? I mean interrupting…," said Lucía, who winced in her confusion while she attempted to keep her smile of innocence.

"I wanted to let you know that Pomeroi castle is just ahead, and an escort of two soldiers have been sent to accompany us to the castle."

"I would like to see the village in passing," said Lucía.

Gómez laughed. "I'm afraid that we already passed it."

"Oh," responded Lucía, and continued, "Oh, very well then. Please continue on."

Gómez pulled down the curtain and, with a laugh, cantered back to the front of the column.

"How do I look, Gabriella?" asked Lucía as she took her hand and pushed back the strands of hair from her face.

"You look as lovely as ever, Lucía."

"My hair. How does my hair look?" asked Lucía as she turned toward Gabriella in a panic.

"Your hair looks fine, Lucía. They will welcome their duchess with open arms," said Gabriella, who sensed that Lucía was nervous and tried to reassure her.

"Now should I wear the wimple or not?"

Sir Guillaume had remained quiet during this time but now attempted to try to be of some assistance and make his thoughts known. "I would say not and let your natural beauty shine for all to see."

Lucía looked at him and said, "Merci, Sir Guillaume, if I want your opinion, I will ask for it. Besides, you have caused enough commotion for one day."

"I'm just offering my advice. That's all."

"Hmm," responded Lucía with a raised brow, and then she turned to Gabriella. "Gabriella, please help me. Should I wear a wimple or not? I value your opinion."

"Well, let's see. You're young and not married—" reasoned Gabriella but was interrupted by Lucía.

"But I want to make a good impression. I don't want to appear neither as a nun nor as a whore," interjected Lucía.

Sir Guillaume started to laugh.

With the roll of her eyes, Lucía quickly turned to him, and said, "And what is so humorous, Sir Guillaume?"

Sir Guillaume didn't say a word but shook his head and continued to laugh.

"Grrrrr." Lucía stared at Sir Guillaume. "Only a fool laughs at nothing," added Lucía, and Sir Guillaume started to laugh even harder.

"You're impossible," said Lucía, and she again turned to Gabriella. "Well, what do you think?"

"I think you are their duchess, and however you appear will be satisfactory to them. Besides, Sir Guillaume is right. They will want to get a good look at you."

"All right. I will not wear a wimple," said Lucía.

"Well, thank God that decision has been made," said Sir Guillaume, who was coming out of his laughter.

"By the bones, Sir Guillaume, your remarks are becoming irritating and infuriating. Really, if you don't mind?"

"I don't mind," said Sir Guillaume calmly.

Lucía looked at Sir Guillaume and shook her head.

Gabriella interceded between the two. "Lucía, try to remain calm. We are almost there."

"Sí, of course. You're right, Gabriella. Do I still look all right?" asked Lucía, and she again started to primp her hair.

"You look fine, Lucía. Stop worrying," responded Gabriella in a calm matter.

Sir Guillaume listened to the conversation without saying a word, but he thought to himself, *Oh the vanities of a young girl.*

The entourage entered the main gates of Pomeroi castle, between two square towers, and was hailed by the guards, who stood at attention on either side of the gate. Lucía could hear the trumpeters heralding her arrival as her transport pulled up to the entrance of the living quarters. After the wagon stopped, there were an awkward couple of minutes of silence. Lucía needed to be introduced to the people who were lined up along the entrance to greet their duchess. Unfortunately, this had not been discussed beforehand. Lucía assumed that Gómez would handle the introduction, but he left the scene with her small army to set up camp in the forest outside the castle wall. This left Lucía without someone to introduce both Gabriella and herself to the people at hand.

With a sigh, Lucía addressed Sir Guillaume in a whisper, "Sir Guillaume, I need for you to introduce Gabriella and me to the people who are patiently waiting for us. I thought that Captain Gómez was going to do it, but he is nowhere to be seen."

"You want me to introduce you and Gabriella?"

"Oui, you are my escort, and now would be a good time," added Lucía, and after a pause, she continued, "before they decide to leave." Lucía had raised her voice above a whisper, and she was becoming annoyed at Sir Guillaume's languidness. "By the bones!" exclaimed Lucía and then quickly stopped herself from using St. James's name in vain. "Will you get out there now? A little celerity would be nice." Lucía could hear unrest among the people outside, who had waited patiently for their duchess to show herself.

Sir Guillaume exited the wagon and introduced himself as Lucía's escort and then assisted Gabriella and introduced her as Lucía's majordomo. Then he introduced Lucía, and there was complete silence, as everyone stared at Lucía without saying a word. The silence was so acute that Lucía thought to herself that she was being judged for not wearing her wimple.

Finally, the seneschal of Lucía's estate walked over to her. "Your Grace, on behalf of your household staff and the people of your duchy, I welcome you," said the seneschal. "Please forgive our staring when you exited your transport, but the resemblance to your mother is most remarkable. Except for the color of your hair, I would swear you were her. You see, many of the staff, as well as I, remember your mother dearly."

Lucía responded to the seneschal's apology with a smile and said, "There is nothing to forgive."

He then introduced her to the household staff, who had lined up on the left of the walkway leading up the steps of the living quarters of the castle. As Lucía was introduced to each servant, each one made a deep curtsy, and after each curtsy, Lucía made a point to embrace each of them.

Gómez had finally returned, and Lucía motioned for him to come to her. He dismounted his horse and walked up beside her at the end of the walkway.

Lucía whispered to him, "This is the time. Please bring me the chest that is under the bench in my transport."

Gómez nodded and instructed two of Lucía's personal guards to fetch the small chest, which was added quietly before Lucía left Segoia and was under Gabriella's seat during the entire journey. He put the chest at Lucía's feet, at which time Lucía made a small speech. "I want to thank all of you for your loyalty over the past many years, which has been deeply appreciated by me, and I know if my mother was here, she would want to express the same sentiment. As a token of my deep appreciation, I have something for each of you. Captain Gómez, will you please open the chest?" Gómez reached down and opened it. Lucía bent down and pulled out a leather purse. "On behalf of my mother and me, I want to present each of you with a purse filled with six gold coins. Captain Gómez will pass one out to each of you."

After the oohs and aahs of the people present, a chorus of "Merci, Your Grace!" could be heard.

The seneschal accompanied Lucía up the steps into the living quarters of the castle, where the great hall was located to the left of the entrance. Lucía peaked in the doorway and saw a huge room that could comfortably seat several hundred guests. At the other end of the long hallway was a door that led to the kitchen, pantry, and buttery. To the right of the entrance, across from the great hall, was an anteroom. Lucía walked into the room and saw among its features a red-carpeted dais at the front of the room on which were two chairs and a table, along with two large wooden gray cabinets on either side of the platform. Below the dais was a polished oak table on which were two silver standing candelabras, along with four chairs and a black chandelier, which was covered with years of hardened dripped wax, hanging above the table. The walls were colorfully decorated with hangings. A huge fireplace completed the décor of the room in the middle of the outer wall to the left of the dais. A rug that matched the wall hangings lay under the table on the stone floor.

Next, the seneschal took Lucía up four flights of winding stairs, which led into a long hallway with three rooms on both sides and a stained-glass window in an alcove at the far end, complete with two wooden benches. Wall torches lit the way down the dark corridor.

The seneschal led Lucía to the far room left of the alcove. "This is your own private room, Your Grace," said the seneschal as he opened the door for Lucía, "This was your mother's room, where she grew up. The room has remained untouched except for the occasional sprucing up. The room directly across from here belonged to your grandfather, Sir Charles. The other rooms on this floor are used for guests and are open for your inspection. You are certainly welcome to make your own room assignments. While you are here, the staff will be obedient to your wishes. The guards are also at your command, Your Grace. I shall leave you now to your own privacy. Are you able to find your way back to the anteroom?"

"Oui, and merci for your kindness," said Lucía.

"Oh, by the way, before I forget to mention it," said the seneschal, "the first room to the right at the entrance at the top of the stairs belongs to a special resident, and once you are settled, I will introduce you to her. If there is anything I can do for you during your stay, please feel free to ask."

"Once again, merci for your kindness," said Lucía.

"Your Grace," said the seneschal, who bowed and left Lucía on her own.

Lucía stood in the large expanse and looked around as tears started to roll down her cheeks, and with those tears of joy, she proclaimed out loud, "I'm here, Mama, and I sense you are here with me too. Your room is so beautiful. I really feel that I am home." Lucía then wiped away her tears and sniffled.

The boudoir was a combination of a bedroom and sitting room. As Lucía looked around the room, the first thing she noticed was the canopied bed with a heavy dark-red curtain on a dais. Lucía walked up the three steps, sat on the bed, and found the mattress to be soft. Next to the dais was a large fireplace with a window on either side that looked down into the courtyard, and to the right, looked over the roofs of the kitchen, pantry, buttery, and the herb garden. A view of the apple orchard could be seen beyond the curtain wall in the distance. The window shutters were open, which let in the sunlight and a cool breeze from the surrounding forest. Across from the canopied bed were a dressing table and a high-back bench lined with pillows. In the middle of the room was another smaller polished oak table with two chairs. Several portable benches could be seen throughout the room. The stone walls of the room were covered with colorful hangings that depicted animal stories, along with a dark-red floor carpet. The window on the other side of the canopied bed caught Lucía's eye as she looked out onto the courtyard and the forest beyond the castle walls.

Lucía went over to the dressing table and removed the large piece of linen that had covered it. The linen cover was so coated in dust that Lucía immediately took it over to the window and shook it out, which caused her to sneeze several times. She took the linen and carefully folded it and placed it on a portable bench. Then something caught her eye under the dressing table. Lucía bent down and found a small locked oak chest.

"What on earth," said Lucía. She pulled the chest from underneath the dressing table and placed it on the polished oak table in the middle of the room. The chest was locked, and there was no key to be found. Lucía immediately went to the dressing table and looked on top and underneath the table, to no avail.

"Where did mother put the key? It has to be here somewhere," Lucía said to herself.

After having had looked in all the obvious places, Lucía decided to pick the less obvious. She went back to the dressing table and studied it for a moment and noticed the mirror, which stood on the dressing table. She sat down on the padded stool that stood in front of the table and carefully examined the mirror. She lifted the heavy circular mirror mounted on a silver stand and placed it on its side. She quickly eyed the bottom of the mirror's base and, to her surprise, found a trapdoor. At a touch, it swung open and revealed the key.

How ingenious! thought Lucía. *Mother was certainly clever.*

Lucía took the key, closed the trapdoor, and placed the mirror right side up on the dressing table. She next walked back to the polished oak table, placed the key in the lock, and opened the small chest to find a treasure trove of items. On top was a piece of parchment folded and sealed in wax. When she broke the seal and opened the parchment, Lucía was completely astounded as to what she read. It was written by her mother and dated the "20th day of March, in the year of our Lord, eleven hundred and eighty-one." It read:

> To my dear daughter, Lucía:
>
> Tomorrow I leave with your grandfather, Sir Charles, for Castile to marry your future father, Don Fernando. I am frightened at the prospect of leaving Pomeroi, the home that I love so much. However, I go with the faith that the Blessed Virgin will guide me on this long journey and to my true calling.
>
> If you are reading this letter, then I am presumed dead, and you have had to find this chest

and brightly figure out how to open it. Please don't be shocked if I call you by your name. I had a premonition that I would not survive your birth and made sure that your name would be Lucía, a beautiful name, which in Latin means "light." Whether I am dead or alive, you will always be my light, and my love for you will be eternal.

All that is in this chest is yours and includes brushes and combs, a couple of broaches, several necklaces, and my diaries. Hopefully, you will get to know me better by reading them. I will also ensure that you will inherit my titles as well as all the privileges and responsibilities that go with them. All that is mine is yours.

From what I have heard, your future father is a fair-minded and a caring man, and I will make him promise that he will take care of you in my absence and provide you with a superb education that I was fortunate enough to have had and will continue to have with a tutor once I reach Spain. I pray that you will have a good life, and I am sorry that I will not be around to share your life with you. However, I will always watch over you.

With much love,
Your mother, Margaret

Lucía put the eerie letter down and wept at what she had just read. She felt that her mother had reached beyond the grave, and for a moment, had touched her with her love and caring soul.

Lucía was lost in thought when she was awakened by a knock on the door. She quickly wiped away her tears, sniffled, and said, "Enter!"

The door opened, and Gabriella appeared with a couple of household servants. "Lucía, your trunks have been brought up from the cart. Should I have the servants bring them in?"

Lucía nodded and responded, "Sí, please do."

The servants brought in the trunks, and Lucía pointed to a spot between the dressing table and the right window by the fireplace. "Please put them there," said Lucía with a smile. The servants struggled with the heavy trunks, placed them in the designated spot, and left.

"Lucía, you must do something with the slabs of stone in those trunks. I watched those two male servants struggle with those trunks up four flights of winding stairs. It took forever, and now I feel tired. And I was only watching them!" voiced Gabriella.

"Sí, I will have the stones removed," said Lucía.

Gabriella looked at Lucía's red eyes and said softly, "You've been crying, Lucía, haven't you?"

"Crying? Me crying? What gave you that idea?" responded Lucía with a guilty look.

Gabriella said with a smile, "Your eyes, Lucía. They give you away all the time. This time they are red."

Lucía walked over to her dressing table, looked in the mirror, and uttered, "Ohhh, so they are."

"Are you all right, Lucía?" asked Gabriella in a concerned voice.

"Of course," answered Lucía.

"Then why were you crying?" asked Gabriella, concerned.

Lucía was about to answer when she was interrupted by her ladies at the door. "May we come in, mi señora?" asked Constance.

"Please," motioned Lucía.

"What a beautiful room," said Geralla as she and the other ladies walked about Lucía's boudoir.

The ladies were fascinated with the wall hangings, which completely covered the stone walls of the room from the top of the ceiling to the floor, and they commented on the many large animals depicted in different vibrant colors.

"This was my mother's room when she was a little girl, and I would presume she found the animals as depicted fascinating."

Beatrix spoke up. She was becoming more confident and lucid in her speech but still had a thick German accent. "I once visited a cousin in Bavaria with similar wall hanging but not as large or as colorful as this. This is truly a work of art and must have been very costly."

"I'm sorry we interrupted you, Lucía, but we were told you are handling the room assignments," voiced Constance.

"Sí, of course." Lucía had Gabriella stay across the hall and divided her ladies between the other two spacious rooms. "You may now have your trunks brought up and placed in your rooms."

"And your servants from Segoia?" asked Constance.

"Sí, well, I'm afraid they will have to bed down in the great hall."

"I will handle the arrangements," said Constance, and she started to usher the ladies to their rooms but was interrupted by Lucía as she addressed the group, "At the top of the stairs to the right of the staircase is a permanent resident of the castle and is not to be disturbed."

The ladies acknowledged Lucía's wishes and went to their rooms.

As Constance was about to leave, Lucía had her fetch two servants to come and take the stone slabs out of her trunks and dispose of them.

Lucía turned next to Gabriella, who stood by the polished oak table. "Have you seen our brave knight?"

"He went to the village with his two friends who appeared earlier."

"Gaston and Étienne, no doubt," responded Lucía, who walked to the window to the left of her canopied bed that had a view, down the steep hill, of the road to Paris with the forest just beyond. She looked out the window and to her far-left, over the curtain wall, she could see the village of Pomeroi. "Probably to the tavern to get drunk and embarrass me further."

As Lucía walked back from the window, Gabriella said, "Lucía, you shouldn't be so hard on Sir Guillaume. He is a good man, and you still deny your love for him."

"It's complicated," uttered Lucía.

"Besides, it must be time for supper. Let's bring the ladies to the great hall for something to eat."

Chapter XXV

The next morning, Lucía awoke early. Servants came in and pulled back the dark-red curtain from around her bed on the dais, opened the window shutters to let in the morning air, and let the bright sunshine through. Gabriella had accompanied them, along with Lucía's ladies, to help her unpack her trunks and pick out her garment for the day.

"And what are your plans for the day, Lucía?" asked Gabriella as she sat on Lucía's bed.

Lucía sat up in bed, stretched, and yawned. "I have the deepest desire to get on a horse, explore the castle grounds, and ride into the village. Perhaps I shall explore in some detail both the vineyard and orchard, and if I get bored with that, then I shall come back here and read my mother's diaries. I shall do all this after I have a meeting with the seneschal."

"Well, that should fill up your day easily," said Gabriella with a laugh.

"Did you sleep well, Gabriella?" asked Lucía with concern.

"Very well. I haven't slept so well in a long time."

"Excellent," uttered Lucía as she rose from her bed and walked over to the polished oak table to a basin of cold water, where she promptly washed her face. She used a piece of linen to wipe her face dry.

While a servant was busy making Lucía's bed, another servant came in with a tray of bread, cheese, and sausage, along with a pitcher of wine, water, and two silver goblets. After she poured the wine, she stood at the head of the table. "Is there anything else I can get for you, Your Grace?" asked the French servant.

"Non, that will be all," said Lucía with a smile as she wiped her hair from her face.

The servant curtsied and left the room.

Lucía, who stood at the polished table and still in her undergarment, turned to Gabriella. "I see that the servants are very attentive here. Anyways, is there any news of our brave knight and his companions?" asked Lucía as she broke off a piece of bread and consumed it.

"Not that I have heard," answered Gabriella.

Lucía sighed and responded, "He is probably somewhere on the castle grounds, drunk and sleeping it off."

"Do you want me to have him found?" inquired Gabriella.

"No, no. Let him find us or not," responded Lucía in disgust.

The ladies had finished unpacking Lucía's trunks for her to pick out her garment and accessories for the day. Adele turned to Lucía. "We are ready for you to get dressed, mi señora."

"I shall wear my green garment, black belt, and black boots," said Lucía. She stood erect by the bed while the ladies dressed her for the day.

When she was dressed, Lucía sat at her dressing table while Beatrix combed her long floor-length hair straight back, braided her hair into two separate lengths, wrapped the two lengths together into one long braid, and let it hang down her back.

Lucía then, after some direction, found a small chapel on the floor beneath her and started the day in prayer, along with her ladies.

After prayer in the chapel, Lucía met the seneschal in the anteroom across from the great hall. When she entered the room, Lucía noticed that the seneschal was already there. He rose from his chair as she approached him.

"Your Grace, please sit here," said the seneschal. He pulled a chair out from the head of the oak table and escorted her to her seat, and then he sat down on the chair to Lucía's right.

"How was your evening, Your Grace? I hope that you found your boudoir comfortable."

"Oui, merci. However, I must apologize to you, though, as I never asked you your name. I try to know people who are in my service. I fear that my conduct was rather ill-mannered, and I apologize," said Lucía.

"Your Grace, you do not owe me an apology. I am your servant. This is your home, and while you are here, you are in command, and I will follow your orders obediently. I am merely an unimportant administrator appointed by King Philip to oversee your interests," said the seneschal. "However, if you wish to know my name, it is Guiscard de Beauchene, originally from a noble family in Orléans."

"How would you like me to address you?" inquired Lucía with a pleasant smile.

"It does not matter, Your Grace. Guiscard would be fine."

"Are you a knight?" asked Lucía.

"Oui," replied Guiscard softly.

Lucía continued with her pleasant smile. "Then I will call you Sir Guiscard."

The seneschal nodded and continued on with the business at hand. "For Your Grace, I have the accounting books for the duchy," said Sir Guiscard as he reached in front of him and placed them in front of Lucía. "For your review, Your Grace. As you can see, a profit has been made in each of the many years that I have administered your interest." The seneschal pointed to the entries in the ledger as he continued on with his explanation.

Lucía interrupted, "How long have you been in Pomeroi?" Lucía noticed that the ledger appeared go back many years.

"I've been here for about seventeen years, Your Grace."

"You knew my grandfather?" asked Lucía.

"Oui, very well. Your grandfather and I were warriors together in the service of King Louis. Since I had administrative skills and was trusted by your grandfather, I was appointed seneschal by King Philip when your mother and Sir Charles left for Castile."

Lucía listened carefully to her seneschal, a man who could easily be her grandfather, as he talked about how he had administered the duchy for those many years. His apparent wisdom matched his age, and Lucía was impressed with Sir Guiscard and how well the duchy was being supervised. She noticed how he would raise his bushy eyebrows whenever he made a point. Here was a man who was happy being in his own skin, an older man with aging dark hair with shades of gray and a few wrinkles on an otherwise clean-shaven face.

Here was a humble man. Here was an honest man. Here was a man that was popular among the people of the duchy. Here was a man that Lucía could count on.

Once Lucía had reviewed the accounting ledgers of the duchy and was more than satisfied with how it was being administered, Sir Giscard asked Lucía if she would like to meet the permanent resident on the fourth floor. Lucía nodded, and they walked from the anteroom together up the narrow staircase to the room to the right at the head of the staircase. When they got to the door, Sir Guiscard knocked on the door.

"Who is it?" asked a feeble voice from inside the room.

"It is Guiscard, and I am here with someone who would like to meet you."

"Please come in," said the feeble voice.

Sir Guiscard entered followed by Lucía. Lucía quickly looked around the room and saw it was large and spacious. However, the fireplace opposite the entrance to her room had no windows. The only window was in the middle of the left stone wall and was closed by two large shutters. There was no dais for the canopy bed, which was next to the fireplace, and the curtain around the bed was white. A polished oak table and two chairs were present in the middle of the room, and the only other pieces of furniture in the room were two high-back chairs in front of the fireplace.

Suddenly, there appeared an old lady with a shawl over her shoulders. She had long gray hair and was a person of significant age. The old lady walked away slowly from her chair and used her hands to guide herself. Lucía could tell by the way she walked that she was completely blind.

"Please stay there," said Guiscard.

"Guiscard, is that you?" inquired the old lady.

"Oui, Madame, it is me."

Lucía followed behind Guiscard as they approached her. Lucía now saw clearly a woman of great age whose face was covered with wrinkles.

"Madame Leclair, I would like to introduce you to Doña Lucía Alvarado, Lady Margaret's daughter from Spain and our duchess."

Madame Leclair could not believe what she just heard, and it took a little time for this bit of news to be completely processed and thoroughly understood. "Did you say Lady Margaret's daughter from Spain?"

"Oui," said the seneschal, and he whispered to Lucía who stood beside him, "She is a little hard of hearing with an aging wit."

Lucía nodded and watched as the old lady fumbled about with her memory.

"Lady Margaret's daughter from Spain," voiced Madame Leclair out loud to herself several times until finally the old lady had an epiphany. "Where is the child?" she asked.

"I am right here," voiced Lucía as she slowly walked over to Madame Leclair and stood in front of her.

Madame Leclair asked Lucía, "Do you mind if I touch your face?"

"Non," said Lucía.

Madame Leclair reached out and put her hands on Lucía's face and felt her forehead, eyes, nose, and mouth. Then she put her hands down and, with tears in her eyes, said, "I never thought that I would ever meet Margaret's daughter. I have certainly been blessed this day."

Despite being blind, Madame Leclair could tell that Lucía was confused as to who she was. She said, "My dear, I was your mother's tutor for many years until she went to Spain with Sir Charles."

Lucía was both excited and enthused that finally there was someone who knew her mother well enough to be able to give her complete insight into her mother's early life and childhood. "You must tell me all you know about my mother, Madame."

"Oui, I would love to do that," said Madame Leclair, who was enthused to have someone to talk to. "Please come over and sit with me." She slowly felt her way back to her chair with Lucía, who followed behind.

As Madame Leclair sat in her chair, Lucía sat in the chair next to her.

"It would appear that both of you have a lot to talk about, so I will excuse myself to attend to other matters at hand," said Guiscard, and he walked toward the door and carefully shut it. Both Lucía and Madame Leclair were so engaged in conversation they did not hear Guiscard leave.

"What do you wish to know about your mother?" asked Madame Leclair.

"Everything," responded Lucía excitedly, "except about the part where my mother was given away. That part was already told to me."

"All right then," said Madame Leclair with a slight laugh at Lucía's blatant inquisitiveness. "Perhaps I should start from the beginning, my dear. I was an attendant to Queen Eleanor, your grandmother, when your mother was born. Due to my education and intellect, Queen Eleanor sent me to be your mother's nurse and, when old enough, her tutor."

Lucía interrupted Madame Leclair apologetically and asked, "When you were in Queen Eleanor's court, did you know a Father Baldwin?"

"Father Baldwin…Father Baldwin…" repeated the old woman. "Oui, come to think of it, I do remember a priest at court sent as a papal legate to Poitiers from Rome. I had forgotten his name, but I do believe that you are correct, Your Grace."

"Please call me Lucía, Madame Leclair."

Madame Leclair smiled and continued, "Your mother was a brilliant student and very docile, an easy child to teach. She especially enjoyed riding through the countryside and would ride so fast that she gave Sir Charles fits on many occasions. She was a fragile creature, as she was a sickly child, but that did not stop her from helping Sir Charles with the apple harvest in the fall or picking grapes in the vineyard."

The two had conversed for quite some time when there was a lull in the conversation, and Lucía asked softly, "Madame Leclair, if I may ask, when did you become blind?"

Madame Leclair paused, and she started to dose off. "I used to read quite a bit. Unfortunately, with age, my eyesight gradually grew dimmer and dimmer until one day everything turned dark."

The conversation ended as Madame Leclair fell asleep. Lucía rose from her chair and went to Madame Leclair's bed, took off the extra coverlet to cover her feet and legs, wrapped her shawl tightly around her shoulders, kissed her on the cheek, and said in a whisper. "I will make sure that you will always be well cared for." Lucía left Madame Leclair's room and carefully closed the door behind her and went back to her boudoir.

When Lucía entered her room, she saw Sir Guillaume and Gabriella both seated at the polished oak table across from each other and appeared to be waiting patiently for her return. Gabriella was embroidering on a piece of linen, and Sir Guillaume was seated and looked bored. Lucía walked up to and stood before Sir Guillaume, who quickly rose from his chair to greet her.

"Well, Sir Guillaume, where have you been? I was becoming concerned that you might have left us."

"I, along with companions, spent the night with Captain Gómez, who offered us warm hospitality and a good night's sleep in your bed inside your tent," said Sir Guillaume and then continued, "He didn't think that you would mind."

"And if I had? Then what?" added Lucía.

"Well, princess, I guess that you would be out of luck," said Sir Guillaume with a sarcastic smile.

"Sir Guillaume, let's get one thing straight. I am a duchess, not a princess."

"Of course, anything you say," said Sir Guillaume with a note of sarcasm and a slight bow.

"Are you mocking me?" asked Lucía, who then shook her head and said, "Oh never mind." She turned to Gabriella and said, "I'm headed for the stables to find a suitable mount to go for a ride in the countryside. Suddenly, I feel the need for some fresh air," said Lucía as she looked at Sir Guillaume with a look of disgust on her face.

As Lucía shut the door on the way out, Gabriella cleared her throat to get Sir Guillaume's attention. As he turned to Gabriella, she said, "Well, Sir Guillaume, what are you waiting for? Go after her."

"So why should I go after her? Let her do what she wants. She is going to do it anyways."

"I have never seen two people who are so fond of each other try to distance themselves from each other as you two always do," voiced Gabriella.

"If you think that I am falling for your duchess, countess, or whatever she is, you've got it wrong. You see, in my way of thinking, she is nothing but a spoiled, stubborn brat," said Sir Guillaume, peeved at Gabriella's remark.

"Of all the gall, Sir Guillaume, you call her stubborn. I have never seen two more stubborn people in my life than you two, and as far as a spoiled brat is concerned, it just goes to show how little you know about Lucía. When you were penniless and walking up the peninsula after your encounter with pirates, who do you think gave you food, weapons, money, and horses at great expense to see you through?"

After a pause, Sir Guillaume said softly, "You mean it was Lucía who did that?"

"Does that sound like a spoiled brat or someone who exceeds generosity?" asked Gabriella with anger in her eyes.

"How could I have possibly known that she was the one who saved us from possible death?" asked Sir Guillaume, who had now softened his tone.

"Perhaps you should try to get to know her better, and then you would be able to see her true feelings," said Gabriella and then continued, "You owe her that much."

Sir Guillaume thought for a minute and then left the room for the stable.

Lucía entered the stable and saw the stable master cleaning out a stall. She walked over to him and cleared her throat to get his attention. The stable master turned, still with pitchfork in hand. "Your Grace. Please forgive me. I did not see you."

"I could see that you were busy at work," said Lucía with a smile.

The stable master rested the pitchfork in an empty stall and walked over to Lucía. "My name is Alain, Your Grace, your stable master."

"It is nice to make your acquaintance," said Lucía.

The stable master paused for a moment, squinted his eyes, and continued, "The resemblance to your mother is remarkable. Her hair was blonder than yours, but outside of that, at a fast glance, I would swear that you are Margaret who has returned."

Lucía could tell his remark was genuine and from the heart. She saw before her an old man, a victim of old age, with a long wrinkly face and skin that hung like leather on a thin frame.

Lucía, with a soft smile, said, "Merci, I will take that as a compliment."

Alain nodded, returned her smile, and then urged Lucía to follow him over to the front of the stable to a stall, where a brown stallion with a white nose and white feet stood with his neck protruding out from the stall door. One look at Lucía, and the horse started to whinny and shake his head eerily, as if he knew her.

Alain laughed and patted his nose. "This is Gelder, Your Grace, your mother's horse. He was named after an old land tax called the geld."

Lucía went over to Gelder, held his chin, and patted his nose. The horse took kindly to her attention and immediately relaxed. Lucía looked him in the eye and kissed his forehead and then turned to Alain. "A geld I don't understand," said Lucía.

Alain continued, "A geld was an old Norman land tax. Sir Charles, who acted on behalf of his wife, Lady Jeanne, the Countess of Bickford, went to collect a land tax from a noble landowner who was short of funds. To pay the geld, which Sir Charles still called the tax, an agreement was made between Sir Charles and the nobleman, whereby Sir Charles would purchase the yearling to pay the land tax and give the horse to his daughter, thus the name Gelder."

Lucía, with a slight laugh, put her face to the horse. She rubbed his head and said to him, "So you were named after an old land tax, were you?"

After a few minutes of giving much due attention to the horse, Lucía turned to Alain and asked, "How old is Gelder?"

The stable master replied, "Oh, he must be about twenty-four years old, Your Grace."

"That's remarkable," said Lucía in complete surprise.

Again, Alain smiled as he went to pat Gelder's head. "Well, he has been well cared for, in good health, and ridden often. Your mother made me promise to do that right before she left to go with your grandfather to Spain, and now you have come full circle." After a pause, he continued, "Would you like to ride him, Your Grace?"

Lucía looked concerned and turned to Alain. "Oui, he appears to be an admirable mount, but I am concerned about his age. I wouldn't want to put any undue strain on him."

"Don't let his age fool you, Your Grace. I assure you he is still full of spirit and enjoys galloping at full speed," said Alain.

Lucía put her face to Gelder and spoke softly, "Would you like me to take you for a ride?"

The horse shook his head and reached for the bridle, which was hanging on the wall of the stall with his teeth. Both Lucía and Alain laughed at Gelder's enthusiasm. Alain took the bridle, opened the stall door, and started to saddle the horse for Lucía.

"He is quite a perceptive animal," said Lucía, and Alain smiled, patted the horse, and continued with the job at hand.

"Do you have a horse at home, Your Grace?"

"Oui, a beautiful white Arabian named Rodrigo. It was a birthday gift from my father on my fourth birthday."

"An Arabian! That must be quite a horse," responded Alain. "Your mother was about the same age when she was given Gelder."

Alain had finished saddling Gelder and led the horse out of the stall. "There you go, Your Grace, all saddled and ready to go."

"Merci," said Lucía, and she mounted Gelder. She was about ready to leave when Sir Guillaume arrived and saw Lucía. "Ah, Your Grace, I'm glad I caught you before you galloped away. Let me saddle my horse. and I will ride with you."

"Too late," responded Lucía, and she left the stable, galloping out the main gate of the castle to the orchard in the back.

Lucía enjoyed the lushness of the vegetation and the cooler summer climate and thought about how the change must have affected her mother, who went to a drier and far warmer summer climate. As

Lucía slowly cantered around the orchard, she saw the peasants from the village and surrounding area busily preparing for the upcoming fall harvest. The trees were filled with small green apples not quite ripe or yet fully grown.

As Lucía continued her tour, she finally found the stream that wound through the back of the orchard and continued into the forest beyond. Lucía had read about it in her mother's diary, as her mother had enjoyed sitting by it to stay cool on a warm summer day. She found a rock on the side of the embankment at the stream's edge large enough and high enough to serve as a seat to enjoy the view of the flow as it gurgled its way over the small rocks and stones farther into the distant forest floor.

Lucía was so mesmerized by the view of the stream, with its trees running along its embankment, deep into the forest beyond, that she did not hear Sir Guillaume approach and was startled by his voice.

"It took a while to find you, but I did, despite almost being decapitated a couple of times from low-hanging branches."

Lucía turned quickly around with a startled look and voiced, "Really, Sir Guillaume, you should learn how to announce your arrival without scaring a girl to death."

"I apologize. I didn't mean to scare you," said Sir Guillaume in a sincere tone. "May I join you, Your Grace?"

Lucía turned again toward Sir Guillaume. "You might as well."

Sir Guillaume sat down next to Lucía, who had cast her eyes back onto the view of the forest in the distance.

After a moment of quiet reflection, Sir Guillaume turned to Lucía, who had her hands braced on the rock. "Gabriella told me of your kind gesture after our first meeting in the lagoon. The supplies and the purse you gave us allowed us to continue our journey home unimpeded, and for that, I want to thank you."

Lucía nodded as she continued her view of the forest in the distance.

After another pause, he continued, "I know now that I've been a fool and misjudged you, and for that, I apologize. I hope we can have a friendlier relationship in the future."

His remarks had struck a chord with Lucía, as she finally heard what she had been waiting to hear from him. It caused her to stand up, and her long braid of hair slipped from her shoulder and fell down her back. Sir Guillaume also rose from the rock, and the two now faced each other.

"What kind of a friendlier relationship are you referring to?" asked Lucía with a welcoming smile. Sir Guillaume gazed into her blue eyes and carefully pushed back the several strands of hair that had fallen to her face.

"Perhaps one like this," said Sir Guillaume as he reached out and embraced her and locked his lips to hers. Lucía was surprised, stunned, and gratified, all in one sensation, and she wrapped her arms around him and totally embraced the moment.

After several minutes of a romantic interlude, Lucía whispered, "It is getting late, Sir Guillaume. We should be heading back to get ready for supper." As the two separated themselves, Lucía heard a rip, and a piece of her green garment was stuck to a chink in his chain mail, in an area where his blue fleur-de-lis surcoat did not cover his armor.

Lucía laughed, and they both tried to unhook the garment. Their struggle caused a further tear until the front of her garment was completely torn away and her undergarment exposed.

"This doesn't look good, does it?" asked Sir Guillaume, and he tried to cover up the portion of her undergarment with the piece of torn cloth.

"Not really." Lucía laughed. "What are you trying to do, Sir Guillaume?" She watched him trying to piece the torn cloth to the garment.

"Repairing your garment," voiced Sir Guillaume.

"Sir Guillaume, the garment is ruined. It's all right. I have plenty more. Please stop fussing about."

"But I don't want you going back looking like this. What are people going to think?" asked Sir Guillaume, who was greatly concerned and embarrassed by the ordeal.

Lucía grabbed his face with her two hands and said softly, "I will simply cover up with my cloak." And then she kissed his lips.

Sir Guillaume then asked, "How can I make this up to you?"

"Oh, I will think of something," responded Lucía with an impish smile. They both walked to their horses and rode back to the castle.

Sir Guillaume walked Lucía back to her boudoir. At the door, she turned to Sir Guillaume as he whispered in her ear, "How about a walk in the orchard after supper?"

"Perhaps, but what about your two friends? Would they mind?"

"You mean Gaston and Étienne?"

Lucía nodded.

"Oh, don't worry about them. They left for Paris this morning."

"Then I accept, if you promise not to wear your armor?"

Sir Guillaume smiled. "I promise." They both embraced for a final kiss before Sir Guillaume departed.

"I'll see you at supper then," said Sir Guillaume as he reached for Lucía's hand and kissed it.

When Lucía entered her boudoir, she found Gabriella still seated at the table and still at work on her embroidery. Gabriella looked up at Lucía as she shut the door and stood in front of it. Her visage was glowing with a silly grin.

"Well?" said Gabriella with a smirk on her face.

"Well, what?"

Gabriella could tell by her glowing expression the answer to her question. With a smirk still on her face, Gabriella then inquired, "Tell me, why are you wearing a cloak on such a warm day?"

"What cloak?"

Gabriella rose from her chair and pointed to it. "That cloak."

"Oh, this cloak," said Lucía, who looked guilty and continued. "I felt a little chill, so I put it on."

"A little chill on such a warm day? Hmm! You'll have to do better than that," responded Gabriella.

"Oh, all right, I'll tell you what happened," exclaimed Lucía as she walked to the middle of the room and waved her arms about.

"I want to know every little detail," expressed Gabriella. She followed Lucía and stood in front of her.

Lucía told Gabriella everything that occurred with Sir Guillaume at the stream, even the romantic interlude, and then she opened her cloak, revealing her torn dress, which incited laughter from Gabriella.

"What have I been telling you all along?"

"Sí, you were right, Gabriella." Lucía then sighed and continued, "But I know that my aunt will not approve of my continued relationship with a penniless knight. She wants me to marry a king so I can become a queen."

"Then you will have to convince her of his worth," added Gabriella.

Lucía sighed again and said, "That is not going to be easy. Anyways, it is time for supper, and I have to change into a new garment. By the way, where are my ladies?" asked Lucía.

"Would you believe that kindly old Madame Leclair up the hallway took an interest in them and invited them in for French lessons?"

"Really!" Lucía laughed.

"They have been in there for several hours, and apparently, they will be having lessons every day, according to the seneschal, who came here earlier looking for you to ask permission for the ladies to attend. I related that I was your majordomo and in charge when you are not around, and I gave permission. The seneschal thanked me and then added that this would give Madame Leclair a new sense of worth. Did I make the right decision?" asked Gabriella.

"You made the right decision, Gabriella. That is wonderful."

"Now let's find a suitable garment for you to wear tonight," said Gabriella as she went searching through Lucía's trunks and found a dark-red garment embroidered with silver trim, along with a belt of connected round silver disks. She also picked a black cloak for Lucía to wear in case the evening produced a chill. A pair of black boots completed her outfit.

After supper, Sir Guillaume and Lucía left the great hall and walked through the courtyard to a small back gate large enough for a man on a horse to ride through, which led directly to the orchard. They walked a distance from the castle into the forest beyond and stopped at a giant oak on the embankment of the stream, which wound around the back of the orchard. It would soon be dark, and a slight chill could be felt in the air. Crickets could be heard chirping, as the forest started to come alive with its nighttime cacophony of sounds. Lucía put on her cloak and backed up against the oak tree. She was enjoying her time with Sir Guillaume, and it showed in her complete change of attitude regarding her newfound love.

Sir Guillaume now felt more relaxed around Lucía, as the hostile environment that was very evident a short time ago was now in the past and a new relationship had suddenly blossomed. Sir Guillaume knew that he had a prize as he stood in front of this petite young girl and gazed into her deep-blue eyes, which lit up her beautiful oval-shaped face. This was a prize he would not let slip through his fingers. This was a prize worthy of keeping through all eternity. He had sensed this from their first encounter.

The two stood against the tree with their lips locked for quite a while. Lucía praised him for trading in his armor for a handsome green tunic, along with green tights. *How comely he looks without his armor*, thought Lucía to herself. Both Sir Guillaume and Lucía talked for some time about their childhood and got to know each better.

Suddenly, the conversation turned to her dear friend, Isabella, and how much she missed her and that she had not received a letter from her at all despite having had written to her on several occasions. "I worry that she is being mistreated by her uncle. What a bad sort he is. My aunt will do nothing about it, except to tell me that he is a blood relative and that I should stay out of it. Despite what she says, if I feel that she is in danger, I will go there and take her home with me myself. My soldiers will follow me," said Lucía emphatically.

"Isabella is lucky to have a friend like you who is watching out for her welfare," added Sir Guillaume, and then he continued, "Perhaps, though, it might be better to convince the queen with proof of her mistreatment before taking action yourself. That to me would be the better course of action."

"Perhaps. I'll see."

"In the name of the saints, Lucía, I would not want to see you in trouble," added Sir Guillaume.

"It would not be the first time," said Lucía. "Besides, I fear it is getting late. We must go."

The two picked their way carefully through the dark forest and orchard and up the hill to the castle. "Who goes there!" shouted the soldier from the guard tower to Lucía and Sir Guillaume below.

"It is all right. It's just Sir Guillaume and me!" shouted Lucía.

"I'm sorry, Your Grace. You can't be too careful these days," said the soldier, and he told the guard at the door to let them enter as he raised the portcullis.

It was very late when Lucía returned to her boudoir. However, the ladies were still awake and awaiting her return. They had a bath already prepared, and although the water was lukewarm, Lucía appreciated the gesture, as the ladies talked about how much they loved and enjoyed their time with Madame Leclair. As they were talking about their time with their newfound friend, Lucía could not help but think of how happy her mother would have been to have known that her tutor had found some happiness from her blind misery.

Chapter XXVI

A fortnight passed, and during this time, Lucía had the opportunity to explore the castle, which included the small chapel that was connected to the living quarters and contained the sarcophagi of her grandparents, the cider mill with its cooper, the vineyard below the castle near the village with its winery and cooper, and the planting fields across the road from the vineyard. She also attended Mass at the village church and mingled with many of the villagers.

When not in the company of Sir Guillaume or having to attend to other business, she continued reading her mother's diaries in the anteroom across from the great hall. Lucía was mystified by a couple of entries, which mentioned a man only known as the black monk, who would come to visit on occasion for a short time and not stay for supper. He always brought a gift with him and came dressed in a black monk's robe with a cowl so deep that her mother could not clearly see the man inside it. She thought him a priest, but he had told her once that he was not but was just a friend of the family. He would always ask Sir Charles about her welfare and if she had enough money to care for herself, after which he always would leave a fat purse. Before he left, he always bent down and gave her a kiss, covering her head completely in his cowl and then would rush off. Lucía was determined to solve the mystery.

Suddenly, a servant broke her concentration, entered the anteroom, and curtsied. "There are two knights who wish to see you, Your Grace."

"They may enter," responded Lucía.

The servant curtsied again, and very quickly Gaston and Étienne entered. "Your Grace, how nice it is to see you again," said Gaston.

Lucía arose from her chair at the table and went to greet them. Gaston took her hand and gently kissed it, followed by Étienne.

"Your Grace, I am sorry to intrude, but the king has requested that Sir Guillaume come to Paris immediately, and we have come to fetch him. Do you know where he is?" asked Gaston as he rubbed his fingers through his long black curly hair.

"Probably with Captain Gómez up the road where the Castilian army is encamped. He spends most of his days there when he is not escorting me around. Is he in trouble?" inquired Lucía, who was concerned.

"I don't believe so. Merci, You Grace." The two bowed and left for the encampment.

A while later, Sir Guillaume entered the anteroom, followed by his two comrades.

Lucía quickly arose from her chair to greet him. "What is going on? Is everything all right?" asked Lucía, who appeared anxious.

"Everything is fine, Lucía. Don't worry. The king only wants to see me, probably to discuss some matter that has developed. I will be gone for a week at most. However, I must be going now. Is there anything I can pick up for you while I am in Paris?"

Lucía shook her head and went over to embrace him as he was about to leave. "Just come back as quickly as you can," said Lucía, and she kissed him goodbye and tried to smile.

Gabriella was about to enter the anteroom just as everyone was leaving. Gaston stopped and looked at Gabriella in the doorway. They both smiled at each other, and Gaston took Gabriella's hand and kissed it. "My lady, an honor to see again. You are such a maiden of exquisite beauty. I will be back."

Lucía and Gabriella went to the courtyard to wave goodbye.

"I didn't know of your fondness for the Lady Gabriella," said Sir Guillaume to Gaston as they mounted their horses.

"That goes to show how much you don't know, Sir Guillaume," said Gaston. They both shared a laugh and rode off.

Lucía turned to Gabriella with a sly look and said, "All right, I want to know every detail."

Gabriella shrugged her shoulders, and they both laughed and went back inside. The mystery of the black monk would have to wait as other more important matters arose.

Lucía realized the time was fast approaching when she would have to prepare for her trip back home, and she tried to make the best use of her remaining time. She started her day with Mass at the private chapel in the castle, followed by private prayer at the main chapel on the castle grounds at the sarcophagi of her grandparents, Sir Charles and the Lady Jeanne, who were buried next to each other in the crypt. Then after a breakfast of a light broth and a small piece of bread, she alternated between working in the orchard and the vine-yard to help prepare for the coming harvest. The peasants enjoyed her company and her interaction with them. At the end of the day, she enjoyed a warm bath scented with rose and lavender.

One morning, Lucía was on her way to mass in the private chapel with Gabriella when she saw a sight she would never forget. Her ladies were leading Madame Leclair carefully down the stairs to the next floor to the chapel for morning Mass. Two of her ladies were on the step below her, holding her hand, and two were on the step in back of her, making sure that she did not fall. She could see the expression of happiness on the face of the poor old blind lady, which was very moving for Lucía, and tears fell down her face on such an act of love and patience. "I hope that you are seeing this, Mama," said Lucía out loud to herself, and Gabriella turned to Lucía with a soft smile. They both stayed far enough behind so as not to attract attention.

That evening, Lucía paid a visit to Madame Leclair. She knocked on her door and was told to enter. Lucía walked in and found her feeling her way toward the door. "It's all right, Madame Leclair. I am right here in front of you," said Lucía.

"Is that you, Margaret?"

"Non, Madame. It's Lucía."

She paused for a moment, then turned to Lucía's voice, and said, "Oh, I am sorry. Of course, you're Lucía. Please forgive my con-fusion, but for just one moment, I thought—"

Lucía interjected, "It's all right, Madame Leclair. I understand." She took her gently by the arm and led her back to her high-back chair and then kissed her on the cheek.

"I don't often get visitors. Once in a while, Guiscard pays me a visit or I talk to a servant or the local priest comes to give me Mass, but that is it," she said as Lucía sat in the high-back chair next to her.

Lucía saw how lonely this poor woman was and wished to do more to make her life happier. She turned in her chair and sat cater-corner to her and saw her staring blindly at the fireplace in front of her. Her white wimple and white garment were too old and showing definite signs of wear.

Then Lucía stated, "If I knew that you could handle the travel, I would love for you to come and live with me in Spain."

Madame Leclair smiled. "Oh, my dear, I do appreciate your sentiment, but as you stated, and rightly so, I am too old for such a journey. Besides, I am blind and would not see what you see. At least I am in a place where I was able to see the beauty around me before I suffered my infirmity. This is where my memories are, and this is where I shall stay."

"I understand," said Lucía. She realized a continuation of the discussion was useless, so she decided to change the subject. "I do want to thank you for taking care of my ladies so."

"I enjoy their company so much, and I am happy to improve their French. Constance is a big help and aids in reinforcing what they learn through practice. I found Beatrix to be my star student. She is a very bright girl despite her heavy German accent," she added with a smile of satisfaction. "I guess I have adopted her in a way."

Lucía knew she would be leaving soon and would have to take her ladies with her, but she did not wish to break Madame Leclair's heart, so she thought to herself of ways to avert such an action. She then decided to change the subject again.

"Madame Leclair, if you could help me out as I grapple with a mystery?" asked Lucía.

"Anything, my dear."

"Well, I've been reading my mother's diaries, and I found several entries regarding a black monk. I wondered if you might know who this black monk was."

Suddenly, there was such complete silence that Lucía thought something was wrong. "Madame Leclair?" No response. "Madame Leclair?" Again no response. Lucía decided to check on her to see if she was all right.

As she was about to leave her chair, Madame Leclair responded slowly, "You don't want to know who that was."

Lucía was dumbfounded by her response, and after a moment of careful thought, she decided to let the subject drop. Perhaps she was tired, and she should leave. After all, Lucía did not want to upset her. Lucía rose from her chair and stood in front of Madame Leclair and gave her another kiss on the cheek.

She said, "It is getting late. I must go. Is there anything I can do for you?"

Madame Leclair then responded on a very strange note, which alarmed Lucía and sent chills up her back. "Lucía, be careful. There is much darkness out there, and danger many times cannot be seen until it reaches out and strangles you. Then it is too late."

Lucía smiled nervously. "Good night, Madame Leclair." She then walked out of her room and headed to her boudoir down the hall.

A week later, Lucía decided to take a ride back to the stream and to listen to the bubbling sounds of water, streaming down the small rocks and pebbles into the distant forest beyond, to help clear her mind. She had read in her mother's diaries that she would often go there with her father on a warm summer day to picnic with a simple fare of bread, cheese, sausage, fruit, and nuts, and then take a walk in the forest.

Lucía, entranced by the forest scene, was startled to have heard a familiar voice greet her from behind. She quickly turned and saw it was Sir Guillaume, who had returned from Paris. She arose from her seat on the rock, slowly walked over to him with a gleeful smile, gazed into his eyes, embraced him, and with quivering lips, locked hers with his. After a couple of minutes of passion, they pulled away from each other as curiosity got the best of Lucía.

"So how was Paris?" she inquired.

"Hot as usual at this time of year."

"Well?" asked Lucía.

"Well what?" responded Sir Guillaume.

"Sir Guillaume, do I really have to drag it out of you? Why were you called to Paris?" she said with a frown and became annoyed at his lack of forthcoming with information.

With a sigh, Sir Guillaume said, "Let's sit down. I have something to tell you, Lucía."

As they both sat on the rock, Lucía sat with her legs to her side while he sat with his hands in his lap with his feet dangling over the edge of the stream. The forest was quiet except for the gurgling sound of the brook. Sir Guillaume turned his head to Lucía, who was patiently waiting for him to say something.

Very slowly, Sir Guillaume said, "The king called me to Paris to tell me that my brother, Giles, was dead. He died while hunting a wild boar. Apparently, the boar got the best of him."

Lucía rested her head on his shoulder. "I'm so sorry, Sir Guillaume."

After a short pause, he continued, "That's all right. My brother was not a well-liked man. He was bad-tempered with bouts of violent behavior, some of which I experienced in my early life first-hand. I've inherited his estate since I am the only surviving member of the family. I have also received the title of duke, the Duke of Guy."

Lucía's expression suddenly changed completely with a combination of surprise and total joy. "I don't believe it. That is something I would never had imaged. It is so wonderful," said Lucía. She stood up, followed by Sir Guillaume, and embraced him with such fervor she almost knocked him down. The two locked lips again for several moments until Sir Guillaume managed to break away and added, "There is one more detail that I must tell you."

"And what is that?" asked Lucía with a big happy smile on her face.

With a sigh, Sir Guillaume added, "King Philip wants me to lead an army of several thousand men to Palestine."

Suddenly, Lucía's jaw dropped, and her expression changed from joy to concern. "How long will you be gone?" inquired Lucía.

"At least a year, but I won't stay there any longer than I have to," exclaimed Sir Guillaume.

Lucía turned to the stream and put her hands to her face as tears rolled down her cheeks. Sir Guillaume went over to her, turned her around, and held her by her shoulders, "Lucía, I did not have a choice in the matter. I have always been loyal to the king and have always done his bidding."

Lucía broke away from Sir Guillaume, turned around, and stared into the distance. "When I was four years old, my father said to me that he would be going to the Holy Land on crusade and that I should not to worry for he would not be gone long. Ten years later, I am still waiting for his return, and now I have found someone that I truly love, and he is also going to that godforsaken place," cried Lucía as she started to weep.

Sir Guillaume went to comfort her, but she shook him off, ran past him, mounted Gelder, and galloped back to the stable. Once there, she left Gelder to the care of Alain, ran to her boudoir, shut and locked the door, and wept uncontrollably on her bed.

After a period of time, Lucía lifted her head, as she heard people talking in the courtyard below. She arose from the bed, wiped away her tears, along with the hair from her face, and went to the window. When she looked out, she saw Gabriella talking to Gaston. Although she could not hear their conversation, she could tell there was a bit of intimacy involved. Shortly thereafter, the conversation stopped as Gaston kissed her hand and went toward the stable, and Gabriella, with a big smile on her face, came up the steps into the main entrance of the castle.

Once Lucía realized that Gabriella was on her way to her boudoir, she went over to the door, unlocked it, and tried to act as if nothing had happened. Gabriella soon entered and gazed upon Lucía, who was standing by the table and very quickly noticed her red eyes.

"You've been crying again," said Gabriella in a sympathetic voice.

Lucía started to weep and could barely be understood. "Sir Guillaume has been made a duke, but he has to lead an army to the Holy Land, and I won't see him for at least a year, if then. It's my father all over again," wept Lucía.

Gabriella went over to Lucía, embraced her, and then said, "I know. Gaston told me about Sir Guillaume's good fortune, and I think it's wonderful. Now you can approach your aunt and tell her that you have fallen in love with a duke. She can't deny your seeing him now."

Lucía walked over to the window, which overlooked the courtyard. "She'll want to meet him, but he will be in the Holy Land," sniffled Lucía.

"Lucía, it will be all right. You will see," said Gabriella as she faced Lucía by the window. "Meanwhile, an angel has shined upon both you and Sir Guillaume with his good fortune. That is something to celebrate. Enjoy your time together now, and do not waste it in sorrow, for tomorrow will be here soon enough."

Lucía again wiped the tears from her face and acknowledged Gabriella's good sense. She turned to her friend. "You're right, Gabriella. Tomorrow will come soon enough." Then she continued, "But what about you and Gaston?"

"Well, both Gaston and Étienne will be following Sir Guillaume to the Holy Land as well, also by order of the king," added Gabriella.

"You have feelings for Gaston, don't you?" asked Lucía, quite concerned.

Gabriella smiled. "Sí, but we will have to wait and see."

"I am so sorry, Gabriella, carrying on like this while you are going through the same fears and concerns I am going through—and handling it more gracefully, I might add."

"Lucía, never mind me. Just go to Sir Guillaume and spend your remaining time together with him."

Lucía smiled and said, "Gracias for helping me come to my senses, Gabriella." She left her boudoir, walked to the stable, and found Sir Guillaume discussing strategy with Gaston.

That night, Lucía planned a special supper to celebrate Sir Guillaume's dukedom with everyone at the castle in attendance, including Madame Leclair. After which, both Sir Guillaume and Lucía spent the rest of the evening at the stream.

The next day, Lucía went to visit Guiscard in the anteroom and found the horseman she had heard ride into the courtyard waiting for her. The seneschal was seated at a table on the dais and was working on various items as the messenger waited patiently and stood at attention below it. When he saw Lucía enter, he approached her and said, "Mi señora, a message from Her Highness, Queen Leonor," he said as he handed it to Lucía.

Lucía took the message, broke the wax seal, read it, and after a slight pause, responded to the messenger. "Tell Her Highness that I will be leaving soon and expect to be home by harvest time."

"Gracias, mi señora," said the messenger, who bowed and left.

"Is everything all right, Your Grace?" inquired the seneschal.

"It's just my aunt wondering if I had forgotten where I live," said Lucía with a smile.

The seneschal laughed. "You must be missed, Your Grace."

"Most likely, she has become bored with no one to yell at," added Lucía.

After they shared a laugh together, Lucía decided that this was the right time to ask the seneschal a question. "May I ask you a question?"

"Of course, anything," responded the seneschal, who walked down from the dais and pulled a chair out from the polished oak table for Lucía to sit in.

The seneschal took a seat across from her. "Now what can I help you with, Your Grace?"

Lucía began, "I have been reading my mother's diaries, and there are several entries that concerned a black monk. Do you know who this black monk was? Madame Leclair told me that I really didn't want to know, but I do."

"I see," said the seneschal and, after an uncomfortable pause, continued, "Madame Leclair called him the devil. The person she referred to was King Henry. He would come here on occasion to visit with Lady Margaret, his real daughter, who was unbeknownst to her until right before she left for Spain. He gave her gifts. I believe he came here maybe four or five times in ten years. He always came dressed in a black monk's robe so Lady Margaret would not know of his true identity."

The seneschal continued, "The last time he came, your mother was, I believe, eleven, about a year before she went to Spain. When he first came that day, he was in good humor all right until a messenger came and delivered him a missive. I was standing at the entrance of the anteroom and saw everything. After he read the missive, he burst out with such rage I had never seen before. He cursed, and he swore. Candlesticks went flying as he took his arm and in anger pushed everything off the table, which included trays of food, vessels of wine, along with the silver cups.

"Sir Charles tried to calm him, but he continued with the rampage. I saw Lady Margaret trembling and shaking with fear, and her eyes were as big as the full moon itself. As he lunged toward her, Madame Leclair stood in front of her to shield her from his abuse. He pushed her away so hard that she took to the ground and was knocked unconscious. Your mother screamed and ran in panic, which caused the guards to come running in, but even they could not restrain him. He was a madman. He finally fell to the ground and even tried to bite the leg off the table. Finally, he was either able to calm himself or was so completely worn out that he became sane again.

"When he realized the destruction he caused, he apologized, gave a fat purse, and left. That was the last time anyone saw him. Madame Leclair was bedridden and unconscious for several days. Your mother sat with her and never left her bedside. When she awoke, she was completely blind. And that is the story, Your Grace."

Lucía put her hand to her face and covered her eyes. "My god!" said Lucía. "No wonder Madame Leclair said I didn't want to know who he was."

"I hope that I did not upset you, Your Grace."

Lucía sighed. "No, and I appreciate your careful detail in relating the story."

"Something else you should be aware of, Your Grace, that I think is important for you to know, which completes the story," said the seneschal.

"Please tell me," responded Lucía, who was curious as to what that might be.

The seneschal continued, "Despite the king's temper, which was well-known, he did care for your mother. Unfortunately, some people have a hard time showing their true feelings. Sir Charles did divulged to me, since I was a trusted official in his court, that one of the reasons why your mother went to Spain was to ensure her safety during the king's dynastic struggles with his sons, all of whom laid claim to certain lands here in France. Her marriage to a Spanish count would provide enough distance away from the center of all the controversy. The arrangement for the marriage between your mother and father was negotiated between King Henry and your King Alfonso." After a pause, the seneschal asked, "Do you have any questions, Your Grace?"

"Non," said Lucía. She sighed, rose from her chair, and turned to the seneschal. "Merci. I appreciated your candor. You have been very helpful and cleared up several matters that have been of concern to me for a long time. Also, I like you and trust you. I do so want you to stay on to administer my estate during my absence and to let me know of anything of importance that occurs."

"Your Grace," said the seneschal. He stood and thanked Lucía as she left the anteroom.

The next day, Lucía was standing under an oak tree on the barren hillside covered in grass. The castle was in the background, along with the adjacent forest, and off to the left farther down the steep hill was the vineyard and village. Sir Guillaume, along with Gaston and Étienne, came riding down the hillside and stopped. Gaston had already said his goodbye to Gabriella. Now it was Sir Guillaume's turn. With Gaston and Étienne a short distance away, Sir Guillaume rode over to Lucía and dismounted. Lucía went over and quickly embraced him, and the two locked lips for a short time.

"I promise I will be back just as soon as I deliver the French troops to Palestine," said Sir Guillaume.

Lucía smiled and accepted the situation at hand. "I'll be waiting anxiously for your return in Segoia."

"I also want to take a lock of your hair to remember you by."

Lucía nodded, and Sir Guillaume removed his dagger from its sheath, cut off a lock of her long hair, and placed it in a leather pouch that hung from his sword belt.

After a final embrace and kiss, Sir Guillaume mounted his horse and rode over to his two friends, and the three, who proudly wore their dark-blue fleur-de-lis surcoats over their chain mail, shouted loudly as they raised their swords in the air, "Longue vie au roi!" Lucía watched them gallop down the hill and onto the road to Paris and disappear from sight.

Lucía knew that it was time to leave Pomeroi. Within a week, Lucía, Gabriella, and her ladies had packed their trunks and were ready to leave, but not before they had a farewell banquet held in Lucía's honor, where she promised that she would return again someday. Also, there was the emotional farewell to Madame Leclair from all the ladies who had gained such benefit from her relationship. Lucía now realized why her mother had cared for and held her in such high regard.

The day had finally arrived when Lucía would start the long journey home. She was awakened before dawn and joined her ladies for early Mass in the oratory for the final time, and then she went for silent prayers at the sarcophagus of Sir Charles and Lady Jeanne in the crypt of the chapel. When she finished her prayers, she arose from the kneeler and went to the head of the sarcophagus and touched her lips with two fingers and then placed her fingers on the lips of the effigy of both her grandparents.

She said in a soft voice, "Adieu mes cheries Je t'aimerai toujours." Then she left to board her wagon in the courtyard.

When she arrived, the seneschal, the servants, and even Madame Leclair were all on hand to say farewell. Alain even brought Gelder out to say goodbye. Lucía took the time to give each servant a kiss on both cheeks and embraced Madame Leclair, who said to Lucía, "Take care, my dear, and remember to beware of the darkness that hides the danger that could befall you."

Lucía gave her a kiss on the cheek and said with a smile, "I will."

She went over and rested the side of her head against Gelder's face and gave him a pat and said, "I shall pray that you will still be here when I return."

As if the horse knew what she had just said, he shook his head and whinnied with such enthusiasm that Alain had a rough time holding on to his reins, to the laughter of all. She then thanked and said her goodbyes to Alain, the trusted stable keeper. Finally, she went over to Guiscard, the seneschal, who was at the head of the line of servants by the steps to the entrance of the castle.

"Merci, and take good care of my duchy for me," said Lucía with a smile.

"Have a safe journey, Your Grace."

Her ladies, servants, and Gabriella were already seated and were waiting for Lucía to board, and once she boarded, the entourage started on the long journey home, with Captain Gómez in the lead. Even the villagers lined the road below the hill to say goodbye and to catch a final glimpse of their young duchess.

Epilogue

Lucía was homeward bound, a little older and perhaps a little wiser. She had come to France, particularly Pomeroi, to learn more about her mother, who was somewhat of a mystery in Lucía's mind throughout her young life. She had learned the reasons why her grandmother had given her away in adoption, why she had traveled to Spain to marry her father, and even though Lucía didn't agree with all of it, she finally had to accept the reality of her mother's fate. Case closed in Lucía's mind, and although there would always be a bond between mother and daughter, she could now move on with her life.

As she looked ahead, there were many areas of concern, especially with Isabella, a friend whom she loved as a sister. She was greatly concerned for her welfare. What to do? Her future relationship with al-Rashid was something to think about, as well as what she would like to do for him and his people, and there was always the ongoing danger from the Moors.

On a more personal note, her new love interest was Sir Guillaume. Would her aunt and uncle approve of the relationship? And how should she tell them? Worst of all, would she ever see him again, or would he disappear, as her father did? Finally, the past attempts on her life, would they continue? Such questions were on her mind, and only time would resolve them, but how much time would it take?

Her travels had broadened her views and made her feel wiser, at least in her mind, but she was still quite young and inexperienced with life's true lessons still ahead. Perhaps she should heed Madame Leclair's warning: "For there will be darkness for this young girl in the years to come until peace and happiness can be truly obtained." And yet can peace and happiness ever really be obtained?

About the Author

TS Nichols has always had an interest in history, especially medieval history. He wanted to be exotic, and he chose Spain to be the setting for his book. Upon doing research, he found Spain to have been the vanguard of Europe at the forefront of preventing the Moors from advancing beyond the Pyrenees. This inspired him to write a story during the time period of the Reconquista when Spain fought hard to drive out the Moors from their homeland, a seven-hundred-year effort.

He is retired and currently resides in New Jersey with his wife, Barbara, and enjoys his six grandchildren.

Lightning Source UK Ltd.
Milton Keynes UK
UKHW010631040121
376386UK00001B/70